THE FOLKLORE OF DISCWORLD

Also by Terry Pratchett

THE FOLKLORE OF DISCWORLD

Legends, myths and customs from the Discworld
with helpful hints from planet Earth

Terry Pratchett
and
Jacqueline Simpson

Doubleday

LONDON · TORONTO · SYDNEY · AUCKLAND · JOHANNESBURG

TRANSWORLD PUBLISHERS
61–63 Uxbridge Road, London W5 5SA
A Random House Group Company
www.rbooks.co.uk

First published in Great Britain
in 2008 by Doubleday
an imprint of Transworld Publishers

A CIP catalogue record for this book
is available from the British Library.

ISBN 9780385611008

Addresses for Random House Group Ltd companies outside the UK
can be found at: www.randomhouse.co.uk
The Random House Group Ltd Reg. No. 954009

The Random House Group Limited supports The Forest Stewardship
Council (FSC), the leading international forest-certification organization. All our
titles that are printed on Greenpeace-approved FSC-certified paper carry the FSC logo.
Our paper procurement policy can be found at
www.rbooks.co.uk/environment

Typeset in 11/15.5 Sabon by
Falcon Oast Graphic Art Ltd.
Printed and bound in Great Britain by
Clays Ltd, Bungay, Suffolk

4 6 8 10 9 7 5 3

Contents

Introduction
by Terry Pratchett

A number of things conspired to cause this book to be written.

There was the time when I was in a car with several other grown-up, literate people and we passed a sign to the village of Great Dunmow, in Essex. I said aloud, 'Oh, yes. Home of the Dunmow Flitch.' They had not heard of it, yet for centuries a married man could go to that village on a Whit Monday and claim the prize of a flitch (or side) of bacon if he could swear that he and his wife had not quarrelled, even once, during the past year. And that he had never wished he was a bachelor again. Back in the late fifties and early sixties the Flitch ceremony used to be televised, for heaven's sake.

Not long after this I did a book-signing on the south coast, when I took the opportunity to ask practically every person in the queue to say the magpie rhyme (I was doing research for *Carpe Jugulum*). Every single one of them recited, with greater or lesser accuracy, the version of the rhyme that used to herald the beginning of the 1960s and 70s children's TV programme *Magpie* – 'One for sorrow, two for joy'. It wasn't a bad rhyme, but like some cuckoo in the nest it was forcing out all the other versions that had existed around the country (some of which will appear in a later chapter). Then a distinguished-looking lady was in front of me with a book, and I asked her, with some inexpressible hope in my heart, how many versions of the magpie rhyme she knew. After a moment's thought, she said 'about nineteen'.

And that was how I met Jacqueline Simpson, who has been my friend and occasional consultant on matters of folklore, and once got me along to talk to the British Folklore Society, where I probably upset a few people by saying that I think of folklore in much the same way a carpenter thinks about trees.

Some of the things in this book may well be familiar, and you will say 'but everybody knows this'. But the Discworld series, which on many occasions borrows from folklore and mythology, twisting and tangling it on the way, must be the most annotated series of modern books in existence. And one thing I have learned is this: not many people know the things which everyone knows.

But there are some things we shouldn't forget, and mostly they add up to where we came from and how we got here and the stories we told ourselves on the way. But folklore isn't only about the past. It grows, flowers and seeds every day, because of our innate desire to control our world by means of satisfying narratives.

I used to live a short distance away from a standing stone which, at full moon and/or Midsummer's Eve, would dance around its field at night, incidentally leaving unguarded a pot of gold which, in theory, was available to anyone who dared to seize it and could run faster than a stone. I went to see it by daylight early on, but for some reason I never found the time to make the short nocturnal journey and check on its dancing abilities. I now realize this was out of fear: I feared that, like so many stones I have met, it would fail to dance. There was a small part of me that wanted the world to be a place where, despite planning officers and EU directives and policemen, a stone *might* dance. And somewhere there, I think, is the instinct for folklore. There should be a place where a stone dances.

For those who feel the same way we have included a short reading list, in theory for those readers who would like to know more, but also because people who love books always want to recommend them to other people at the least excuse.

Introduction
by Jacqueline Simpson

Ah yes, I remember it well, that book-signing on the south coast! A misty, moisty November evening in 1997, a long queue inching its way towards a very impressive black hat, the eager voice demanding, 'Tell me *everything* you know about magpies!'

A little ahead of me in the queue, one woman had been explaining to all and sundry as we waited that it was for her nephew, not herself, that she wanted a signed copy of *Jingo*. She herself never, ever read novels of any kind, let alone fantasy fiction. 'I only want facts. What's the point of reading about things that aren't real? As for a world flying through space on a turtle . . .' Her voice died out in a splutter of indignation, and the combined arguments of a dozen Discworld readers couldn't budge her one inch. I was not surprised to learn what her job was; she was an accountant – which is to say, very nearly an Auditor of Reality. Give her a small grey robe with a cowl, and she would find a perfect niche on the Disc.

The truth of the matter is, the Disc is the Earth, but with an extra dimension of reality. On the Discworld, things that on Earth are creatures of the imagination (but sometimes quite powerful, even so) are alive and, in some cases, kicking. Sometimes we recognize them at once (is there anyone who doesn't know a dragon when they meet one?). Sometimes we simply feel that something is deeply familiar and completely right, but we have no idea why. Hours, days or weeks later, we may find the key, when the rich soil that accumulates at the back of the mind suddenly yields the fruit of memory.

Then we realize that the key to the familiarity lies in folklore.

Whatever is folklore on Earth finds its mirror in the reality of the Disc. Of course it's perfectly natural that Mrs Gogol's house moves about on four large duck feet, because Baba Yaga's hut spins around on chicken legs in the forests of Russia; of course the Nac Mac Feegle are *pict*sies, not pixies, because of stories the Scots told about Picts; of course there's an ancient king sleeping in a cavern deep under a mountain in Lancre, because that's what King Arthur does in England and Scotland, and the Emperor Barbarossa in Germany. We've known about such things for ages, even if we called them fairy tales, myths, and folklore; now that we're on the Disc, they are real, and we feel quite at home.

Well, then, what is the 'folklore' of Earth, and more specifically of British tradition? It's the sum total of all those things people know without ever having been officially *taught* about them, all those stories and images which drift around with no apparent source, all those funny little customs people follow simply because everyone has always done them (and, usually, it's fun). If we were bookish children, we may remember precisely when we first discovered some of them. Terry still has the copy of Brewer's *Dictionary of Phrase and Fable* which he bought second-hand when he was twelve years old, and read from end to end (it cost him 10/6 – OK, OK, 50p, about three weeks' pocket money). I remember the hot summer day I spent sitting against a haystack, aged thirteen, and embarking for the first time on the genuine full-length tales of King Arthur and his knights, as written by Sir Thomas Malory in the 1460s, funny spellings and weird words included. But most people, most of the time, just grow up having always known how and when to touch wood or cross their fingers, and what happens when a princess kisses a frog or a boy pulls a sword from a stone. They take for granted that there will be pancakes on Shrove Tuesday, pumpkins and scary costumes at Halloween, bonfires on Guy Fawkes Night, mince pies at Christmas. (Non-British readers, please adjust to fit your own traditional foods and calendars.)

So who are the 'folk' who have all this 'lore'? The answer is, 'any of us'. It's a mistake to think that the only folklore worthy of the name is what you get by finding the oldest crone in the dirtiest cottage in the poorest village in the remotest mountain valley, and cross-examining her on her deathbed. Every group and sub-group in society has its jokes, its beliefs, its tales and traditions. At this very moment, there are children in the playground giggling over the latest naughty joke (it may or may not be one their great-grandparents knew too); young mothers who take for granted that little girls *must* wear pink; college students teaching each other the equivalent of Nanny Ogg's 'Hedgehog Song'. And because where there is fun there is also money to be made, there's a large-scale trade in birthday cards, Easter eggs, Mother's Day cards, Halloween masks and so forth, which no parent dares ignore. And any town or pub or castle which wants to attract tourists will go looking for colourful local legends and customs to exploit.

The days are long gone when scholars insisted that 'real folklore' must always be something passed on by word of mouth, not in print. This was never very realistic, at any rate in literate societies, where generations of poets and novelists and dramatists have drawn material from myth and folk tale, twisted and embroidered it, and then handed it on to future readers. And then, maybe, the readers become tellers in their turn, and hand it on again. The Tree of Folklore has no objection whatever to creative carpenters.

Stories and beliefs grow and multiply in all the media available, old and new; they are forever feeding on, and then feeding back into, the rich soup of tradition. Take vampires, for instance. How much of 'what everybody knows who knows anything about vampires' comes from the basic five-hundred-year-old East European folklore, and how much from novels, films, comics, TV? Specialists can work it out, but does it really matter? Here and now, in the twenty-first century, all vampire lore has blended together into a luscious soup.

Folklore may *look* as if it never changes, but if you keep a watchful eye on it, you will notice some things dying out and others springing up. In Britain nowadays, people do not wear mourning for months on end after a death in the family, but because grief needs an outlet a new custom has appeared out of nowhere and is spreading fast – thirty years ago nobody built roadside memorials of flowers and mementoes at the site of tragic accidents, but now this is felt to be right and proper. Customs also travel from one country to another much faster and more frequently than they once did; since the 1980s Britain has learned from America that if you tie a yellow ribbon to a tree or a fence, this means you're praying for the safety of some prisoner or kidnap victim who is in the news. In fact, variously coloured ribbons and plastic wrist-bands in support of good causes are popping up all over the place now, in the way that lapel badges used to do, and everyone understands what each one means.

On the Discworld, folklore is much more stable. New symbols sometimes arise – the black ribbon recently adopted by reformed vampires, for instance (its Earthly parallel was the blue ribbon of Victorian teetotallers), and the commemorative spray of lilac which Vimes and some others in Ankh-Morpork wear on one day of the year, as explained in *Night Watch* – but nothing ever seems to be discarded and forgotten. This makes the Discworld a wonderful place in which to rediscover the solidity, the *depth* which tradition brings to a society, and learn to cherish it.

So when Terry invited me to join him in exploring this incredibly rich network of links, I had only one misgiving. Is it wise to *explain* so much? Might it not be best to let readers enjoy the glimpses and hints and clues half understood, and gradually make their own discoveries?

But as Terry has said elsewhere, a conjurer is more entertaining than a wizard because he entertains you twice: once with the trick, and once with the trickery.

So now, there's a drum-roll, the curtains part, and you can watch how the conjurer works . . .

Chapter 1

THE COSMOS: GODS, DEMONS *and* THINGS

VERY VAST IS THE EXPANDING rubber sheet of the space-time continuum. Should we not call it infinite?

No, as a matter of fact, we should not, not unless we want to get into an interminable argument with both physicists and philosophers – the kind of argument where people steeple their fingers and say, very slowly, '*We-ell*, it all depends on what you *mean* by "infinite".' And go on saying it, with variations, till the beer runs out. If you are very unlucky, they will explain how infinities come in different sizes.

What we can fairly safely say is that there are clumps of matter on that rubber sheet, moving about and organizing themselves into complicated systems. Billions of them. Two of these deserve our close attention. One consists of a rather lumpy and intensely hot spherical core of iron and rock, much of it in a molten state, held together by its own pressure, and wrapped in a thin solid crust. It is whirled through space by the force of gravity. This is the Earth, which is round-like-a-ball. The other is round-like-a-plate, and is moved at a more sedate pace by a team of elephants and a turtle. This is the Discworld.

What they have in common is that each carries through the cosmos a cargo of conscious, imaginative – we could even say, charitably, intelligent – living species. Over the many centuries of their existence, these species have generated an accumulation of thoughts, information, emotions, beliefs and imaginings which envelops their world like a mental atmosphere, a *noosphere*. Within this noosphere patterns have formed, driven by the irresistible force of narrativium, the narrative imperative, the power of story. Some scholars call the patterns *motifs*, others *topoi*, others *memes*. The point is, they're there, everyone knows them, and they go on and on. More remarkably, some of the strongest can replicate themselves and go drifting off across the multiverse as particles of inspiration, which leads to some truly amazing similarities between the Earth and Discworld.

THE ELEPHANTS AND THE TURTLE

The absolutely central, incontrovertible fact about the Discworld is that it is a disc. At least, it's incontrovertible unless you adhere to the Omnian religion, in which case you must controvert it like billy-o. This disc rests upon four gigantic elephants (named Berilia, Tubul, Great T'Phon and Jerakeen), whose bones are living iron, and whose nerves are living gold. These elephants themselves stand upon the shell of the Great A'Tuin, a ten-thousand-mile-long star turtle, which is swimming through space in a purposeful manner. What this purpose may be, is unknown.

> A child once asked, 'Why does the Turtle swim?'
> A wise man replied, 'Child, there is no Why. IT ... IS ... SO.'
> And that could be said of many things.

On Earth 'everyone knows' that people used to believe that their planet was also flat, if they thought about it at all. In fact for several thousand years a growing number of educated people have shared the knowledge that it is a globe. Generally speaking it was wisest not to shout about it in the street, though, because of the unrest this could cause. No doubt scholars in the ancient Hindu India partook of this knowledge, but since truth comes in many forms, the age-old epic poems of India declare the world to be a disc.

Further details of Hindu cosmology vary. According to one myth, there are four (or eight) great elephants named the *diggaja* or *disāgaja*, 'elephants of the directions', guarding the four (or eight) compass points of this disc, with a type of god called a *lokapala* riding on the back of each one. But the oldest texts do not claim that they *carry* the world. According to another myth, however, the world rests on the back of a single elephant, Maha-Padma, and he is standing on a tortoise named Chukwa. Finally, it is said in yet another myth that the god Vishnu once took on the form of a vast tortoise or turtle (*kūrma*), so huge that Mount Meru, the sacred central mountain of the world, could rest on his back and be used as a stick to churn the ocean. At some stage, though nobody knows just when, these insights began to blend, with the result that some (but not all) Hindu mythographers now say the world is a disc supported by four elephants supported by a turtle.

Variations of the myth spread out from India to other areas of the globe.[1] One that has proved particularly popular involves an infinite regression of turtles. It is said that an arrogant Englishman once mocked a Hindu by asking what the turtle stood on; untroubled, the Hindu calmly replied, 'Ah, Sahib, after that it's turtles all the way down.'[2] Another variation, briefly mentioned in the film *A Thief of Baghdad*, involves different creatures but is of value because it adds one vital factor, that of movement. It tells how the world rests on seven pillars, carried on the shoulders of a huge genie, who stands on an eagle, which perches on a bull, which stands on a fish – and this fish swims through the seas of eternity.

Chinese mythology also knows of an immense cosmic turtle, but with a difference. According to the Chinese, our world is not balanced upon the creature's back (with or without elephants), but is sloshing about inside it. Its plastron contains the oceans upon which all our

---

[1] And some may be locally grown. Humanity seems predisposed to see the turtle as a massive carrier.

[2] Yes, we know that there are several versions of this story!

continents are floating, and when we look up at the dome of the night sky we are seeing the inside of its vast carapace, studded with innumerable stars.

Clearly, fragments of information have drifted through the multiverse and taken root here and there. But the full and glorious Truth is known only on the Discworld. The Turtle Moves!

And beyond that Truth lies an even deeper mystery, one hinted at in the legends of the dwarfs – the legend of the Fifth Elephant. For the dwarfs of Uberwald say there was once a fifth elephant supporting the Disc, but it crashed:

> They *say* that the fifth elephant came screaming and trumpeting through the atmosphere of the young world all those years ago and landed hard enough to split continents and raise mountains. [*The Fifth Elephant*]

Nobody actually saw or heard this, but the dwarfs *say* that the vast deposits of iron ore, gold and fat under their mountains are all that remains of the Fifth Elephant. Also that the crash buried thousands of acres of prehistoric sugar cane, creating a mass of dense crystalline sugar which can now be mined. These raw materials form the basis for a flourishing trade in confectionery and in very fine-quality candles, soaps and lamp-oils.

The iron, the gold and the fat undoubtedly exist. Yet the legend itself poses great problems. If the Four Elephants mark the four quarters, where did the Fifth stand? Centrally, to form the pattern known as a quincunx? If it slipped and fell from the Turtle's back, how could it strike the Disc – did it fall *upwards*? And if so, wouldn't it strike the underside of the Disc rather than crashing down through the atmosphere? Did it perhaps briefly go into orbit? Dwarfs are a secretive race, so we are unlikely ever to learn the truth of this.

Some philosophers in Ephebe, hearing the tale, have concluded that the Fifth Elephant is not a gross material being subject to normal physical laws, but the pure, subtle, ethereal Quintessence of Cosmic

Pachydermacy. It is nowhere to be seen because it is present everywhere. Without it, the whole Universe of the Discworld would cease to exist. By a remarkable coincidence, this is exactly how the Earth philosophers of Ancient Greece described their hypothetical Fifth Element – the invisible, impalpable, ethereal Quintessence which provides the essential counterbalance to the four material elements of Earth, Air, Fire and Water, the five together making up their universe. Or it may just be a legend. Legends don't have to make sense. They just have to be beautiful. Or at least interesting.

THE GODS

At the last count, the number of major gods known to research theologians on the Discworld was 3,000, and rising. The potential number is unlimited, since at any moment a new one may be called into existence by the mere fact that it has occurred to a human being (or to a member of any other sentient species) to believe he, she or it exists, and to feel an urge to worship him, her or it. The greater the number of devotees, rituals, shrines, temples, sacrifices, and sacred books which develop from this initial urge, the greater the status of the deity. Conversely, of course, since belief is the life-force and nourishment of gods, in the course of time particular gods can and do lose power as the number of their believers drops. Rarely, however, do they dwindle into total insignificance, and any good dramatic miracle quickly restores them to their previous status, as was proved by the events narrated in *Small Gods*. Two of them, Fate and Luck (The Lady), are almost certainly immune to change – they don't have temples, but there can hardly be anybody, anywhere in the multiverse, who does not believe in *them*. In addition, dwarfs have formulated the notion of a Creator quite distinct from any individual gods, whom they call Tak; we shall have more to say on this in the next chapter.

Discworld people vary considerably in their attitude to the gods.

Certain groups, notably witches, wizards, policemen and dwarfs, ignore them. Not that anybody would actually deny that they exist – it is known that they are quick with a thunderbolt if they detect actual atheism – but it is perfectly possible to get on with one's life without thinking about them. Similarly, the citizens of Ephebe do not pay very much attention to their numerous divinities. On the other hand, the land of Djelibeybi is swarming with local gods, in whose honour devoted priests carry out an endless round of sacred rituals. In Omnia and Borogravia, every aspect of life is dominated by the very demanding cult of a single god, Om and Nuggan respectively. As for Ankh-Morpork, it is rather a paradox. Street after street has a temple in it, enough of them to suit every ethnic group, yet nobody could call it a pious city, exactly. The citizens seem willing to worship any god at all, provided he or she is good for trade. In that city, we learn (in *Making Money*), there is even a god-of-the-month club. And a deity currently in the ascendant is Anoia, goddess of Things That Get Stuck in Drawers. That's life in the big city for you. People will take a chance on heaven, but they would like to get their hands on the corkscrew right now, amen.

The major gods, loosely organized into a rather grumpy pantheon, have chosen to make their home on the peak of a truly remarkable mountain, Cori Celesti – a spire of rock and ice, ten miles high, rising above the clouds at the very centre and hub of the Disc. The home itself is of course a vast marble palace, a pile of pillars, pilasters, pinnacles, pyramids, parapets, peristyles, porticos, porches, portals and pavilions, which they have decided to call Dunmanifestin. Gods are not noted for good taste or a sense of the ridiculous, nor indeed, in most cases, for intelligence.

If the gods have the ability to look into other dimensions, then they will see some remarkable resemblances to themselves in the cosmic soap operas of Earth. One thing they have apparently taken notice of is fashions in divine accessories and lifestyles – thunderbolts, goat's feet, a jackal's head, and so on – whatever. If Zeus and his gang have a Mount Olympus, and Vishnu and *his* gang have a

Mount Meru, they get themselves their Cori Celesti, and it's higher than the other two put together. This passion for keeping up with the Zeuses means that anyone with a working knowledge of inter-dimensional mythology who drops in at Dunmanifestin will feel quite at home there.

The Disc gods will have noticed, too, that all pantheons pass their time in banqueting, and that many also like playing board games. For example, one of the first things the Norse gods did when they had finished creating the cosmos was to settle down for a happy session of *hnefatafl*, played with pieces made of pure gold. As *hnefi* is 'fist' and *tafl* is 'table' or 'board', the name means roughly 'The Punch-up Board-Game'; it is a bit like draughts but much more like the Discworld game of Thud. It is thought that the run of play determines the destinies of men, gods, giants and the world itself. Apparently the game will be disrupted and the pieces scattered when gods and monsters fight at Ragnarok, the War at the End of the World, also known as the Doom of the Gods and the Twilight of the Gods. Afterwards, according to the Old Icelandic prophetic poem *Völuspá*, a new world will arise and the surviving younger gener-ation of gods will restore both the cosmic order and the game which expressed it:

> Then once again in the grass are found
>> Draughtsmen all of gold,
> The wondrous draughtsmen the gods had owned
>> In the earliest days of old.

On Earth, however, not everyone relishes the idea of being a pawn in a game played by gods. The twelfth-century Persian poet Omar Khayyám made a resigned but gloomy comment on life in his *Rubáiyát*:

> 'Tis all a Chequer-board of Nights and Days
> Where Destiny with Men for Pieces plays:

Hither and thither moves, and mates, and slays,
And one by one back in the Closet lays.

The gods of the Discworld lack the patience and imagination to play chess, draughts, *hnefatafl*, or even chequers; their idea of amusement is a form of Snakes and Ladders (played with greased rungs), accompanied by heavy betting and a good deal of bluffing and cheating, which brings it nearer to poker. The currency staked is the souls of men. The gaming board is a finely carved map of the Disc, overprinted with squares. Occasionally, the playing pieces represent monsters; more often, they are beautifully detailed models of those human beings who have foolishly done something to get themselves noticed. It is said that these unfortunate mortals sometimes faintly hear, as they hasten to their doom, the rattle of dice in the celestial (skull-shaped) shaker.

This is one of the reasons it's wise to steer clear of the gods, as the wizard Rincewind knows:

'I don't like the idea of going *anywhere* near the gods. We're like toys to them, you know. And they don't realize how easily the arms and legs come off.' [*The Last Hero*]

Or maybe (and even Rincewind in his darkest moments didn't think of this) they *do* realize, and find it funny. That at any rate is what Will Shakespeare thought when he wrote *King Lear*, in one of *his* darkest moments:

As flies to wanton boys are we to the gods;
They kill us for their sport.

The gods have an age-old feud with the Ice Giants, a species of super-troll the size of large houses, craggy and faceted, and composed entirely of ice which glints green and blue in the light – apart from their small, deep-sunken, coal-black eyes. Just as Zeus and the

Olympians defeated the gigantic Titans and imprisoned them inside volcanoes such as Etna (where they still wriggle about, causing eruptions and earthquakes), so Blind Io and the other Discworld gods defeated the Ice Giants and imprisoned them under the eternal ice at the Hub. There is, however, a prophecy. A very Norse-sounding prophecy, a prophecy of End Time doom:

> At the end of the world they'll break free at last, and ride out on their dreadful glaciers and regain their ancient domination, crushing out the flames of civilization until the world lies naked and frozen under the terrible cold stars until Time itself freezes over. Or something like that, apparently. [*Sourcery*]

Whether it comes with ice ages, global warming, a nasty bang or a little whimper, the end of a world is never much fun.

Blind Io

Io is the chief of the gods. He is elderly, white-haired and white-bearded, dressed in a toga and wearing a white blindfold which conceals the blank skin where his eyes should be. Despite this, and despite his name, he sees everything that is going on, since in fact he has a number of detached eyes (several dozen of them) which hover around him and keep a sharp look-out in all directions. His throne too is encrusted with eyes. He is the Supreme Thunderer, having absorbed every other thunder-god on the Disc into himself. However, he keeps a stock of seventy hammers, double-headed axes, and thunderbolts, each of a different design, to blend in with local expectations wherever he may appear. This avoids unnecessary distress to worshippers.

At one time he employed a pair of ravens to fly hither and yon and keep him informed of everything going on in the world. In another universe Odin, chief of the Norse gods, had had exactly the same idea; his two ravens were named Memory and Thought. From the god's point of view, it's a good plan, efficient and energy-saving. From the ravens' point of view, regrettably, Io's free-floating eyeballs were altogether too much of a temptation (Odin's one eye is firmly fixed in his head, so in his case the problem did not arise) and after some embarrassing scenes Io's ravens had to be dismissed.[3]

Earth is well stocked with thunder-gods, including Zeus, Jupiter, Thor, Perkun, Indra and Jehovah. Usually, a thunder-god is also the ruler of his particular pantheon, but Thor is an exception, taking second place to Odin (god of war, magic, death and poetry). Blind Io's insistence on being the Disc's *only* Thunderer is an example of how Discworld gods love to outdo those of Earth in displays of status. It's the same with his lavish use of detached eyeballs, whereas on the Earth even the mightiest deities are satisfied with only one. These are mostly to be found in Ancient Egypt, where the Eye of a major god such as Ra, Atum, or Horus embodied the concentration of his divine power and could be sent out to act on his behalf. The separated Eye, called the *wedjat*, was often shown in religious art, and worn as an amulet. It was sometimes identified with the sun or the moon, and sometimes personified as itself a goddess. That's something Io has not yet thought of.

Dagon

A very ancient, mysterious and probably unpleasant god, believed to have been once worshipped on the mud-flats where the city of Ankh-Morpork was later built. At least, *something* happened not so long ago when the late Mr Hong opened a takeaway fish bar on the site of an old temple in Dagon Street, at the time of the full moon – or, some say, of a lunar eclipse. Everybody has heard about it, in general terms, but nobody says just *what* it was . . .

Traditions of the Earth are fuller. It appears that Dagon was first worshipped there some four thousand years ago by Philistines and

---

[3] Only to find a job with Miss Treason (see page 228). Mythology loves ravens.

Phoenicians in the Middle East; there were temples to him in Gaza and other coastal towns. According to the Bible (1 Samuel 5), his statue stood in a mighty temple at Ashdod, but when the captured Jewish Ark was brought into this temple the statue crashed to the ground and its head and hands broke off, leaving only a stump on the threshold.

There is argument among scholars as to what he looked like, and what it was he was god of. The older generation thought his name came from a word for 'fish' and that he must have been the god of fishes, shaped like a merman, human above the waist and fishy below. Most poets and occultists agree. More recent scholars say no, the name comes from a word for 'corn', and he was a god of farming (no fish tail required). The matter could easily be settled if one could find an old temple of his and set up a bakery in one corner and a fish-and-chip shop in the other, and see what happened.

One writer who had no doubts at all on the matter was the American H. P. Lovecraft, whose eerily receptive mind picked up many strange influences from the worlds of gods and demons, and indeed from the dreaded Dungeon Dimensions. In 1917 he published a story, 'Dagon', in which a shipwrecked man reaches an unknown land of mud and rocks, newly risen from the ocean floor. There are weird buildings there, with repulsive carvings. Then he sees, emerging from a deep abyss, a vast and loathsome monster with scaly arms, webbed hands and feet, shockingly wide and flabby lips, and bulging, glassy eyes. Though he escapes, he remains haunted by the thought of huge nameless things crawling and floundering at the bottom of the ocean until the day when they will come to destroy mankind:

Once I sought out a celebrated ethnologist, and amused him with peculiar questions regarding the ancient Philistine legend of Dagon the Fish-god; but soon perceiving that he was hopelessly conventional, I did not press my enquiries.

This may well be significant, since it is strongly suspected on the Discworld that Dagon had some connection with the sunken land of Leshp, which occasionally rises to the surface of the Circle Sea, as described in *Jingo*. On Leshp, there are fragments of buildings with an uncomfortably non-human look about them, a bodeful atmosphere, and plenty of pretty mosaics showing squid and octopuses. All in all, it seems probable that Dagon is actually one of the Things from the Dungeon Dimensions still lurking on the Disc, like Bel-Shamharoth (see below).

Fate

This, possibly, is the god most feared and hated by men. He is proverbially stern and implacable. Some Earthbound poets have claimed that he is blind, but this is far from true; anyone who looks into his dark and bottomless eyes will see that they are holes opening on to the blackness of infinite night. He enjoys gambling and chess, largely because when he plays, the roll of the dice is always fixed and there are always two queens on his side of the board – unless, of course, his eternal rival the Lady has a hand in the game, in which case there is a million-to-one chance that somebody might cheat Fate.

In the mythologies of the Earth, Fate is sometimes personified as three old women, the Fates – three because triplicity symbolizes power. More often, however, he remains an abstract figure.

The gods of Djelibeybi

In the river kingdom of Djelibeybi, the national religion has been accreting and fermenting and bubbling away for seven thousand years, during which time nobody ever threw away a god, in case he might come in useful one day. As a result, the gods are far too numerous to list. One might start by mentioning Scrab the Pusher of the Ball of the Sun, Thrrp the Charioteer of the Sun, Jeht the

Boatman of the Solar Orb, Vut the Dog-Headed God of Evening, Bunu the Goat-Headed God of Goats, Ket the Ibis-Headed God of Justice, Hat the Vulture-Headed God of Unexpected Guests, Bast the Cat-Headed Goddess of Things Left on the Doorstep or under the Bed . . . From which, two things are already obvious: they just love fooling around with funny faces, and most of them reckon they can do the top job. They can also be quarrelsome:

> There was a monstrous splash out in the river. Tzut, the Snake-Headed God of the Upper Djel, surfaced and regarded the assembled priesthood solemnly. Then Fhez, the Crocodile-Headed God of the Lower Djel, erupted beside him and made a spirited attempt at biting his head off. The two submerged in a column of spray and a minor tidal wave. [*Pyramids*]

There are remarkably close and no doubt wholly coincidental similarities here to the pantheon of Ancient Egypt, where many of the deities have the heads of animals or birds, and where it was perfectly possible for several of them to be credited with the same important function. Thus, Amun, Aten, Atum, Ptah, and Ra were each said to have been the creator of the world, and all except Ptah were also sun gods. This does not seem to have caused any quarrels, either among the gods themselves or among their priests. In Egypt, as in Djelibeybi, priests, very much in the way of advanced physicists, took for granted that mutually incompatible statements could still both be true, and that in any case the *really* important thing was to carry out rituals correctly.

The kings of Djelibeybi, also called pharaohs, are regarded as gods even while still alive; the divine part of their souls comes from the sun in the form of a bird – in the case of Teppicymon XXVII, a seagull. Kings have the power (and duty) to make the sun rise every morning, and to make the river Djel flood the land in due season; they do this by carrying out daily rituals as tradition requires. There may be minor supernatural manifestations too – rivers flowing more strongly as a pharaoh passes by, grass and corn springing up in his footsteps, and so on. On the Earth, the pharaohs of Egypt had similar powers and responsibilities.

It has to be said that the Egyptian pantheon fits snugly into the Discworld way of thinking with barely more than a few changes of name. At one point the author of *Pyramids* declared: 'I bought half a shelf of books on Ancient Egypt, and after a while I decided to make things up, because when you got down to details the real thing was just too weird.'

Herne the Hunted

Wherever humans go in for hunting, because they need the meat, or just because it's such good fun, they tend to create a god (or goddess) of the hunt. They pray, and make offerings. They believe the god (or goddess) will provide a good fat deer or buffalo or wild boar for them, and ensure that they don't break their necks as they gallop after the deer, or shoot one another by accident, or get gored by the boar. But it never occurs to them that the prey could be praying too, though probably not to the same deity.

On the Discworld, where divinities are called into existence by the very fact that someone hopes and believes that they exist, this often urgent prayer is catered for. There, in the mountains and forests of Lancre, lives Herne the Hunted, who is a god of the chase, though not in the usual sense:

> Herne was the god of the chased and the hunted and all small animals whose ultimate destiny is to be an abrupt damp squeak. He was about three feet high, with rabbit ears and very small horns. But he did have an extremely good turn of speed. [*Lords and Ladies*]

His role as a deity is to hear the occult voice of the prey. He is a good listener, but his success rate at answering prayers is not high. His worshippers, unfortunately, tend to die shortly after calling upon his name.

How he got his name is an interesting example of interaction between one universe and another. At any one time there are millions of particles of inspiration and information pulsating through the multiverse, pouring out from the minds of various sentient species. One of the most powerful sources was on Earth, in the creative mind of a human being named William Shakespeare. In the world of Shakespeare's imagination – to be precise, in his play *The Merry Wives of Windsor*, written in 1597 – there is a Herne the *Hunter*. The two heroines of the play decide to make a fool of a man who is pestering them by persuading him to disguise himself as a ghost and meet them at midnight under an oak tree in Windsor Park. Describing this ghost, one says:

> There is an old tale goes, that Herne the hunter,
> Sometime a keeper here in Windsor Forest,
> Doth all the winter time, at still midnight,
> Walk round about an oak, with great ragg'd horns;
> And there he blasts the trees, bewitches cattle,
> And makes the cows yield blood, and shakes a chain
> In a most hideous and dreadful manner.

According to another version of the play, some mothers used Herne as a bogeyman to frighten children:

> Oft have you heard since Herne the hunter dyed,
> That women, to affright their little children,
> Say that he walkes in shape of a great stagge.

Shakespeare tells us nothing more about Herne's life or death, but about two hundred years later, in 1792, a writer called Samuel Ireland says he had heard say that Herne was a gamekeeper who had turned to crime, and who hanged himself on the oak, fearing he was about to lose his job. This fits the traditional belief that suicides haunt the scene of their death. The rattling chain is also standard equipment for a ghost, but the stag's antlers are not. Perhaps Shakespeare felt they matched the forest setting. Or perhaps he just wanted to get a laugh; Elizabethan audiences thought horns side-splittingly funny, even better than custard pies, and this is a comedy after all.

To Shakespeare, Herne was simply an earthbound ghost, for ever walking round and round one particular tree, in the same way as the ghostly kings of Lancre must never move far from the stone walls of their castle. But the job-description 'hunter' caught the eye of Jacob Grimm, a German expert on mythology in the early nineteenth century, and started up a whole new train of thought. It reminded him of the Wild Hunt – a horde of phantom riders who, according to European folklore, gallop across the night sky during midwinter storms. Their leader is sometimes said to be a lost soul who is doomed to hunt for ever, sometimes the Devil pursuing the souls of sinners, occasionally a god hunting forest elves. Maybe, said Grimm, Herne had once been a Wild Huntsman, not a common-or-garden gamekeeper's ghost.

This is Grimm's theory, *not* Will Shakespeare's. But people liked the idea, and so on the Earth Herne the Hunter, the stag-headed god of hunting, was born. He has enjoyed a brilliant career, thanks to those fascinating antlers. In the 1930s, people started wondering if he could be connected with various old Celtic gods who had horns or antlers on their heads, especially a Gaulish one to whom sailors raised an altar in Paris early in the first century AD, calling him Cernunnos, 'Horned One' (or possibly 'Old Horny'). Others thought he might even have as his remote ancestor a prehistoric man painted on the wall of a French cave, wearing a skin and antlers. By now, there are many, many people ready to swear that Herne is an age-old god, the lord of wild nature. But there is the truth and, then again, there is The Truth, in the face of which truth can only shrug and grin.

According to a popular 1980s British TV series, Robin Hood

used to meet a horned man in the forest, and this was none other than Herne. Well, maybe so – provided Robin had an efficient time machine to whisk him forward two or three centuries to Elizabethan times, or backwards to the first century AD to meet up with Cernunnos.

And so, while Will Shakespeare lies giggling in his grave, the story goes drifting off across the dimensions, twisting itself into other shapes, and creating Herne the Hunted. Stories and folklore always tangle, and never more than on Discworld.

Hoki the Jokester

Hoki is a localized nature-god, only to be found in the deep forests of the Ramtops. Sometimes he manifests himself as an oak-tree, sometimes as half a man and half a goat, and pretty well always as a bloody nuisance. He plays the flute, very badly.

Hoki has a typically mix-and-don't-match approach to the business of filching attributes and character traits from the gods of another universe. He admired and copied the shaggy goat-legs and the pipes of Pan, a cheerful, sexy little nature-god living in Arcadia in Ancient Greece. His name, however, he took from that of the Norse Loki, a trickster and trouble-maker, whose most infamous deed was a murder-by-proxy: he caused the death of the popular and handsome young Baldur by getting a blind god to throw a twig of mistletoe at him, supposedly as a joke. Hoki must have got to hear about this, since it is said that he was thrown out of Dunmanifestin for playing 'the old exploding mistletoe trick' on Blind Io.

The oak-tree manifestation is something Hoki picked up more recently. In some countries of the Earth over the past fifty or sixty years there has been a revival of paganism, and sexy male nature-gods are once again in fashion, including a Green Man who manifests himself as a face sprouting leaves, peering through leaves, or entirely made up of leaves. Sometimes, they are oak leaves. Observing this, Hoki decided to go one better and be the whole tree.

The Lady

Though everyone believes in her and longs to win her favour, nobody ever calls her by her true name, or tries to summon her, for this would make her vanish. Her eyes are pure green, from edge to edge, and green is her favourite colour. Her realm is that of the throw of the dice, of uncertainty and chance, especially the million-to-one chance. She thwarts the rigid rules of Fate.

And on the Earth too, that's exactly how things are. Except as regards the colour green. That information has not seeped through into our world, where many people regard green as unl— er, quite the opposite.

Nuggan

Nuggan, the god of Borogravia (and also of paperclips, desk stationery sets, and unnecessary paperwork), is small and podgy, and has the sourest face one could wish never to see, with a fussy little moustache. He has revealed himself unto his faithful people via the holy *Book of Nuggan*, which – unlike other holy writs – is published in a ring binder, since it is permanently incomplete, especially as regards the List of Abominations. Updates appear regularly as an appendix. At the last count, the things that are Abominations in the eyes of Nuggan included garlic, chocolate, certain mushrooms, dwarfs, cats, babies, shirts with six buttons, cross-dressing, jigsaws, and the colour blue.

Nuggan's temper being notoriously tetchy, Borogravians mostly pray to their ruler, the Duchess Annagovia, whom they call Little Mother, and whose icon is displayed in every house. She herself is never seen, having shut herself away in a castle for years, in mourning for her husband who was gored by a wild boar when hunting, they say. (Another instance of trans-dimensional parallels, since on the Earth Adonis, a human lover of the Greek goddess Aphrodite, met his death in just the same way.) She may possibly be dead. She is (or was) human, of course, yet somehow rather more, as the

Ankh-Morpork consul to Zlobenia explained to Commander Vimes:

> 'The royal family in Borogravia have always had a quasi-religious status, you see. They're the head of the church, and the peasants, at least, pray to them in the hope that they'll put in a good word with Nuggan. They're like ... living saints. Celestial intermediaries. To be honest, that's how these countries work in any case. If you want something done, you have to know the right people. And I suppose it's easier to pray to someone in a picture than to a god you can't see.'
> [*Monstrous Regiment*]

According to Commander Vimes, Nuggan has dwindled away to a mere voice, and it is time for the Borogravians to find themselves a new god. The Duchess herself agrees; speaking through her most fervent devotee, she declares:

> Fight Nuggan, for he is nothing now, nothing but the poisonous echo of your ignorance and pettiness and malicious stupidity. Find yourselves a worthier god. And let ... me ... go! All those prayers, all those entreaties ... to me! Too many hands clasped, that could more gainfully answer your prayers by effort and resolve!

A *very* unusual message for a divinity, or a semi-divinity, to give unto the faithful, in any universe, but it might bear repeating.

Offler the Crocodile

Offler is a very old god, who first arose from steamy swamps in the hot dark land of Klatch, and finds worshippers anywhere where there is a large river and a warm climate, including Djelibeybi and Ankh-Morpork. He is sometimes known as 'Offler of the Bird-Haunted Mouth', because of the flock of brave and holy birds which attend upon him, pecking out those little shreds of meat which are such a nuisance when they get stuck between your fangs. Apart from his crocodile head, he is of normal human shape, though he has occasionally manifested himself with six arms instead of two. He lisps, because of the fangs.

His counterpart on the Earth is the Egyptian Sobek, son of the primeval waters, whose name means 'the Raging One' and who manifested himself either as an entire crocodile wearing a crown, or as a man with a crocodile head. He lived in the marshes by the Nile, and was ardently worshipped by prudent river fishermen. Nile crocodiles are notoriously savage.

Om

The Great God Om is the sole god of the land of Omnia, his devotees having zealously exterminated everybody who worshipped any others. By nature he is very liable to outbursts of Wrath, expressed through cursing, trampling of infidels, and smiting with lightning. According to the Omnian priests, he spoke – indeed, he spake – to a series of chosen prophets, dictating to them a vast number of Laws, Precepts and Prohibitions which are enshrined in numerous sacred writings, not to mention some Codicils written on slabs of lead ten feet tall. Sometimes, it is said, Om did his spaking from out of a pillar of flame. Sometimes the chosen prophet sprouted glowing horns, for Holy Horns are Om's symbol.

The priests also claim that Om made the world, and revealed to them that it is not a disc carried by a turtle, but a perfectly smooth ball moving in a perfect circle round the sun, which is another perfectly smooth ball; this has become a vital dogma in the Omnian Church. Actually, Om now denies that he ever said this, or that he made the world – and if he *had*, he says, he wouldn't have made it as a ball. Silly idea, a ball. People would fall off. Come to that, Om has only very vague memories of having met any prophets, and doesn't recognize the things he is supposed to have said to them.

Om's views on these matters are known because he spent three years or so in the world in the form of a tortoise. This was an embarrassing accident. He had meant to manifest himself briefly in some suitably impressive avatar – most likely, a bull – but what he got was a tortoise. Not a vast mountain-bearing tortoise such as the Hindu god Vishnu once chose, but a mere common-or-garden tortoise. And he found he was quite unable to get back to his own shape. This humiliating failure of god-power was due to the fact that hardly any Omnians had real, true, deep-down belief in Om. Possibly, only one. The rest *thought* they believed in him, but what they really believed in was the terrifying authority of the Omnian Church and its Quisition. As the philosopher Abraxas wrote:

> Around the Godde there forms a Shelle of prayers and Ceremonies and Buildings and Priestes and Authority, until at Last the Godde Dies. Ande this maye notte be noticed. [*Small Gods*]

To make matters worse, Om-as-tortoise found his physical life in danger. Far too many people he met knew that 'there's good eating on one of those'. He was also being hunted by an eagle who had found out that if you carry off a tortoise in your talons and drop it on a rock from a great height, the result is a shattered shell and a rather fiddly meal. If, on the other hand, you drop it on somebody's head, then you are recreating the Earth legend which claims that the Ancient Greek dramatist Aeschylus was killed when a flying eagle dropped a tortoise on his bald head, mistaking it for a rock.

That eagles in some places have learned to drop tortoises in order to crack them open has been attested to by various sources, and our suspension of disbelief in a bird's ability to target humans in the course of breaking its lunch was occasioned by a *Daily Telegraph* obituary of Brigadier John Mackenzie. In the Second World War he worked with partisans in the mountains of Greece, and '. . . on one occasion a brigade rifle meeting on a mountain was disrupted when a flock of vultures carrying various small tortoises in their talons decided to drop them on the mountainside to crack their shells. Two soldiers sustained fractured skulls from the tortoises and there were other injuries; the meeting was abandoned.'

Om has been affected by his spell as a humble tortoise. The Omnian Church has now disbanded its Quisition. Divine smitings have become noticeably rare. Om's devotees grudgingly allow foreigners to worship their own deities without being massacred, and his missionaries simply afflict the infidel with hymns and excruciatingly boring tracts. Clearly, this is all made up and the story has nothing to do with any 'Earthly' deity.

Valkyries

Valkyries form a group of very specialized goddesses honoured by Barbarian Heroes; their name means 'Choosers of the Slain'. They are found both on the Discworld and in the Nordic and Germanic myths of Earth, where they serve Odin the God of War (also known as Wotan or Woden). They became even better known through a nineteenth-century opera by the German composer Wagner. They are tall, powerfully built women, wearing chain mail and horned helmets, and riding magnificent airborne horses. Since Wagner's time, a good singing voice is also a requirement for the job, for they ride to a rousing chorus of 'Hi-jo-to! Ho! Hi-jo-to! Ho!'

The task of a Valkyrie is to hover over battlefields where her chosen Hero is fighting, bringing him good luck for as long as the God of War decrees. Then, when the fated time comes for the Hero to be killed, she swoops down and carries his soul to Odin's Valhalla, 'Hall of the Slain' – or to its Discworld equivalent, the Halls of Blind Io – where he will enjoy a blissful afterlife of quaffing mead and feasting on roast boar. The Valkyries will be on hand to make sure the drinking horns are kept filled. And there is other fun to be had too, as the medieval Icelandic writer Snorri Sturluson explained in his account of heathen Nordic mythology, The Edda, in the 1220s:

'What sport is there for the Chosen Warriors when they aren't drinking?' asked Gangleri the Wanderer.

The High One said: 'Every day, when they have dressed they put on their armour and go out into the open country and have a battle, and they kill one another, every one of them. That is their sport. And when the time for the evening meal comes round, they ride back home to Valhalla and sit down together to drink again.'

It's a magnificent option, an offer one can't refuse. But sometimes, sometimes – well, maybe only once in all the centuries of the Discworld, and never on Earth – there come Heroes like Cohen the Barbarian and his Silver Horde, who do refuse it, as is told in *The Last Hero*. As their confederate Mr Saveloy had once pointed out (in *Interesting Times*), it does sound like spending forever in a room full of sports masters. And it involves hobnobbing with gods, which isn't to everyone's taste. Instead, Cohen and the Horde choose to ride away to the stars.

DEMONS OF THE NETHER PIT

Demons have existed on the Discworld for as long as the gods, whom in many ways they closely resemble. There are millions of them. They find it very galling that those stuck-up bastards in Dunmanifestin refuse to take them seriously.

The demons live in a spacious dimension which is more or less on the same space-time continuum as that of humans, and which they have tastefully decorated in shades of flame and keep heated to roasting point, as tradition requires. It is arranged in eight circles, surrounding a bubbling lake of lava-substitute, from which rise the majestic towers of Pandemonium, the Demon City. Demonic society is strongly hierarchical, murderously competitive, and devoted to tradition. Its higher ranks have added impressive titles to their sonorously supernatural names – Lord Astfgl, Duke Vassenego, Earl Beelzemoth, Duke Drazometh the Putrid. This, incidentally, is equally true on Earth, where the famous grimoire known as the *Lemegeton*, attributed to King Solomon, is intensely class-conscious. It lists seventy-six aristocratic demons: eighteen kings, twenty-six dukes, fifteen marquises, five earls and twelve presidents, besides various minor groups.

Demons take a lively interest in observing human affairs, partly out of curiosity and partly because they do so much admire human ingenuity when it comes to devising ways of hurting one another. Like the gods, they can peer across multidimensional space, and take note of events and ideas on the Earth as well as on the Disc. This is useful to them, since they are about as capable of original thought as a parrot is of original swearwords. Their Infernal Regions would have been pretty bleak without the picturesque notions they pinched from human imaginations. From the Bible they got the idea of a lake of fire, mentioned in the Apocalypse (Book of Revelation); from the medieval Italian poet Dante, the idea that Hell is a deep funnel-shaped pit, with circular terraces running round it – Dante talked of nine circles, but the Discworld demons opted for eight, the preferred magical number in their universe. In Milton's *Paradise Lost*, it is said that devils built themselves a palace in Hell by the power of magic and music, and called it Pandemonium:

> Anon out of the earth a fabric huge
> Rose like an exhalation, with the sound
> Of dulcet harmonies and voices sweet –
> Built like a temple, where pilasters round
> Were set, and Doric pillars overlaid
> With golden architrave; nor did it lack
> Cornice and frieze, with massive sculptures graven;
> The roof was fretted gold . . .

And so on and so forth – brazen doors, marble pavements, starry lamps, a jewelled throne – the lot. But still, it was just one palace. The Discworld demons can do better than that: *their* Pandemonium is a whole city.

Most demons are rather old-fashioned as regards their personal appearance, liking to look as disgusting as possible. Thus Urglefloggah, Spawn of the Pit and Loathly Guardian of the Dread Portal, who welcomes newcomers to Hell, has various well-fanged mouths and more tentacles than legs, though fewer arms than heads. First impressions are *so* important. Then there was Quezovercoatl the Feathered Boa, a demon who went off to become a god to the humans of the Tezuman Empire and teach them how to cut the hearts out of one another on top of pyramids. It is thought that he had picked up his ideas from the Aztecs of Mexico, and likewise (more or less) his name. He was half-man, half-chicken, half-jaguar, half-scorpion, and half mad. However, he was also only six inches high, so when forced to manifest himself physically he came to a sad, squishy end.

At the time of the events described in *Eric*, Hell was ruled by a relatively new king named Astfgl, who was determined to modernize everything, including his own appearance. His predecessors had gone in for hoofs and shaggy hind legs, but such things were beneath him. Nor would he ever consider tentacles, or grotesque faces in unseemly places. Instead, he favoured a red silk cloak and gloves, crimson tights, a cowl with two rather sophisticated little horns on it, and a trident. A brief glance at the theatrical archives of Britain had been enough to show him that this is the correct formal dress for a Demon King. Regrettably, whenever he lost his temper his neat costume would get ripped apart in a sudden sprouting of claws and wings.

Lord Astfgl also revamped the whole infernal regime to conform to up-to-date business practices. He abolished good traditional tortures such as pushing a rock uphill only for it to roll down again, or having your liver eaten by an eagle every day – both copied from excellent models in Greek myth, the punishments of Sisyphus and Prometheus. Instead, he issued memos, policy statements, and morale-boosting notices to staff. In agonies of outrage and boredom, the lesser demons conferred on him the title of Supreme Life President of Hell and gave him a luxurious but remote office to himself, where he is still happily busy compiling an in-depth analysis of the role, function, priorities and goals of the demon race. After which, the old familiar flames flickered once again. It was for the best (or, technically, for this is Hell, for the worst). It is only a matter of time before he invents the first-ever mission statement, causing his world to end in self-defence.

It is a curious fact that demons, powerful though they are in their own dimension, can nevertheless be summoned into the human world and told to make themselves useful. In theory, this requires elaborate magic circles, runes, pentacles (on Earth) or octograms (on the Discworld), plus special robes, wands, knives, swords, candles, talismans, and incense, all of which come expensive. Then there are the chants and invocations, which go on and on and on. Part of a conjuration composed in the 1640s by the learned Elias Ashmole (antiquary, alchemist, astrologer, and founder of Oxford's Ashmolean Museum) runs as follows:

> I, Elias Ashmole, adjure thee Elaby Gathen, straightly charge and command thee by Tetragrammaton, Emmanuel, messias, sether, panton, cratons, Alpha and Omega, and by all other high and reverend names of Almighty God both effable and ineffable . . . that thou appear meekly and mildly in this glasse, without doinge hurt or daunger unto me or any other living creature . . . and truly, without fraud, dissymulation or deceite, resolve and satisfye me in and of all manner of such questions and commands and demandes as I shall either aske, require, desire or demande of thee . . .

Demons love this kind of language. They think it shows proper respect. And so long as you are ceremonially robed and equipped, and chanting jargon by the bucket-load, they manage to forget that what's actually going on is that they are being *ordered about* by a human.

They are less happy if someone cuts out the frills, as the three witches of Lancre did in an emergency. Being in Nanny Ogg's washroom at the time, they used a sharp and terrible copper-stick, scattered some rather old washing soda and extremely hard soap flakes, and bound the demon by the names of the bald scrubbing brush of Art and the washboard of Protection. And if the Summoning was unorthodox, the Dismissal was frankly insulting:

> '*May I go now?*'
>
> 'Um?'
>
> '*Please?*'
>
> Granny jerked upright again.
>
> 'Oh. Yes. Run along,' she said distractedly. 'Thank you.'
>
> The head didn't move . . .
>
> '*You wouldn't mind banishing me, would you?*' said the demon, when no one seemed to be taking the hint.
>
> 'What?' said Granny, who was thinking again.
>
> '*Only I'd feel better for being properly banished. "Run along" lacks that certain something,*' said the head . . .
>
> 'Certainly,' said Magrat. 'Right. Okay. Um. Begone, foul fiend, unto the blackest pit—'
>
> The head smiled contentedly as the words rolled over it. This was more like it.
>
> It melted back into the waters of the copper like candlewax under a flame. Its last contemptuous comment, almost lost in the swirl, was, '*Run aaaalonggg . . .*' [*Wyrd Sisters*]

Finally it has to be said that on the Disc there are certain low-grade demons who stay permanently in the human world, working inside pocket watches, picture-making devices, personal disorganizers, and similar contraptions. Some are eager to please, others distinctly surly. The great lords of Hell never, ever, mention this.

THINGS FROM THE DUNGEON DIMENSIONS

It is well known on the Discworld that *Things* from the shadowy, chaotic wastelands outside space and time which some call the Dungeon Dimensions are always trying to break through into the little circle of candlelight loosely called 'the real world'. They prowl round its flimsy stockades, searching for places where the fabric of reality has worn thin. Their shapes are unstable, but nasty, with random combinations of tentacles, talons, mandibles, spindly limbs, and wings; this reflects their sad, mad, incoherent minds. They hoot and howl and buzz, giggle and flutter, and produce a horrible chittering sound. Any large concentration of magic attracts them. They crave the solidity, light, and life of real worlds, and hate all living creatures with a deep and jealous hate; if they did gain a foothold on the Disc they would inevitably drain all life from it. Occasionally some deluded power-seeking magician imagines that he can safely invoke and control them – or manages to trap the even more mysterious parasitic entity known as the hiver, described in *A Hatful of Sky*. This brings disaster on the magician himself, and on others. More often, someone accidentally creates a point of entry by, for example, conducting a powerful magical or religious ceremony at a spot where the walls between the dimensions are already weak. So far, the breaches in the walls have always been healed and the Things repulsed before too much harm has been done.

It appears from the obscure writings of some exceptionally erudite wizards that the Things were once Dark Gods, existing on the Discworld until they were driven out by even more ancient and powerful beings, the Old High Ones. Their names are listed in the utterly forbidden and totally perilous grimoire known as the *Necrotelicomnicon* or *Liber Paginarum Fulvarum* (Book of Yellow Pages) compiled by the Klatchian necromancer Achmed the Mad. The first edition of this dread opus is kept in conditions of maximum security in the vaults of Unseen University, and students are only permitted to read tenth- or twelfth-hand copies.

Awareness of these occult matters first reached the Earth through the receptive mind of the American writer H. P. Lovecraft, creator of horror fantasies in the 1920s and 30s. He too described monstrous beings from other dimensions forever trying to break through into the normal world; he too wrote of a potently evil book of spells written by a mad Arab, the *Necronomicon*, which could be used to summon and worship them. Alarmingly, it appears from his writings that these creatures have more than once managed to establish themselves in isolated parts of America. One can only hope he was mistaken, but sometimes one fears he was not.

BEL-SHAMHAROTH

It is hard to know how to classify this extremely unpleasant entity.

On the one hand, it could be argued that he should be considered a god, since he inhabits a black eight-sided temple deep in the forest of Skund, near the Hub. He lurks there under an eight-sided stone slab in a hall with eight walls, reached by eight corridors and lit by the dim, eldritch glow of eight-sided crystals. Whether he currently has any worshippers is a very moot point – those who built the temple died long ago, and people who enter it now have an extremely short life-span. However, the level of belief they experience during the few moments that they are face to face with Bel-Shamharoth is so exceptionally intense that it keeps him in existence. His appearance is totally non-humanoid. He looks rather like a spider, or maybe an octopus or squid, or maybe something altogether more strange; something black, at any rate, that is all suckers and tentacles and mandibles, with a single great glaring eye in the middle.

On the other hand, the gods of Cori Celesti have never accepted Bel-Shamharoth as one of their number. The Lady went so far as to say on one occasion that he should never have been spawned, and that she thought all such creatures had died out at the beginning of Time. This seems to imply that he was one of the Old Dark Gods that once existed on the Discworld, and that he managed to remain there when the others were driven out to the Dungeon Dimensions.

One of his powers, we are told in *Equal Rites*, is an ability to enter people's dreams. Amazingly, this is so strong that he has been able to reveal something of himself even in another universe. His title of 'Soul-Eater' is echoed in the mythology of the Ancient Egyptians, who believed that when the dead entered the Afterlife their hearts were weighed against the Ostrich Feather of Truth. If they failed this test, they would be devoured by a hideous monster which crouched beside the scales, called the Eater of Souls. It did not, however, *look* like Bel-Shamharoth, simply being part lion, part crocodile, and part hippopotamus – no tentacles or suckers whatsoever.

Many centuries later, the image of a monstrous tentacular creature stamped itself deeply on the mind of H. P. Lovecraft. He described an incredibly ancient being named Cthulhu, one of the Old Ones who once ruled the Earth, now banished below the ocean bed, but still remembered and worshipped by some. A small stone figurine, of unfathomable antiquity, shows Cthulhu as 'a monster of vaguely anthropoid outline, but with an octopus-like head whose face was a mass of feelers'. Even more appalling is the Dunwich monster, child of a human mother and Yog-Sothoth, another of the Old Ones; this creature is bigger than a barn, made of what looks like squirming ropes, 'an octopus, centipede, spidery kind of thing' with great bulging eyes all over it, and ten or twenty mouths all opening and shutting . . . Definitely an echo or emanation of Bel-Shamharoth.

THE AUDITORS

The most deeply negative and destructive forces in the cosmos of the Discworld have no fangs, no tentacles, no red glowing eyes. They look like small grey hooded robes, with nothing whatsoever inside. They are the Auditors of Reality, who see it as their job to make sure that the universe functions smoothly and efficiently, without unpredictable interruptions. Above all, they distrust and reject the notion of individual personality, since they hold that to have a personality means to have a beginning and an end, and hence to forfeit immortality. The way to be immortal, they maintain, is to avoid living. Therefore they operate entirely by consensus, never permitting themselves to show personal tastes, feelings or opinions; if any of them becomes aware of itself as an individual, it self-destructs instantly. They are the enemies of all imagination, creativity and emotion, and hence of life itself.

Mercifully, their power on the Discworld has so far been restricted. On Earth, their presence grows daily.

Chapter 2

DWARFS

IN A MINE, there are many levels. Some, anybody can visit. But lower down, there are hidden galleries, closed-off corridors, places which only the oldest and wisest miners know. And so it is with dwarfs. Pretty well everyone on the Discworld has *seen* a dwarf, but very, very few really understand what it is like to *be* a dwarf.

What you *see* is easily told. A dwarf is a smallish humanoid (about four foot tall on average), strongly built, bearded, dressed in layer upon layer of leather, plus chain mail and helmet if circumstances warrant it, and never without an axe. This description applies to both male and female dwarfs, though some close observers have claimed that the beards of the latter are silkier. All dwarfs are tireless, highly skilled workers; their traditional, ancestral occupations are mining and smithing, but they are also excellent engineers, jewellers, printers, and so forth. Thousands of them have migrated to Ankh-Morpork, where they work hard and mostly keep themselves to themselves; some of the young ones, regrettably, like to congregate in dwarf bars where they drink too much, sing interminable songs about gold, and get into fights.

These facts find close parallels in the myths and legends of Earth, especially in pre-Christian Scandinavia and the Germanic areas. There, tradition tells of a race of small beings who live inside rocks and under mountains, and are so skilled in metalworking that they make magical weapons and rings for the gods themselves. They are old, wise, and very rich. Female dwarfs are never mentioned (unlike she-elves and giantesses), so one must assume that on our world, as on the Discworld, they looked just like the males and worked at the same crafts. Although in later centuries the names for various types of small supernatural beings have become seriously confused, one can be sure that those that inhabit human mines (as gnomes and kobolds do in Germany, and knockers in Cornwall) and those that work as smiths are kin to the true ancient dwarfs.

One need only look at the names, nicknames and patronymics of many Discworld dwarfs to find confirmation of this link with Nordic and Germanic dwarfdom – from their ancient king B'hrian Bloodaxe to the modern Albrecht Albrechtsson or Bjorn Stronginthearm, there are echoes everywhere. Other dwarf names (Ringfounder, Helmcrusher, Hammerhock) allude to battle prowess and craftsmanship. But from time to time, curiously unsuitable ones occur, such as Cheery, Snorey, Dozy, and Bashfull; these must be due to some alien influence, possibly that which affected the Discworld during the time when moving pictures were being made at Holy Wood. It was certainly at that time that some dwarfs first felt an urge to sing the irritating, and previously unknown, Hiho Song (which is utterly undwarfish, since it does not mention gold and is less than an hour long).

These are only the upper levels of their culture. To understand the nature of a Discworld dwarf, one must dig much deeper. There, dwarfish identity is not defined by mere genetics and size, but by a whole complex culture of laws, taboos, customs, moral principles and traditional knowledge. It is not precisely a religion, but it is as vital to their sense of selfhood as any religion could be. Height, in Discworld dwarf culture, plays no part in defining a dwarf. Dwarfishness is about what you do, not how high you do it. Captain Carrot Ironfoundersson, for example, happens to have been born of human parents and to be well over six foot tall, but his upbringing has made him socially and spiritually a dwarf. As he explains to Vimes:

'Adopted by dwarfs, brought up by dwarfs. To dwarfs I'm a dwarf, sir. I can do the rite of *k'zakra*, I know the secrets of *h'ragna*, I can *ha'lk* my *g'rakha* correctly . . . I am a dwarf.'

'What do those things mean?'

'I am not allowed to tell non-dwarfs.' [*The Fifth Elephant*]

The legal aspects of this culture are known collectively as *kruk*. Outsiders think of this as 'mining law', which is true as far as it goes, but as Carrot explains:

'It's a lot more than that. It's about . . . how you live. Laws of ownership, marriage laws, inheritance, rules for dealing with disputes of all kinds, that sort of thing. Everything, really.'

Each dwarf mine[4] has its own 'king' (a title roughly equivalent to 'chief engineer'), but in disputes where the *kruk* is unclear the final arbiter is the Low King, whose authority extends over all dwarfish communities. He is chosen by the senior dwarfs, usually from among the leading families, and is crowned sitting upon the Scone of Stone. He must sit on it to give his judgements, as all Low Kings have done ever since the days of King B'hrian Bloodaxe, fifteen hundred years ago. This scone is the supreme example of a traditional dwarf bread – a highly prized product used by dwarfs as a food of last resort, and regarded as utterly inedible by all other races. It also serves as a weapon. Some observers claim to have seen it being fashioned with hammer and anvil. Specimens kept in museums for decades, if not centuries, show little change from the day they were baked. That, however, is not why the Scone is held in deep reverence and guarded with the utmost care. King B'hrian Bloodaxe, fifteen hundred years ago, sat on it while it was still soft, and left his impression upon it. It is now the very seat of majesty, conferring legitimacy on each new ruler.

---

[4] Any assembly of dwarfs for a common purpose is technically a 'mine', even if it is a boat or a farm.

This should not seem surprising to us. Pretty well every country can show at least one rock on to which some ancient hero or holy man has stamped his footprints – or hand-prints, or the mark of his knees, or the hoof-prints of his horse. Many are sites of pilgrimage. Some, in Britain and Ireland, are symbols of authority. One famous Scottish one was the Stone of the Footprints on the island of Islay in the Hebrides, a rock about seven foot square marked with two prints; at his inauguration, each chief of the MacDonalds would set his feet in them and stand there, sword in hand, to take his oath. This showed that he would walk in the ways of justice established by his forebears, and held his power by right. This particular stone, alas, was destroyed some three hundred years ago.

The most famous of all inauguration stones is the Stone of Scone, on which generations of medieval kings of Scotland were crowned. Some say it originally came from Ireland, and is identical with the legendary Liafail, which screamed a greeting when a rightful high king of Ireland stood on it; if so, it is at least 2,300 years old. It does not, however, bear any imprints. It was removed from the castle of Scone, near Perth, in 1296 by Edward I of England after his victory over the Scots; for centuries it was kept in Westminster Abbey, built into an ornate wooden throne on which every monarch (including the present Queen) has sat for her or his coronation. In 1950 it was stolen, and recovered a few months later – or was it? Some say what was recovered was only a replica. In any case, real or replica, the Westminster stone was returned to Scotland in 1996, and is now in Edinburgh Castle. Clearly the Stone of Scone and the Scone of Stone echo one another across the multiverse.

Curiously, and we advance it with some caution, our world may offer a more direct parallel with the Scone of Stone. In her book *Footprints in Stone* Janet Bord mentions a local legend that there's said to be a stone behind the main altar in Reims cathedral with the marks of Christ's *buttocks*. He was helping masons build the main doorway, and felt a bit tired. So many comments spring to mind, but the only one we will allow to spring further is that stories of Jesus helping in the construction were endemic during the cathedral-building era, and this one has the feel of a workmen's legend, especially the sort which would be told to wide-eyed apprentices.

Let us return to the Discworld. There, dwarfs are famous workmen. As Captain of the City Watch, Vimes had to learn about the folkways of this important ethnic minority. When one of the city dwarfs was murdered, and later when one who had joined the multiracial City Watch was killed in the course of his duties, Vimes learned a good deal. For one thing, a dead dwarf's tools are always melted down, however fine they are, since no one else would want to use them:

> 'What, use another dwarf's actual tools?' Carrot's mouth twisted in distaste. 'Oh no, that's not . . . right. I mean, they're . . . part of him. I mean . . . someone else using them, after he's used them all these years, I mean . . . urrgh!' [*Men at Arms*]

And a weapon, of the finest quality, will be placed in his grave. Vimes, examining the murdered Bjorn Hammerhock's workshop, noticed a particularly heavy axe etched with intricate patterns. This, Carrot explains, is a burial weapon:

> 'It's made to be buried with a dwarf. Every dwarf is buried with a weapon. You know? To take with him to . . . wherever he's going.'
> 'But it's fine workmanship! And it's got an edge like— aargh,' Vimes sucked his finger, 'like a razor!'
> Carrot looked shocked. 'Of course. It would be no good facing them with an *inferior* weapon.'
> 'What them are you talking about?'
> 'Anything bad he encounters on his journey after death,' said Carrot, a shade awkwardly.

This is so essential that Cuddy, the dwarf watchman, flatly

refuses to depart into the afterlife because his axe has been shattered in the fall that killed him. He protests to Death that he needs a good weapon:

> 'If I'm not going to be properly buried, I ain't going. My tortured soul will walk the world in torment.'
> IT DOESN'T HAVE TO.
> 'It can if it wants to,' snapped the ghost of Cuddy.

Many, many human societies in this world have agreed with the dwarfs that the dead should be given their weapons, and anything else they might need on the journey. And archaeologists are very grateful to them – especially to the ones who carefully laid the stuff in the grave, rather than those who tossed it on to a funeral pyre, even if from the ghost's point of view both methods are equally good. Obviously, archaeologists can't tell from material remains whether in these old societies the living also felt (as Carrot does) that there's something disgusting about using weapons and tools that had belonged to the dead, but it would not be surprising if they did. In the modern world, Gypsies traditionally approve of the idea of burning a dead man's caravan and all its contents, though this means such financial loss to the family that nowadays it is rarely done. So too on the Disc, the Chalkland shepherds burned Granny Aching's hut after her death, knowing none of them would dare use something she had made so much her own (see *A Hatful of Sky*).

One of us recalls a metalwork shop staffed by very old men. When one of them died, his personal tools were left on the bench where he'd put them, untouched, and were gradually buried under workshop debris. It does not need a fevered imagination to see that in the days when tools were an expensive lifetime investment, shaped over the years to their owner's hand, there would be a certain unfocused distaste for handling them after a workmate's death.

*

Outsiders often assume that because all dwarfs look, dress and behave alike, have masculine names, and refer to one another as 'he', they are in fact all male. This is completely untrue – the population, as with other humanoid races, is fifty per cent male and fifty per cent female. But very, very, *very* few dwarfs would ever admit this statistic in public. And (until very recently) *none* would let it be publicly known that they themselves belong to the female fifty per cent.

Even when outsiders know about this, they underestimate the distress it can cause. When the dwarf Cheery Littlebottom joined the Ankh-Morpork Watch, the werewolf Angua guessed that 'he' was really 'she', but couldn't understand why being spotted was so shattering:

> Cheery sagged on to a seat. 'How could you tell? Even other *dwarfs* can't tell! I've been so careful!'
>
> 'I don't know why you're so upset,' said Angua. 'I thought dwarfs hardly recognized the difference between male and female, anyway. Look, there's plenty of women in this town that'd love to do things the dwarf way. I mean, what are the choices they've got? Barmaid, seamstress, or somebody's wife. While *you* can do anything the men do . . .'
>
> 'Provided we do only what the men do,' said Cheery.
>
> Angua paused. 'Oh,' she said. 'I *see*. Hah. Yes, I know *that* tune.' [*Feet of Clay*]

Encouraged by Angua, Cheery gradually yields to her suppressed longing for a bit of jewellery and a dab of lipstick; eventually and with much nervousness, she dons a mid-calf leather skirt (still keeping helmet, breastplate, and beard, naturally). Some other dwarf watchmen react with horror:

> 'That's . . . *female* clothes, isn't it?'
>
> 'Well?' she quavered. 'So what? I can if I want to.'
>
> 'That's . . . my mother never even . . . urgh . . . That's

disgusting! In public too! What happens if kids come in? I can see your *ankles*!'

As it turns out, other she-dwarfs in Ankh-Morpork soon follow Cheery's lead and pluck up courage to 'come out'. But when her duties take her to the old homelands in the mountains, she has to face traditionalists who think it an obscene abomination, a denial of all true dwarfishness, for a female even to admit her gender, let alone to flaunt it by her appearance. The fact that the relatively liberal King Rhys Rhysson accepts her presence, and actually shakes hands with her, is for them a major culture shock.

It is fascinating to compare the way Discworld dwarfs view femininity with the rules, taboos and superstitions about women in many Earthly societies, past and present. At first glance, they seem to be opposites. Dwarfs expect females to conceal their gender, to dress exactly like males, to be warriors, miners, blacksmiths and so forth, just like males. On Earth, on the contrary, societies and religions which feel strongly on questions of gender abominate the idea of a woman dressing like a man. They expect her to wear distinctively female cloth-ing, obeying rules as to what is or is not 'modest': the most important concerns usually being the length of the skirt and how much of the hair, head and face should be concealed. In extreme cases, women end up looking more like small perambulating tents than human beings. So, although their garb proclaims their gender, at the same time it hides it, as surely as that of a Discworld she-dwarf.

As regards work practices, however, Discworld dwarfs are not hampered by the same taboos as Earth's older traditional societies, where it would be out of the question for a woman to take up man's work. Even in European countries in recent times, in some ultra-masculine occupations it was believed that the mere presence of a woman brought bad luck. Women were not allowed to go down mines or on board fishing boats – indeed, simply to meet a woman on the road down to the beach would make a fisherman give up his plans for the day and head back home.

Behind this, rarely mentioned openly, is a deep-rooted horror of menstruation, regarded as a source of magical harm in primitive societies, and as a pollution in the Bible. Sir James Frazer's *The Golden Bough* gives examples of taboos among the native peoples of Australia, North America and elsewhere: a menstruating woman must not touch a man, or his tools and weapons, or any object he may use, or he will surely die; she must not touch freshly killed meat, or it will go bad; she must not go anywhere near the pastures, or the cows will die. There is a whole list of similar notions in the writings of the Roman naturalist Pliny, who regarded them as proven scientific facts: her touch will turn milk sour, cause plants to wither, blunt razors, cloud mirrors, and so on. Most of them crop up again in relatively modern European folklore. As recently as 1846 Victor Hugo noted that menstruating women were not allowed into parts of the Paris catacombs where mushrooms were grown, as their presence would make the mushrooms rot. And to this day some Orthodox Jews will not shake hands with a gentile woman, for fear she might be having her period (a Jewish woman would know she must keep out of their way at this time).

Dwarfs say of themselves that they are not a religious race. True, they have been heard to utter some rather strange words, which *may* be the names of gods, if they drop something heavy on their toes. They also talk about Agi Hammerthief, a mischievous sort of sprite who hangs about in mines and makes off with the tool you were quite sure you'd put down just *there*. Sometimes, in a dark tunnel, you can hear his distant laughter. But they don't count these things as religion; they don't take them seriously.

What dwarfs do take very seriously indeed are the Laws, which were called into existence, at the beginning of time, by Tak. Who Tak was or is, is something they do not discuss, but every dwarf knows the Tale of the Things Tak Wrote:

The first thing Tak did, he wrote himself.
The second thing Tak did, he wrote the Laws.

The third thing Tak did, he wrote the World.
The fourth thing Tak did, he wrote a cave.
The fifth thing Tak did, he wrote a geode, an egg of stone.
[*Thud!*]

When the geode hatched in the twilight of the cave, the First Man and the First Dwarf were born, but only the First Dwarf found the Laws Tak had written. Finally came the First Troll. The conclusion of the Tale was deliberately distorted for thousands of years in order to justify the hatred dwarfs felt for trolls, but the true text has now been recovered. It runs:

> Then Tak looked upon the stone and it was trying to come alive, and Tak smiled and wrote 'All things strive'. And for the service the stone had given he fashioned it into the First Troll, and delighted in the life that came unbidden. These are the things that Tak wrote!

This, as any Earthbound reader can see, is a philosophically and morally profound Creation Myth, and Tak a more impressive figure than any of the gods on Cori Celesti. We can no longer accept that dwarfs are a non-religious race.[5]

Yet in some dwarf communities devotion to the Laws spawned an outlook as rigid as the unchanging ritualism in the kingdom of Djelibeybi, though not as cruel as the enforcement of dogma by the Omnians. At the time of the events described in *The Fifth Elephant* and in *Thud!* the influence of traditionalist mountain dwarfs, especially those from Schmaltzberg, had grown strong. They held that those who had moved to Ankh-Morpork and other lowland cities were *d'rkza*,

---

[5] For a given value of 'non-religious'. Study of the text suggests that Tak, in the dwarfs' understanding, is both the creator of, and immanent in, the fundamental laws of the universe. There is no act of worship, any more than gravity is worshipped, although it may be argued that living a 'right life' is such a thing. Even then the dwarf laws seem open to slow change by long argument. Dwarfs are artisans, after all; tools that don't work are recast.

'not proper dwarfs', because they had become lax, they had let the old ways slide. If Albrecht Albrechtsson had become Low King, he would have declared all these city-dwellers *d'hrarak*, 'non-dwarfs'; this would have made their marriages and business contracts invalid, and would have meant that old dwarfs would not be allowed to be buried back home.

Albrecht did not become Low King, so this did not happen. Instead, traditionalists themselves began coming to Ankh-Morpork, hoping to re-establish orthodoxy by their teaching and example. They are called grags. They are greatly respected by the city dwarfs; they conduct marriages and other necessary ceremonies, give judgement in disputes and advice on problems:

> Please come and say the death-words over my father . . . Please advise me on the sale of my shop . . . Please guide me in my business . . . I am a long way from the bones of my grandfathers, please help me to stay a dwarf. [*Thud!*]

The grags, or deep-downers, go beyond even the strictest letter of the Laws. They have dug themselves new dwellings under the cellars of existing houses, where they live as much as possible underground; if they do have to come up to the surface, they wear heavy black leather robes and hoods with a mere slit for the eyes, and are carried about in curtained sedan chairs, so as never to commit the crime of seeing daylight. The strictest among them form enclosed communities, and never come out. They send a junior novice, called 'the daylight face', to do any errands above ground and to speak with visitors in an antechamber. They claim that everything that happens underground should be governed by *kruk*, 'mining law', not by the laws of Ankh-Morpork. This is something Commander Vimes vigorously rejects; city law, he argues, applies just as much *below* the city as *in* the city.

It should not be too difficult to find parallels to all this in other universes, including ours. One thinks of fundamentalist movements in various religions, of cultic communities, of the rules of enclosed orders of monks and nuns. Humans and dwarfs think the same way. Regrettably, here there is no Commander Vimes around to put a stop to the endless revival of Koom Valley . . .

Chapter 3

THE ELVES

IT'S EASY, ALL TOO EASY, for people nowadays to get hold of the wrong end of the stick if you tell them there are 'elves' about. And if you say 'fairies', that just makes matters worse. People think of tall, shining figures dancing in rings in the moonlight to the loveliest music one could hope to hear; or tiny dainty creatures with butterfly wings, fluttering round flowers.

And in a way, some of this is true. For elves do generally choose to appear tall, beautiful and glamorous to humans. Their real appearance is thin, dull, and grey, with triangular faces and big slanty eyes (oddly, they occasionally let themselves be seen like this by the people of our world, who then label them 'aliens' and 'extra-terrestrials', and get very excited). They do sing and dance, and sometimes they laugh a lot, though you would probably not like it if you knew what they are laughing about. And there are indeed little flying ones, though they have more in common with hornets than with butterflies. In truth, elves and fairies are a predatory, cruel, par-asitic race, who will use other living beings, and hurt them, because this is fun. They break into a world through those strange places where the barrier between dimensions is just a bit too *thin* for safety. Places which are like a door, half open. Places where it's wise to put a marker of some kind – a solitary tree, say, or some standing stones – to warn everybody to keep away.

And yet, foolish people *will* go there. In Lancre, for instance, a group of men in a wood, looking for somewhere private to rehearse a play:

'Let's go right,' said Jason.

'Nah, it's all briars and thorns that way.'

'All right, then, left then.'

'It's all winding,' said Weaver.

'What about the middle road?' said Carter.

Jason peered ahead.

There was a middle track, hardly more than an animal path, which wound away under shady trees. Ferns grew thickly alongside it. There was a general green, rich, dark feel to it, suggestive of the word 'bosky'.

His blacksmith's senses stood up and screamed.

'Not that way,' he said.

'Ah, come *on*,' said Weaver. 'What's wrong with it?'

'Goes up to the Dancers, that path does,' said Jason. [*Lords and Ladies*]

The blacksmith Jason Ogg knows that the Dancers – a ring of eight stumpy man-sized stones, one of which is The Piper – are to be avoided, though he doesn't know why. Nor does his conscious mind know why he fears the ferny path; it is his instincts which (as we shall see) have picked up a warning from the lore of another world. These are signs of a gateway, a short cut between dimensions, a place where elves can enter.

One clue that elves have broken in, or are just about to, is that crop circles start appearing in cornfields; the growing wheat bends over sharply, breaks, and lies down in a circle. This strange phenomenon has been observed several times in Lancre, and also on the Earth in recent years.

Earlier generations on Earth got no such warnings, but then they didn't need them. They knew for sure that there were elves and fairies lurking in pools and streams, in deep woods and inside mounds and rocks, and sweeping across the sky in the wild winter winds. And they knew that these beings were cold-hearted, revengeful, often cruel, however beautiful their faces and however enchanting their music. Any countryman in Ireland or the Scottish Highlands 150 or 200 years ago would have known of a dozen cases of someone who died, or lost his wits, or became paralysed, or simply was 'never the same again' after meeting them. Similarly in England, at an earlier period – in 1684, for instance, a writer named Richard Bovet reported that he knew someone (completely reliable, of course) who knew a man who had once seen fairies holding a market on Blackdown Hill in Somerset and foolishly tried to join them. He felt a sudden pain, and by the time he got home 'lameness seized him all on one side' and he remained so, though he survived for many years. We still call such a thing a 'stroke', even if we have forgotten who did the striking. And we still say of somebody who seems vague, dim-witted, or slightly crazed that he or she is 'away with the fairies'.

In Eastern Europe, the fear of elves and fairies was still powerful in quite recent years. The American folklorist Gail Kligman, working in Romania in 1975, learned about wondrously beautiful but malevolent fairy maidens called *iele*, which literally means 'They' or 'Themselves', since it is dangerous to utter their true name. They live in woods and wild places. They travel by night, singing and dancing, but those who listen to their music or join their dance will regret it – at best, they will be deaf for life, and may well be crippled, or go mad. There is hardly any limit to the sickness and trouble which the *iele* can inflict on humans, even those who have never offended them. In Russia and other Slavonic lands, there are forest elves who trick travellers into leaving the path to wander helplessly among the trees until they starve to death, and water elves who catch and drown the unwary. Beautiful? Yes, usually. Nice? Never.

Wherever elves go they feed on the awe, the terror, the superstition they inspire. They take control of people's minds. They enslave. When they invaded Lancre, as is told in *Lords and Ladies*, Granny Weatherwax warned King Verence II:

'When they get into a world, everyone else is on the bottom. Slaves. Worse than slaves. Worse than animals, even. They take what they want, and they want everything. But worst of all, the worst bit is . . . they read your mind. They hear what you think, and in self-defence you think what they want. And it's barred windows at night, and food out for the fairies, and turning around three times before you talks about 'em, and horseshoes over the door.'

Horseshoes are important, and so are the blacksmiths who make them, since almost the only protection humans have against fairies is the power of iron. It is known throughout the multiverse that all creatures of this species fear and detest iron, which causes them intense pain. Various more or less foolish theories have been proposed to account for this. On the Earth, it is often claimed that it shows 'fairies' are nothing more than a folk memory of some prehistoric human society which did not have iron weapons, and fled from others who did. But on the Discworld people know the real reason. Elves have a powerful sixth sense based on awareness of magnetic fields, and use it to know precisely where they are, and where and what all other living creatures are. So to them iron is:

. . . the terrible metal that drinks the force and deforms the flux universe like a heavy weight on a rubber sheet and blinds them and deafens them and leaves them rudderless and more alone than most humans could ever be. [Lords and Ladies]

The other picture people have of fairies, the picture of their beauty and charm, is partly created by the fairies themselves as they infiltrate the collective memory and imagination of humanity. Nanny Ogg knows this, yet even she finds it hard to keep a clear mind when thinking about elves:

People didn't seem able to remember what it was *like* with the elves around. Life was certainly more interesting then, but usually because it was shorter. And it was more colourful, if you liked the colour of blood. It got so people didn't even dare talk openly about the bastards.

You said: The Shining Ones. You said: The Fair Folk. And you spat, and touched iron. But generations later, you forgot about the spitting and the iron, and you forgot why you used those names for them, and you remembered only that they were beautiful.

Elves! The bastards . . . and yet . . . and yet . . . somehow, yes, they did things to memory.

We only remembers that the elves sang [thought Nanny Ogg]. We forgets what it was they were singing about.

How completely people forget depends very much on when, where and how they live. In the cities – in London, New York, or Ankh-Morpork – elves and fairies are nothing more than fantasy, just a bit of fun for the kids. But people who live on the land, especially in remote and wild parts of the country, those people know they are real. And they remember that though they *might*, just occasionally, bring good luck, they are far more likely to inflict diseases, kidnap people, and steal human babies, replacing them with their own sickly and mentally deficient 'changelings'.

Changelings were a particularly sad obsession. A healthy young couple out in the country and in a world without modern medical understanding or any idea of the meaning of the term 'limited gene pool', give birth to a child who looks like a little old man, or is beautiful but very backward, or eats incessantly but nevertheless fails to thrive . . . and the only reason the family can find lies in folklore: 'the fairies stole our beautiful child and left one of their own.' A horrible thought, yet not *quite* so horrible for the parents as one religious alternative: 'It's our own fault the baby is like this, it's a judgement on us for our sins.'

In a disturbing but fascinating paper published in the journal of the Folklore Society in 1988, Susan Shoon Eberley cites many accounts of the appearance and behaviour of changelings as they were described in nineteenth-century sources, and maps them against dozens of childhood disorders which produce children that look and act 'like the fairies'. The Victorian medical establishment was coming to grips with the idea that these children were victims of disease; but the common people fell back on folk myth, which was reinforced with every case.

Folk myth also supplied a cruel remedy. You had to make life so miserable for the changeling that it would flee and the 'real' child would miraculously return. Custom handed down various 'remedies', including putting the child in a hot oven or leaving it out on the midden all night – child abuse at best, socially condoned infanticide at worst. The wonderful child did not return, but at least there was no longer the inconvenient changeling in the cradle, and everyone nodded and understood . . .

Nanny Ogg, a midwife, knew what she was doing when she took the king of the elves to task in *Lords and Ladies*. A society does not want elves in the driving seat.

Yet by the nineteenth century, in much of Europe, memories were fading, and people spoke of elves and fairies without such fear. Their world was under attack by education and street lights and medicine and technology; the telegraph could beat Puck when it came to putting a girdle round the earth.

And thus their decline continued. Though people still told stories about changelings and abductions, on the whole they believed (or half believed, or suspended disbelief) that the Hidden Folk could be good neighbours to humans, and were just mischievous, not truly dangerous. They could lead you astray even in woods which you knew quite well, so that you felt hopelessly lost and would maybe fall into a ditch, but that was just their fun (and in any case it was easier to blame the fairies than the cider). They would do you no harm, provided you were careful not to offend them. The rules were clear: don't cut down their favourite trees, don't damage the mounds where they live, don't build a road across their paths, be careful where you throw dirty water, keep your house clean and your hearth swept in case a fairy comes there in the night.

There was even one type, the house-elves, whom humans welcomed. The English called them hobs, pixies or pucks, the Scots brownies, the Scandinavians nisses and tomtes. These would actually live in a farm and bring it luck; they would help with harvesting, tend the animals, even do housework, in exchange for an occasional bowl of milk or porridge – provided nobody spied on them or laughed at them. Russian country folk said there were several on each farm; the most important one lived behind the stove, others guarded the barn, the bath-house, the henhouse, and so on. On the Discworld, only the Wee Free Men have ever done such a favour for humans, and then only once, in the very special circumstances created by their bond with Tiffany Aching. Their reward was Special Sheep Liniment, which smells suspiciously like whisky.

Another sign that people in Europe were forgetting the true nature of elves, and no longer took them seriously, is that they so often thought of them as *small*. The Little People, the Wee Folk. Some people said they were about the size of a rabbit; others, that of a six-year-old child. Some said they were really, really small – like the little farm-elf in Sweden who sweated and panted as he dragged a single ear of wheat into the barn, but went off in a huff when the farmer laughed at him; once he was gone, the farm went to rack and ruin. So he had his revenge. Even so, one can't be seriously scared of something a few inches high (unless, of course, it is a Nac Mac Feegle).

Why did the menace of elves dwindle in this way? How can they have been so reduced? Once again, it was Will Shakespeare's plays which nudged the human imagination on to a new path. In *A Midsummer Night's Dream* he gave elves sweet but silly names: Peaseblossom and Cobweb, Mustardseed and Moth. They were, by his reckoning, just about big enough to kill a red-hipped bumble-bee on top of a thistle. True, he also wrote about Puck, who was bigger and more active and enjoyed playing practical jokes, but there is no real malice or danger in Puck's tricks. In *Romeo and Juliet* he described Mab, Queen of the Fairies, who controls people's dreams, like the Fairy Queen whom Tiffany encounters in *The Wee Free Men*. But whereas *that* Queen is terrifying, Queen Mab is a delightful little thing as she drives her tiny, dainty chariot across the bodies of sleeping humans:

> Her waggon-spokes made of long spinners' legs;
> The cover, of the wings of grasshoppers;
> The traces, of the smallest spider's web;
> The collars, of the moonshine's watery beams;
> Her whip, of cricket's bone; the lash, of film;
> Her waggoner, a small grey-coated gnat . . .

This new image of fairies and their world proved irresistible. From Shakespeare's time right down to the twentieth and twenty-first centuries it has gone on spreading in literature, painting, children's books, films, television. So now there are plenty of pretty fairies and quaint little elves on Earth – they make a good story to entertain a child. And so some become Santa's Little Helpers, and some bring money for a tooth, and there are fairies at the bottom of the garden (it's not so very, very far away). There's one who says she'll die if children don't clap their hands to prove they believe in her. And for very young children, just to get them properly addicted to tweeness, there are dumpy little baby-fairies in romper suits, with horns, living in a land where it's all trees and flowers and sunshine. So nice. Such good fun.

There is another way in which Earthly folk have tamed the notion of the elf, and this too involves children. Adults who have stopped believing in elves can make damn sure that their children are still scared of them, because that way they'll stay away from dangerous places, and learn to obey the rules. They turn elves and fairies into Nursery Bogeys: 'Don't play in the woods after sunset, the hytersprites will get you' – 'Don't stand at the edge of the pond, Jenny Greenteeth will drag you in and gobble you up' – 'Behave yourself while I'm out, remember the tomte who lives under the stairs will be watching you'.

Nanny Ogg understands this principle. Consider the copper in her washhouse:

> The water under the lid was inky black and, according to rumour, bottomless; the Ogg grandchildren were encouraged to believe that monsters from the dawn of time dwelt in its depths, since Nanny believed that a bit of thrilling and point-less terror was an essential ingredient of the magic of childhood. [*Wyrd Sisters*]

But not *entirely* pointless. After all, a toddler could drown in a copper.

However, fashions in child-rearing change. In many parts of the Earth it is now considered quite wicked to deliberately frighten a child, even for its own good, so Nursery Bogeys are an endangered species. Some have reinvented themselves as Funny (but Nice) Fairies in order to survive. In Iceland, children used to be told that in the thirteen nights leading up to Christmas thirteen hideous hobgoblins would come down from the mountains and creep into the house, one by one; they would carry off any child who was naughty, and probably eat it. Nowadays, this simply won't do. The Thirteen Christmas Lads still *look* hideous, but that's just a joke, and nobody is afraid of them. In fact, each of the Lads pops a sweet, or some other little present, under the child's pillow. Perhaps this delicacy is because we think we know of more complex monsters now? But we always have. The world of the fairy tale is a map of prohibitions: do not open that door/enter that wood . . . and above all, young lady, don't talk to the wolf.

There have been many theories as to what the true home of the elfin races is like, and where it may be found – if indeed they have a home, for they might simply be alien nomads, creating the illusion of a

Fairyland in any territory they invade. The Nac Mac Feegle (who ought to know, as they are fairies of a sort themselves) say that there *is* an elf-world, but it's a mere parasite. One of them tells Tiffany Aching: 'It floats around until it finds a place that's weak on a world where no one's payin' attention, and opens a door. Then the Queen sends in her folk. For the stealin', ye ken.'

The Wee Free Men is the story of how elves 'open a door' between standing stones on the Chalk hills, and how Tiffany crosses into their world to rescue her little brother, kidnapped by the Queen, and also, incidentally, an older boy named Roland. One can't properly describe this 'Fairyland', for it is full of human dreams and nightmares, which keep on changing. But in its true nature, before the illusions begin, it is a cold, snowy land which somehow does not feel like a real place. There is no sun in the sky. The woods are full of dimness and shadows, and no birds sing. Nothing grows older there, because nothing grows at all.

Yet the Nac Mac Feegles tell Tiffany that 'Fairyland' was not always such a terrible place. It has been ruined by a domestic dispute:

'It wasnae so bad then. It wasnae perfect, mark you, but the Quin wasnae as cold in them days. The King was still aroound. She was always happy then.'

  'What happened? Did the King die?'

  'No. They had words, if ye tak' my meanin',' said Rob.

  'Oh, you mean like an argument—'

  'A bit, mebbe,' said Rob. 'But they was *magical* words. Forests destroyed, mountains explodin', a few hundred deaths, that kind of thing. And he went off to his own world. Fairyland was never a picnic, ye ken, even in the old days. But it was fine if you kept alert, an' there was flowers and burdies and summertime.' [*The Wee Free Men*]

There are mysteries here. Will Shakespeare must have picked up some echo of them, since his *Midsummer Night's Dream* tells of a quarrel between the King and Queen of Fairyland, whom he calls Oberon and Titania, ending in reconciliation. Whether there can be the same happy ending elsewhere in the multiverse remains to be seen. But where, meanwhile, has Oberon's Discworld counterpart disappeared to? And who is he? The witches of Lancre know the answer. He is the powerful antlered figure who lies in the cavern beneath the barrow known as the Long Man, dreaming the days away in his steam-filled sweat-house. One day, maybe, he will return. Meanwhile (as we learn in *Lords and Ladies*), he occasionally intervenes to frustrate the plans of his Queen.

When Tiffany asks the Nac Mac Feegles what will become of her brother if she can't rescue him, they explain that he will probably return one day, *but . . .*

> 'Time passes slower the deeper ye go intae this place. Years pass like days. The Quin'll get tired o' the wee lad after a coupla months, mebbe. A coupla months *here*, ye ken, where time is slow an' heavy. But when he comes back intae the mortal world, you'll be an old lady, or mebbe you'll be deid. So if youse has bairns o' yer own, you'd better tell them to watch out for a wee sticky kid wanderin' the hills shoutin' for sweeties, 'cos that'll be their Uncle Wentworth. That wouldna be the worst o' it, neither. Live in dreams for too long and ye go mad, ye can never wake up prop'ly, ye can never get the hang o' reality again . . .'

The grim picture of a sunless land where time does not run true matches some accounts in the folklore which took shape before Shakespeare's influence was felt. Take the story of Thomas the Rhymer, also called Thomas of Erceldoune, a poet and seer who lived on the borders between Scotland and England at the close of the thirteenth century. Some time in the next couple of hundred years, someone wrote a ballad about him (it is still sung today). It tells how

Thomas, resting on a hillside near Edinburgh, saw the Queen of Elfland ride by on a milk-white horse with silver bells on its mane; she summoned him to be her harpist, he kissed her and mounted behind her on her horse.

> O they rade on, and farther on,
>   The steed gaed faster than the wind;
> Until they reached a desert wide,
>   And living land was left behind.

In that desert is a place where three paths meet, just as they do in Lancre. One is a narrow path, thick beset with thorns and briars; this, says the Queen, is the Christian Path of Righteousness. The second is a broad path through flowery meadows, and that's the Path of Wickedness. As for the third:

> 'And see ye not yon bonny road,
>   That winds about the fernie brae?
> That is the road to fair Elfland,
>   Where thou and I this night maun gae.'

But the bonny road among the ferns isn't so very bonny after all:

> O they rade on, and farther on,
>   And they waded rivers abune the knee,
> And they saw neither sun nor moon,
>   But they heard the roaring of the sea.

> It was mirk, mirk night, there was nae starlight,
>   They waded thro' red blude to the knee;
> For a' the blude that's shed on earth
>   Runs through the springs o' that countrie.

Finally they reach a garden, where the Queen gives Thomas an apple as his wages, and with it the unwelcome gift of 'a tongue that can never lie'. He eats (one should *never* eat the food in Elfland),

> And till seven years were gane and past,
> True Thomas on earth was never seen.

It could have been worse. He was away only seven years, after all, and when he returned he became a famous seer and prophet, thanks to his truth-telling tongue.

People who are kidnapped by elves can be rescued, but this needs courage and a cool head, as there won't be a second chance. Sometimes the rescuer has to go deep into Elfland (as Tiffany does). Sometimes, according to our own tales, it is enough to go back a year later to the place where the person was taken – a fairy ring, perhaps, where elves gather to dance, or some crossroads which they pass when they ride out hunting – and wait and watch. When they appear, their human captive will be seen among them. The rescuer must drag him or her out of the dance, or off the horse, and hold on tight, no matter what monsters and terrifying illusions the elves call up. Another method, known in Scotland, is to throw a dagger over the captive's head. Some would-be rescuers have lost their nerve, but others do not:

> 'I remember a folksong about a situation just like this,' said Magrat. 'This girl had her fiancé stolen by the Queen of the Elves and she didn't hang around whining, she jolly well got on her horse and went and rescued him. Well, I'm going to do that too.' [*Lords and Ladies*]

The song Magrat remembers is known in Scotland as the ballad of Tam Lin. To save him, his lover Janet must pull him off the fairy horse and hold on as he turns into a snake, a deer, and a red-hot iron, before returning to human form. She has the courage, and Tam is free and unharmed.

Others were not so lucky. Some never escaped, others fell victim to the distortion of time in Fairyland. An Irish hero, Bran the son of Febal, heard an elf-woman singing and followed her to her magical island in the western seas. He remained there for a year (so he thought), but then he and his companions grew homesick. She told them they were allowed to sail close to the coast of Ireland and speak with anyone standing on dry land, but must not step ashore themselves. And so they anchored in a harbour, and shouted to the men on the beach. Nobody recognized them, though someone remembered that there were old stories about a man called Bran who once, long ago, had sailed into the West. One of Bran's friends jumped into the water and swam ashore, but as soon as he touched land he crumbled to dust. As for Bran, he put out to sea again, and has never been seen since.

And it's not only bards, seers and heroes – quite ordinary people get taken too. During a wedding dance on a Danish farm the bride went out for a breath of air, and walked as far as a little mound in one of the fields, a mound where elf-folk lived. It had opened up, and elves were dancing there too, and one of them came out and offered her some wine. She drank. She joined in the dancing, just one dance, and then remembered her husband and went home. But the village and the farm looked different; she couldn't recognize anybody, and nobody recognized her. There was just one old woman who listened to her story and exclaimed, 'Why, you must be the girl who disappeared a hundred years ago, at my grandfather's brother's wedding!' At these words, the bride's true age came upon her in an instant, and she fell dead.

In tales such as this, told in the European countryside, elves were often lurking in quite normal, familiar places. Just a little mound in a field which you pass every day, nothing particularly eldritch about it, no marker stones to warn you off. It might of course be an ancient burial mound, like the one on the Chalk Downs which the Wee Free Men take as their home, but on the other hand it might be a simple natural hillock. But if you lie down and press your ear to the ground, you hear faint music . . . Then one day it is standing open, and there

They are. They are the Hidden People, the Underground Folk, the Good People, the Good Neighbours. Maybe they've come to do you a favour, or to ask for one. There's no need to be frightened, is there? Is there?

Yet long after the 'enlightened' and well-educated generations had lost their faith and fear, after the wild elves had been safely reduced to Peaseblossoms, an occasional artist recaptured the older image. The crazed painter Richard Dadd did so in his sinister picture *The Fairy Feller's Master Stroke*, which he worked on from 1855 to 1864, while living in an asylum. So did the composer Rutland Boughton in the key aria of his opera *The Immortal Hour* (1914), based on a poem by Fiona Mcleod:

How beautiful they are,
The lordly ones
Who dwell in the hills,
In the hollow hills.

Their limbs are more white
Than shafts of moonshine.
They are more fleet
Than the north wind.

They laugh and are glad
And are terrible.
When their lances shake and glitter
Every green reed quivers.

How beautiful they are,
How beautiful,
The lordly ones
In the hollow hills.

Beautiful, yes. And terrible.

Chapter 4

THE NAC MAC FEEGLE

THE WEE FREE MEN, also known as the Nac Mac Feegle (and, sometimes, as 'the defendants'), are a fiercely independent species, organized into numerous interrelated clans. Outsiders sometimes call them gnomes. To humans, they are one of the most feared of the fairy races – indeed, they can put trolls to flight, and even Nanny Ogg's cat Greebo retires under the furniture at the sight of them. They have shaggy red hair, and are covered all over with blue tattoos and blue paint, in patterns which indicate their clan. They wear kilts or leather loincloths, use feathers, bones or teeth as decorations, and carry swords almost as large as themselves – though they go in for kicking and head-butting too. They are about six inches tall.

Originally, they were denizens of Fairyland, and served its Queen as her wild champion robbers who went raiding on her behalf into every world there is, but all that is over. Why so, is not certain. Some say they were thrown out of Fairyland for being drunk and disorderly, making rude gestures, and using language which would be considered offensive by anybody who could understand it. They themselves say they left in disgust because the Queen was a spiteful tyrant, and ordered them to steal from the poor as well as the rich, 'But we said it's no *right* to steal an ol' lady's only pig, or the food frae them as dinnae ha' enough to eat.' Whatever the truth of it, they are now out-and-out rebels against any authority whatsoever. Their war-cry is 'Nac Mac Feegle! The Wee Free Men! Nae king! Nae quin! Nae laird! Nae master! We willna be fooled again!'

They now live in the human territories of the Discworld, but it is hard to say just where they are at any one time. Not only do they stay well hidden, but they often shift from one area to another at high speed, rather like a swarm of locusts, while indulging in their favourite occupations: drinking, stealing, and fighting anything that gets in their way. They get such pleasure from this that they think they're dead, and gone to heaven, where there's lovely sunshine (not like the perpetual half-light of Fairyland), good hunting, and plenty of monsters to fight:

> An amazing world like this couldn't be open to just *anybody*, they say. It must be some kind of a heaven or Valhalla, where brave warriors go when they are dead. So, they reason, they have already been alive somewhere else, and then died and were allowed to come [to the Discworld] because they have been so good. [*A Hatful of Sky*]

They don't mourn much for those that actually get killed while fighting on the Disc:

> 'Oh, they've gone back to the land o' the livin'. It's nae as good as this one, but they'll bide fine and come back before too long. No sense in grievin'.' [*The Wee Free Men*]

They do not limit themselves to the Discworld, for, as one of their leaders, Rob Anybody, proudly declares, 'We've been robbin' an' runnin' aroound on all kinds o' worrlds for a lang time.' Their running around within a particular world is done normally, with feet (though very, very fast); but their transit from one universe to another is done by magic. They are unwilling to discuss the process, which they call 'the crawstep'. Those who have seen them actually doing it say they simply thrust out one leg straight ahead of them, wiggle the foot, and are gone.

For many centuries, one of their favourite places was an area of the Earth called Scotland. They were already there in the time of the Ancient Romans, who spoke of them as *picti*, 'painted men'; Julius Caesar himself records that the tribes of Northern Britain had 'designs carved into their faces by iron', a clear reference to tattooing. Needless to say, they refused to submit to the Empire, conducting such a persistent guerrilla war that the Romans gave up hope of conquering Scotland, and the Wee Free Men remained both wee and free.

Later generations of Scottish humans were well aware of their presence, and called them Pehts, Pechs, Pechts or Picts. They themselves like the last version best, and have adopted it for their own use, in the form 'pictsies'. (Be careful, however, never to confuse them with the 'pixies' of Devon and Cornwall, since pixies are an altogether inferior race, whom the Feegles despise as 'wee southron shites', whatever that means.) Several Scotsmen have described the Pechs, who were somewhat taller than the Discworld clans, but in other respects pretty similar. They were 'unco wee bodies, but terrible strang', wrote a certain James Knox in 1831, and lived in underground chambers and burial mounds. Indeed, for generations the Scots took it for granted that any odd stone structures found underground were 'Picts' houses'. Robert Chambers, in his *Popular Rhymes of Scotland* (1870), wrote: 'Short wee men they were, wi' red hair, and long arms, and feet sae braid that when it rained they could turn them up owre their heads, and then they served for umbrellas. The Pechs were great builders; they built a' the auld castles in the kintry.'

This refers to the brochs, a type of ancient round tower, which Scotsmen called 'Picts' castles'. Why they built them is a mystery, since they never lived in them; perhaps they had struck some bargain with the local human ruler, broch-building in exchange for hunting rights, or the like. It was said they could raise a broch in a single night, quarrying the stones, forming a long chain from the quarry to the chosen site, flinging the stones from hand to hand, and then piling them into massive walls. This is much the same technique as that of the Feegles when fighting people bigger than themselves; they work in groups, running up one another's backs to form a pyramid, till the top one is high enough to punch the enemy, or, preferably, to head-butt him. Once he is down, it is all over bar the kicking.

Feegles can easily lift things far heavier than themselves; to steal a sheep or cow, for instance, needs only four of them, as Nanny Ogg explains:

'Four. One under each foot. Seen 'em do it. You see a cow in a field, mindin' its own business, next minute the grass is rustlin'. Some little bugger shouts "Hup, hup, hup," and the poor beast goes past, voom! without its legs movin'. Backwards, sometimes. They're stronger'n cockroaches. You step on a pictsy, you'd better be wearin' good thick soles.' [*Lords and Ladies*]

Another clan of Feegles settled in Ireland, where they changed their way of dressing to suit local fashions, but continued to spread undiluted terror. People there were too scared to use their proper name, so they called them 'the good folk', hoping they might take the hint. It didn't work. The poet William Allingham records the lament of some Irish humans:

Up the airy mountain,
Down the rushy glen,
We daren't go a-hunting
For fear of little men.
Wee folk, good folk,
Trooping all together,
Green jacket, red cap,
And grey cock's feather.

On the Discworld, Feegles initially took up residence on the high moors of Uberwald, but some came into conflict with vampires who objected to the presence of any others of the 'old races'. Since vampires can fly and Feegles can't (except on large birds), the former had an unfair advantage, and the latter decided to move on. They arrived in Lancre, where, in return for timely help given to King Verence, they were granted possession of an island on a lake, with lots of fish around, and the chance of good hunting up the valley, provided they promised not to go cattle-raiding.

There are other Feegle clans on the Downland Chalk. One group lives inside the large burial mound of some ancient king, whose bones don't bother them at all, and whose gold occasionally comes in useful. These particular Feegles are probably unique in that some of them have actually been seen doing chores for a human girl, Tiffany Aching, a young witch whom they greatly respect. In general, however, we must repeat the warning that pictsies are not pixies. As Nanny Ogg has remarked, if you leave a saucer of milk out for them, hoping they'll do the washing-up while you're asleep, all that'll happen is that the 'little buggers will break into your cottage and steal everything in your drinks cabinet'.

Very occasionally, for reasons unknown, an individual Feegle may leave his clan for a while, to get a taste of city life. One such is Wee Mad Arthur, rat-catcher and pest-destroyer in Ankh-Morpork, who plays a crucial role in *Feet of Clay*. The locals refer to him as a 'gnome', but his accent, his strength and his fondness for head-butting all show he is a true Feegle.

No one could clear out rats like Wee Mad Arthur. Old and cunning rats that knew all about traps, deadfalls and poison were helpless in the face of his attack, which was where, in fact, he often attacked. The last thing they felt was a hand gripping each of their ears, and the last thing they saw was his forehead, approaching at speed. [*Feet of Clay*]

The same may well be true of the 'gnome' Buggy Swires, a recently recruited Corporal in the City Watch, where he is the head (and only member) of the Airborne Section, as mentioned in *Monstrous*

Regiment. He patrols the skies by riding on a large female buzzard named Morag, who was trained by pictsies and is well worth the crate of whisky she cost the Watch. Typical! Shakespeare's Ariel thought himself a fine fellow because he could fly on a bat's back, but only a large bird of prey will do for a Feegle.

The time that the Feegles or their ancestors spent in Scotland has had a deep influence on them (unless, who knows, it was the other way around). Besides the tattoos and the kilts, they have developed a taste for strong liquor, and even for haggis. Each clan keeps a bard and musician, called a gonnagle, with a repertoire of heroic lays, laments, and martial music played on the mousepipes. Such performers are invaluable in battle, for terrorizing the enemy. When Tiffany Aching and the Feegles of the Chalk are attacked by a pack of fairy grimhounds, the venerable William the gonnagle takes out his pipes:

> 'I shall play,' he announced, as the dogs got close enough for Tiffany to see the drool, 'that firrrm favourite, "the King Underrr Waterrr".'
>
> As one pictsie, the Nac Mac Feegles dropped their swords and put their hands over their ears.
>
> William put the mouthpiece to his lips, tapped his foot once or twice, and, as a dog gathered itself to leap at Tiffany, began to play . . .
>
> The dog in front of her went cross-eyed and, instead of leaping, tumbled forward.
>
> The grimhounds paid no attention to the pictsies. They howled. They spun around. They tried to bite their own tails. They stumbled, and ran into one another. The line of panting death broke into dozens of desperate animals, twisting and writhing and trying to escape from their own skins. [*The Wee Free Men*]

What had happened was that William had played 'the notes of

pain', pitched too high for human ears, but agonizing to dogs. There is precedent for such skill in our world. According to ballad singers in Shetland, there was once a King Orfeo whose wife had been slain by a dart flung by the King of Fairies. So Orfeo went into Fairyland to win her back. He entered in at a grey stone, and played his pipes at the Fairy Court. First he overwhelmed his hearers with pain, then filled them with joy, and finally played a wild dance tune to make their hearts whole again:

> An first he played da notes o noy,
> An dan he played da notes o joy,
>
> An dan he played da göd gabber reel
> Dat meicht ha made a sick hert hale.

Naturally, his wife was given back to him. And, unlike the Ancient Greek Orpheus, he did *not* lose her by looking back.

The title of office for a Feegle bard, 'the gonnagle', is a touching tribute to the memory of William McGonagall (born 1825), a famously excruciating Scottish poet. He had grasped one basic point about poetry, namely that it should rhyme, eventually, but since he had not the faintest conception of rhythm he was capable of stretching a line of verse like chewing gum. As for his choice of words, the less said the better. His most celebrated production was a lament over the collapse of a railway bridge. It is long, so the first and last verses must suffice:

> Beautiful Railway Bridge of the Silv'ry Tay!
> Alas! I am very sorry to say
> That many lives have been taken away
> On the last Sabbath Day of 1879,
> Which will be remembered for a very long time.
>   . . .

Oh! Ill-fated Bridge of the Silv'ry Tay,
I must now conclude my lay
By telling the world fearlessly without the least dismay
That your central girders would not have given way,
At least many sensible men do say,
Had they been supported on each side with buttresses,
At least many sensible men confesses,
For the stronger we our houses do build,
The less chance we have of being killed.

The Feegles of the Chalk have an aspiring young bard who has mastered this style to perfection, and deploys it when they are under attack from vicious little flying fairies, rather like dragonflies. Standing with one hand pressed to his heart and the other outstretched very theatrically, and rolling his eyes, he utters a long-drawn mournful moan, and launches forth.

'Ooooooooooooooiiiiiit *is* with great lamentation and much worrying dismay,' the pictsie groaned, 'that we rrregard the doleful prospect of Fairyland in considerrrable decay . . .'

In the air, the flying creatures stopped attacking and began to panic. Some of them flew into one another.

'With quite a large number of drrrrrreadful incidents happening everrry day. Including, I am sorrrry to say, an aerial attack by the otherwise quite attractive fey . . .'

The flyers screeched. Some crashed into the snow, but the ones still capable of flight swarmed off amongst the trees.

'Witnessed by all of us at this time, And celebrated in this hasty rhyme,' he shouted after them.

And they were gone.

The old bard congratulates the young one:

'That, lad,' he said proudly, 'was some of the worst poetry
I have heard for a long time. It was offensive to the ear and
a torrrture to the soul. The last couple of lines need some
work but ye has the groanin' off fiiine. A' in a', a verrry
commendable effort! We'll make a gonnagle out o' ye yet!'
[*The Wee Free Men*]

The speech of the Feegles is markedly Scottish, to the point that,
though it is not technically a foreign language (unlike, for example,
that of dwarfs), most people in Lancre and Ankh-Morpork find it
very hard to follow. Yet it's a good language, as Nanny Ogg says,
'with a hint of heather and midden in it'. Most of it is a form of
Lowlands Scots peppered with Glasgow slang, but there are several
words adopted from Gaelic, the Celtic language of the Highlands and
Isles, one of which is of considerable folkloric significance. In its
original tongue it is *Cailleach*, pronounced approximately 'kall-yack'
and meaning 'old woman, hag'. Like 'hag', it often implies magical
power, and so can mean 'witch'. In the Feegle language it has
developed two quite different forms. The first, used light-heartedly in
ordinary speech, is 'callyake'. For example, a Feegle who had been
startled by Greebo shouted at Nanny Ogg, 'Ach, hins tak yer scaggie,
yer dank owd callyake!', which appears to mean, 'Oh, devil take
your moggy, you daft old woman!' But the second form, 'kelda', is a
title to be used with the deepest respect.

Feegles are matriarchal. Each community is ruled by a kelda,
who has come from some different clan when young, to choose one
of them as her husband and be their Queen and their Wise Woman
for the rest of her life. Like a queen bee, she bears an incredible
number of offspring, but in her case (unlike the bee's) all but one or
two of them are male. This means that all the men of the clan are
either her sons or her husband's brothers, apart from a few of her
own brothers who came with her as bodyguards, and probably the
gonnagle, since these travel from clan to clan. Keldas are rather taller
than the male Feegles, and very, very fat, looking just like the little

figurines of goddesses carved on Earth way back in the times of ice and mammoths. Their word is law, as truly as if they were indeed goddesses. As for the title itself, though centuries of use have worn it down, its origins can still be guessed. It comes from Cailleach Dubh, 'the Black Hag', a supernatural figure in Scottish and Irish tradition who shapes the landscape, rules the seasons, protects wild animals, and confers power on favoured humans. The Cailleach Dubh was a true Mother Goddess, and the language of the Feegles honours her memory.

And what of their own name? Here again we see the influence of the Scottish and Irish lore they picked up during their stay on the Earth (or vice versa). 'Mac Feegle' means 'Sons of Feegle', and 'Feegle' is clearly a variation of 'Fingal', the eighteenth-century Scottish name for a great hunter and warrior hero in Celtic tradition. Tales about him under his older name of Finn or Fionn mac Cumhaill have been popular for over twelve hundred years in Ireland, and almost equally long in Scotland, where he is called Finn MacCool. He was the chieftain of the *fianna*, a band of wild young men who lived by hunting deer and wild boar, fighting, cattle-raiding and robbing. At times they might take service under some king and fight in his wars; at other times they chose an independent life. All were fearless in confronting any enemy, natural or supernatural. Fionn himself more than once entered some sinister region of the Otherworld and had to fight his way out against great odds. It is very understandable that the race now known as the Nac Mac Feegle should wish to take his name.

Chapter 5

TROLLS

TROLLS ARE A UNIQUE life-form because their 'flesh' is composed of silicon in various complex combinations. At least, so it is said. They *look* rocky. Lichen grows on their heads. They have carbon as well as silicon in their make-up – in their teeth, which are of diamond – and from time to time, at intervals of many centuries, there appears a King of Trolls who is pure diamond. In one sense, therefore, trolls belong in the mineral kingdom, and exposure to strong sunlight often puts them into a fully stony state until nightfall – although in truth it is heat rather than light that slows down their brains.

At the same time, they do have most of the attributes of animal life: they eat and drink (mineral and chemical substances only), walk and talk, are male or female, make love and have children. Their given names are always related to geology – Mica, Bluejohn, Flint, Morraine (or Brick, for one born in the city). They can be killed by force, but do not (as far as is known) ever die a natural death. Instead, after several centuries of active life, a troll withdraws to some remote mountain area and settles down in one spot among the rocks to think long, slow thoughts about nothing in particular. Gradually he becomes more and more rock-like, till he is to all intents and purposes simply a landscape feature.

Many have come down from the Ramtop Mountains, which for most of them is their native region, and have come looking for work in towns and cities. Being immensely strong and intimidating, they are welcome wherever a hired fist is needed – as private bodyguards, barmen, bouncers or splatters (who carry out the same duties, but with messier results). One, who has adopted the human name of Big Jim Beef, is employed as a customs officer and frontier guard for the kingdom of Lancre; when not making checks on travellers, he lives under the Troll Bridge. It is not a good idea to mention billygoats in his hearing. Unfortunately, some of the young city-dwelling trolls give themselves unpleasantly thuggish airs; they go in for elaborate body-carving and real skull pendants, and become addicted to various brain-rotting substances (and practically anything can slow down a troll's brain).

The best-known troll is Detritus, who was recruited into the Ankh-Morpork City Watch by Captain Vimes, and has proved a most keen and loyal Sergeant, if a little slow on the uptake. Trolls are not in fact stupid, despite what most people think, but their brains function properly only at low temperatures (because of the silicon), so the warm climate of the valleys and plains makes them very sluggish, especially in the daytime. Detritus now gets some help from a small fan attached to his helmet, but it was only when he was accidentally shut in the refrigerated Pork Futures Warehouse that his true intelligence was revealed – as he gradually froze, he scratched calculations worthy of Einstein all over the iced-up walls. There are hints that trolls have age-old cultural traditions which no outsider knows anything about; there is talk of their history chants and stone music, for instance, and of their Long Dance. They think of Time in a curious though logical way: the future, they say, must be behind you, since you can't see it, but the past, which you can see in your memory, must be ahead.

There is an age-old feud between trolls and dwarfs, possibly arising from the fact that both races live in the same mountain regions, and that dwarfs spend their lives mining and tunnelling through rock – something which trolls find it upsetting to think about. It is even rumoured that dwarfs have occasionally tunnelled into the underside of a particularly stony and immobile troll. Be that as it may, the feud led to the disastrous battle of Koom Valley, said to be the only occasion in military history where each army ambushed the other. It was long ago and far away, but has never been forgotten. Koom Valley has become a myth, a state of mind.

> Where any dwarf fought any troll, there was Koom Valley.
> Even if it was a punch-up in a pub, it was Koom Valley. It was
> part of the mythology of both races, a rallying cry, the ancestral
> reason why you couldn't trust those short, bearded / big, rocky
> bastards. [*Thud!*]

And yet . . . and yet . . . if *other* myths can be trusted, the first man, the first dwarf and the first troll all originated in a single egg of stone, a geode, more than 500,000 years ago, and are therefore, in some sense, brothers. This myth was mentioned above, in the section on dwarfs. Its implications, together with the story of what *really* happened in Koom Valley, are explored in *Thud!*.

Trolls also have a dislike of druids, who can be found in the small, rainy, mountainous kingdom of Llamedos. There is no mystery about the reason, for the druids of the Disc went around erecting huge stone circles in much the same way as (some folk used to say) British druids did at Stonehenge. Regrettable errors occurred:

> Any sapient species which spends a lot of time in a stationary,
> rock-like pose objects to any other species which drags it sixty
> miles on rollers and buries it up to its knees in a circle. It tends
> to feel it has cause for disgruntlement. [*Soul Music*]

Even the dragging on rollers is not the worst of it. It is said (as recorded in *The Light Fantastic*) that one particularly skilled group of druids found a way to quarry huge slabs of high-quality stone and *fly* them hundreds of miles along ley-lines to the snowy Vortex Plain, where they set them up as an immense construction of concentric circles, towering trilithons, and mystic avenues, to be a great computer of the skies. It proved hopelessly inaccurate. This act of wanton cruelty to minerals made trolls still more bitter towards druids.

On Earth, there are two quite different races claiming the name 'troll'. One lot is to be found in Denmark: these are smallish mischievous goblins with red hair, living inside mounds and hillocks near farmland. They can be disregarded here since, apart from the name, they have nothing in common with Discworld trolls, and seem akin to Feegles.

The other ones, however – the huge mountain trolls who live in Iceland and Norway – are remarkably like those of the Discworld, but wilder and more hostile to human beings. They are thought to be the direct descendants of the dangerous Giants of Scandinavian myth, but differ from them in being generally solitary creatures. They are immensely old and strong, and probably not as stupid as humans say they are. They have had a considerable impact on the landscape – quite literally so, since they often quarrel and hurl huge boulders at one another, and never clear the pieces away afterwards. They also send avalanches and rock-falls crashing down on anybody who annoys them by shouting among the mountains. Many of them object to humans building churches in their district, partly because they dislike Christianity itself, and partly because they hate the noise of bells. The troll's solution is always the same: heave a large rock at it. He always misses. At least, so the stories say, but can we be sure that there are no squashed churches under *any* of the rocks that litter the landscape? Has anyone checked?

There was once a Norwegian troll who tried a different plan. Hearing that St Olaf was trying to build himself a church at Trondheim, he volunteered his services as a stonemason. But this was in fact a plot to kill Olaf. 'I'll build your church for you,' said the troll, 'but I'll take the sun and the moon and the heart out of your breast as my fee – unless you can guess my name before the last stone is in place.' The troll turned out to be not only extremely strong but also a remarkably quick worker, and in no time the walls were done, and the tower was rising fast. But then one night as the saint wandered gloomily along the mountain paths, he heard the voice of a she-troll from inside the rocks, as she sang her little ones to sleep: 'Hushabye, hushabye, your daddy Finn will soon be home, and he'll bring you the sun and the moon to play with, and the priest's heart too.' Next morning St Olaf strolled up to the church, just as the troll was setting the last course of stones on the tower. 'Splendid work, Finn,' said Olaf. Now, it is one of the basic rules of folklore that to know a magical creature's name gives you the power to destroy him – and another, that somehow or other the secret is sure to get out. So the troll crashed down dead, but Trondheim cathedral is still there.

The physiology of Earth's mountain trolls must be based on silicon, like that of their Discworld counterparts, judging by the way they all too easily turn into large boulders, which in their case are permanent. One variety, the Icelandic Night-troll, hides in caves all day and only comes out at night, because any ray of direct sunlight petrifies it at once. There are several spectacularly tall rocks offshore which are said to be trolls caught unawares by the sunrise while wading out to sea.

Naturally, the best defence against a Night-troll is to keep it talking till the sun comes up. There was once an Icelandic girl who had been left at home on Christmas Eve, to look after her baby brother while everyone else went to church. In the middle of the night she heard a deep voice outside the window, serenading her.

Fair seems your hand to me,
Hard and rough mine must be,
    Dilly-dilly-do.

But she did not look round. Instead, she sang to the baby in the cradle:

Dirt it did never sweep,
Sleep, little Kari, sleep,
    Lully-lully-lo.

When the troll praised her eyes and her feet, she told the baby that she had never looked on anything evil, never trodden on dirt. And so it went on all night, till dawn broke and the girl sang in triumph:

> Stand there and turn to stone,
> So you'll do harm to none,
>   Lully-lully-lo.

And when the family came home from church, they found a huge boulder on the path between the farm buildings, which had certainly not been there the night before.

As this tale shows, one difference between the way trolls evolved on Earth and in the Discworld is that the Earth ones can get amorous towards humans, an idea which would never enter the head of a troll on the Disc. Icelandic she-trolls sometimes kidnap a handsome young man to be their mate, or lure him up into their caves by magic chants. There, they do all they can to seduce him, and to persuade him to eat trolls' food; they rub him with strange ointments, stretch his limbs, and bellow into his ear, to make a troll of him. It is said that men who do not manage to escape gradually do turn into trolls themselves. In the Norwegian legend of Peer Gynt, the King of the Mountain wanted Peer to marry his daughter, who was apparently quite good-looking, whereas it is unlikely that a female Discworld troll would ever appeal to a male human, no matter how cheap the beer and however bad the club lighting.

Earthly trolls can, in fact, look like humans and humans can become trolls, and it has been suggested that trolls have their origins in 'folk memories' of earlier races (even Neanderthals) who were pushed to the edges of the habitable world by the stumbling advance of civilization, and then into myth and story. This attractive and beguiling idea is very familiar to folklorists as an explanation for 'fairy' folk of any sort (who look outlandish and have strange powers), and so we will back tactfully away and leave it to the anthropologists.

It's worth adding that Discworld trolls cannot digest human beings (though they have been known to try), whereas those of Earth find them both tasty and wholesome. In Norway, men have heard she-trolls bellowing to one another among the crags, discussing their cooking: 'Sister, can I borrow your big pot?' – 'What for?' – 'Here's Jon the woodcutter coming up this way, I want to make a stew of him.' – 'All right, Sister. When you skim the broth, save some of the fat for me.' Somehow, bellowing across the landscape that you are waiting in ambush seems so very troll.

Trolls were still being talked about in Iceland as late as the nineteenth century. There were certain cliffs where seabirds nested, and it was said that when men went over the edge on ropes to gather eggs or to catch the birds themselves for food, great, grey, shaggy hands carrying very sharp knives would reach out from caves and cut the ropes, and so kill the men who hung there. So then some priest would be sent for to drive the trolls out by going down on a rope and blessing the cliff, while men on the cliff-top sang psalms as loud as they could. The really intelligent priests would bring a hammer, and chip away the sharp ridges on the cliff face as they blessed it – after which, the ropes hardly ever frayed and broke. But there remain a few cliffs which were never blessed, and where egg-gatherers never go, however many birds there may be. This is because once, when a bishop had gone down on a rope and was working his way along the cliff face, a voice from inside the rocks called out: 'Don't bless anything more! The wicked do have to have *somewhere* to live!' And the bishop, being a fair-minded man, left this place unblessed.

GARGOYLES

Although gargoyles are very different from a standard troll in size, appearance, habitat and habits, they are in fact a subspecies which has evolved to fit an urban environment. They are, if anything, even more stony; they squat motionless on some rooftop, which they are very reluctant to leave. On the other hand, their digestive system is quite different from that of trolls; they are carnivores, preying on pigeons. Their main occupation is absorbing rainwater from the gutters and ejecting it vigorously, through their gaping jaws, on to the heads of pedestrians below. When they do move, it is in slow, grinding jerks; their mouths are permanently fixed open, making it hard to understand their speech. But their endless patience and keen eyesight make them valuable members of the Watch in Ankh-Morpork, somewhat like CCTV cameras in a modern city on Earth.

Gargoyles are also a familiar sight on the roofs of Earth's medieval churches and castles, where they got their name. It suits them well, for they gurgle, gargle and glug in their gullets, and most of them goggle too. But there are few, if any, stories about them, probably because they are too high up for anyone to see them properly.

SEA-TROLLS

It should be mentioned that 'trolls' of one sort or another apparently exist elsewhere in the multiverse. The wizard Rincewind, in one of his early adventures described in *The Colour of Magic*, was almost swept over the Edge of the Disc, where an endless cascade of ocean pours away into space. Instead, he crashed into the Circumfence – a single rope, suspended a few feet above the water from occasional wooden posts, and extending for tens of thousands of miles round the rim of the Disc. This particular section was patrolled by a sea-troll, a creature of a pleasantly translucent blue colour, apparently composed of sea-water and very little else. As for size, he gradually swelled as the hours went by, then just as gradually shrank; owing to the strength of the Discworld moon, he was suffering from chronic tides.

The sea-troll was not native to the Discworld. He came from a *different* disc, quite a small one (mostly blue), where the seafolk lived in thriving civilized communities on its three oceans. Unfortunately, he had been blown over the edge in a great storm, fell through outer space (which froze him solid), and eventually landed on the Disc. Curiously, the name of his own world is Bathys, which on Earth is Greek for 'ocean depths', and the troll's personal name is Tethis, remarkably close to that of the Ancient Greek sea-nymph Thetis.

Interestingly, the Norwegian artist Theodor Kittelsen, who painted a large number of what we now call fantasy paintings, did several based on trolls, including, in 1887, a fearsome sea-troll. Alas, it is not transparent.

Chapter 6

OTHER SIGNIFICANT RACES

VAMPIRES

THE CHILDREN OF THE NIGHT are an increasing presence in Ankh-Morpork these days, thanks to the efforts of the Uberwald League of Temperance. Sensible vampires have realized that a diet of black pudding and blood sausage *and* a stake in a growing economy is much to be preferred to just a stake. However, it was not always thus: the vampire – or at least the *image* of the vampire – has evolved quite markedly over the centuries.

Do vampires suck blood? Silly question, nowadays. If there's one thing everybody knows about vampires, it's that they suck your blood, leaving you with two neat puncture marks at the base of your neck. Of course, what everyone knows is wrong, and nearly everyone knows it. At least, we think so; the trouble with what everyone knows is that you can never be sure that everyone knows it. But surely everyone knows that vampires, like werewolves, have stepped out of folklore and into popular culture. The movies, of course, were the major influence; in the 1950s and 60s a generation grew up (thanks to Hammer Films) *knowing* that female vampires *always* wore underwired nightgowns, and male ones a high-collared black cloak with a red satin lining.[6]

---

[6] And also that in the inevitable chase scene the coach would always break down in the same place in Black Park, near Pinewood Studios – according to Terry. This may not be strictly true, but it gave him the idea for Don'tgonearthe Castle.

But it was not always so. In the folklore of the Balkans, Greece, and Central Europe a vampire, also known as a *nosferatu*, a *vryko-lakas*, or a *nachzehrer*, was simply an Undead revenant – a corpse that gets out of its grave and wanders about. Some sucked blood, others didn't. Instead, they might breathe on you and give you plague, cholera or consumption; or sit on your chest and give you nightmares; or strangle you; or beat you black and blue; or simply get into your house and smash the furniture. Subtle and elegant they were not. Their close relative, the *draug* of medieval Iceland, would break every bone of your body, and of your cattle too.

Early European vampires were not aristocrats, but village folk. They did not look like noble gentlemen in black cloaks, or luscious women in low-cut ball gowns. They looked like what they were, corpses. To be precise, corpses that have been buried long enough to begin decaying, but not long enough to turn into nice clean skeletons. When terrified locals dug into the grave of a suspected vampire to destroy him, they would find a body bloated with gases, and there-fore plumper and bigger than when alive; the skin taut; the blood no longer congealed, but runny, and often oozing from the mouth or nose; the face puffy and red, or in some cases dusky. If they jabbed a stake or spade into it, nasty reddish liquids gushed out. They might even hear a sort of grunt or squawk as the blow forced the gases out through the windpipe. Who could doubt that this was an Undead?

Such a corpse must then be destroyed by burning. If this is too difficult (dead bodies take a lot of burning), at least it can be muti-lated or pinned down in some way, so that it will never walk again. Which is where staking comes in, or beheading, or tearing the heart out.

Vampires as the Earth knows them now are rather different. They were created by English writers in the Romantic and Victorian periods, and perfected by that most powerful myth-making medium, the cinema. The first was Lord Ruthven in John Polidori's story 'The Vampyre' (1819), an evil blood-sucking deathless aristocrat. Then in 1872 came Joseph Sheridan Le Fanu's story about the beautiful young Carmilla, who (like Salacia in *Thud!*) assumed she could evade discovery by making anagrams of her name – Millarca, Mircalla. She was gentler than Lord Ruthven, but she too brought death; she was eventually found in a blood-filled coffin, staked, and decapitated.

And then, in 1897, Bram Stoker's *Dracula* appeared, presenting the sinister but elegantly seductive Count, his female victims, and three erotic female vampires. Stoker stole the Count's name from the real-life Vlad Dracul, also known as Vlad Tepes the Impaler, one of the great warrior-princes of Romanian history, who in his native country is respectfully remembered as a hero, and is never, *never* thought of as a vampire. Stoker also adopted many details from East European folklore. For over a hundred years now, the Dracula figure and its variants have been fixed in modern popular mythology – fangs, swirling black cloaks with red linings, brocaded waistcoats, a haughty manner, and an escort of bats, rats, and wolves.

On Discworld, the Count de Magpyr is a magnificent example of the aristocratic vampire, sprung from an ancient family whose motto is *Carpe Jugulum*, 'Go for the Jugular'. His son Vlad is very much the dandy; his daughter Lacrimosa is a thin girl in a white dress, with very long black hair and far too much eye make-up. Their home is a castle on a crag in Uberwald, complete with sinister ancestral portraits. One of these shows Aunt Carmilla, a far more savage figure than Le Fanu's heroine of the same name; she used to bathe in the blood of up to two hundred virgins at a time, just as the real-life Hungarian Countess Elizabeth Bathory was rumoured to do. It was a good cosmetic. There is also the portrait of the *old* Count de Magpyr (father of the present one, and remembered by some as 'Old Red Eyes'):

A bald head. Dark-rimmed, staring eyes. Two teeth like needles, two ears like batwings, fingernails that hadn't been trimmed for years . . .

That's something known on this world too. That's Nosferatu, perhaps the most terrifying vampire in the history of the cinema, as created in 1922.

But the current Count de Magpyr is adapting to modern times. To the fury of his servant Igor, whose attitude can be described as more-gothic-than-thou, he and his family wear full evening dress in the evenings only, not all the time, as his father the *old* Count did; the rest of the time, it's fancy waistcoats for the men and lacy skirts for the women. In the castle, squeaky door-hinges must now be oiled, guttering candles removed, spiders chased out of the dungeons. There must be no black plumes on the coach or its horses – coaches looking like hearses are not at all cool.

The Count's aim is to train his family, little by little, to overcome all the taboos which limit a vampire's freedom, and which are only cultural conditioning – a conditioning which, strangely, seems to be much the same on the Discworld and the Earth. He believes that with a little effort and practice, modern vampires could and should learn to drink . . . wine, go out in sunlight, cross running water, eat garlic-flavoured canapés, bear the touch of holy water, and look at any sacred symbol without wincing. By and large, the plan seems to be succeeding. But they still can't enter a house unless invited.

As was noted above, quite a number of Discworld vampires hope to become integrated into society as a whole, and so have joined the Uberwald League of Temperance; members have forsworn the drinking of human blood – or, as they prefer to call it, 'the b-word'. They carry their badge, a small twist of shiny black ribbon, and gather regularly in mutual support groups for a nice singsong with cocoa and a bun. One Black Ribboner is Otto Chriek, a brilliant iconographer on the staff of the *Ankh-Morpork Times*. He dresses as the cinematic stereotype requires, and speaks (when he wants to) with a thick Uberwald accent – deliberately so, to make people laugh. That way, no one fears him, or hates him. Since Otto personally has not overcome his hereditary allergy to strong light, he suffers intensely whenever he has to use a flash, sometimes even crumbling to dust. He carries a card for such emergencies:

DO NOT BE ALARMED. The former bearer of this card has suffered
a minor accident. You vill need a drop of blood from any
species, and a dustpan and brush. [*The Truth*]

If some kind person dribbles a drop or two from, say, a piece of raw
steak on to the dust, it mushrooms up into the air, becomes a mass
of coloured flecks, and once again is Otto Chriek.

From the information so far available, it looks as if all Discworld
vampires become such either by their genetics, or by being bitten.
Admittedly, one may suspect that the genes of the late Count
Notfaroutoe were pretty reluctant to be activated in the unlikely DNA
of his only remaining relative, his nephew Arthur Winkings, who was a
coming man in the wholesale fruit and vegetable business. And Arthur
was even more reluctant to receive them, as we learn in *Reaper Man*.
But that's how it goes – if you inherit the title and the estates, you get
the coffin and the batwings too. Genetics, or a bite. Take your choice.

On the Earth, this is true in the literary and cinematic mythology,
but in European folklore there are plenty of other reasons why the
dead become vampires. They may have lived an evil life, committed
suicide, or practised black magic; they may have been conceived in
sacrilege, their parents having had sex on a holy day; they may have
been born with teeth, or a tail, or two hearts,[7] or a caul. In Romania,
anyone with red hair and blue eyes is regarded as a potential
vampire. In many parts of Europe, a corpse will become a revenant
if it is left unburied, or buried secretly without proper rites. If it is
laid out at home, it should be in a lighted room, and there should
always be somebody keeping watch; no dog or cat should be allowed
to jump on to or over it. Break any of these rules, and you will soon
have a vampire in the village.

---

[7] As we will see later, two hearts are magical. However, the only known person with two hearts on
the planet Earth is Doctor Who.

And when you do, what do you do about it? As the Quite Reverend Oats, self-appointed Omnian missionary to Lancre, explained to Nanny Ogg,

> 'It depends exactly where they're from, I remember. Uberwald is a very big place. Er, cutting off the head and staking them in the heart is generally efficacious . . . in Splintz they die if you put a coin in their mouth and cut their head off . . . in Klotz they die if you stick a lemon in their mouth – after you cut their head off. I believe that in Glitz you have to fill their mouth with salt, hammer a carrot into both ears, and then cut off their head . . . And in the valley of the Ah they believe it's best to cut off the head and boil it in vinegar . . . But in Kashncari they say you should cut off their toes and drive a nail through their neck.'
>
> 'And cut their head off?'
>
> 'Apparently you don't have to.' [*Carpe Jugulum*]

Decapitation was the folk method in parts of Europe too, especially among Germans and western Slavs, with the addition that the severed head must be placed between the legs of the corpse, behind its buttocks, or below its feet – so that it couldn't find it and put it back on. The southern Slavs preferred staking the corpse; Greeks cremated it, often cutting the heart out first; Russians would throw it into a lake or river. Danes staked revenants; medieval Icelanders beheaded and/or burned them.

There was no need to stick to one method at a time. In Germany, one woman who 'walked' was dug up, decapitated, and then reburied at a crossroads with her mouth full of poppy seeds. Another corpse was taken to a border between two districts, cut open, staked through the heart, and beheaded; a stone was put in the mouth, and both body and head were left lying there, for animals to eat.

Of course, it was best if you could stop the corpse from leaving its grave at all, by giving it something to do which would keep it there. For example, Oats told Nanny Ogg, you can defeat vampires by stealing their sock:

> 'They're pathologically meticulous, you see. Some of the gypsy tribes in Borogravia say that if you steal their sock and hide it somewhere they'll spend the rest of eternity looking for it. They can't abide things to be out of place or missing . . . They say in some villages that you can even slow them down by throwing poppyseed at them. Then they'll have a terrible urge to count every seed. Vampires are very anal-retentive, you see?'

Paul Barber, a notable American authority on vampires, has similarly stressed their 'limited, rigid, and compulsive nature'. This makes it easier to stop them from coming home after burial. For instance, they have to re-enter the house in the same way they left it, so if you lift the coffin out through a window or a hole in the wall, instead of using the door, and then shut the window or refill the hole, they'll never find the way back. If you bury them face down, when they try to dig themselves out they'll just go down deeper and deeper. If you put seeds or sand in a vampire's mouth or coffin, or on the path to the graveyard, this activates his compulsions: 'he must collect the grains one at a time, and often only one grain per year. This so engages his attention that he is obliged to drop all other pursuits.' Nets and knitted stockings in the coffin are just as good; he has to unpick them, one knot or stitch per year. As for putting coins, pebbles, dirt or food in the corpse's mouth, that gives him something satisfying to chew on.

So a girl setting out to be a vampire-slayer in Uberwald needs a big sack, to be ready for all possibilities. She must carry a stake and mallet, a spade, and a strong knife; nets, seeds, coins, sand, salt, stones, lemons, garlic, assorted vegetables; thorns and needles to stick in the vampire's feet to stop him walking, and in his tongue to stop him sucking; a flask of holy water and the sacred symbols of all major gods.

But, as Nanny Ogg could tell her, there is a better way. She could simply borrow Greebo the cat, and wait till a very large red-eyed bat comes by. For that would be a flabberghast ('which is foreign for bat,' Nanny Ogg explains), and a flabberghast is a shape-shifted vampire. And it would very soon learn the useful truth set down in *Witches Abroad*:

> Vampires have risen from the dead, the grave and the crypt, but have never managed it from the cat.

BANSHEES

These unpleasant (and mercifully rare) creatures, native to the Uberwald mountains, are the only humanoid species on the Discworld that has evolved wings, apart from certain small elves; vampires who fly, such as the Count de Magpyr and his family, simply do so by a form of levitation. However, there may possibly be some remote genetic connection between the two races, since a banshee has two hearts, which, according to some folk traditions, is a characteristic of vampires. No research has been done on this topic, nor is likely to be.

A Discworld banshee is about the same size as a man, but far more lightly built, consisting almost entirely of thin bones and very strong sinews, several rows of pointy teeth, and huge claws. At first glance, you would think it is wearing a black leather cloak. This, as you will soon discover, is its wings. And then there is its scream.

> It was harsh, guttural, it was malice and hunger given a voice. Small huddling shrew-like creatures had once heard sounds like that, circling over the swamps. [*Going Postal*]

It is well known that to hear the banshee's scream means that you are going to die. With the more civilized banshees, all this means is that they have taken on the job of a death-omen, and will sit screeching on your roof to make sure you get plenty of warning that Death is on his way. Indeed, in Ankh-Morpork there is one solitary and gloomy banshee named Ixolite who suffers from a speech impediment and just writes OoooEeeeOoooEEEeee on a scrap of paper and slips it under your door. But the wild banshees, such as the Mr Gryle described in *Going Postal*, do the whole job themselves. One minute you hear the scream, next minute there's a swoop and a pounce and some quite remarkable claws.

Over in our own parallel universe, banshees are only to be found in one particular habitat, namely Ireland. The name, if not the species, must have originated there, since *bean sí* makes good sense in Irish, though it is mere gibberish in Discworld languages. It means 'woman of the otherworld' – for in Ireland the creature is invariably female. Her mission is to announce the imminent death of someone in one of the old aristocratic Irish families, by screaming and wailing near their homes. She is more often heard than seen, but when she does let herself be glimpsed it is as an old woman with long, loose white hair which she combs as she wails. Sometimes she is seen crouching by a river, washing a winding-sheet. In some parts of the country she is also known as the *badhbh chaointe*, pronounced 'bo-heenta' and meaning 'the keening scaldcrow', though she does not nowadays actually appear in crow-shape.

Though the Irish banshee is no predator, it is best to be wary of offending her. There was once a man who saw a banshee combing her hair on the riverbank at twilight, crept up behind her, and snatched her comb. He ran home with it. That night there were terrifying shrieks all around his house, and something was hammering on his window. So he opened the window just a little way and pushed the comb out, holding it in the big iron tongs from the fireplace. And it was well for him that he did so rather than putting his hand out, for the thing that grabbed the comb grabbed the tongs too and threw them to the ground, all bent and twisted. Such is a banshee's strength.

GOLEMS

In all societies there is a good deal of boring, dirty, heavy work which nobody really wants to do, whatever the pay. So what could be better than to find a race of strong, tireless, silent workers to take on these jobs? Especially if they don't need paying.

The historical solution, in Ankh-Morpork, is the golems – large, powerful creatures made of baked clay, roughly humanoid in form but seven or eight foot tall. They need no food or sleep; they can work underwater, or in extremes of heat or cold, or in total darkness; they cannot feel pain or boredom. They can repair themselves, and last for centuries. Their triangular eyes have the faint, dark red glow of a banked fire, and on the rare occasions when they open their mouths you get a brief glimpse of an inferno. According to the original specifications they cannot speak, though they can write; this, however, was changed at the insistence of Commander Vimes, after the events recounted in *Feet of Clay*.

A golem's head is hollow, and flips open when you press a line across the forehead; inside is a yellowing scroll bearing words in Cenotine, an ancient sacred script, the language of a dead religion. This has to have been written by a priest. Take out the scroll, and the light in the golem's eyes goes out, and its life (if it can be called life) ceases. Put it back, and it comes 'alive' again. When the golem Dorfl is asked to explain itself, it writes on a slate:

I am a golem. I was made of clay. My life is the words. By means of words of purpose in my head I acquire life. My life is to work. I obey all commands. I take no rest . . . Golem must work. Golem must have a master. [*Feet of Clay*]

The written commands in a golem's head are those which the Cenotine god is said to have given to the first people on earth, after he had baked them out of clay. 'Thou shalt labour fruitfully all the days of your life' is one of them, and another is 'Thou shalt not kill', and a third 'Thou shalt be humble'.

Not surprisingly, factory owners are prepared to pay a good price for golems. There are stories that sometimes one of them overdoes things, being too stupid to stop work unless actually ordered to, so your house gets flooded as it brings pail after pail from the well. This, however, always seems to have happened somewhere else, some good while ago, and can be disregarded. One minor snag is that just occasionally they down tools and go off for a few hours, leaving a message that today is for them a holy day. Apart from that, they are perfect machines for work.

Few in Ankh-Morpork remember who first made a golem, or why, or how. Recent archaeological discoveries (described in *Making Money*) indicate that particularly fine specimens existed in the ancient City of Um, back in the Clay Age some sixty thousand years ago. When Rincewind visited the Counterweight Continent (see *Interesting Times*) he accidentally roused a vast Red Army of seven thousand terracotta golems, which were standing guard inside the burial mound of some very ancient emperor – but again, nothing is known of their making. To learn more, one must turn to the more recent traditions of Jewish communities in Central and Eastern Europe. For there, by one of those remarkable freaks of cosmic resonance, the story of the making of the golem first appeared in fifteenth-century Germany, and by the seventeenth century had become famous.

In Hebrew, the word 'golem' means an unshaped lump of matter, an imperfect or incomplete creation. According to legend, various extremely learned and pious rabbis knew how to create a humanoid being out of clay, thanks to the magical power of holy words and letters, especially the four letters forming the Name of God. The act echoed that of God Himself in forming Adam from the dust of the earth, and for that reason most rabbis never put their knowledge into practice, for fear of blasphemy. But a few did, to get themselves a servant, or to get help in times of great danger.

The fullest and most famous story is about Judah Loew ben Bazalel, Chief Rabbi of Prague towards the end of the sixteenth century. In 1580 the Jews of Prague were under attack from anti-Semitic fanatics, and Rabbi Loew received a divine message telling him to create a golem for their protection. Four elements would be required: earth, fire, water and air. He went with two disciples to the bank of the River Vltva, and moulded a human form of clay. Then one disciple danced round it seven times from right to left, saying certain words which invoked the element of fire, causing it to glow like red-hot metal. The other disciple danced round it seven times from left to right, saying words to invoke the element of water, and by the time he had finished steam was rising, and the golem's hair and nails had begun to grow. Finally Rabbi Loew himself danced round seven times, breathed air into the golem's nostrils, and put a parchment with a word on it into its mouth – or, some say, wrote a word upon its brow.

Then the golem came to life and stood up, though it lacked the power of speech. Rabbi Loew said: 'Your mission is to walk the streets of Prague and keep my people safe from persecution. You will obey my commands, and go wherever I send you – into fire, into water, or down to the floor of the sea.'

What was the word that gave a golem life? Some say it was *schem*, which means 'name', and refers to the Tetragrammaton JHVH, the never-to-be-spoken Holy Name of God. Others say it was *emeth*, 'truth', and that one could destroy the golem by rubbing out the first letter, leaving *meth*, which means 'death'. For eventually, all legends agree, something will go wrong, and the golem will have to be 'killed'. Perhaps it has grown so big and powerful that its maker can no longer control it. Or perhaps he has forgotten to give it its orders for the day, and it has gone berserk through having nothing to do, and is about to devastate the city.

In Prague, Rabbi Loew kept his golem till 1593, but then, know-ing the danger of persecution had passed, he and his disciples reversed their rituals, reducing it to a mere mass of clay. This they sealed up in the attic of the Synagogue, and Rabbi Loew ordered that nobody was ever to set foot in that attic again. And nobody ever has.

Such was the sad destiny of Earth's golems. In the Discworld, thanks to the ferocious sense of justice of Commander Vimes and the pragmatism of Lord Vetinari, golems are now in process of buying their freedom from their masters, and have acquired speech and independence of thought. The words in their heads are those they have chosen themselves. Still untiring and sternly moral, some have found a role as law enforcers (one instance of this is described in *Going Postal*). Naturally, this requires a certain modification of one of the basic Laws of Golems, which now runs: 'You shall not harm a human being, or allow a human being to come to harm – unless ordered to do so by a properly constituted authority.' As we have said, Lord Vetinari is a *pragmatic* ruler. That is not the same as nice.

WEREWOLVES

Wherever wolves are found in the multiverse, there are werewolves too, yet the condition of werewolfery (or lycanthropy, as those of more scientific bent prefer to call it) remains mysterious. What can be the cause? Is it voluntary or involuntary? Is it a magical power, or a form of madness? Are werewolves heroes, victims, or criminals?

The clash of theories is obvious on Earth. Several Ancient Greek writers blamed religious cannibalism, allegedly practised in honour of Lycean (i.e. 'Wolfish') Zeus in the wild hilly region of Arcadia. According to Pausanias, a Greek geographer writing in AD 166, the first werewolf was a certain King Lycaon of Arcadia, whose very name means 'wolf'.

Lycaon brought a human baby to the altar of Lycean Zeus and sacrificed it and poured out the blood upon the altar, and they say that immediately after the sacrifice he was turned into a wolf. For my own part I believe the tale: it has been handed down among the Arcadians from antiquity, and probability is in its favour. They say that from the time of Lycaon downwards one man has always been turned into a wolf at the festival of Lycean Zeus, but that the transformation is not for life, for if while he is a wolf he abstains from human flesh, in the ninth year afterwards he changes back into a man, but if he has tasted human flesh he remains a beast for ever.

About a hundred years earlier, the Roman author Petronius had included a werewolf story, more or less as a joke, in his comic novel *Satyricon*. To him, it was simply magical shape-shifting: a young soldier deliberately turned into a wolf by taking off his clothes in a graveyard by moonlight and pissing round them, and went off to kill cattle and sheep – but then, like many shape-shifters before and since, he was wounded while in animal form, and so his secret was discovered.

In later European folklore, all sorts of explanations were suggested. Some said it was a magic art of warriors, who went into battle as wolves by wearing a wolf's pelt. Others, that it was due to a spell which a witch could lay on a man by striking him with a wolf-skin glove. Others, that it came from accidentally eating a particular magic plant, or bathing in a particular lake. Others, that it was a curse that a child was born with, as a punishment because his parents conceived him on a holy day when sex was not allowed,[8] or because his mother used magic to avoid a painful childbirth. Others, that the man had made a deliberate pact with the Devil, and went about murdering people while in his wolf form. In more recent centuries, it has been generally assumed that lycanthropy was a madman's delusion. Attitudes varied according to the theories – wolf-warriors

---

[8] See the section above on vampires, where this same thing is mentioned as one possible cause for the condition. For much of the early history of these creatures (that is, before the days when vampires dressed snappily and werewolves generally managed to keep their trousers on) they were in most cultures pretty much the same thing. Someone who was a werewolf when alive would keep up the bad work by becoming a vampire when dead.

were admired as heroes, the victims of spells and curses were to be pitied as well as feared, the lunatics were to be locked up, but murderous Satanist werewolves were to be tried and hanged.

There are no such crazy notions on the Discworld. There, everybody knows that being a werewolf is just something that you're born with, something that runs in families. It's not supernatural, but it's very, very embarrassing. Especially if you live in a town. Most humans and dwarfs find werewolves both frightening and disgusting, so werewolves do all they can to keep their condition secret, and most of the time they can pass as human. But if when in wolf shape they were to meet real wolves, they could never pass as wolf – the scent is quite different. And for the most part real wolves *detest* werewolves. So, one way and another, werewolves lead a lonely life.

The genetic laws governing Discworld werewolfery are logical, but far more complex than the transformation rules of Earth, since the condition can show itself in different forms. Ludmilla Cake, who is a 'classic bimorph' werewolf, is a tall, strong girl for three weeks in every month, though a careful observer might note that her hair is unusually thick and long. In the week of the full moon, however, she becomes a wolf and stays in her room, so as not to upset the neighbours. Sometimes preliminary signs appear a day or two before what her mother coyly refers to as 'your Time':

> Something came in from the back yard. It was clearly, even attractively female in general shape, and wore a perfectly ordinary dress. It was also apparently suffering from a case of superfluous hair that not all the delicate pink razors in the world could erase. Also, teeth and fingernails were being worn long this season. You expected the whole thing to growl, but it spoke in a pleasant and definitely human voice. [*Reaper Man*]

Mrs Cake's forebears had originally come from the Ramtop Mountains, and she suspected that Ludmilla was a throwback to this distant past; she was pretty sure that her own mother had once alluded circumspectly to a Great-Uncle Erasmus who sometimes had to eat his meals under the table.

The exact opposite of a werewolf is a wolfman. For three weeks in every month he is simply a wolf, but as soon as he sees the full moon he *stops* howling, most of his hair temporarily falls out, and next minute he's standing up, walking and talking. The problem is, no clothes. So when the full moon is due to rise, a canny wolfman takes care to get back to where he keeps a pair of trousers stashed. It is to be hoped that Lupine the Wolfman and Ludmilla the Werewolf have managed to find happiness together, despite having to pay more attention to the calendar than most couples.

Sergeant Angua of the Ankh-Morpork City Watch is different again. Like Ludmilla, she is compelled to become a wolf during the time of the full moon, but in addition she has the power to shape-shift at will, by day or night, at any time of the month. This gift is a great advantage to her in police work; when in wolf form she has a superb sense of smell, thanks to which she can track anyone anywhere and decipher subtle clues at crime scenes. And, as many a villain has found out, it is most disconcerting to chase an attractive and unprotected girl into a dark alley, only to find a pile of discarded clothes and a large she-wolf, teeth bared. However, she has certain weaknesses. For a day or two before her Change she becomes irritable, due to Pre-Lunar Tension. When she is in wolf form the touch of any silver object gives her intense pain, and (like werewolves on the Earth) she is vulnerable to silver bullets. Some strong smells overwhelm her delicate nose, bringing on the equivalent of acute hay fever.

Angua's parents are the extremely aristocratic Baron Guye von Uberwald (also known as Silvertail) and Baroness Serafine von Uberwald (also known as Yellowfang). The Baron spends most of his time in wolf form, to the annoyance of his wife. Angua had a brother named Wolfgang, a magnificently built and very athletic young man, with strongly Nietzschean views, who made a terrifying wolf and would have felt quite at home in the SS. Even his father was afraid of him. But, as she tells Carrot, she also has another brother, Andrei, and she did have a sister named Elsa, till Wolfgang killed her.

'He *said* it was an accident. Poor little Elsa. She was a yennork, just like Andrei. That's a werewolf that doesn't change, you know? I'm sure I've mentioned it. Our family throws them up from time to time. Wolfgang and I were the only classic bi-morphs in the litter. Elsa looked human all the time, even at full moon. Andrei was always a wolf.'

'You mean you had a human sister and a wolf brother?'

'No, Carrot. They were both *werewolves*. But the, well, the little ... switch ... inside them didn't work. They stayed the same shape. In the old days the clan would kill off a yen-nork quickly, and Wolfgang is a traditionalist when it comes to nastiness. He says they made the blood impure. You see, a yen-nork would go off and be a human or a wolf but they'd still be *carrying* the werewolf blood, and then they'd marry and have children ... or pups ... and, well, that's where the fairytale monsters come from. People with a *bit* of wolf, and wolves with that extra capacity for violence that is so very human. But Elsa was harmless. After that, Andrei didn't wait for it to happen to him. He's a sheepdog over in Borogravia now. Doing well, I hear. Wins championships.' [*The Fifth Elephant*]

Not surprisingly, Angua has broken with her family.

But the existence of the yennork explains a lot. No doubt the aristocratic werewolves guard their pedigrees carefully, but mistakes will happen, even in the best regulated families.

IGORS

The Igors are a very numerous humanoid family in the Uberwald region, each of whom is named either Igor or Igorina. They are not, of course, undead, but are usually standing very close to a corpse. They are, in fact, a big nod to the cinematic cliché that whenever there is a brain to be collected or a big crackling switch to be pulled, then there is an Igor, or someone who looks very much like him, ready and willing to do the job.

Igors are heavily built, with a strong tendency to lurch and shamble, and they speak with a heavy, spluttering lisp. For generations many of them have gone into service in the households of aristocratic vampires in Uberwald, where it is their pride and joy to ensure that massive doors creak, candles gutter, cobwebs abound, and carriages look as much like hearses as possible. They have a keen appreciation of all the traditional trappings of horror. Sadly, Earthly vampires, unlike those of the Disc, seem never to have employed Igors. As we have pointed out, they did not have many visitors.

Another reason why Igors like working for vampires is that their castles usually have large, deep, cool cellars where an Igor can quietly pursue his real interests. The whole clan has a remarkable hereditary skill in surgery, especially transplants and wound repair, including the replacing of severed limbs. This they practise both on themselves and on others. You can always recognize an Igor by his distinctly patchwork look and interestingly individual scar patterns, and maybe an extra thumb or mismatched eyes. In many cases, you could place a ball on the top of his head, and it would not roll off.

The Igorinas, on the other hand, use their skill to look absolutely stunning, but always include some fetching little detail – a beautifully curved scar under one eye, a line of decorative stitching round the wrist – to maintain the Family Look.

Since Igors hate discarding any body part that could be recycled, an elderly member of the clan will make arrangements for the best bits of himself to be shared out among his kin when the time comes. They have a great fondness for heirlooms; among Igors, 'he's got his grandfather's hands' is likely to be literally true.

There is a tradition among Igors that the ancestor who first learned surgery was working for a mad doctor at the time. A more recent member of the clan, who diversified into extremely delicate clock-making, produced references from a series of employers whose hold on sanity appears to have been shaky – Mad Doctor Scoop, Crazed Baron Haha (crushed by a burning windmill), Thcreaming Doctor Bertherk (died of blood poisoning caused by a dirty pitchfork), and Demented Doctor Wimble, who discovered how to make the perfect clock while working on a scheme to extract sunshine from oranges. This particular Igor has a passion for electricity and thunderstorms, as described in *Thief of Time*.

There are few echoes of the Igors on Earth. And those that there are are only to be found in modern cinema and comic strips, not in age-old folklore. However, they do support the idea that an Igor once worked for a Doctor Frankenstein (who was definitely crazy) on a job which involved a great deal of stitching body parts together and exposing them to lightning. The Doctor wouldn't have got far without his help.

Despite the people they work for, Igors are generally well-intentioned, nay, spiritual beings. Most religions teach that the body is just an outer garment, to be shed in due time, and Igors think, in a provident way, that items with some wear left in them should not be wasted.

ZOMBIES

It is not strictly accurate to include the Discworld zombies in this chapter, since (unlike werewolves, golems or Igors) they do not constitute a separate race or species. On the contrary, a zombie is simply a human being who obstinately remains sort-of-alive when he has in fact died. He ought to lie a-mouldering in his grave, instead of wandering around looking vaguely grey, with fingers dropping off occasionally. No one knows why some people are natural zombies; it may simply be stubborn bloody-mindedness, an inborn refusal to kowtow to any authority, even that of Death. What Death thinks of this situation has not been recorded.

On the Disc, it would seem that zombies keep the personalities they had when alive, more or less intact, with the result that the four we know best are strikingly different. One is Mr Slant, the eminent lawyer who can count most of the upper-class families in Ankh-Morpork among his clients. He is dry-as-dust, in a very literal sense, and though he would never (of course) do anything illegal, it is not wise to cross him. He knows family secrets going back for an uncomfortable number of generations. At the opposite end of the city's social and political spectrum is Reg Shoe. In life he saw himself as a romantic revolutionary; in death he devotes most of his energies to protesting at society's unjust prejudice and discrimination towards the Undead. Then there is the old wizard Windle Poons, who finds his time as a zombie considerably more exciting than his actual life had been, as we learn in *Reaper Man*; in his case, however, it is merely a temporary state – the default setting for someone who happens to die when Death is not around to do whatever it is he does with his scythe. And in distant Genua there is Baron Saturday, a zombie who may be something more than just that. His name and his appearance suggest that he has an Earthly counterpart in the sinister Baron Samedi in Haiti – a being who is not himself a zombie or ghost, but a spirit Lord of the Dead. He is seen at crossroads and in cemeteries, and can be recognized by his black tuxedo, white top hat, dark glasses, and skull-like face. He is greatly feared.

Earth's zombies, who are only to be found in the traditional beliefs of Haiti, are very, very different, despite the identical name, and despite the fact that they too are Undead humans. Their condition is due to the spells of some voodoo sorcerer who has called them from their graves – and who, some say, was responsible for putting them down there in the first place, having sent them into a death-like trance by a secret poison, concocted from the liver of a very rare fish (it appears, from a conversation recorded in *Reaper Man*, that the wizards of Unseen University have heard rumours about this). When Haitian zombies emerge, their minds and souls have gone; they have become mere robots, incapable of speech, who must serve the sorcerer as his slaves. However, there is one way to rescue a zombie: give him salted food, or salt water to drink, and his soul and his power of speech will be restored.

It is said there was once a girl who died and was buried, but she was seen three years later, working very long hours in a boutique; she looked much the same as in the past, except that her neck was twisted – and that was because her coffin had been too small, and they had had to force her head down. But she spoke to nobody, and her eyes had no life in them.

Reg Shoe, the tireless revolutionary and champion of the Rights of the Undead, would be unspeakably angry if he knew the plight of the poor, exploited, downtrodden zombies of Haiti.

Chapter 7

BEASTIES

I T IS ONE OF THE MYSTERIES of the multiverse that animals which
exist as normal flesh-and-blood creatures in one world are regarded
as imaginary, legendary or folkloric in another – and yet, in many cases,
the descriptions tally almost perfectly. Whether this is due to the
perpetual drifting of particles of knowledge through cosmic space, or
whether such species did once inhabit all worlds and have regrettably
become extinct in some of them, is a matter of debate.

But nobody can deny that the fauna of the Discworld is particularly rich in species which other worlds have dreamed of. Not for
nothing does the old song run:

> All beasts bright and beautiful,
>   All monsters big and small,
> All things weird and wonderful,
>   The Discworld has them all.

DRAGONS

On our world, the image of the dragon is so widespread and so deep-
rooted that it can truly be said that its origins are lost in those famous
mists of time. It's a persistent image, too. Even after the last land
masses had been explored, and map-makers were forced to admit
that 'Here be *no* dragons', people still reported seeing sea-serpents,

and huge scaly things in lakes. And to this day there are innumerable storytellers and artists, still eagerly creating and re-creating dragons in their works. There must be a powerful flow of draconicons still pouring into the Earth from some other universe. It seems likely that the source is the Discworld, which can boast of two flourishing species and has some awareness of a third.

(a) Draco vulgaris

Visitors to Ankh-Morpork and other Discworld cities have often commented on the charming fashion for society ladies to wear small, colourful dragons on their shoulders; in the winter months, they are also popular as muffs and foot-warmers. These are miniature specimens of *Draco vulgaris*, the Common Swamp Dragon, which probably no longer exists in the wild but has been bred in captivity for many generations. The basic type is the Common Smut, familiar to all, from which numerous distinct varieties have been developed; some three dozen are recognized for show purposes (details obtainable from the Cavern Club Exhibitions Committee). Most are of amiable disposition, but it should be noted that the Golden Deceiver retains some characteristics of its wild ancestors; it makes a good watch dragon but should not be allowed near children.

To own a pedigree Swamp Dragon is a mark of taste and refinement, but also requires a degree of patience which, alas, all too few would-be owners possess. Where dragons are kept, damage to furniture and clothing is inevitable, and chemical effluvia are frequently emitted which some persons of delicate constitution may find offensive. Most dragons are highly strung, excitable little creatures, so great care must be taken in approaching and handling them, if the owner wishes to avoid scratches, bites, and unsightly loss of hair through sudden flaming at close range. The owner can also expect much expense on vets' bills, since dragons suffer from a multitude of ills – Slab Throat, Skiplets, The Black Tups, Storge and Staggers, to name but a few (see *Diseases of the Dragon*, by Sybil

Deirdre Olgivanna Ramkin). Their digestive systems are liable to catastrophic malfunctions, notably Blowback, which is invariably fatal. Needless to say, all varieties readily explode under stress.

There has been much debate as to how so delicate and vulnerable a species can have evolved and survived. True, their native habitat in the swamps of Genua was fairly inaccessible, and they had no natural predators; the only external danger was from callous young men who had worked out that the simplest way to set yourself up as a hero was (in the words of Sir Samuel Vimes) 'to come plodding into the swamp to stick a sword into a bag of guts that was only one step away from self-destruction anyway'. Yet their entire metabolism seems radically unsuited to Discworld conditions. Leonard of Quirm has proposed the bold theory that swamp dragons did not originate on the Disc but are descended from the non-discly species *Draco nobilis* (see below), showing adaptations for a heavy-air environment. The difference in size would thus be an example of evolutionary dwarfism, a process well attested in isolated populations.

(b) Draco nobilis

Everyone on the Discworld and on Earth has heard of the Noble or Great Dragon – a creature many times larger than the Swamp Dragon, fierce, untameable, with scales and claws and breath like a blast furnace, coiled up in its secret lair on top of a great hoard of gold. In traditional tales, such dragons fed on virgins and could only be slain by heroes (preferably the long-lost heirs of kingdoms), and we shall have more to say on this in a later chapter. But were they myth, or were they real?

At the time of the events recounted in *Guards! Guards!* the most that could be said was that they were a great mystery. Lady Sybil Ramkin knew that they used to turn up from time to time, full of vim and vigour, but had ceased coming. She believed they had migrated to somewhere where gravity wasn't so strong, where they could fulfil their potential and be all that a dragon should be. Lord Vetinari was positive that they were extinct, despite the fact that something large, hot and angry was incinerating portions of the city. The Unique and Supreme Lodge of the Elucidated Brethren of the Ebon Night were using rituals to summon and control a Great Dragon. They discovered that if summoning is hard, control is much, much harder. But at least nobody could still argue that *Draco nobilis* was a myth. Ensuing events confirmed that *Draco vulgaris* and *Draco nobilis* are indeed related, but gave no clue as to the latter's current habitat.

The wizard Rincewind claimed to have learned, in the course of a very alarming early experience of his own, that most of the time they do not exist as people generally understand 'existence', but only potentially:

> The *true* dragon is a creature of such refinement of spirit that they can only take on form in this world if they are conceived by the most skilled imagination. And even then the said imagination must be in some place heavily impregnated with magic, which helps to weaken the walls between the world of the seen and unseen. Then the dragons pop through, as it were, and impress their form upon this world's possibility matrix. [*The Colour of Magic*]

Some years later, Rincewind revised his views on the mystery in the light of fresh discoveries. When the intrepid voyagers on Leonard of Quirm's flying machine landed briefly on the Disc's moon (as recounted in *The Last Hero*), they found a population of magnificent silver dragons of all sizes, feeding on moon-plants with metallic silver leaves. They were completely unafraid of humans; indeed, the little ones would swarm all over people, like kittens. It is plausible to assume that these superb creatures are a variety of *Draco nobilis*. How we yearn to know more about them! But it seems the gods have decreed that no more flying machines shall be built. Probably this is for the best. Let the Moon Dragons enjoy their serene life, safe from the deplorable impact of humanity. The true dragon-lover must rejoice for them.

(c) *Draco maritimus immensis*

No other dragon species has actually been observed on or near the Disc, but according to Scandinavian mythology there was (or is) a third one on Earth, the aquatic Midgardsorm or Middle-Earth Worm (*Draco maritimus immensis*). It is written that it lies on the seabed, encircling the whole Earth, where it will remain till the end of the world, when it will emerge, and a particularly stupid Norse god named Thor will clobber it with a hammer. It is some comfort that it is also written that its dying breath will poison him.

This myth is hard to believe. The distribution of land masses on the Earth is so untidy that no dragon could encircle the whole planet while lying on the seabed without suffering painful and possibly fatal dislocations of its spine. However, somewhere there exists another universe which was once briefly summoned into a prism by the gifted young wizard Simon, and this one does appear to contain a Middle-Earth Worm.

> A prism . . . held another slowly turning disc, surrounded by little stars. But there were no ice walls around this one, just a red-gold thread that turned out on closer inspection to be a snake – a snake big enough to encircle a world. For reasons best known to itself it was biting its own tail. [*Equal Rites*]

This is confirmed by something the sea-troll Tethis told Rincewind (see *The Colour of Magic*). While tumbling through space after being swept off the edge of his own world, Tethis passed within a few leagues of a world with a strange ring of mountains round it – mountains that turned out to be 'the biggest dragon you could ever imagine, covered in snow and glaciers and holding its tail in its mouth'. A dim awareness of this universe may explain the Earth myth of *Draco maritimus immensis*, and also the image of the *ouroboros* or tail-biting serpent known to alchemists and hermetic philosophers as the symbol of the ever-circling eternity of time and space.

THE BASILISK AND THE CHIMERA

The basilisk is a particularly dangerous species of serpent, which can kill any other animal merely by glancing at it with its fierce, fell and fiery eyes; its breath destroys all vegetation, so it is necessarily a desert-dweller; its blood is said to be of great value to magicians. On Earth, it was first identified by the Ancient Greeks, who gave it a name meaning 'little king', because (as the Roman naturalist Pliny explained) it has a golden mark like a crown on its head.

Later, during the Middle Ages of western Europe, people believed that it wore an actual coronet of pure gold, and some described it as a snake with four pairs of legs. They gave it a second name, 'cockatrice', and said it was a mortal enemy of crocodiles. They also claimed to know how it is born: when a farmyard cock lives longer than is normal for his species, in the last stage of his life he starts to lay eggs, and if, in the hottest days of summer, some venomous serpent or toad coils itself round such an egg and hatches it, what comes out is the cockatrice or basilisk. It has the head and legs of a cockerel, but its body tapers down to a snake's tail, ending in a dart. It was much feared for its death-dealing glance, until a method of destroying it was devised. Writing a *Historie of Serpents* in 1608, the naturalist Edward Topsell mocked the legend:

> I cannot without laughing remember the old wives' tales of the vulgar cockatrices that have been in England, for I have often-times heard it confidently related, that once our nation was full of cockatrices, and that a certain man did destroy them by

going up and down in glasse, whereby their own shapes were reflected upon their own faces, and so they died.

Topsell was wrong to laugh. The method is perfectly valid. It exploits an instinct which can also be seen in young male swamp dragons in the breeding season, when they are so eager to drive off a rival that they will attack their own reflections (as Chubby did in *Men at Arms*).

On the Discworld, the basilisk inhabits the burning deserts of Klatch. On one occasion, as we read in *Sourcery*, a hungry basilisk which lay panting in the baking shade of a rock, dribbling corrosive yellow slime, heard the thumping of hundreds of little feet. This, the creature thought, must mean that its dinner was on the way. But what was approaching was the wizard Rincewind's fearsome Luggage, which was in a particularly foul mood because it had become separated from its master and had recently had to fight its way across a river infested with alligators.

> The basilisk blinked its legendary eyes and uncoiled twenty feet of hungry body, winding out and on to the sand like fluid death.
>
> The Luggage staggered to a halt and raised its lid threateningly. The basilisk hissed, but a little uncertainly, because it had never seen a walking box before, and certainly never one with lots of alligator teeth stuck in its lid. There were also scraps of leathery hide adhering to it, as though it had been involved in a fight in a handbag factory, and in a way that the basilisk wouldn't have been able to describe even if it could talk, it appeared to be glaring.
>
> Right, the reptile thought, if that's the way you want to play it.
>
> It turned on the Luggage a stare like a diamond drill, a stare that nipped in via the staree's eyeballs and flayed the brain from the inside, a stare that tore the frail net curtains on the windows of the soul, a stare that—

The basilisk realized something was very wrong. An entirely new and unwelcome sensation started to arise just behind its saucer-shaped eyes. It started small, like the little itch in those few square inches of back that no amount of writhing will allow you to scratch, and grew until it became a second, red-hot, internal sun.

The basilisk was feeling a terrible, overpowering and irresistible urge to blink . . .

It did something incredibly unwise.

It blinked. [*Sourcery*]

The Luggage went on its way, with a few traces of yellow slime rapidly drying on its lid. What a tragic misunderstanding! If only the basilisk had been less hungry that day, and the Luggage less ill-tempered, they would have seen how much they had in common – a domineering gaze, a dislike of alligators and crocodiles, perhaps even a multiplicity of feet, if some pictures of basilisks can be trusted. A beautiful friendship might have been born. But it was not to be.

Pursuing its erratic course across the dunes of Klatch, the Luggage next encountered a Chimera, which was sitting on a stone pinnacle the shape and temperature of a firebrick. Before recounting the outcome, it will be useful to see what books from our own world can tell about this monster – legendary here, but real enough on the Discworld.

According to John Milton, a chimera is just about the worst thing you could meet on a guided tour of Hell. In Book 2 of his *Paradise Lost* he lists the horrors in the infernal landscape at some length, and caps them all with the assertion that Hell is a place

Where all life dies, death lives, and Nature breeds
(Perverse) all monstrous, all prodigious things,
Abominable, inutterable, and worse
Than fables yet have feigned, or fear conceived,
Gorgons, and Hydras, and Chimaeras dire.

After which it comes as a bit of a let-down to find that, according to Ancient Greek poets, the Chimera was a rather muddled female monster, consisting of a fire-breathing nanny-goat with a lion's head and a snake's body. An alternative view, supported by Ancient Greek artists who had to draw the damn thing, was that she had two heads at the front end, one leonine and one capriform, and a long scaly tail at the back end, terminating in a snake's head. The Greek Chimera's family was an unpleasant one. Her father Typhon, the god of storms at sea, was nothing but a writhing mass of serpents from the waist down, and had snakes instead of fingers, while his wings darkened the whole sky; her mother was a sea-monster, half woman and half snake, who ate humans raw; her siblings included Cerberus, the three-headed Hound of Hell, and the hundred-headed Hydra.

The Greek Chimera did her best to be dire; she tried to look as abominable and inutterable as she could, but the goat component undermined the effect. Her biggest asset was her fiery breath, yet even this turned out to be unhelpful when the hero Bellerophon was sent to kill her, on the orders of an enemy of his, who assumed this was a mission impossible – indeed, fatal. But Bellerophon was as canny as he was good-looking, and devised a cunning plan. Mounted on his good flying horse Pegasus, he swooped over the Chimera, firing arrows at her, and when she opened her lion's jaws to puff flame at him he dropped a lump of lead down her throat. The heat of her stomach melted the lead, sealing her doom from the inside.

The chimera of the Discworld may be related, but separate evolution has brought about several differences, including some unexpected wings. According to Broomfog's bestiary *Anima Unnaturale*,

> It have thee legges of an mermade, the hair of an tortoise, the teeth of an fowel, and the winges of an snake. Of course, I have only my worde for it, the beast having the breathe of an furnace and the temperament of an rubber balloon in a hurricane. [*Sourcery*]

Such was the creature which attacked Rincewind's Luggage.

> The chimera's technique was to swoop low over the prey, lightly boiling it with its fiery breath, and then turn and rend its dinner with its teeth. It managed the fire part but then, at the point where experience told the creature it should be facing a stricken and terrified victim, found itself on the ground in the path of a scorched and furious Luggage.
>
> The only thing incandescent about the Luggage was its rage. It had spent several hours with a headache, during which it seemed the whole world had tried to attack it. It had had enough.
>
> When it had stamped the unfortunate chimera into a greasy puddle on the sand, it paused for a moment, apparently considering its future . . . [*Sourcery*]

There is a distinct possibility that the Discworld chimera, always an endangered species, is now extinct.

THE SPHINX

Though there can be no doubt that Prince Teppic of Djelibeybi once met a Sphinx, there has been much argument over whether the creature is truly part of the Discworld's fauna. Teppic himself was unclear as to where he was when he encountered it. Space and time had been behaving strangely. A spokesman for Unseen University expressed the view that:

> The Sphinx is an unreal creature. It exists solely because it has been imagined. It is well known that in an infinite universe anything that can be imagined must exist somewhere, and since many of them are not things that ought to exist in a well-ordered space-time frame they get shoved into a side dimension. [*Pyramids*]

To which Teppic replied that that's as may be, but he was in no doubt that either he broke into the Sphinx's dimension or it broke into his, and that what has happened once may happen again. Provisionally, therefore, the Sphinx has been listed as a potential (if unwelcome) denizen of the Discworld.

On Earth, its existence is better documented. According to ancient writers, a Sphinx is a creature with the body of a lion or lioness and a human head; one subspecies has wings and human female breasts; another has a serpent's tail; yet another exists only in the form of conjoined twins. The name means 'throttler' in Greek. They were native to Egypt, where they guarded the borders of the kingdom, the entrances to temples, and the approaches to important pyramids and tombs. They were not normally dangerous to humans. Many statues of them were made, and can be seen to this day.

The Egyptians themselves had no generic word for sphinxes, each one (and there were hundreds of them) having a name of its own. Tourists visiting the Great Sphinx of Giza should address it, cautiously, as Horemakhet Khepri-Ra-Atum. If they get the pronunciation right, it may choose to reveal some of the hidden treasures which it guards. If they get it wrong, it may choose to reveal its claws.

The Great Sphinx of Giza has two aims in its existence. The first is to guard the royal tombs at Memphis, which it has successfully done for some 4,500 years; the second is to keep itself, and the town of Giza, free from drifting sand, because sand makes it ache in all its limbs. This has been a sorry failure. After a mere eleven hundred years it was buried in dunes right up to the neck, until it was dug clear by Prince Thutmose, whom it gratefully made Pharaoh. Other people have had to dig it out again since then, but they don't now get to be made Pharaoh. In fact, the Great Sphinx seems to have pretty well given up on its sand-repelling duties, allowing Giza to be engulfed, and relying on humans to give it the occasional brush-up. The

Arabs say it is sulking because a holy man smashed its nose.

According to Greek mythology, the goddess Hera brought a single female sphinx from Egypt to Greece, for vindictive reasons; she must have hoped that, as so often, the introduction of a foreign species would seriously damage the local ecology, but since she neglected to provide it with a mate it did not breed, and the devastation it caused ended with its life.

This Greek Sphinx was more active, more malevolent, than her Egyptian relatives. She perched herself on a rock overlooking the main road into Thebes, where she forced every traveller to try to guess her utterly perplexing Riddle: 'What animal walks on four legs in the morning, two at midday, and three in the evening, and is at its weakest when it has most legs?' If they couldn't answer, she throttled them, and ate them. And so it went on, until one day Oedipus came along, and replied, 'That animal is Man. As a feeble baby, he crawls on all fours; as an adult, he walks upright; as an old man, he uses a stick.' The Sphinx was so furious that she beat her brains out against the rock.

Prince Teppic's Sphinx, like the Egyptian one, guarded a border – in this case, a fold in the space-time continuum which was a border between dimensions. Like the Greek one, it relied upon The Riddle to provide it with entertainment and with innumerable meals. Now Teppic, despite being a fully qualified Assassin, was not a man of violence, and had a proper concern for wildlife, even in its more alarming forms. He tried polite conversation ('We've got any amount of statues to you at home'), but the Sphinx, though flattered, could not be sidetracked for long, and challenged him with its Riddle. Teppic admitted defeat, so the gloating Sphinx itself gave him the explanation.

Now, Teppic had been born into a culture profoundly distrustful of metaphors, symbolism, allegories, and figures of speech of every sort. The people of Djelibeybi took all religious, poetic, and meta-physical statements as literal physical truths; to them, a metaphor was a lie. Furthermore, Teppic had recently visited Ephebe, where he had heard the philosopher Xeno expounding his famous logical proof that if you shoot an arrow at a tortoise you cannot possibly hit it.

So Teppic launched an attack, not on the Sphinx, but on its metaphor. Combining the deadly literalism of Djelibeybi with the debating skills and logic of Ephebe, he demanded clarifications. Did all this actually happen in one day, to one individual? Well, no, the Sphinx admitted, it is a figure of speech, but what's wrong with that? 'An element of dramatic analogy is present in all riddles,' it claimed. 'Yes, *but*,' said Teppic, 'is there internal consistency within the metaphor?' Step by step, the hapless Sphinx was forced to concede that in an analogy where the human lifespan of seventy years is represented by twenty-four hours, the crawling stage only lasts for about twenty minutes, and can't be called 'morning', as it comes just after midnight. There are other problems too. Since some old folk need no sticks while others use two, would it not be more accurate to say that after supper-time 'it continues to walk on two legs or with any prosthetic aids of its choice'?

When everything had been settled to their mutual satisfaction, the Sphinx repeated its challenge. But of course Prince Teppic already knew the answer. The Sphinx itself had told him, earlier on. He now gave it, and the Sphinx had to let him go free. He got away just in time as an angry bellow erupted behind him, when the Sphinx finally worked out what had happened.

Should the creature ever reappear on the Discworld or in our own universe, people will now know how to deal with it.

THE PHOENIX

Everyone agrees that the phoenix, also known as the firebird, is extremely beautiful, and that it is the rarest bird that has ever existed, or could ever exist, anywhere in the multiverse. It's said, both on the

Discworld and on Earth, that you only get one phoenix at a time, that it lives to be five hundred years old, and that when it feels its death approaching it builds a nest, in which it lays a single egg. Then it bursts into flame and burns itself up, so that the warmth will hatch out the new bird from the ashes. This way of life, and death, makes it extremely useful as an allegory or metaphor. It also makes some people think that it is only a mythical creature.

However, there are people in Lancre who, having observed nature closely, think the commonly accepted story cannot be accurate. Both Hodgesaargh the falconer and Granny Weatherwax have found the occasional phoenix feather, a small flickering flame-like thing which nothing can quench. Granny keeps hers in a little glass bottle. One day the other witches are examining it:

'I saw her pick that thing up years ago,' said Magrat. 'It was around this time of year, too. We were walking back through the woods and there was a shooting star and this sort of light fell off it and we went to look and there it was. It looked like a flame but she was able to pick it up.'

'Sounds like a firebird feather,' said Nanny. 'There used to be old stories about them. They pass through here. But if you touch their feathers you'd better be damn sure of yourself, because the old stories say they burn in the presence of evil—'

'Firebird? You mean a phoenix?' said Agnes.

'Haven't seen one go over for years,' said Nanny. 'Sometimes you'd see two or three at a time when I was a girl, just lights flying high up in the sky.'

'No, no, the phoenix . . . there's only *one* of it, that's the whole point,' said Agnes.

'One of anything's no bloody use,' said Nanny. [*Carpe Jugulum*]

On the Discworld, the firebird is said to have its main home in the hot deserts of Klatch, even though its seasonal migrations take it over Lancre. So, the best place to look for its equivalent on Earth would be in the hot deserts of Ancient Egypt. And there, sure enough, it is – not yet called the phoenix, but the Benu Bird. The name probably means 'rise-and-shine'. According to one Egyptian myth it is the oldest of all creatures; its cry was the first sound ever heard, when it perched, glowing, on the first mound of earth to rise up out of the primeval sea – or, others said, on the first sacred obelisk, the Benben stone at Heliopolis. It was usually described as a heron, or as a huge golden hawk with a heron's beak.

Many generations later, in the fifth century BC, the Greek writer Herodotus visited Heliopolis, where he was told about a marvellous red-gold bird which would come to the temple of the sun there once every five hundred years. He called it 'phoenix', meaning that its brilliant colouring was as fine as the richest Phoenician purple dye. This bird, he was told, would arrive carrying an egg which it had formed from the ashes of its parent mixed with myrrh; the next phoenix would be born from this egg.

Later writers changed the bird's homeland from Egypt to Arabia, and gave a different explanation of its death and rebirth. An aged phoenix, they said, would build itself a nest full of spices, and settling there would sing a last sad song. Then it would burst into flame and burn itself to ashes. But from the ashes a new young bird would arise.

Thanks to this story, the phoenix is famous in poetry and folk-lore as a symbol of indestructible life. As Will Shakespeare put it:

> Thus when
> The bird of wonder dies, the maiden phoenix,
> Her ashes new-create another heir,
> As much to be admired as she herself.

The witches of Lancre would not entirely agree. 'Bird of wonder', yes; 'maiden', no. For, as Granny Weatherwax pointed out, 'One of anything ain't going to last for very long, is it?'

THE SALAMANDER

Salamanders are a species of lizard, pinkish in colour, sluggish in behaviour, and in no way dangerous. The only interesting thing about them is that they do not eat in the normal sense of the word; instead, they subsist entirely on the nourishing quality of octarine, the eighth colour in the Discworld's sunlight, which they absorb through their skins. Since the wavelengths corresponding to the other colours have no food value for them, they store this surplus light in a special sac and discharge it when the sac is full, or when they are alarmed, causing a vivid flash. A cage of salamanders is a very useful piece of equipment for anyone who wants to keep a pictorial record of events (such as Twoflower the tourist, or Otto Chriek the journalistic iconographer), for the flash enables the imp in the picture-box to function even in the dark.

On Earth the name was applied, in the days of the Ancient Greeks, to what must be a related species – a lizard that lives in the midst of fire, remaining unharmed because its body is so intensely cold that it extinguishes the flames around it. Centuries later, the alchemist Paracelsus taught that each of the four elements (earth, air, fire and water) had its own elemental spirit, and that of fire was a salamander. These dramatic creatures are now regarded on Earth as mere myths, useful only in poetry and heraldry. Confusingly, however, there are also on that world several species of flesh-and-blood lizards which are called 'salamanders'. Throwing them into a fire as an experiment is not considered an environmentally friendly act.

THE UNICORN

This elegant but sometimes ferocious beast is an elvish creature, not native to the Discworld. The one which appeared in Lancre (as told in *Lords and Ladies*) came from an alternative universe where it was the Elf Queen's pet; it had crossed accidentally, at one of those places where worlds come too close together, and the wall between them is thinner than one would wish. It could not return. Terrified and enraged, it became a danger – for a large stallion with a twelve-inch razor-sharp horn growing from its forehead is not to be treated lightly.

Yet Granny Weatherwax was able to cope. When the unicorn charged at her, she created an invisible wall into which it crashed, and as it writhed on the ground she let down her hair, and broke off a single hair at the root.

> Granny Weatherwax's hands made a complicated motion in the air as she made a noose out of something almost too thin to see. She ignored the thrashing horn and dropped it over the unicorn's neck. Then she pulled.
>
> Struggling, its unshod hooves kicking up great clods of mud, the unicorn struggled to its feet.
>
> 'That'll never hold it,' said Nanny, sidling around the tree.
>
> 'I could hold it with a cobweb, Gytha Ogg. With a *cobweb*.'

And so indeed she does, dragging the unicorn to Jason Ogg's forge, where its hooves are shod – not with iron, of course, since that would kill an elvish animal, but with silver horseshoes made from Granny's own best tea-set. Her ability to control the beast should not surprise anybody, for, as Nanny Ogg says, there are some things which *everybody* knows about trapping unicorns – 'who is qualified to trap 'em is what I'm delicately hintin' at.' It takes a maiden to do it, in any universe. And Granny may be old, but she *is* qualified.

> Granny emerged from the forge, leading the unicorn . . . It walked politely alongside the witch until she reached the centre of the square. Then she turned it loose, and gave it a slight slap on the rump.

It whinnied softly, turned, and galloped down the street, towards the forest . . .

'*She'll* never get it back, though she calls for it for a thousand years,' said Granny, speaking to the world in general . . .

The unicorn reached the forest, and galloped onwards.

There are clear affinities here with what people on Earth have long been saying, though, regrettably, in that world the fate of the captured unicorn is more cruel. As early as the seventh century, the Spaniard Isidore of Seville described the unicorn, and how to hunt it:

The unicorn is a most savage beast. It has this name because in the middle of its forehead it has a horn, four foot long. And that horn is so sharp and so strong that it knocks down or pierces everything it strikes. This beast often fights against the elephant and pierces him in the belly and throws him to the ground. And the unicorn is so strong that he cannot be taken by the might of hunters. But men who write about the nature of animals say that a maiden is brought where the unicorn may come; and she opens her lap and the unicorn lays his head on it, and abandons all his fierceness, and falls asleep there. And thus the beast is caught, and slain by the huntsmen's spears.

Granny's device of using a hair as a noose and leash is a remarkable piece of magical skill, and very rare. In Earthly legends one occasionally reads about a maiden tying a defeated dragon with the girdle of her robe and leading it away – St Martha did this, at Tarascon in southern France, and so did the girl St George rescued – but a hair, no. However, a few malevolent hags in the Scottish Highlands did know the trick. If one of these hags found a huntsman sheltering in a mountain bothy, she would kill him, provided she was safe from his dog. So she would ask him to tie the dog up with one of her own long hairs. When she cried, 'Tighten and choke, hair!' the dog died.

But that is an unpleasant thought. Instead, let us turn to what the poet Alexander Pope has to say about a girl's charming ringlets:

Love in these labyrinths his slaves detains,
And mighty hearts are held in slender chains.
Fair tresses man's imperial race ensnare,
And beauty draws us with a single hair.

THE LUGGAGE

Perhaps the strangest of all life-forms on the Disc is the Luggage. It is certainly made of wood, yet its multiple legs and strong aggressive instincts are equally certainly proof that it is no mere plant or plant-product. And very, very certainly it has a mind of its own. 'Vegetable with animal connections' is a fair summary. Yet much mystery remains, even after careful study of various Earthly traditions which help to throw light on its possible evolution.

On Earth, there was a time when travelling was truly Travelling, not just a matter of hopping on to a jet for a five-day break on the Costa del Sol. People said, 'I go south in the winter', meaning they made a habit of spending a couple of months on the Riviera every year; they went off for half their lives to govern a chunk of far-flung Empire; in extreme cases, they went round the world in eighty days. En route, they tended to acquire pterodactyls, mummies, and bits of old temples. So when an English gentleman travelled, a whole host of trunks, crates, chests, portmanteaux, packing cases, suitcases, dressing-cases, shoe-cases, hatboxes, bandboxes, Gladstone bags, carpet bags, and pistol cases travelled with him. Arriving at his destination, he would leave most of them at the quayside or station and enter his hotel with a mere smattering of hand baggage (say, as much as two porters could carry), telling the manager, 'My luggage will follow'. And so it would, pushed on handcarts, or carried on the backs or heads of porters.

But as time rolled on, the race of porters became mysteriously extinct, and evolutionary pressures caused luggage itself to develop mechanisms enabling it to obey its instinct to *follow*. The first scientific record of this phenomenon was by Terry himself, when he wrote in 1988:

> Many years ago I saw, in Bath, a very large American lady towing a *huge* tartan suitcase very fast on little rattly wheels which caught in the pavement cracks and generally gave it a life of its own. At that moment the Luggage was born. Many thanks to that lady . . . [Dedication of *Sourcery*]

The Discworld environment is hostile to things with little rattly wheels, as we learn in *Reaper Man*, when it is menaced by an incursion of alien supermarket trolleys. Therefore on the Disc evolution has produced a more elegant solution: the Luggage hurtles across the landscape (and, if need be, through space, time, and dimensions) on several hundred energetic but retractable little legs, always following the person it has adopted as its owner.

If that were all, one could reasonably claim to understand the origins and characteristics of the Luggage. But it has more mysterious properties, whose equivalents on Earth are obscure, though not beyond all conjecture. Outwardly it looks like a pirate's treasure-chest, the kind one expects to find brim full of ill-gotten gold and jewels, but its interior is larger than its exterior, and probably does not occupy the same space-time framework. Sometimes it does indeed contain bags of gold, at other times food and drink, or its owner's neatly folded clothes, smelling of lavender; but when it is in fighting mode it opens its lid menacingly to reveal rows and rows of large square teeth, as white as bleached sycamore or tombstones, and a red, pulsating, mahogany tongue. It is wholly impervious to magic, being itself made of sapient pearwood from the Counterweight

Continent, possibly the most concentrated magical substance on the Disc. When angry (as it so often is) it is a fearsome enemy, as was amply demonstrated during a fight in the Broken Drum.

> The door burst open. Two trolls hurried through it, slammed it behind them, dropped the heavy bar across it and fled down the stairs.
>
> Outside there was a sudden crescendo of running feet. And, for the last time, the door opened. In fact it exploded, the great wooden bar being hurled far across the room and the frame itself giving way.
>
> Door and frame landed on a table, which flew into splinters. It was then that the frozen fighters noticed that there was something else in the pile of wood. It was a box, shaking itself madly to rid itself of the smashed timber around it . . .
>
> A raven swooped down from its perch in the rafters and dived at the wizard [Rincewind], talons open and gleaming.
>
> It didn't make it. At about the half-way point the Luggage leapt from its bed of splinters, gaped briefly in mid air, and snapped shut.
>
> It landed lightly. Rincewind saw its lid open again, slightly. Just far enough for a tongue, large as a palm leaf, red as mahogany, to lick up a few errant feathers. [*The Colour of Magic*]

It would be reassuring to think that no such devastating piece of carpentry exists, ever has existed, or ever could exist elsewhere in the multiverse. But the myths of olden time and the inspirational insights of modern authors both show that a race of deadly chests has evolved on Earth, with all the destructive power of the Luggage, and none of its usefulness and charm.

The first hint of their existence comes from Plutarch, a Greek writer living in Rome who died in AD 126; he visited Egypt, whose ancient religion fascinated him, and wrote a book *Concerning Isis and Osiris* based on the legends current there in his time. He recounts in detail how the virtuous king Osiris was murdered by his evil brother Seth. Seth secretly obtained the exact measurements of Osiris, and had a magnificent chest made; he then displayed it during a feast, promising to give it to whoever could fit inside it exactly. Many tried, but in vain. Finally Osiris laid himself in the chest, which immediately became a perfect fit for him; Seth promptly bolted it shut, sealed it with lead, and threw it into the Nile. It floated magically for many miles, and when it washed ashore in the Lebanon it grew at once into a marvellous tree, still containing the dead body of Osiris; then it was cut down and made into a pillar in a king's palace. Isis, wife of Osiris, claimed the pillar and had it opened, revealing the chest/coffin, which held the wonderfully preserved corpse; it thus became the prototype for all Egyptian mummy-cases.

Another death-dealing chest is recorded in Norse tradition as the property of the legendary goldsmith Volund (or, in English, Wayland). A cruel king held him captive on an island, forcing him to work at making golden treasures; his sword had been taken from him, and he had been deliberately lamed to prevent any escape. The king had two young sons, who one day went hunting on that island and came to Volund's forge. There they saw a great chest, and asked Volund for the key. He opened it, and they looked in. It held great evil, but to the boys it seemed filled with gold rings and fine jewels. 'Come back tomorrow,' said Volund, 'and all this will be yours. But tell no one that you are visiting me.' And so they did, and, as the Old Icelandic poem *Völundarkviða* says:

> They came to where the great chest stood,
>   Asked Volund for the key;
> When they looked in, there was revealed
>   Evil and enmity.

He struck off the heads of those two boys
  As they bent down to gaze,
And under the pit of the anvil there
  He buried their bodies.

'He struck off the heads' . . . but how, as he had no sword? One has a nasty suspicion that the chest did the deed itself, using its lid as a weapon.

Suspicion also surrounds a tragic event chronicled by Thomas Haynes Bayly in his poem 'The Mistletoe Bough' in the 1820s. It was in the times of Merrie England that one of our typical Merrie barons was holding a typically Merrie Christmas dance in his typically Merrie castle, together with his retainers (who all were blithe and gay), his newly married daughter, and the latter's bridegroom, young Lovell. Seized by a sudden Merrie whim, the bride decided to play hide-and-seek, challenging Lovell to find her secret lurking place. But it all went horribly wrong:

They sought her that night! They sought her next day!
And they sought her in vain when a week passed away!
In the highest – the lowest – the loneliest spot,
Young Lovell sought wildly – but found her not.

Many, many years passed by, and then:

At length an oak chest, that had long lain hid,
Was found in the castle – they raised the lid –
And a skeleton form lay mouldering there,
In the bridal wreath of that lady fair!
Oh! Sad was her fate! In sportive jest
She hid from her lord in the old oak chest.
It closed with a spring! – and, dreadful doom,
The bride lay clasp'd in her living tomb!

Sheer accident? The corresponding tragedy in the history of Lancre does indeed seem so, judging by Nanny Ogg's account:

> 'I remember years ago my granny telling me about Queen Amonia, well, I say queen, but she never was queen except for about three hours because of what I'm about to unfold, on account of them playing hide-and-seek at the wedding party and her hiding in a big heavy old chest in some attic and the lid slamming shut and no one finding her for seven months, by which time you could definitely say the wedding cake was getting a bit stale.' [*Lords and Ladies*]

Yet over in our own world, suspicion lingers. Did the chest Bayly speaks of have some rudimentary capacity for bloody-minded malevolence? And how exactly had it managed to lie hidden while everybody was searching the castle from turret to dungeon? There is a sinister mystery here.

A later generation glimpsed what may be a related phenomenon in Robert Louis Stevenson's *Treasure Island* (1883). Jim Hawkins, looking back on the adventure of his boyhood, recalled how it began on the day the 'brown old seaman with the sabre cut' arrived, *followed* by his sea-chest, and took lodgings at the inn which Jim's parents owned.

> I remember him as if it were yesterday, as he came plodding up to the inn-door, his sea-chest following behind him in a hand-barrow ... I remember him looking round the cove and whistling to himself as he did so, and then breaking out in that old sea-song he sang so often afterwards:–
> 'Fifteen men on the dead man's chest –
>   Yo-ho-ho, and a bottle of rum!
> Drink and the devil had done for the rest –
>   Yo-ho-ho, and a bottle of rum!'

This ill-omened shanty echoes again and again through the story, and is never completed, or explained. Jim writes that 'At first I had supposed the "dead man's chest" to be that identical big box of his upstairs in the front room', the great sea-chest which none of them had ever seen opened. The thought gave him nightmares, as well it might. For how could fifteen men be on one chest? Knowing what we now know of the Luggage, we must query the correctness of the preposition. Not *on* but *in*, perhaps? Let us recall Rincewind's conversation with Conina, on an occasion when the Luggage had just emerged from the Shades with several arrowheads and broken swords sticking in it. She asks him if it is dangerous.

> 'There's two schools of thought about that,' said Rincewind. 'There's some people who say it's dangerous, and others who say it's very dangerous. What do you think?'
>
> The Luggage raised its lid a fraction . . .
>
> Conina stared at that lid. It looked very like a mouth.
>
> 'I think I'd vote for "terminally dangerous",' she said.
>
> 'It likes crisps,' volunteered Rincewind, and then added, 'Well, that's a bit strong. It *eats* crisps.'
>
> 'What about people?'
>
> 'Oh, and people. About fifteen so far, I think.' [*Sourcery*]

Fifteen, eh?

But it would be unfair to take leave of the Luggage without any mention of the gentler, more domestic side of its nature. During a brief return to its native country, described in *Interesting Times*, it gallantly rescued a rather charming trunk with inlaid lid and dainty feet (with red toenails) from the unwelcome attentions of three big, coarse cases covered in studded leather. Romance blossomed. Mysterious sounds of sawing and hammering were heard by night on a hillside where pear trees grew. And when the Luggage reappeared it – or shall we say he? – was followed by the dainty-footed Luggage, and then, in descending order of size, four little chests, the smallest being about the size of a lady's handbag. But the Luggage could not deny its inner calling. After one or two sad backward glances, or what might have been glances if it had had eyes, it cantered away through the dimensions, still following Rincewind.

Chapter 8

THE WITCHES OF LANCRE

WHY THREE? WHY 'WYRD'?

THE GREATEST CONCENTRATION of natural magical talent in the Discworld is found in the Ramtop Mountains, especially in the small kingdom of Lancre. There have been witches there for generations, remembered to this day with fondness and fear. And still one can hear the age-old rallying call, as an eldritch voice shrieks through a thunderstorm, 'When shall we three meet again?' To which, after a pause, another replies in far more ordinary tones, 'Well, I can do next Tuesday.'

Which is all very well, but it does raise questions. Lancre witches normally work alone, each having her own personal approach to her craft. So why do these particular witches (Granny Weatherwax, Nanny Ogg, and Magrat Garlick) often meet as a threesome? Why is the first account of their deeds entitled *Wyrd Sisters*, when they are *not* sisters? And isn't wyrd a weird way to spell weird, even if they *are* weird?

As with so many other things, it's all down to Will Shakespeare. His impact on the universe certainly stretches as far as Lancre.

In Will Shakespeare's *Macbeth*, there is a trio of secret, black and midnight hags who forgather in a thunderstorm on a blasted heath, boil up unappetizing brews in a cauldron, and utter tricky prophecies which shape the destinies of kings. The stage directions are quite clear as to what they are ('Thunder and lightning; enter three witches'), and the text is equally clear as to their name. They are the Weird Sisters. That is what Macbeth calls them, and what they call themselves. The Weird Sisters.

Being strong individualists, it would never occur to Granny Weatherwax, Nanny Ogg and Magrat to give themselves a collective name. But the book does. Being receptive to inspiration, it calls them Wyrd Sisters.

That, actually, is how Shakespeare *ought* to have spelled the name of his own three witches, since it is their true and original title. It doesn't mean they were peculiar or crazy. It is the Anglo-Saxon *wyrd*, a word meaning Fate or Destiny, which is now completely forgotten in England, but is still sometimes heard in Scotland, in encouraging remarks such as 'Weel, laddie, ye maun e'en dree your weird' (roughly, 'That's *your* bad luck, son, and you'll just have to put up with it'). Shakespeare's witches could foretell, and probably direct, your destiny.

Shakespeare found their name in the book where he first read about Macbeth's career, Raphael Holinshed's *History of Scotland* (1577). Holinshed was too cautious to commit himself as to what exactly the three women on the heath can have been. He wrote:

> The common opinion was, that these three women were either the weird sisters, that is (as ye would say) the goddesses of destinie, or else some nymphs or feiries, indued with knowledge of prophecie by their necromanticall science, because euerie thing came to pass as they had spoken.

Goddesses, nymphs, fairies, witches, necromancers, prophets? You can take your pick. But there is no doubt that they had power.

But why, in both universes, are there precisely three of them? It is of course true that this suits the theatre, as the great playwright Hwel remarks when he looks through a script which, emanating from the mighty power-source of Shakespeare's mind, has drifted over to the Discworld without too much damage.

There were, he had to admit, some nice touches. Three witches was good. Two wouldn't be enough, four would be too many. They could be meddling with the destinies of mankind and everything. Lots of smoke and green light. You could do a lot with three witches. It was surprising no one had thought of it before. [*Wyrd Sisters*]

But the true reason lies far, far deeper. Three has always been an important number in stories, and in magic. All good things come in threes, and all bad things too. Which is why the Ancient Greeks and Romans spoke of three Fates who held in their hands the thread of each person's life: Clotho spun it on her distaff, Lachesis measured it, and in due time the dreaded Atropos ('She who can't be turned aside') snipped it with the shears of death. They were usually said to be old women, looking much alike, except that the first two wore white robes and the third, guess who, black.

Norsemen too believed in goddesses of destiny, the Norns. According to one poem there were just three, whose names were Urđr, Verđandi, and Skuld – meaning 'what's-happened-already', 'what's-happening-now', and 'what's-bound-to-happen'. But others said there were many of them, and that they came to every child when it was born, to shape its life.

In southern Europe people thought that there were supernatural women who bestowed wishes and gifts on newborn babies. They were a kind of fairy, but it was most unwise to use that word – better to refer tactfully to 'Ladies from outside', or 'Ladies who must not be named'. They were the original fairy godmothers. In Greece and the Balkans, they would arrive on the third night after the birth, and there were three of them. Everyone went to bed early that night, the dogs would be chained up, the door of the house left unlocked. The baby's cot would be placed near the icon in the main room, and beside it a table with three low stools for the Ladies. There would be a candle burning, and heaps of food – bread and wine, fruit, nuts, honey-cakes. Nobody could enter the room till morning, when the midwives and female relatives would eat up the goodies themselves, for the Ladies had already magically taken what they wanted of them during the night.

On one occasion (as recounted in *Wyrd Sisters*), Granny Weatherwax, Nanny Ogg and Magrat saved a baby's life and appointed themselves his godmothers. In normal circumstances, they would certainly have appreciated a cosy midnight feast, if one had been on offer. But the circumstances were far from normal, and they had to bestow their gifts from a distance.

Magrat sighed.

'You know,' she said, 'if we *are* his godmothers, we ought to have given him three gifts. It's traditional.'

'What are you talking about, girl?'

'Three good witches are supposed to give the baby three gifts. You know, like good looks, wisdom and happiness.' Magrat pressed on defiantly. 'That's how it used to be done in the old days.'

'Oh, you mean gingerbread cottages and all that,' said Granny dismissively. 'Spinning wheels and pumpkins and pricking your finger on rose thorns and similar. I could never be having with all that.'

In the end, however, Granny agreed. Each gave her gift separately, and these gifts shaped the child's destiny, for, as the Anglo-Saxons used to say, *Wyrd bið swiðost*, 'Fate is the strongest', and *Wyrd bið full aræd*, 'Fate is inflexible.'

As a result of this episode and of the events in *Witches Abroad*, Fairy Godmothers are officially defined in the *Discworld Companion* as 'a specialized form of witch with particular responsibility for the life of one individual or a group of individuals'.

MAIDEN, MOTHER, CRONE

When Magrat got married, she gave up witching for a while. This caused problems for the other two, because not only is three a good number for witches, but it has to be the *right* sort of three. The right sort of *types*. Nanny Ogg brooded on the matter:

> As a witch, she naturally didn't believe in occult nonsense of any sort. But there were one or two truths down below the bedrock of the soul which had to be faced, and right in among them was this business of, well, the maiden, the mother and the . . . other one.
>
> Of course, it was nothing but an old superstition and belonged to the unenlightened days when 'maiden' or 'mother' or . . . the other one . . . encompassed every woman over the age of twelve or so, except maybe for nine months of her life.
>
> Even so . . . it was an *old* superstition – older than books, older than writing – and beliefs like that were heavy weights on the rubber sheet of human experience, tending to pull people into their orbits.
>
> They needed to be three again. [*Maskerade*]

Nobody would dream of arguing with Nanny on a point like this. The Discworld is about what people *believe* is true. So if Nanny says it's a truth down below the bedrock of her soul that three witches must be of different ages, then – on the Discworld – it is. If she says that it's a superstition older than books, older than writing, then – on the Discworld – it is.

But on Earth it's not. It's just over one hundred years old, actually. Will Shakespeare's witches were all the same age. So were the three Fates, the three Norns, the three Graces, the three Mothers in early Britain, the three War Goddesses in Ireland, and other female trios in old mythologies.

It was in 1903 that a Cambridge scholar, Jane Ellen Harrison, decided that all the many goddesses in ancient religions could be tidily sorted out into three aspects of one great Earth Goddess: the Maiden, the Mother, and a third she did not name. She was mainly interested in the first two; so was her colleague Sir James Frazer (he of *The Golden Bough*), who thought they were a mother-and-daughter pair like Demeter and Persephone in Greece.

The first writer to pay much attention to the third one was the magician Aleister Crowley, who called her 'the crone' and identified her with the sinister Hecate, a Greek goddess of darkness and black magic. He seems to have loathed her. In his novel *Moonchild* in 1921, he wrote:

> Artemis [the moon goddess] is unassailable, a being fine and radiant; Hecate is the crone, a woman past all hope of mother-hood, her soul black with envy and hatred of happier mortals; the woman in the fullness of life is the sublime Persephone.

And then the idea took root in the mind of the poet Robert Graves, and grew into his book *The White Goddess* (1948), the picture of a lovely, cruel threefold deity who brings both life and death, inspiration and despair. Her third aspect is the crone, the hag, the destroyer, but beyond the pain she represents there is a promise of reward and renewal, so she is not to be seen as evil. This powerful image which Graves created is now firmly imprinted on the minds of modern occultists on Earth, where the trio of identical figures which Shakespeare knew has faded away, morphing into the sharply differentiated group of Maiden, Mother, and Crone.

But if Nanny Ogg is right (and she always is) it all began on Discworld way back in the mists of time. There is leakage between universes.

So she and Granny Weatherwax had to find some way of setting up a threesome of the right type, to spread the load. They began by recruiting shy young Agnes Nitt (also known, in the recesses of her own mind, as Perdita) to replace Magrat and carry out the traditional tasks of the Maiden, which consist mainly of fetching the tea and getting bullied. But then Magrat had a baby, and so would be qualified to return as Mother. This, however, is Nanny Ogg's natural role, seeing as she has had fifteen children, and revels in an ever-growing horde of grandchildren and great-grandchildren. In literal years, Nanny belongs to the same generation as Granny, but in these matters it is not literal facts that count. It is no accident that her cottage is called Tir Nani Ogg, which, as Tiffany Aching rightly suspects, means 'The Land of the Ever-Young' (*Tir nan Og*) in the ancient Celtic speech which the Nac Mac Feegles brought to the Discworld – and *not*, regrettably, 'Nanny Ogg's Place' [*Wintersmith*].

It is understandable that when it seemed that Granny might be about to withdraw from witching, Nanny disliked the consequences for herself: 'Can't say I fancy being a crone. I ain't the right shape and anyway I don't know the sound they make.'

So, for the present at least, the threesome is a quartet, and who-stands-for-what still has to be sorted out. Nevertheless, Granny and Nanny have grown into their roles during the course of the series: Nanny is the notionally soft big-hearted one, an expert on midwifery, while Granny is the one you will, with some trepidation, call in when death is in the air.

BORROWING IS NOT SHAPE-CHANGING

Granny Weatherwax is the most skilful Borrowing Witch in all Lancre. While her body lies cold and rigid in her bed, her mind goes off and borrows the consciousness of any bird or animal she chooses. Steering it gently, she sees with its eyes, feels its pleasures and fears and appetites, absorbs any knowledge it has. In due course she guides it into her bedroom, and quietly slips out of its mind. Then she has a short lie-down, just to get used to the feel of her own body again. And then, since things have to balance, for the next few days she will put out some food for the creature whose mind she entered.

She is so skilled that she has even Borrowed a swarm of bees:

'She's going to swank about this for *weeks*,' said Nanny Ogg. 'No one's ever done it with bees. Their mind's everywhere, see? Not just in one bee. In the whole swarm.'

'I done it with beezzz! *No one* can do it with beezzz, and I *done* it! You endzzz up with your mind all flying in different directionzzz! You got to be *good* to do it with beezzz!' [*Lords and Ladies*]

Which also goes to show that some of what you've Borrowed stays with you for a while, such as, in this case, a certain confusion in the vocal cords, plus a need for a bunch of flowers, a pot of honey, and someone to sting. The bees themselves – or the owl, bat, hare, or whatever – remain almost unaware that a human mind has been riding them. At least, that is how it should be. If someone ruthless does it, an Elf Queen for example, she goes through the animal's mind like a chainsaw, leaving it half crazed.

There are dangers, of course. No magical procedure is without risks. A young inexperienced witch with a natural talent can become so intoxicated by the joy of Borrowing that she sinks too deep in, and stays there. So can an old one, come to that. For years Nanny Ogg used to put out lumps of fat and bacon rind for a bluetit that she was sure was old Granny Postalute, who went out Borrowing and never came back. Even Granny Weatherwax knows that she must be careful. It's addictive, like a drug.

There is also the practical problem that someone might mistake your body for a corpse, and pop it into a coffin before you can get back. To avoid this embarrassment, Granny Weatherwax always holds, in her rigid hands, a small card which says I ATE'NT DEAD.

Not all Discworld witches are able, or willing, to Borrow, while on Earth the skill is almost unknown. There, one of the very few accounts of what appears to be a Borrowing Witch comes from St Briavels in Gloucestershire, and was reported in the journal

Folk-Lore in 1902. There was a girl there who, for some reason, had to share a bed one night with a certain old woman and her daughter.

> During the night she happened to wake, and was alarmed to feel how very cold the old woman was. She shook her, but in vain. So she then woke the daughter, crying, 'I do believe your mother's dead!' – 'Dead?' laughed the daughter. 'Her bain't dead, her be out and about now!'

Shape-changing witches, on the other hand, are extremely common in the lore of this world. The difference is that whereas a Borrower sends her separated mind to 'ride' in an animal (which has its own real existence, before, during and after the process), the shape-changer changes herself entirely, body and mind together, into the *appearance* of an animal. There is no real animal there at all, simply the transformed witch.

Witches of the Earth could turn into any animal they wanted, but hares seem to have been the favourites, with cats a close second. Being a hare was especially good fun because it gave them the chance to infuriate huntsmen. Stories about this were told throughout Britain well into the twentieth century, for instance one which was collected by members of a local Women's Institute for their book *It Happened in Hampshire* (1937):

> When I was a boy, they did say there was a woman over to Breamore that could turn herself to a hare up there on the Downs. If the dogs did press her too much she could turn herself back again and they wouldn't see nothing but a woman combing her hair. One day the dogs were after her, just as she was getting near her cottage. She did shoot through the keyhole, but they were after her. The children cried out, 'Run, Granny, run! or the dogs'll have 'ee.' But her was up on the top of the old brick oven so they never had her. Whether 'twas true or whether it wasn't, that is what I did hear when I was a boy.

The witch-hare did not always escape. If the hounds were particularly fast, or if the huntsman was a good shot with a bullet made from a silver sixpence, she might get bitten or shot in the rump as she bolted indoors. And next day everyone would see that she was limping badly.

People on the Discworld have heard about this somehow, and those who do not understand Granny Weatherwax sometimes think this is what she gets up to. Thatcher the carter, for instance:

'Cor, she frightens the life out of me, her. The way she looks right through you. I wouldn't say a word against her, mark you, a fine figure of a woman, but they do say she creeps around the place o' nights, as a hare or a bat or something. Changes her shape and all. Not that I believes a word of it, but old Weezen over in Slice told me once he shot a hare in the leg one night and next day she passed him on the lane and said "Ouch" and gave him a right ding across the back of his head.' [*Lords and Ladies*]

In *Equal Rites*, there is an argument on this point between Esk, an intelligent little girl, and her brothers Gulta and Cern:

'They say,' said Gulta, 'she can turn herself into a fox. Or anything. A bird, even. Anything. That's how she always knows what's going on. They say there's a whole family over Crack Peak way that can turn themselves into wolves. Because one night someone shot a wolf and next day their auntie was limping with an arrow wound in her leg, and . . .'

'I don't think people can turn themselves into animals,' said Esk, slowly.

'Oh yes, Miss Clever?'

'Granny is quite big. If she turned herself into a fox what would happen to all the bits that wouldn't fit?'

'She'd just magic them away,' said Cern.

'I don't think magic works like that,' said Esk.

But occasionally, very occasionally, Granny does shape-shift, or appears to do so. This happened during her confrontation with Archchancellor Cutangle of Unseen University, as described in *Equal Rites*. The Archchancellor had unwisely hurled white fire at her, and she had deflected it towards the roof. Then:

Cutangle vanished. Where he had been standing a huge snake coiled, poised to strike.

Granny vanished. Where she had been standing was a large wicker basket.

The snake became a giant reptile from the mists of time.

The basket became the snow wind of the Ice Giants, coating the struggling monster with ice.

The reptile became a sabre-toothed tiger, crouched to spring.

The gale became a bubbling tar pit.

The tiger managed to become an eagle, stooping.

The tar pit became a tufted hood . . .

This is what students of folklore on the Earth have labelled The Transformation Combat. A typical instance would be the battle recorded in the medieval Icelandic *Saga of Sturlaug Starfsama*, between an Icelandic youth and a Lapland wizard. To the bewilderment of the observers:

They set upon one another and fought fiercely, so swiftly that they could not be followed with the eye, but neither managed to wound the other. When men looked again, they had vanished, and in their place were two dogs, biting one another furiously; and when they least expected it, the dogs disappeared too, and they heard a noise going on in the air. They looked up and saw two eagles flying there, and each tore out the other's feathers with claws and beak so that blood fell onto the earth. The end was that one fell dead to the ground, but the other flew away, and they did not know which one it was.

That was a well-matched fight, but sometimes one of the magicians is simply trying to escape. A medieval Welsh tale tells how the witch Ceridwen has spent a year and a day boiling a magic potion. She sets a boy called Gwion to keep the fire going under the cauldron. But the potion splutters, and three scalding drops splash Gwion's finger, so he automatically sucks it – and all the magic power becomes his. He flees, in the form of a hare. The furious Ceridwen turns into a greyhound. He runs to the river, and changes into a fish. She chases him, as an otter. He becomes a small bird, she a hawk. He becomes a grain of wheat, and she a high-crested black hen – and swallows him. And that, Ceridwen must have thought, was that. But not so. The grain of corn made her pregnant, and the son she bore (who was really Gwion) grew up to be the great seer and poet Taliesin.

It is interesting that in her contest with Cutangle, Granny Weatherwax does not counter-attack aggressively, but chooses forms which restrain and control. For the snake, an Indian snake charmer's basket; for the dinosaur, a coating of ice; for the tiger, sticky tar; for the eagle, a falconer's hood. Granny is always a careful minimalist in the magic arts.

CHANGING THE SHAPES OF OTHERS

Throughout the multiverse, there is a persistent story that if you annoy a witch she will utter a curse which turns you into some small and unpleasant animal, probably a frog. And an animal you will be for ever, unless somebody finds a way to break the spell. This idea is common in fairy tales and old ballads, where the witch is quite often the victim's Wicked Stepmother. In this world, there used to be people who seriously believed that a witch might change you temporarily into a horse, if she wanted to ride to a sabbat. At Pendle in Lancashire in 1633, according to the records of a witch trial there, a young boy accused a neighbour of having done this to him. He later admitted he was lying.

The annals of the Discworld record only three clear instances of such a transformation. One occurred when the malicious witch Lilith of Genua turned two coachmen into beetles, and *trod* on them, as told in *Witches Abroad*. The second case concerns the talking toad which is the familiar of Miss Perspicacia Tick, a witch of the Chalk Country (see *The Wee Free Men*); though initially suffering from memory loss, he later recalls that he was once a human lawyer, who foolishly took a witch to court for supplying substandard magic. The third was when Tiffany, under the influence of the hiver, turned a useless wizard, Brian, into a frog, as described in *A Hatful of Sky*. Admittedly, there have also been one or two occasions when Granny Weatherwax messed with someone's head, causing him to *believe* that he was a frog, but she knew the effect would wear off fairly soon.

What is far more common on the Disc is the reverse process, where a witch uses her power to transform an animal's outward appearance (and, to a lesser extent, its behaviour) into that of a human. But here too the result is unstable. The three witches of Lancre encountered some nasty examples of this type of magic when they travelled to Genua (as told in *Witches Abroad*) – the work of Lilith (real name Lily), whose hobby was to enslave the wills of those around her and force them to re-enact the plots of fairy tales, whether they wanted to or not. She, meanwhile, kept all true power in her own hands, because she was the one in charge of the stories. As part of her plans, she had turned a swamp frog into a prince – but the spell held only during daylight hours, so at night he turned back into his old shape, and had to have a pond in his bedroom. Lilith also turned two snakes into apparent women, to guard the potential heroine of the tale she was concocting, and mice into horses to draw her coach.

Faced with this cruelty, Nanny Ogg persuades the other two that it is right to fight fire with fire, using her own beloved one-eyed cat, Greebo, who she thinks is nearly human anyway. 'And it'll only be temp'ry, even with the three of us doing it,' she said. And so the three of them concentrated.

> Changing the shape of an object is one of the hardest magics there is. But it's easier if the object is alive. After all, a living thing already knows what shape it is. All you have to do is change its mind.
>
> Greebo yawned and stretched. To his amazement he went on stretching.
>
> Through the pathways of his feline brain surged a tide of belief. He suddenly believed he was human. He wasn't simply under the *impression* he was human; he believed it implicitly. The sheer force of the unshakeable belief flowed out into his morphic field, overriding its objections, rewriting the very blueprint of his self.

In his human form, Greebo is a grinning, swaggering, six-foot bully-boy in black leather, with a broken nose, an eye-patch, and an excitingly lascivious smile. He is just as keen on fighting and love-making as when he was in cat-shape. And there can still be claws on his hands, if he so wishes. A few hours later he reverts to his natural felinity, but it turns out that he has been left with a problem seldom encountered by cats. It is one of the laws of magic that no matter how hard a thing is to do, once it *has* been done it becomes a whole lot easier, and will therefore be done a lot. For the rest of his life, part of Greebo's soul knows that he has one extra option for use in a fight, and that is: Become Human. He has become a spontaneous shape-changer, even if the effect never lasts long – fortunately for him, and for others.

THE DIS-ORGANIZATION OF WITCHES

There have been times and places in the multiverse when people got really paranoid about witches. For about three hundred years in most countries of Europe, they felt sure that there was a huge conspiracy of malevolent women, hundreds of whom would gather to hold sabbats where they worshipped the Powers of Evil, plotted magical murder and mayhem, and held unimaginably sexy orgies. German and Swedish witches were said to choose the peak of a bare mountain for these gatherings.

In England, early in the twentieth century, one scholar (Margaret Murray) maintained that witches had indeed been members of a real secret society, but that they did no harm – all they were doing was to keep an old religion going, honouring gods and goddesses of earth and moon, of sex and seasons and crops. She claimed that they were tightly organized into covens of thirteen, and had been holding exactly the same ceremonies to mark the seasons on the same dates all over Europe for hundreds of years. Nobody seems to have reminded her that spring in, say, Italy doesn't come in on the same date as in, say, Sweden, weather being rather more relevant to the idea of a 'season' than the mathematics of the calendar.

Nowadays, historians and folklorists think Murray's theory is an elaborate house of cards built up on hardly any evidence at all. On the other hand, a whole new religion called Wicca sprang up in England in the mid twentieth century, based on her ideas. Wiccans worship the powers of nature as personified by a Triple Goddess and a Horned God, and yes, many of them do gather in groups of thirteen. They tend to say that it doesn't matter too much what the facts of history may have been. What matters is whether their magic works *for them.*

Whatever may or may not have happened on this planet, the true witches of Lancre don't form covens and secret societies, and they don't go in for sabbats. They are totally dis-organized, though they do hold periodic competitive Witch Trials, where each can display her skills. Each is an individual, working in her own way, and often alone, though when she grows old she will probably take on a girl and train her (in exchange for a bit of help with the housework), so as to hand over the area to her when she dies. Even those witches who act as a threesome only do so on the understanding that the arrangement is entirely voluntary and non-hierarchical. Except, naturally, that Granny Weatherwax gives the orders, and Magrat makes the tea.

> Your average witch is not, by nature, a social animal as far as other witches are concerned. There's a conflict of dominant personalities. There's a group of ringleaders without a ring. There's the basic unwritten rule of witchcraft, which is 'Don't do what you will, do what I say.' The natural size of a coven is one. Witches only get together when they can't avoid it. [*Witches Abroad*]

Yet something of the notion of a coven has leached into the Discworld, particularly affecting the minds of beginners in the craft. In her younger days, Magrat yearned for one:

> It had seemed such a lovely idea. She'd had great hopes of the coven. She was sure it wasn't right to be a witch alone, you could get funny ideas. She'd dreamed of wise discussions of natural energies while a huge moon hung in the sky, and then possibly they'd try a few of the old dances described in some of Goodie Whemper's books. Not actually *naked*, or skyclad as it was rather delightfully called . . . that wasn't absolutely necessary . . .
> What she hadn't expected was a couple of crotchety old women who were barely civil at the best of times and simply didn't enter into the spirit of things. [*Wyrd Sisters*]

Occasionally, there were Lancre girls who preferred a more intellectual and ritualistic kind of magic, more like wizardry – the kind which involves chalk circles and Cones of Power and candles and Tarot cards, and which promises spectacular displays (on Earth, it's often called High Magick). Such a girl has had an education. She probably wears a big floppy black hat, and black lace, and lots of occult silver jewellery. She paints her fingernails black. She adopts a new, flamboyant name. Arrogant and domineering, she creates a coven which she runs entirely to suit herself, bullying and mocking her followers. One such girl was Diamanda (real name Lucy Tockley), who thought she could challenge Granny Weatherwax, and became dangerously involved with elves, as is told in *Lords and Ladies*.

THE TOOLS OF THE CRAFT

Young witches tend to attach too much importance to their tools. Magrat, for instance, at the start of her career, used to read grimoires, drew sigils on her cottage walls, and owned a fine assortment of wands, robes, crystals, grails, crucibles, magical knives, mystic coloured cords, candles, incense, and occult jewellery, including bracelets bearing the hermetic symbols of a dozen religions. (She would have felt quite at home among the Wiccans and Neo-Pagans of Earth today, in a society where a pentacle is just another ornament; fifty years ago most people would simply think you were Jewish but hadn't thought to count the points on your star.)

But older witches avoid showy items of magical equipment. Crystal balls, for example. Granny Weatherwax loathes crystal balls, especially big expensive quartz ones ('Never could get the hang of this damn silicon stuff. A bowl of water with a drop of ink in it was good enough when I was a girl'). Instead, both she and Nanny Ogg use old green glass ones, which had once been buoys for fishing nets.

Pondering on this fact, young Agnes Nitt sees that there are good historical reasons for it.

A glass fishing float, five hundred miles from the sea. An ornament, like a shell. Not a crystal ball. You could use it like a crystal ball, but it wasn't a crystal ball . . . and she knew why that was important . . . Witches hadn't always been popular. There might even be times – there *had* been times, long ago – when it was a good idea *not* to advertise what you were, and *that* was why all these things on the table didn't betray their owner at all. There was no need for that any more, there hadn't been in Lancre for hundreds of years, but some habits get passed down in the blood.

In fact things now worked the other way. Being a witch was an honourable trade in the mountains, but only the young ones invested in real crystal balls and coloured knives and dribbly candles. The old ones . . . they stuck with simple kitchen cutlery, fishing floats, bits of wood, whose very ordinariness subtly advertised their status. Any fool can be a witch with a runic knife, but it took skill to be one with an apple-corer. [*Carpe Jugulum*]

There are practical reasons too. If you believe that a spell will only work if you wear your robes and use the right coloured ink on the right kind of parchment while burning the right kind of incense on the right day of the week, you will be helpless if an emergency arises and you don't have all your paraphernalia at hand. The three Lancre witches once needed to invoke a demon, but as they were in Nanny Ogg's washhouse at the time Magrat protested:

'Oh, but you can't. Not here. You need a cauldron, and a magic sword. And an octogram. And spices, and all sorts of stuff.'

Granny and Nanny exchanged glances.

'It's not her fault,' said Granny. 'It's all them grimmers she was bought.' She turned to Magrat.

'You don't need none of that,' she said. 'You need headology.' She looked around the ancient washroom.

'You just use whatever you've got,' she said. [*Wyrd Sisters*]

And in fact the demon was successfully summoned by means of a copper, its paddle, a scrubbing brush, a washboard, and a lump of soap. Magrat learned the lesson well, and not long afterwards was able to bring surging life back into the long-dead timbers of a dungeon door, by sheer force of imagination and will, with no artificial aids whatsoever.

Yet tools can be very, very useful for impressing the client, especially when combined with a few little white lies. Take healing, for example. Magrat is a good healer because she knows a lot about herbs, but Granny is an even better one because of her skill in stage-management and the use of props. She gives people a bottle of coloured water, tells them they feel better, and they do. As she explains to young Esk:

> 'I saved a man's life once. Special medicine, twice a day. Boiled water with a bit of berry juice in it. Told him I'd bought it from the dwarves. That's the biggest part of doct'rin, really. Most people'll get over most things if they put their minds to it, you just have to give them an interest.' [*Equal Rites*]

Similarly on Earth, the village healers who were known as 'cunning folk' or 'wise women' knew just how important it was to add a touch of drama. In County Clare in Ireland in the nineteenth century there was a woman called Biddy Early with a great reputation as a healer. She used all sorts of herbal brews, but what impressed people most was the small blue bottle which she kept always at hand, and used as a focus for her Second Sight when she was scrying (which is the same as crystal-gazing, only without the crystal). When a sick person came to consult her she would shake it, stare fixedly into its cloudy depths, and then tell him what ailed him, and what he must do to get well. Some said this bottle had been given to her by fairies. It is said, too, that on her death-bed she made her family swear to throw it into a lake, on pain of some terrible curse if they disobeyed. So they did, but as soon as she was dead they hurried down to the lake to fish it out again – after all, she hadn't expressly told them not to, had she? But they never found it, and though many people have tried, no one has yet. At least, that is one story; another is that the parish priest threw it into the lake. And there is another, which says that later on, a dark stranger appeared in the village, went to the lake and—

But that's another story, and stories cling to Biddy like iron filings to a magnet. There is a consensus that she was born in County Clare in 1798 and died in Kilbarron, near Feakle, in 1874. In between, she has become folded and moulded by narrativium, and defined by the kind of accounts that begin, 'I heard tell when I was a boy'. In short, for the purposes of this book, she could be thought of as Granny Weatherwax and Nanny Ogg rolled into one. By all accounts she had a fine grasp of practical psychology as well as some expertise in folk medicine, and was famous for her cures; she was said to have got her powers from the fairies or some similar 'sponsor' and probably did nothing to discourage this belief. She liked a drink, too, and when it came to payment she was on the Whiskey and Chickens standard. She must also have liked men, because she had four husbands.

Nowadays, if you go looking for 'Biddy Early's Cottage', you will eventually be directed to a lonely, tumbledown building at the far end of a weed-choked path. You will find that others have been there before you, leaving their tokens on windowsill and doorstep – coins, flowers, strips of cloth, candles, beer bottles. She is not forgotten.

In fact Biddy Early needs a book of her own, and our bibliography has at least two.

OF HATS AND BROOMS

There is of course the pointy hat. And the broomstick. Every Discworld witch uses these, and as far as we know they always have. Yet the broomstick is merely a convenience, and the hat is not in itself magical. Its secret – and it is one of the great secrets of witchcraft – lies elsewhere. When Granny challenges clever young Esk to discover it, Esk examines the hat carefully.

> There was nothing particularly strange about it, except that no one in the village had one like it. But that didn't make it magical . . . It was just a typical witch's hat. Granny always wore it when she went into the village, but in the forest she just wore a leather hood . . .
>
> 'I think I know,' she said at last.
>
> 'Out with it, then.'
>
> 'It's sort of in two parts.'
>
> 'Well?'
>
> 'It's a witch's hat because you wear it. But you're a witch because you wear the hat. Um.'
>
> 'So –' prompted Granny.
>
> 'So people see you coming in the hat and the cloak and they know you're a witch and that's why your magic works?' [*Equal Rites*]

On Earth too, some people who practised magic for a living appreciated the value of eye-catching clothes and headgear, though there was no uniform style. There was Mother Redcap, for instance, a fortune-teller in Camden Town in London in the seventeenth century, whose appearance was definitely eccentric. She was strikingly ugly, kept a huge black cat, and always wore the red bonnet which gave her her nickname, plus a grey shawl with strange black patches. From a distance, they looked like flying bats. Then there was Billy Brewer, the most famous fortune-teller and magical healer in nineteenth-century Somerset, who practised in Taunton from the 1840s till his death in 1890 and called himself the Wizard of the West; he went about the streets wearing a long Inverness cloak, a tattered brown wig, and a sombrero, with gold and silver rings glittering on every finger. This did wonders for his reputation.

In the matter of pointy hats and broomsticks, it is a curious fact that nowadays, as soon as you say 'witch' people just *see* the hat and the broom, and yet three hundred years ago they were very, very rare. Many people believed that witches could fly through the air, but they were said to do this by riding on all kinds of everyday objects and animals, not just brooms. The fashion for broomsticks began in late medieval France and Flanders, and only started spreading after about 1600; in Germany, cooking sticks were preferred; in Britain, pitchforks and hurdles. In Russian fairy tales, there's the famous witch Baba Yaga, a child-eating ogress who lives in the forest; she often travels high above the tree-tops, sitting in an iron kettle or a stone mortar.

As for the hat, nobody, in all the witch trials of the sixteenth and seventeenth centuries, ever stepped into court and said, 'I know she's a witch because she wears a pointy hat.' No paintings, prints or pamphlets of that period show it; if a witch is wearing any headgear at all, it is that of ordinary everyday dress. But then things change. If we look at William Hogarth's cartoon of 1762 which mocks 'Credulity, Superstition and Fanaticism', we can see a preacher brandishing a doll dressed as a witch. She's an ugly old woman. In a pointy hat. Astride a broom. Something remarkable must have happened, since Hogarth obviously expected everybody to know what his picture meant. And that was only the beginning, because now there are broomsticks, black cloaks and pointy hats in every toyshop in the run-up to Halloween. They are spreading fast, even in countries which had never heard of them fifty years ago. In Sweden, for instance, until quite recently witches wore aprons and headscarves when they gathered for their annual Great Sabbat (held at Easter), but now it's cloaks and pointy hats for them too.

So what can have happened? There can only be one explanation – this costume was invented on the Discworld and rightfully belongs there, but the image it creates is so powerful that it is seeping out across the multiverse, and before long people will recognize it in every other world there is.

SO WHAT DO WITCHES ACTUALLY DO, THEN?

Whatever might be the case elsewhere and elsewhen, in Lancre witchcraft is seen as an honourable profession. Witches get respected. They don't go in for fancy titles, but use good old-fashioned homely names which speak volumes for their solid respectability – Dame this, Old Mother that, Gammer t'other, and of course Granny and Nanny. It is to them that the village turns when a child or a cow falls desperately sick, when a woman is having a difficult labour, when those who are dying cannot actually die. It is then that the witch has to bring help – and take responsibility. Nobody knows this better than Granny Weatherwax.

> There were stories that were never to be told, the little secret stories enacted in little rooms . . .
>
> They were about those times when medicines didn't help and headology was at a loss because a mind was a rage of pain in a body that had become its own enemy, when people were simply in a prison made of flesh, and at times like this she could *let them go*. There was no need for desperate stuff with a pillow, or deliberate mistakes with the medicine. You didn't push them out of the world, you just stopped the world pulling them back. You just reached in, and . . . showed them the way . . .
>
> She'd been a witch here all her life. And one of the things a witch did was stand right on the edge, where the decisions had to be made. You made them so that others didn't have to, so

that others could even pretend to themselves that there *were* no decisions to be made, no little secrets, that things *just happened*. You never said what you knew. And you didn't ask for anything in return. [*Carpe Jugulum*]

Well, true enough, you didn't *ask*, but, as Nanny Ogg says, 'There's ways and ways of not askin', if you get my meaning. People can be very gen'rous to witches. They do like to see a happy witch.' And it was indeed amazing how many people would pop round to a witch's cottage from time to time with a basket of this or a bottle of that, and would volunteer to do a bit of digging, or to check that the chimneys were OK.

Magrat once grumbled that Granny Weatherwax hardly ever did 'real magic' – 'What good is being a witch if you don't do magic? Why doesn't she use it to help people?'

To which Nanny Ogg replied that it was precisely because she knew how good she would be at it that she didn't. Nanny meant that magic is power, and where there is power, there is always the temptation to abuse it. Granny steered clear of that temptation, knowing its strength only too well. Moreover, she thought that you could not help people with magic, though you could certainly help them by headology and hard work.

All this is very much like what used to go on on Earth up to a hundred years or so ago – maybe even more recently, in some parts. There were women who knew charms and cures, who told fortunes, who acted as midwives and nurses, who knew what counter-spells to use against bewitchment. And men too. You could find them in both villages and towns, and their clients came from miles around. Some openly made a career of it, taking payment in cash for their services, others used Nanny Ogg's technique (with an edge to it). A Sussex village witch in the 1890s, for example, was described to a folklorist in 1941, in the *Sussex County Magazine*.

Her reputation was very valuable to her. If she stopped a child and said, 'What a fine crop of plums your mother had down Crabtree Lane, dearie,' the result would be a basket of the best plums, as otherwise the tree would wither and die. So she kept herself provided with good things.

But you had to be careful what you called such people, since on Earth the word 'witch' so often meant someone who uses magic to harm, not to help. It was more polite to say 'wise woman', 'white witch', 'charmer', 'cunning man', even 'wizard' – and latterly a 'District Nurse'. But shorn of the little nods to superstition, what they had and have in common has been a certain strength of character, practical experience and the ability to take charge of a situation.

Yet, in spite of these parallels, there are important differences between magical practitioners in the two universes.

The most far-reaching concerns the source of their power. On the Earth it was generally assumed that magic power must originate in some non-human source, and that the witch had received it as a gift or reward, or through some pact or bargain. Those who feared and hated witches accused them of having pledged their souls to devils. Some of the more learned magicians boasted that their knowledge came from angels and spirits. Some Scottish wise women claimed they had been taught charms and remedies by elves, whom they would visit in the hollow hills, or by the dead. In other lands, gods and the spirits of ancestors were the power sources.

The witches of Lancre have no such ideas. Their skill and power are their own innate gifts, carefully honed by practice and observation. They have no dealings with the gods or the dead, despise demons, and rightly regard elves as dangerous and evil. Nor do they depend on 'familiars' to act on their behalf, as Earthly witches were said to do – these being minor demons, usually in the form of toads, mice, or cats, who were loaned to witches by the Devil and would perform magical tasks in exchange for a few drops of blood. (The cat Greebo is no demon; he is nothing more, and nothing less, than a cat. Miss Tick's toad appears to have no magical abilities at all; his power of speech is merely the residue of his previous human faculties.)

Another major difference is that on the Discworld witches undertake one dangerous duty that 'our' witches have no idea of. It is their responsibility to defend their homeland against insidious supernatural invasions. Blatant attacks by Creatures from the Dungeon Dimensions are usually dealt with by the wizards of Unseen University, who can be relied on to recognize a tentacular threat when it turns up on their doorstep, but it takes a witch to fight the more subtle menace of vampires or elves. Their epic struggles on behalf of Lancre are recounted in *Lords and Ladies* and *Carpe Jugulum*. Never, in the field of inter-species conflict, was so much owed by so many to so few. But do the people of Lancre appreciate this? Do they, hell! They don't even notice. Which is perhaps how it should be.

WICKED WITCHES

The witches of Lancre remember stories about other witches long ago, or maybe not so long ago, whom they disapprove of. Witches who have gone to the bad, who have crossed over to the Dark Side. There is something of the dark in the Weatherwax heredity, and Granny was for a long time worried about her own Nana, Alison Weatherwax, who disappeared in Uberwald and was rumoured to have hobnobbed with vampires. Fortunately, the rumour was false. She didn't hobnob with them, she staked them.

Then there was Black Aliss. Not exactly a bad witch, but so powerful that one couldn't really tell the difference, and deeply affected by narrative patterns similar to those which the Brothers Grimm recorded on Earth. Magrat asked about her once.

'She was before your time,' said Nanny Ogg. 'Before mine, really. She lived over Skund way. Very powerful witch.'

'If you listen to rumour,' said Granny.

'She turned a pumpkin into a royal coach once,' said Nanny.

'Showy,' said Granny Weatherwax. 'That's no help to anyone, turning up at a ball smelling like a pie. And that business with the glass slipper. Dangerous, to my mind.'

'But the biggest thing she ever did,' said Nanny, ignoring the interruption, 'was to send a whole palace to sleep for a hundred years until . . .' She hesitated. 'Can't remember. Was there rose bushes involved, or was it spinning wheels in that one?' . . .

'Why did they call her Black Aliss?'

'Fingernails,' said Granny.

'And teeth,' said Nanny Ogg. 'She had a sweet tooth. Lived in a real gingerbread cottage. Couple of kids shoved her in her own oven at the end. Shocking.' [*Wyrd Sisters*]

One sign that things weren't quite right with Black Aliss was that she used to cackle. So one day when Granny Weatherwax uttered a cackle (though she swore it was just a rather rough chuckle), Nanny Ogg warned her:

> 'You want to watch out that you don't end up the same way as she did. She went a bit funny at the finish, you know. Poisoned apples and suchlike.' [*Wyrd Sisters*]

But Black Aliss wasn't really bad, not out and out bad. It was just that she got so involved in old stories – those rural myths that happen over and over again and everyone knows about – that they sent her weird in the head, so she lost track of what was real and what wasn't. 'I mean, she didn't ever really *eat* anyone,' said Nanny. 'Well. Not often. I mean, there was talk, but . . .'

Her name can't have helped, for names shape people, and this one carries sinister echoes drifting across from the Earth. There, in the city of Leicester, a hideous hag called Black *Annis* lived in a cave in the Dane Hills, just outside the town. She had a dark blue face, and her nails were long sharp talons. There can be no doubt that *she* ate people – naughty children mostly, but good ones too if they stayed out late. She would lurk in a tree overhanging the mouth of her cave, ever ready to spring like a wild beast on any stray children passing below; then she would scratch them to death with her claws, suck their blood, and hang up their skins to dry. If memories from Black Annis's mind had infected Black Aliss, it's a wonder that she didn't become far more wicked than she did.

Names shape people. When a young witch gives herself a new name, it tells you who and what she wants to be – who and what she will inevitably become. Most times, all it means is a little vanity, a little snobbishness and misplaced romance. If a girl named Violet prefers to be 'Magenta', or an Agnes becomes 'Perdita', that does no great harm. But if a Lucy turns into a 'Diamanda', that shows she's already a bright, hard little bitch, and intends to become brighter and harder.

So what of that most powerful and evil of witches, who began her life in Lancre as plain Lily Weatherwax, but took the name Lilith when she moved to Genua? How did it come into her mind? Surely it must have arrived as a particle of inspiration, originating in a parallel universe. For in Earthly myth and legend 'Lilith' is the name of a terrible female demon, noted for pride as well as cruelty. It is said that she was Adam's first wife, but refused to submit to his authority and fled from Eden into the desert, where she consorted with demons and became a demon herself. Ever since, she has exploited her beauty by seducing sleeping men in their dreams, and satisfied her cruelty by killing women in childbirth and strangling young babies. She feeds on their blood and sucks the marrow from their bones. And so, in her own way, does Lilith of Genua. She takes people's lives and twists them, sucking away their will-power and personality, forcing them into the patterns of old stories where she, and she alone, is in control. Yet all the time she is enslaving them, she convinces herself that she is the good godmother, the good witch. And if that's not being a wicked witch, what is?

Chapter 9

THE LAND OF
LANCRE

LANCRE LANDMARKS

The Dancers

WHEN PEOPLE HAVE LIVED in the same place for generations, they know every inch of the countryside as if it were their own backyard, which it often is. They like things to have reasons, a name, a history, an explanation. Particularly an explanation. Everything inexplicable demands an explanation. Narrativium takes over, the land becomes filled with stories, and the result is a fine crop of folklore. On the Discworld the process is most obvious in Lancre and on the Chalk, though much the same thing would be found in every country if anyone went to look.

Of course, there are always people who wouldn't take a folk tale seriously even if it jumped up and bit them (which, given the power of narrativium, it might quite well do). Consider the case of Eric Wheelbrace, that most resolute and rational of ramblers, now alas missing and presumed dead. Among interesting features noted in his essay 'Lancre: Gateway to the Ramtops' (included in *A Tourist Guide to Lancre*), he briefly mentions the Dancers, a group of standing stones on a small area of moorland about midway between Lancre River and the Ramtops:

There are eight of them, in a circle wide enough to throw a

stone across. They are reddish, about man height, and barely thicker than a man as well. Local legend has it that they are a gateway into the kingdom of the elves but the truth is likely to be much more prosaic. They are typical of a style of silicon chronograph constructed in the dawn of time by our ignorant forebears. Basically, they are an underused resource, and I for one intend to organize a Lancre Music and Dance Festival next year, based round the stones, which are in a perfect location for that sort of activity. It is my belief that the stories are put about by the locals in order to keep people away, but we will not be deterred. [*A Tourist Guide to Lancre*]

Oh deary, deary me. Eight of them, a magic number. And called The Dancers, too, with a Piper and a Drummer among them. This looks very much like a warning that something eldritch happened there in the olden days, and maybe could happen again. The witches have done their best to make sure everyone avoids the place. Even the more stupid locals have some notion of the dangers:

'I remember an old story about this place,' said Baker. 'Some man went to sleep up here once, when he was out hunting.'

'So what? I can do that,' said Carter. 'I go to sleep every night, reg'lar.'

'Ah, but *this* man, when he woke up and went home, his wife was carrying on with someone else and all his children had grown up and didn't know who he was.' [*Lords and Ladies*]

These weird tricks of time always happen when someone is taken out of their own world into Elfland, as we noted in an earlier chapter. But in what sense are the stones themselves Dancers? Since the locals didn't tell Wheelbrace, or if they did he wasn't listening, we must look to the Earth for the explanation, thanks to some of those remarkable parallels and echoes between one universe and another.

Stone circles are powerful or, at least, become cloaked in powerful stories. In various parts of England – Cornwall, Devon, Dorset, Derbyshire – there are circles of stones known as the Nine Ladies or Nine Maidens or Merry Maidens. There may or may not actually be nine of them (it's a magical number, like eight is on the Disc), but their story is everywhere the same: there were once some girls who loved dancing so much that they would go off to the hills to dance together whenever they could, even on Sundays when they should have been in church. So one Sunday they were smitten by the Wrath of God, which turned them to stone. No more dancing for them – except maybe for the ones near Okehampton in Devon, where (some people say) they are allowed to take a few steps every day at noon. Sometimes one stone in the circle, or close beside it, is named the Piper or Fiddler; it is said he was playing the music for the girls to dance to, and was smitten too.

Back in Lancre, Eric Wheelbrace insisted that there was a right of way across the Dancers, and that he would organize his Festival there. Dismissing local objections as mere superstition, and declaring that a determined rambler will laugh with scorn at threats, he set off to cross the circle one Midsummer Eve. His boots were found frozen solid, in a hedge a mile away. He has presumably now discovered that the Dancers are indeed, as legend claims, 'a gateway into the kingdom of the elves', and he may even understand that such gates are meant to be kept *shut*. That's why the stones chosen for the job are reddish and magnetic; they contain a good deal of iron, a tried and trusted elf-repellent.

The Standing Stone

On the crest of a moor in the Ramtops, there is a solitary bluish Standing Stone (well, sometimes there is). It is a painfully shy megalith, so although there is only one of it, nobody has ever been able to count it. If it sees anyone approaching with a calculating look, it shuffles off to hide among the gorse bushes or flops into a peat bog. There are rumours that other huge standing stones on the moor are mobile too, but are too keen on their privacy to let themselves be seen when on the move.

The folklore of Earth is, as so often, remarkably close to the facts of the Disc. It is almost commonplace on Earth to be told that at midnight, or at dawn, a particular standing stone will spin round on its base, or dance, or walk down to the river to drink. But if someone tells you about this, do listen carefully – it could be folklore, or it could be a leg-pull. If what he said was, 'That stone turns round whenever it hears the church clock strike midnight', he's speaking a very literal kind of truth, and what you have to ask yourself is, 'How often does a stone *hear* a clock?' Never, actually. That's the leg-pull. On the other hand, if what he said was, 'That stone turns round when the church clock strikes midnight', he's folk, and that's lore.

As for counting, Earthly megaliths absolutely hate being counted, and will do anything to prevent it. Stonehenge used to be very good at this – a rumour got around that anyone who reckoned up its stones and got the number right would be sure to die. And those who did try got wildly different results. Yet Daniel Defoe, writing in the 1720s, said he had seen them counted four times, and each time the total was 72; the only problem, he thought, was that many were fallen and half buried, so one could not easily tell whether one was seeing two parts of one stone, or two separate stones. In 1740 the antiquary William Stukeley published *his* count, making it 140 and exclaiming triumphantly, 'Behold the solution of the mighty problem, the magical spell is broke which has so long perplexed the vulgar.' Modern archaeologists disagree with them both; having tidied the place up and mapped it, they have settled on 96.

In several places where there are 'countless stones', people have had the same bright idea: take a basket of loaves, count them, and put one on top of each stone till you have gone all round the ring, then see how many loaves are left, do a simple sum, and, bingo, that's it. This did work with The Hurlers in Cornwall, but not at Stonehenge, nor yet at Little Kit's Coty in Kent. There, some say, a baker who tried this trick ended up with more loaves than he started out with; others say he completed his calculations but dropped dead before he could announce the result.

Some people might suggest that all you need to do is chalk a number on each stone as you go, but somehow that just doesn't do the trick, lore-wise. It lacks style. Besides, there's sure to be *Something* that comes creeping up behind you to rub the figures out.

The Long Man

In a valley a few miles from Lancre's solitary Standing Stone is an even more significant landmark, the Long Man. This name could mislead someone from our world, since *here* the Long Man is a giant human figure carved into the chalk of a hillside at Wilmington, on the Sussex Downs. Lancre has no chalk, and hence no hill-figures, but it does have plenty of burial mounds ('barrows'), housing the dead of long-gone generations, and sometimes housing the Wee Free Men as well. Some have partly collapsed, exposing their huge stones to the sky, and attracting folklore of their own. There's one that's supposed to be the workplace of an invisible blacksmith; people put a sixpence on the stone and leave a horse there overnight to be shod, just as people of this world used to do at Wayland's Smithy on the Berkshire Downs. There, this magic worked (or so they say); in Lancre, both coin and horse would be gone by morning, people there having more of a sense of humour.

What Lancre calls 'the Long Man' is a group of burial mounds close together, two round ones at the foot of a long one. Nanny Ogg says that the first time she saw them from the air she laughed so much she nearly fell off her broomstick. She has also given a pithy description of a much-loved Lancre custom, the Scouring of the Long Man.

This takes place about every twenty years in early May, when the men and the married women go up to the Long Man and cut away all the bracken and seedlings which have grown up since the last Scouring. Says Nanny: 'Unmarried girls ain't allowed to join in, but it's amazin' what a good view you can get from up a tree and if you ain't got brothers you can get an education there which will prevent surprises later in life. When it's decently dark there's a pig roast and then people wander off and make their own entertainment.' [*A Tourist Guide to Lancre*]

If the memories of Nanny Ogg's great-grandmother can be trusted, things had been a good deal wilder in the old days, when the menfolk used to go up to the Long Man for strange rites which no woman ever saw (unless, being an Ogg, she hid in the bushes):

'She said they just used to build sweat lodges and smell like a blacksmith's armpit and drink scumble and dance around the fire with horns on and piss in the trees any old how. She said it was a bit cissy, to be honest. But I always reckon a man's got to be a man, even if it *is* cissy.' [*Lords and Ladies*]

In Lancre Town, as Eric Wheelbrace notes, one can buy 'vulgar and inappropriate souvenirs which allegedly depict the Long Man and some of the legends attached to it'. Well, well.

There is nothing on the Earth which fully matches the three-dimensional majesty of Lancre's Long Man, where, as Nanny Ogg puts it, the landscape itself is boasting, 'I've got a great big tonker.' The poor old Long Man of Wilmington, in fact, has no tonker at all. In Dorset, however, there is the Cerne Abbas Giant, which is the outline of a huge man with an erect penis, carved into the chalk. It requires to be scoured every seven years, to keep it clear of grass and weeds. There is a strong local tradition that couples who want a child but have failed to conceive should visit the Giant and make love at the appropriate spot. We are not certain if an appointment is required.

The Scouring of Lancre's Long Man, though, would seem to have more in common with the periodical Scouring of the White Horse, a magnificent and very ancient figure carved into a hillside near Uffington in Berkshire (see the section on the Chalk). On irregular occasions the Horse was cleaned up, and this became the occasion for a fair and games such as chasing cheeses down a hill, climbing the greasy pole, cudgelling, wrestling and, as the ale and the sun both went down, brawling, drunkenness and, after dark, 'making your own entertainment'.

But there is more to Lancre's Long Man – much, much more. At the foot of the long mound three large irregular stones form a low cave. One wall has a drawing scratched on it, showing an owl-eyed man wearing an animal skin and horns, who appears to be dancing. A shaman, performing a magical hunting ritual? A god, half human and half beast? A shaman, dressed as this god? Whoever and whatever he is, he has an identical twin brother on Earth, painted several thousand years ago on the wall of the Trois Frères cave in the south of France.

Force the stones apart, and the opening reveals steps leading down into the vast underground network of the Lancre Caves. This too is an entrance to an elf world – but this is the *other* elf world, the one the Queen's elves don't talk about, the one which is an integral part of Lancre, not a malevolent, parasitic universe. A spiral path goes further and further down under the Long Man, till one comes to a hot, dark, steamy tent of skins, a shaman's sweat-lodge. There, sprawled half asleep beside a bowl of red-hot stones, lies the huge figure of the Antlered One, the only god for whom Nanny Ogg has a soft spot. He is the Lord of the Elves, the Queen's estranged husband; at Nanny's request, he forces the Queen to give up her attack on Lancre, as described in *Lords and Ladies*.

Will Shakespeare, whose finely tuned mind often unconsciously picked up the particles of information which drift from one universe to another, echoed the strained relations between the Elf Queen and her husband when he described the quarrel of Titania and Oberon in his play *A Midsummer Night's Dream*. Yet he had no inkling of the true nature and appearance of the Antlered Elf Lord. In fact, it is less than a hundred years since this image began to coalesce in the imaginations of English witches and pagans. It has been built up out of bits and pieces of various myths, some far older than others – the figure in the Trois Frères cave, the Greek Pan, the Celtic antlered god Cernunnos, the medieval idea that the Devil has bull's horns and goat's feet. Plus the fact that horns are a natural, universal symbol of a male animal's strength and sexuality. Put all this together, and you get what modern witches call The Horned God – the incarnation of maleness, the personification of the ever-renewed vital force of Nature. Some now say he is the oldest god man has created. And on the Discworld, he is real.

Sleeping Warriors

There are other things too in the labyrinthine Lancre Caves, for these are one of those areas where the normal rules of time and space do not apply. When Nanny Ogg goes there with the dwarf Casanunda, they pass a certain cavern:

> There were hundreds of dust-covered slabs ranged around the cavern in a spiral; at the centre of the spiral was a huge bell, suspended on a rope that disappeared into the darkness of the ceiling. Just under the hanging bell was one pile of silver coins and one pile of gold coins.
>
> 'Don't touch the money,' said Nanny. ''Ere, watch this, my dad told me about this, it's a good trick.'
>
> She reached out and tapped the bell very gently, causing a faint *ting*.
>
> Dust cascaded off the nearest slab. What Casanunda had thought was just a carving sat up, in a creaky way. It was an armed warrior . . . He focused deepset eyes on Nanny Ogg.
>
> 'What bloody tyme d'you call *thys*, then?'
>
> 'Not time yet,' said Nanny.

'What did you goe and bang the bell for? I don't know, I haven't had a wynke of sleep for two hundred years, some sodde alwayes bangs the bell. Go *awaye*.'

The warrior lay back.

'It's some old king and his warriors,' whispered Nanny as they hurried away. 'Some kind of magical sleep, I'm told. Some old wizard did it. They're supposed to wake up for some final battle when a wolf eats the sun.' [*Lords and Ladies*]

The legend of the Sleeping Warriors recurs so often that its narrativium drive must be unusually powerful. On the Discworld it has been found in at least three other places, far from Lancre.

First, in a huge burial mound on the Counterweight Continent there are seven thousand terracotta warriors, each seven foot tall, who form an invincible Red Army when aroused. Their Earthly counterparts were discovered by archaeologists some years ago, drawn up in military array in pits all round an Emperor's grave in China; wisely, nobody has yet attempted to arouse them. It is as yet unclear whether the golems who have come to Ankh-Morpork, as is told in *Making Money*, and who were last seen digging themselves into trenches round the city, will be taking on a similar role. Secondly, inside a hill at Holy Wood, there is a gigantic knight in golden armour lying on a dusty slab in front of a silver screen, and beside him is the gong to wake him. And thirdly, in the limestone caverns under Koom Valley, there is the Kings' Cave, where Dwarf King and Troll King, encased in stalactites, sit eternally at their game of Thud, as they were when death overtook them:

There was the dwarf king, slumped forward across the board, glazed by the eternal drip, his beard now rock and at one with the stone, but the diamond king had remained upright in death, his skin gone cloudy, and you could still see the game in front of him. It was his move; a healthy little stalactite hung from his outstretched hand. [*Thud!*]

Many European traditions tell of an ancient king who lies asleep inside a mountain. Some say he will awake in the hour of his country's greatest need, and return to save his people; others, that when he wakes it means the End of the World is near. In France, he is Charlemagne; in Britain, King Arthur; in Denmark, Holger Danske; in Germany, the Emperor Frederick Barbarossa ('Red Beard'). Barbarossa is in Mount Kyffhausen:

> He sits on a bench at a round stone table, resting his head on his hand, sleeping, nodding his head and blinking his eyes. His beard has grown long – according to some, right through the stone table. But according to others, the beard grows around the table, and when it has encircled it three times it will be the time of his awakening. It has now grown around twice.
>
> A shepherd was once led into the mountain by a dwarf. The emperor rose and asked him, 'Are the ravens still flying round the mountain?' When the shepherd assured him that they were, he cried, 'Now I am going to have to sleep for another hundred years.' [*German Legends of the Brothers Grimm* (1816), no. 23; transl. Donald Ward, 1981]

In Britain, the sleeper is King Arthur. Many people claim to know the very place where he and his knights are lying in some cavern under a hill, with their horses and hounds beside them – inside Alderley Edge in Cheshire, inside Cadbury Hill in Somerset, under Sewingshields Crag in Northumberland, under Richmond Castle in Yorkshire, in the Eildon Hills near Edinburgh. If you can find your way in and reach the place where Arthur sleeps, you may see a pile of gold; you are allowed to take some *once*, but don't ever go back to get more. There will certainly be significant objects – maybe a bell, maybe a sheathed sword, a garter, or a horn. There are just two problems: first, you have to know whether you must or must not touch them in order to wake the king (assuming that is what you want to do); and then, you have to keep your nerve. So far, things have never worked out properly. At Richmond Castle, one man who found his way down to the sleepers' vault saw a sword and a hunting horn. He drew the sword half out of its scabbard, and the sleepers began to stir, but this terrified him so much that he thrust the blade back. An angry voice called out:

Thompson, Potter Thompson,
If you'd drawn the sword or blown the horn,
You'd ha' been the luckiest man
That ever yet was born.

The man who got into the vault at Sewingshields did a bit better. He saw a sword, a garter, and a bugle. He drew the sword right out of the scabbard, and Arthur and the knights opened their eyes. Then he cut the garter, and this too was the right thing to do, and they slowly sat up. But then he stopped. The spell took hold again, and the king and his warriors sank back on their couches, but not before Arthur had cursed the man:

O woe betide that evil day
On which this witless wight was born
Who drew the sword, the garter cut,
But never blew the bugle horn!

The Gnarly Ground

Gnarly ground is hard to see, let alone describe. There's a patch of it on the highest part of the moorlands, beyond the forest and among the mountains. If you look at it in one way, it's just a pathless stretch of heather and furze, less than a mile across (even if the furze is horribly matted and thorny), and at one point there's a little stream which has cut a groove among the rocks, scarcely more than a foot deep. You could easily jump it. Yet somebody has laid a broad stone slab across it, as a bridge. Now look at the scene the *other* way . . .

You see an endless, nasty-looking, desolate expanse; a long, narrow, dizzying bridge spanning a ravine; a raging torrent far below. They say a deer will sometimes run on to gnarly ground if hard-pressed in the hunt, but it has to be pretty desperate.

'What *is* gnarly ground?' said Agnes.

'There's a lot of magic in these mountains, right?' said Nanny. 'And everyone knows mountains get made when lumps of land bang together, right? Well, when the magic gets trapped you . . . sort of . . . get a bit of land where the space is . . . sort of . . . scrunched up, right? It'd be quite big if it could, but it's like a bit of gnarly wood in an ol' tree. Or a used hanky . . . all folded up small but still big in a different way.' [*Carpe Jugulum*]

In *Carpe Jugulum*, Granny Weatherwax sets out alone to cross the gnarly ground, and the younger witches go after her. Their socks, knitted from Lancre's toughest, most wiry wool, protect them from the savage spikes of furze. But then comes the gorge, an abyss so deep one can barely see the river below, and a high, slender bridge that shifts and creaks underfoot. And then a cavern, some tunnels, a flash of fire.

It is a strange, perilous journey, but not unparalleled. Time and again, in myths and folk tales from all parts of the multiverse, those who take the road to the Otherworld must pass a water barrier by way of a Bridge Perilous. A Scottish ballad describes one leading from Purgatory to Paradise:

The brigge was as heigh as a tower,
And as scharpe as a rasour,
    And naru it was also;
And the water that ther ran under
Brennd of lightning and of thunder,
    That thought him mikle wo.

The closest match for Granny's journey is the strange medieval funeral chant known as 'The Lyke-Wake Dirge', which Yorkshire women sang, as late as the sixteenth century, as they kept watch over a corpse. The tale it tells was already old; it had begun (in so far as such things can be said ever to begin) four hundred years before, as a vision which came to a German monk called Gottskalk in December 1189, as he lay sick of a fever. He saw the souls of the dead gathering on the edge of a great wild heath covered with thorns and furze. There was a tree nearby, its branches loaded with pairs of shoes, but the newly dead soul must cross the thorny ground barefoot – unless, while alive, he or she had given socks and shoes as alms to the poor. And so the Yorkshire women sang:

If ever thou gavest hosen or shoon,
    Every night and all,
Sit thee down and put them on,
    And Christ receive thy soul.

If hosen and shoon thou never gave none,
    Every night and all,
The whinnies shall prick thee to the bare bone,
    And Christ receive thy soul.

Having passed over Whinny Moor, the soul comes to The Bridge of Dread, which is 'no broader than a thread', and finally to Purgatory Fire. Those who once gave food and drink to the needy will not shrink from its flames; those who never did will be burned to the bare bone. The song stops at this point, but since in Christian belief Purgatory is never a final state, simply the last stage on a sinner's journey to God in Heaven, we can assume a happy ending.

As for Granny Weatherwax, the message she sends the world is, I ATE'NT DEAD YET.

BELIEFS OF LANCRE

The people of Lancre are, on the whole, remarkably free from irrational beliefs. Things which in another universe would be considered superstitions are plain commonsensical everyday facts in Lancre. People there don't *believe* that a horseshoe over the door keeps you safe from elves, they *know* it, and if you ask them why it works they can explain just why (the magnetic effect of iron disrupts the sixth sense so vital to an elf's well-being). Beekeepers are careful to tell their bees everything important that concerns the family and household – births, marriages, deaths, a new set of curtains, and suchlike. But that's not superstition, just the practical observation that if you don't tell them, they will fly indoors to find out for themselves.

Or take the matter of controlling horses. On the Earth, there were farriers and farm workers who had learned the secret magic of the 'Horseman's Word'. They could make any horse follow them, or utterly refuse to move on, by whispering it into its ear. To become a Horse Whisperer or Toadman wasn't easy. In Scotland, you had to be initiated into a secret society and swear blood-curdling oaths. In East Anglia, you had to kill a toad, leave it on an ant-hill for a month till the bones were picked clean, then on the next night of the full moon put the bones in a stream (ignoring the eldritch sounds which would break out just behind you). One single bone would float *upstream*. Take it home, rub it with oils, grind it to powder. That powder holds the power.

In Lancre, the blacksmith and farrier Jason Ogg has no need of all that palaver, but he does have a more immediately practical approach. He can calm the wildest stallion by whispering a definitely non-magical Word in its ear – he simply points out what all those pliers and hammers *could* be used for, 'if you don't stand still right now, you bugger'.

Royal Phantoms

Curiously, the royal family of Lancre have one strong superstition, though it only affects them once they are dead. They believe that they are bound to the stones of their ancient castle (especially if they happen to have been murdered on the premises), and must haunt it indefinitely. When this happened to King Verence I, he found he disliked most of his fellow-ghosts:

> Champot was all right, if a bit tiresome. But Verence had backed away at the first sight of the Twins, toddling hand in hand along the midnight corridors, their tiny ghosts a memorial to a deed darker even than the usual run of regicidal unpleasantness.
>
> And then there was the Troglodyte Wanderer, a rather faded monkeyman in a furry loincloth who apparently happened to haunt the castle merely because it had been built on his burial mound. For no obvious reason a chariot with a screaming woman in it occasionally rumbled through the laundry room. [*Wyrd Sisters*]

Being not entirely stupid, King Verence found a way of escape. He persuaded Nanny Ogg to help him, pleading, 'Pray carry a stone out of the palace so's I can haunt it, good mother, it's so bloody boring in here.' So he left the castle, clinging to a bit of rock that Nanny broke off the battlements and put in her apron pocket, and took up residence in her cottage. Unfortunately all the other ghosts came along too, but she got used to them in the end.

Magpies

Creatures which in other parts of the multiverse are a topic for wild rumour and proliferating legend are regarded in Lancre simply as rare and interesting species. To see the occasional phoenix or unicorn is sometimes a surprise, always a pleasure, but never an omen, either for good or ill. (Details of these and other remarkable fauna are to be found in the chapter on 'Beasties'.) But there is one exception – magpies are definitely bodeful.

The magpies which come down into Lancre from Uberwald are the spies and messengers of a powerful vampire, Count de Magpyr. But even apart from that, magpies are unpopular there for their thieving ways and for being omens.

Something chattered at them from a nearby branch . . .

'Good morning, Mister Magpie,' said Agnes automatically.

'Bugger off, you bastard,' said Nanny, and reached down for a stick to throw. The bird swooped off to the other side of the clearing.

'That's bad luck,' said Agnes.

'It will be if I get a chance to aim,' said Nanny. 'Can't stand those maggoty-pies.'

' "One for sorrow",' said Agnes, watching the bird hop along a branch.

'I always take the view there's prob'ly going to be another one along in a minute,' said Nanny, dropping the stick.

' "Two for joy"?' said Agnes.

'It's "two for mirth".'

'Same thing, I suppose.'

'Dunno about that,' said Nanny. 'I was joyful when our Jason was born, but I can't say I was *laughin'* at the time.'

Two more magpies landed on the cottage's antique thatch.

'That's "three for a girl—",' said Agnes nervously.

' "Three for a funeral" is what I learned,' said Nanny. 'But there's lots of magpie rhymes.' . . .

' "Seven for a secret never to be told",' said Agnes.

' "Seven's a devil, his own sel' ",' said Nanny darkly. 'You've got your rhyme, I've got mine.' [*Carpe Jugulum*]

*

Things are much the same on the Earth, where magpies (also known as pies, pyats, mags, or maggoty-pies) are sinister and unpopular birds. They are shameless thieves, snatching anything bright and glittery and carrying it off to decorate their extremely untidy and badly built nests – behaviour which earned one of them a vital but non-singing role in Rossini's opera *The Thieving Magpie*. It is said they will even fly down into Hell if there is a bag of gold to be found there. They love gossiping, chattering, and causing trouble; they are evil birds who know far more than they ought, always peering about and prying into other people's business. They have always enjoyed disasters. Even in the days of Noah's flood, the magpie refused to enter the Ark, preferring to perch on the roof and jabber with glee at the sight of the drowning world.

Magpies are so malicious that Spanish peasants say each one has seven bristles from the Devil's beard among its feathers, and seven bladders of bitter gall in its body. They are the Devil's spies and messengers. In Russia, too, they are considered the Devil's forces; there are said to be forty of them perched on fir trees to guard a bog where he sits enthroned on a white rock.

Throughout England and Scotland for the past two hundred years and more, there have been rhymes to warn you what to expect if you see magpies flying across your path. However, as Nanny Ogg would certainly point out, they are not very reliable, since they are not the ones the magpies know themselves. There are many versions, all agreeing that a single magpie brings bad luck, but two bring good. With three and four, there is more choice:

One for sorrow,
Two for joy,
Three for a girl,
And four for a boy.

Or:

One for sorrow,
Two for mirth,
Three for a wedding,
Four for a birth.

Or on the other hand, in the oldest known version (from Lincolnshire in 1780) it is:

Three for a wedding,
And four for a death.

After which things become more complicated. You can have:

Five for silver, six for gold,
Seven for a secret never to be told.

Or:

Five for rich, six for poor,
Seven for a witch, I can tell you no more.

Or:

Five for England, six for France,
Seven for a fiddler, eight for a dance.

Or:

Five for heaven, six for hell,
Seven, you'll see the devil himsel'.

To be on the safe side when a magpie crosses your path, and to turn aside the bad luck, you can draw a cross on the ground, or lay two straws or sticks crosswise; or bow to the bird, saying 'Good day, Mr Magpie!', or blow a kiss towards it; or recite this charm:

I crossed the magpie, and the magpie crossed me;
Devil take the magpie, and God save me!

CUSTOMS OF LANCRE

For some years now, the Ankh-Morpork Folk Dance and Song Society has been compiling an archive of old folk customs and fertility rituals from the countryside around. One summer a lady folklorist arrived on Nanny Ogg's doorstep, demanding information. 'Well,' said Nanny, 'there's only one fertility ritual that I knows of and that's the one that comes nat'rally.' But the lady said, 'No, there's got to be loads of folk stuff hanging on because I am writing a book, and I will give you this handsome silver dollar, my good woman.'

So Nanny Ogg gave her what she reckoned was one dollar's worth, but no more. This included the Scouring of the Long Man, as described above, and two or three others, which will be found in *A Tourist Guide to Lancre*:

The Seven-Year Flitch. This is an old custom datin' back to one Miscegenation Carter who left some money in his will to set it up to provide a flitch of bacon for the deservin' poor. It is held every five years. It is open to any man who has been married for more than seven years to appear before the Flitch Court, which consists of six old married couples, an' swear that in that time he has never had a cross word with his wife or regretted bein' married. If he does, he is beaten near senseless with the flitch for lying, but brought round with strong drink and the rest of the day is a fair. So far no man has ever convinced the Court an' the flitch is the original one, which is as hard as oak now.

The Lancre Oozer. The Oozer, attended by people dressed up as his Squeasers, dances from house to house in every village on Old Hogswatch Eve until people gives them money to go somewhere else. It is said that any maiden kissed by the Oozer is sure to be pregnant before the year is out but this is an odds-on bet in these parts anyway.

The Slice Mummers' Play. This is performed on the first Saturday after Marling Day, when the characters of Old Hogfather, Death, Merry Hood and the White Knight perform an age-old ritual tellin' of the death and resurrection of really bad acting. This is the high spot of the Slice Fair and Revels. There is not a lot to do in Slice. Well, not that isn't mostly banned everywhere else.

The similarities to Earthly customs here are truly astonishing. Anyone who knows anything about English traditions will recognize the name of the Dorset Ooser, a large, heavy wooden head with bull's horns, goggle eyes, and movable snapping jaws. Folklorists found out about it in 1891, at which time it was kept by a family in Crewkerne, but could get no information on how it was used. It has since disappeared, or perhaps it took a dislike to the folklorists and ran away. Its Discworld counterpart behaves very much like the May Day Obby Oss at Padstow in Cornwall, which dances from house to house through the narrow streets, led by a Teaser, and accompanied by singers and a massed band of accordions and drums. This goes on all day. If the Oss catches a woman, she will be married and/or pregnant within a year.

Mumming Plays can be seen in many towns and villages of England, Lowland Scotland, and parts of Ireland around Christmas time (or Easter, in Lancashire). They always involve a lot of shouting of bad verse, two or three fights, a death, and a resurrection brought about by a quack doctor. And then someone takes up a collection from the spectators. Folklorists used to think this was some sort of

extremely ancient fertility ritual, but eventually got around to notic-
ing the collection, and the odd fact that performances used to take
place outside rich men's houses, and nowadays at a pub.

As for the Seven-Year Flitch, this recalls something which has
been going on, off and on, for at least six hundred years at Great
Dunmow in Essex. Originally, any man who, having been married
for more than a year, could convince the monks at Little Dunmow
Priory that he had never once had words with his wife or wished he
was single again, would be given a flitch of bacon and carried in procession. Successful claims were few and far between. When the
monastery was closed down at the Reformation, successive Lords of
the Manor took responsibility for keeping the custom going, and did
so till 1751, when they dropped it. Fortunately, in 1854 the best-
selling novelist Harrison Ainsworth wrote an enthusiastic
description, *The Flitch of Bacon, or the Custom of Dunmow* (it can
still be found). This inspired a revival, which has flourished ever
since. Nowadays there is a mock trial, with the wives giving
evidence, and the whole thing is treated as a joke.

Soul Caking

If the lady folklorist from Ankh-Morpork had produced another
dollar, she could have learned about the excitements of the Soul Cake
Days, which are celebrated in the Ramtops and on the Sto Plains on
the first Tuesday, Wednesday and Thursday after first half-moon in
the month of Sektober. Readers attempting to work out this date
should bear in mind that on the Discworld it is extremely dangerous
to utter the magic number 'eight', or any of its derivatives, in any
language.

According to the *Discworld Almanak*, the Soul Cake Days are
'celebrated by Dwarfs and Men with great fires, much noise, and
mysterious customs, too many to catalogue, and some too moist to
recommend'. It is known that Morris Dancing is involved; also that
dwarfs play at Bobbing for Toffee-Rats on a Stick, and human

children go Trickle-Treating. Lady folklorists in Ankh-Morpork assume that this is just a local pronunciation of 'Treacle-Treating', meaning that the kids who dress up and go from house to house are hoping to be given treacle gob-stoppers as their treat. Male folklorists hold the opinion (never mentioned in print, or in the hearing of their female colleagues) that the name arose because people who refuse to hand out any treats later find a rather nasty trickle on their doorstep.

Lancre children are also given eggs with funny faces on them (Nanny Ogg is a dab hand at painting them). There must be some connection with the Soul Cake Tuesday Duck, a magical creature which lays chocolate eggs for children in Ankh-Morpork, as will be described in a later chapter. And this in turn links up with the fact that the duck-hunting season begins that Tuesday. The good people of Ubergigl (in Uberwald) mark the date by 'The Running of the Ducks', when maddened untamed ducks run, more or less, through the streets, pursued by young men who vie with one another to snatch the coveted rosette from the beak of the biggest drake. Perhaps their minds have been affected by some floating awareness of the Running of the Bulls, which is done every July at a fiesta at Pamplona in Spain.

All of which is well and good, but does not even begin to explain what souls, and cakes, have to do with it. Here, by remarkable co-incidence, English traditions can again cast light on the problem. In the Middle Ages 2 November, All Souls' Day, was the day when Christians prayed particularly for the souls of the dead, to speed them on their way from Purgatory to Heaven (as is still done in Catholic countries); on this and the preceding days, it was customary for those who could afford it to give away little cakes to the poor, asking them too to pray for the donor's dead family and friends. Long after the religious purpose had been forgotten, people made fancy cakes at this time of year, and called them 'soul cakes'; in the nineteenth century in the rural parts of Cheshire and Shropshire, the poorer people went from farm to farm asking for money, food or drink, with the song:

Soul, soul, for a souling cake,
I pray you, good missis, for a souling cake,
Apple or pear, a plum or a cherry,
Anything good to make us merry.
Up with your kettles and down with your pans,
Give us an answer and we'll be gone.

They said they were 'Going Soul Caking', but secretly they hoped there'd be some beer to go with the cakes, or, better still, some money. By the end of that century the custom had died out among adults; children, however, were still keeping it up in the 1950s. Though sometimes they forgot about the cakes:

Soul, soul, for an apple or two,
If you've got no apples, pears will do;
If you've got no pears, ha'pennies will do;
If you've got no ha'pennies, God bless you.

Morris Dancing, Light and Dark

There are some things Nanny Ogg took good care not to mention to the lady folklorist from the city – the things she calls the 'real stuff', things like the Dark Morris. The lady would be bound to get them all wrong anyway.

Now, even ordinary Morris dancing, what we may for convenience call the Light Morris, is a curious thing, both on Earth and on the Disc. A typical dance involves six men in two lines of three, facing each other; they are all dressed alike, usually in white, with coloured baldrics and decorated hats, and possibly with ribbons and rosettes too; they clash sticks in time to the music, miraculously avoiding one another's fingers by a hair's breadth, or wave large handkerchiefs, or clap; they have bells strapped to their ankles and knees. There will be one or two reserve dancers in the team, to replace anyone who retires exhausted or injured; a musician playing an accordion, or a fiddle, or in earlier centuries a pipe and tabor; a Fool; and someone to go round taking the collection.

On one level it's a public display of skill, strength, stamina and sheer bloody-mindedness, which some people in Lancre think of as entertainment and others as a form of martial art (especially when sticks and buckets are involved). There is a definite competitive edge to it. You can have events like the Fifteen Mountains All-Comers' Championships, which the Lancre Morris Men have won no fewer than six times. It gives the teams a chance to dress up and swagger around, to be someone special.

In Elizabethan England, the strict Puritans thought the swaggering was much too much fun, both for the dancers and the crowd. In 1583 Philip Stubbes complained furiously in his *Anatomie of Abuses* that at village festivals there would be Morris Men dressed in 'green, yellow, or some other light wanton colour':

> And as though that were not gaudy enough, I should say, they bedeck themselves with scarfs, ribbons and laces, hanged all over with gold rings, precious stones and other jewels; this done, they tie about either leg twenty or forty bells, with rich handkerchiefs in their hands, and sometimes laid across their shoulders and necks, borrowed for the most part from their pretty Mopsies or loving Betties, for bussing them in the dark . . . Then march this heathen company towards the church and churchyard, their pipers piping, their drummers thundering, their stumps dancing, their bells jingling, their handkerchiefs fluttering above their heads like mad men, their hobby horses skirmishing among the throng.

On a second level – at any rate in England, where it has flourished (off and on) for at least six hundred years – Morris dancing used to be an excellent way for working men in country districts to get free beer and food and some extra cash. They would appear at seasonal festivals such as May Day and Whitsun, and also at whichever date the local fair was held; in winter they would go round performing outside the houses of the wealthy. This was a great asset when times were hard, as they so often were in the eighteenth and nineteenth centuries. Nowadays, Morris teams usually perform outside pubs and in town centres; they still take up a collection, but simply to cover their expenses or for a charity.

Some English teams used to go out on tour for several weeks, and even visit towns. At a fair in London in 1823, for example, there was:

> a group of young rustics attired in garments decorated with numerous bows of ribbon. They had small jingling bells fastened to their knees and ankles. Some waved white handkerchiefs and others wands . . . keeping time by striking their wands against one another.

It was so pleasant, wrote another London eyewitness in 1830,

> to observe the monotony of some long dull street of dingy houses broken by the simple music of the pipe and tabor, and the ringing of the bells on the legs of the morris-dancers . . . There seems a patch of old-time merriment in the active motions of the ruddy and sunburnt countrymen.

Just *how* old was the merriment? When and why did it come to be such an essential part of the rose-tinted picture of the happy, simple, country life of Old England? A theory popular in the eighteenth century was that the name 'Morris' was a corruption of the Spanish word *morisco*, 'Moorish', and that it was a fashion introduced from Spain in the fourteenth century. This would imply that at first it was danced by the upper classes, not among country folk, and that they called it 'Moorish' not just for being foreign, but because it was so wild and energetic, in contrast to the stately dances of the Court. It is a plausible suggestion, but apart from the name itself there is no actual evidence for it.

Then, in the later nineteenth and early twentieth centuries, a dramatic new theory emerged and became instantly popular and widely accepted. The origins of the Morris, it was claimed, lay in the fertility rituals of prehistoric Europe; the noisy bells, the waving hankies, and aggressive sticks were meant to drive away evil spirits; the high leaps into the air were meant to make the crops grow tall. On this level, the third and for many people the most important one, Morris dancing is an immensely ancient magical rite for the promotion of life. There is no evidence for this either, but as the English scholar Keith Chandler recently wrote, 'viewing a dance which is supposedly several thousand years old appears to satisfy some indefinable need in the human psyche'.

Whether or not this theory holds good on Earth, it is well known to be the truth of the matter on the Disc. There, Morris dancing is done to bring good luck and drive bad things away; there's nothing like the jangle of little iron bells for getting rid of elves. What's more, it's all about the cycles of growth and decay, summer and winter, life and death. It involves the Light Morris, yes, but the Dark Morris too.

This is why there's one village in the Ramtops, the one where they really do know what they are doing, where the Morris Men dance twice, and twice only, in every year (we shall have more to say on this in the next chapter). The first time is at dawn on the first day of spring, and everyone is welcome to watch. But the second time is in autumn, and it's private.

On a certain day when the nights are drawing in, the dancers leave work early and take, from attics and cupboards, the *other* costume, the black one, and the *other* bells. And they go by separate ways to a valley among the leafless trees. They don't speak. There is no music. It's very hard to imagine what kind there could be.

The bells don't ring. They're made of octiron, a magic metal. But they're not, precisely, silent bells. Silence is merely the absence of noise. They make the opposite of noise, a sort of heavily textured silence.

And in the cold afternoon, as the light drains from the sky, among the frosty leaves and in the damp air, they dance the *other* Morris. Because of the balance of things.

You've got to dance both, they say. Otherwise you can't dance either. [*Reaper Man*]

This is the Dark Morris Nanny Ogg was keeping quiet about. If it is danced elsewhere in the multiverse – and it surely is – people there are keeping quiet about it too. (Well. Not that quiet. Terry is occasionally informed of a sighting, and once saw it danced in Chicago.)

Chapter 10

THE WITCHES
OF THE CHALK

HOSTILITY TOWARDS WITCHES

IN THE LOWLANDS and in the Chalk country, witches do not receive the same respect as in Lancre. There have been times when they were systematically persecuted, even burned, and though that no longer happens many of the Chalk people still distrust them, and are quick to blame them when there is trouble. So witches who go there are wary, and try not to attract attention. They wear ordinary clothes, and disguise their true craft behind a slightly more socially acceptable calling, such as teaching. That is why, when Miss Perspicacia Tick visits the Chalk, or surrounding villages, she wears what looks like a simple black straw hat smothered in paper flowers, but is actually a collapsible stealth model. Press a spring, and it unfolds into the classic pointy shape. Among the paper flowers lurks a talking toad which she refers to as her familiar, though so far it has not displayed any magical powers – unlike the toad-familiars of English witches in Wessex, which are so dangerous that the worst threat their mistress can utter is, 'I'll set my toads on 'ee!'

Miss Tick's equipment too looks far from witchy. She does her scrying by pouring a few drops of ink into rainwater in a cracked saucer which she carries about in one of her many pockets. Also in her pockets are other insignificant objects – twigs, loose beads, string, a reel of cotton, a holed stone, a few feathers, scraps of coloured paper. These she can thread together to make a 'shamble', a powerful magic-detector and projector which looks a bit like a particularly complicated cat's cradle, a bit like a broken set of puppet-strings, and a bit like a very untidy dream-catcher. To do this requires high skill in making string-figures, an art practised in various parts of the multiverse, and often linked to myths and magic. On Earth, Germans call it *das Hexenspiel*, 'the Witch's Game'.

A shamble won't work if you buy it ready-made. You have to make your own, fresh every time, out of whatever there happens to be in your pockets. In the centre you put something alive – an egg, say, or a beetle or small worm – and pull the strings, and as the objects twirl past or even through one another, the device works. In the presence of really powerful magic, it may explode. But if you pull the right bit of string, it all falls apart in a moment and becomes just a small pile of harmless rubbish. Nothing suspicious. Nothing that makes people say 'witch'.

Because once people think you're a witch, things can go terribly, terribly wrong, as they did for poor old Mrs Snapperly, who died in the snow one winter, but who probably wasn't a witch at all. As Tiffany Aching tells Miss Tick, Mrs Snapperly used to live alone in a strange cottage in the woods, and had no teeth, and talked to herself. And she had a cat, and she squinted. So when a young boy went riding in those woods one summer day and never came back, people said she'd killed him, and maybe cooked him in her oven too.

'And so after he vanished they went to her cottage and they looked in the oven and they dug up her garden and they threw stones at her old cat until it died and they turned her out of her cottage and piled up all her old books in the middle of the room and set fire to them and burned the place to the ground and everyone said she was an old witch.' [*The Wee Free Men*]

To make matters worse, this lost boy was the Baron's son, and the Baron (whose family had held the Chalk for generations without ever changing their minds about anything) was full of taken-for-granted prejudices. He too blamed Mrs Snapperly, and gave orders that nobody was to have anything to do with her, and that any witch found in the country should be tied up and thrown in a pond. The old woman managed to live through the autumn, begging and stealing food here and there and sleeping where she could, but there came a cold night when no one would open their doors to her, and it snowed, and by morning she was dead.

Thankfully, such small rural tragedies are now rare on Discworld, but they were common on Earth until modern times. As late as the 1920s, in one Sussex village there was an old widow called Betsey Shadlow who was forced into isolation by the fears and suspicions of her neighbours. She was a wicked old woman, they said, and had 'powerful books with a deal of evil written in them'. She lived alone and in poverty, and was crippled with rheumatism, but nobody would help her dig up her potatoes for fear of what she might do to them. When she went to the farm to buy milk, the farmer wouldn't let her pass the gate in case she bewitched the cows, so she had to stay in the road and yell until somebody heard her. There came a time when people realized that they hadn't seen her around for a couple of weeks, so the Rector called at her cottage and found her sick in bed, too ill to move. The man who told her story to the *Sussex County Magazine* in 1943 remembered how it all ended:

The workhouse people came next day and took her away. One of the head men stayed behind to sort out her belongings. She hadn't much furniture, but they found a pile of books. My neighbour, who was very fond of reading and very curious as well, asked the official if he could have them, or at least read them, but we said it wasn't right, and anyway we didn't want anyone else learning the secrets and playing us up – Betsey Shadlow was trouble enough – and we asked the workhouse chap to burn them. He looked at them, and said they were rubbish anyway. It's a strange thing, but when they came to set fire to all the unwanted stuff from the cottage along with those books, we lookers-on saw *green* flames coming from the fire!

The Baron's notion that the thing to do with witches is to throw them into ponds must be one of those thought-particles drifting through the multiverse and taking root in any suitable mind. It echoes a practice once common in many countries of the Earth, the 'swimming test'. It began in the Middle Ages as a way of discovering whether someone was or was not a witch, and reached its peak in the first half of the seventeenth century. The suspect would be tied up, hands to feet, and thrown in. It was believed that if she was guilty, water, being a pure and holy element, would reject her, and she would remain floating on the surface; if she was innocent, she would sink – and, hopefully, someone would haul her out before she drowned. Though popular, this was not actually legal, and the vast majority of lawyers and church leaders refused to accept it as evidence in court. One famous writer who did believe in the test was King James VI of Scotland and I of England, who linked it with the idea that witches had rejected the Christian faith in which they had been baptized:

> So it appears that God hath appointed, for a supernatural sign of the monstrous impiety of witches, that the water shall refuse to receive into her bosom those who have shaken off them the sacred water of baptism and wilfully refused the sacred benefit thereof.

There came a time when all laws against witchcraft were dropped, and people could no longer take a woman to court if they thought her spells had harmed them. So, remembering the old ways, village mobs sometimes took matters into their own hands by 'swimming' her themselves, not as a test but as a punishment. Even in Victorian England, there were one or two cases where people died of this, by drowning or by pneumonia. In view of the Baron's decree, it is fortunate that Miss Perspicacia Tick is good at untying knots with her teeth and swimming underwater, and can lurk under the weeds, breathing air through a hollow reed.[9]

WITCHES HAVE A DUTY

As in Lancre, so on the Chalk a witch has a duty to her land and her people. It is because young Tiffany Aching has an instinctive ability to accept responsibility, to cope with threats to herself and others, that she is a natural born witch. As the kelda of the Wee Free Men tells her: 'Ye're the hag noo, the witch that guards the edges and the gateways. So wuz yer granny, although she wouldnae ever call hersel' one.'

Granny Aching had lived and died as a shepherd. The chalk and flint were in her bones, the sky was her hat and the wind her cloak. All spring and summer she stayed out on the hills, sleeping in her old wheeled shepherding hut, which could be dragged across the downs to follow the flocks. Tiffany knew (probably by reading *The Goode Childe's Booke of Faerie Tales*) that any old woman who lived in a house that *moved about* must be at least slightly a witch. She was sure of this, even though she had never heard of Mrs Gogol, the swamp-witch in Genua whose hut paddled along on duck's feet, let alone Baba Yaga in Russian fairy tales, whose cottage stood on hen's legs and spun round and round.

Granny Aching was a supremely skilful and conscientious shepherd, with all the toil and responsibility this entails.

---

[9] Regrettably, some things don't change. Terry recalls a case in the USA some years ago when a somewhat New Age lady got a visit from her local sheriff after a neighbour reported that she was 'saying spells' in her garden. She'd been singing a Christian hymn – in Latin.

[One would see] Granny Aching's light, weaving slowly across the downs, on freezing, sparkly nights or in storms like a raging war, saving lambs from the creeping frost or rams from the precipice. She froze and struggled and tramped through the night for idiot sheep that never said thank you and would probably be just as stupid tomorrow, and get into the same trouble again. And she did it because not doing it was unthinkable. [*The Wee Free Men*]

She used no magic, though some shepherds' tricks look like magic if you don't know how they're done. But she had wisdom, and authority, and sometimes anger too; she saw to it that where there was injustice there would be a reckoning, since 'Them as can do, has to do for them as can't, and someone has to speak up for them as has no voices.' Within two or three years of her death, the memory of her had grown into something larger than life, something like a spirit of the downs:

There were always buzzards over the Chalk. The shepherds had taken to calling them Granny Aching's chickens, and some of them called clouds like those up there today 'Granny's little lambs'. And Tiffany *knew* that even her father called the thunder 'Granny Aching cussin''.

And it was said that some of the shepherds, if wolves were troublesome in the winter, or a prize ewe had got lost, would go to the site of the old hut in the hills and leave an ounce of Jolly Sailor tobacco, just in case . . .

No wonder that when monsters and elves from another world appear in the Chalk country, Tiffany's first thought is that Granny would have known how to deal with them. But Granny is dead. It is now young Tiffany who must become the witch-as-shepherd, guarding the borders, driving invaders away, keeping an eye on things. She has a duty.

BECOMING A WITCH

How does a girl become a witch? First, she must have some natural inborn talent, even if she does not yet realize it. Here, heredity can help, and in Tiffany's case it does; the Achings, like the Weatherwaxes, have witching in their blood. It *might* also be significant that she is the seventh daughter. On the Earth it certainly would be, for in that universe many a magical healer and fortune-teller has found that being a seventh son (or daughter) is good publicity. But the supreme magical number on the Discworld is eight, not seven, so it is usually the eighth son (or daughter) who is born with power, as we learn in *Equal Rites* and *Sourcery*.

The really unmistakable sign that Tiffany is destined to be a witch is her name – a sign all the more powerful for being the result of sheer chance (if there *is* such a thing as chance). In the languages of the Discworld 'Tiffany' has no meaning, but the kelda of the Wee Free Men tells her that in their Old Speech (a Celtic tongue, learned in another universe) its true form is Tir-far-Thóinn, meaning 'Land Under Wave'.[10] Chalk hills are land which was once under the waves, land formed from the shells of countless millions of sea creatures. Knowing this, and knowing what her name means, is the core of Tiffany's power.

> She saw herself set her boots firmly on the turf, and then . . .
> . . . and then . . .
> . . . and then, like someone rising from the clouds of a sleep, she felt the deep, deep Time below her. She sensed the breath of the downs and the distant roar of ancient, ancient seas trapped in millions of tiny shells. She thought of Granny Aching, under the turf, becoming part of the chalk again, part of the land under wave. She felt as if huge wheels, of time and stars, were turning slowly around her.

---

[10] But in the languages of Earth it comes from the same Greek root as 'epiphany', meaning 'revelation of god".

She opened her eyes and then, somewhere inside, opened her eyes again.

She heard the grass growing, and the sound of worms below the turf. She could feel the thousands of little lives around her, smell all the scents on the breeze, and see all the shades of the night . . .

The wheels of stars and years, of space and time, locked into place. She knew exactly where she was, and who she was, and what she was. [*The Wee Free Men*]

However, even if you are born with an aptitude for magic, there are still skills to be learned, and it is not wise to try to learn witching all by yourself. Get one little thing wrong, and you're stuck among dangers you don't understand. Even if you make no mistakes, you'll be desperately lonely. Unless you can meet people of your own sort, you may end up mad – or bad.

Things aren't so bad for boys who are potential wizards, since they can go to Unseen University. Occasionally, in those few times and places in the multiverse where girls have been allowed to study the same things as their brothers, there has been some talk of boarding schools for young witches, and even of co-educational establishments. But on the Disc there is nothing like that. When Miss Tick tells Tiffany that yes, there is indeed such a school – very magical, nowhere else quite like it – this is a trick or test. The true 'school', as Tiffany soon understands, is all around you, once you know how to open your eyes and then open them again. As for the detailed skills of the craft, they are passed on from elderly witches to young ones on a one-to-one basis, together with some very necessary guidance and protection. It is Miss Tick's responsibility, as a secret witch-finder, to pick out girls with talent and make suitable arrangements for them.

So when Tiffany was eleven, she left her home in the Chalk country and travelled to the mountains, where she went into service with Miss Level, partly as a maid and partly as an apprentice. She learned about herbs, and broomsticks, and tried patiently to make a shamble. She accompanied Miss Level round the villages and isolated farms doing medicine and midwifery, and learned that though a witch never expects payment and never asks for it, there is a constant interchange of gifts and favours. There was nothing romantic about this work, nothing dramatic, no magic potions to cure the sick in an instant. Witchcraft, said Miss Level, was mostly about helping people by doing quite ordinary things. This has been the task of the true Wise Woman in every universe, and we can assume (though evidence is lacking) that girls who became Wise Women on Earth learned their skills and duties by some similar informal apprenticeship.

However, cures and advice are more likely to be accepted if they *sound* magical, as Tiffany learned. Miss Level had been carefully telling one family that their well was much too close to their privy, so the water was full of tiny, tiny creatures which were making the children sick. They listened politely, but did nothing. Then Granny Weatherwax visited them and told them the illness was caused by goblins who were attracted to the smell of the privy, and that very day the man of the house and his friends began digging a new well at the other end of the garden. A story gets things done.

Yet there was part of Tiffany's mind which hankered for power and drama and picturesque paraphernalia. This is a very common weakness in young witches, and Tiffany meets one group of girls who practise 'The Higher MagiK'.

'Magic with a K?' said Tiffany. 'MagiK*kkk*?'

'That's deliberate,' said Annagramma coldly. 'If we are to make any progress at all we *must* distinguish the Higher MagiK from the everyday sort.'

'The *everyday* sort of magic?' said Tiffany.

'Exactly. None of that mumbling in hedgerows for *us*. Proper sacred circles, spells written down. A proper hierarchy, not everyone running around doing whatever they feel like. Real wands, not bits of grubby stick. Professionalism, with respect. Absolutely no warts. That's the only way forward.' [*A Hatful of Sky*]

Annagramma has learned this approach from Mrs Letice Earwig, a tall thin witch who wears so much silver that she gleams, uses words like 'avatar' and 'sigil', and writes books. This has earned her Granny Weatherwax's heartfelt contempt. 'That's just wizard magic with a dress on,' and 'She thinks you can become a witch by going shopping,' are two of Granny's milder comments.

Annagramma runs a coven of young girls, whom she bullies and sneers at, and chivvies through complex ceremonies involving such things as the Wand of Air, the Cauldron of the Sea, the Shriven Chalice, the Circlet of Infinity. They all go in for robes and occult jewellery, and patronize the very expensive shop of Zakzak Stronginthearm, a dwarf craftsman who supplies everything the Higher MagiKkkkian might require: wands of metal or rare woods, elaborately pretty ready-made shambles, crystal balls, luxurious cloaks, star-spangled hats, rings, pendants, your personal grimoire ('Book of Night', or 'Book of Shadows') bound in heavy leather with an actively rolling eye on the cover.

It is really remarkable how similar ideas spring up across the multiverse. On the Earth groups like this have become common over the past hundred years or so. There too, some of them insist on an eccentric spelling for what they do, calling it Magick, to make sure that nobody mistakes it for that boring old-fashioned folk magic. They go in for formal initiations, oaths, grades, and hierarchies, and their founders and leaders (generally men) are notably authoritarian. They take grandiose names for themselves, their organizations, their ritual ceremonies, and the objects used in ritual. And the Zakzaks of our world do very good business. Well, whatever ... but one instinctively feels that Granny's 'every stick is a wand, every puddle is a crystal ball' is closer to the truth. Or *a* truth, at least.

'SEE ME'

The most remarkable of Tiffany's abilities was one which she ought really to have mentioned to Miss Tick, but she didn't, being too young and inexperienced to know how unusual, and how risky, it was. Closing her eyes and concentrating, she would say 'See me'. Then, reopening her eyes, she would find herself standing a few feet away from herself. She had walked out of her own body, and now her detached self could move around, looking at her physical self from every side. When she had seen all she wanted, she would say 'See me not', and the two selves were instantly reunited.

As a child, Tiffany simply thought of this as a handy little trick to use if you didn't have a proper mirror. She had no notion that it is the basis of Borrowing, that supreme skill of great witches. Still less did she suspect that if you just walk out of your body and leave it there, without taking proper precautions, there are creatures only too ready to move in and take control.

This ability, or something very like it, has been observed elsewhere in the multiverse, though not under the deliberate control of those who have it. One form is the 'Near Death Experience', much discussed nowadays on the Earth. People who are semi-conscious from heart failure or anaesthetic, and almost on the point of death, feel the mind detaching itself from the inert body and floating upwards; they can watch the body from above, and see what is going on around it, but eventually are reunited with it and regain consciousness.

Older Earthly sources speak of the soul, rather than the mind, separating itself from the sleeping body and wandering off on its own. According to folk tradition, it is possible for an observer to see this happening, for the soul emerges in visible form, as a small animal, an insect, or a puff of smoke. This is said to have happened once to King Guntram of the Franks, who ruled Burgundy from 561 to 592; the story was written down some two hundred years later.

One day, Guntram felt tired while out hunting, and took a nap under a tree, while a courtier kept watch. This man saw that while the king was asleep a little animal slithered out of his mouth and went down to a tiny brook, where it ran to and fro on the bank, looking for a way to cross. Amused at this, the courtier laid his sword across the brook. The little creature crossed at once, and disappeared into a hole on the opposite bank. After a bit, it returned across the sword bridge, and slipped back into the king's mouth. Then Guntram woke up, and said to his companion, 'I must tell you what a strange dream I've just had. I saw a very large, very wide river, and across it a great iron bridge had been built. I crossed the bridge, and went into a cave in the side of a towering mountain, and it was filled with treasure!' Then the courtier told the king what had actually happened, and they decided to dig into the bank of the brook, and sure enough, there was a treasure buried there.

It is important that no one should touch or shake or shift the unconscious body while its soul is away, because if the soul cannot find its way back, the person will die.

MAKING A MYTH OF ONESELF

Tiffany's next post is as apprentice to an extremely odd – nay, terrifying – witch named Miss Eumenides Treason, one hundred and thirteen years old, quite blind, and quite deaf. Yet these disabilities scarcely bother her, because she is skilled at Borrowing and uses the eyes and ears of any nearby animal as if they were her own. On occasion, she even Borrows Tiffany's eyes, which is rather irritating of her.

Whereas Miss Tick is a stealth witch, Miss Treason flaunts witchery in every detail of her lifestyle. All witches like wearing black, but she has gone further; the walls and floors in her cottage are black, and so, of course, are her candles; she keeps black goats and black hens; even cheeses must be coated with black wax.

Everything has been carefully crafted to match images stamped deeply into the human psyche by the force of narrativium, since it is her aim to turn herself into a myth, in life and in death. She knows exactly how to do it.

Every witch has her particular skill, and Miss Treason's is to deliver Justice. People would come to her from miles around with disputes about land, or cows, or rent, or legacies, and she would sit in judgement. So, how does the image fit the role?

First, blindness. Everyone knows that when Justice is personified she wears a blindfold, and so does Miss Treason – a black one, naturally. So indeed does Blind Io, chief of the gods, who has blank skin where his eyes should be and an impressive number of detached eyeballs floating round him. It is not known whether Miss Treason is deliberately mocking him; it is not impossible, for witches don't have much respect for gods. What is quite certain is that she strikes terror into the hearts of disputants when she removes the blindfold from her pearly grey eyes and prepares to give judgement, saying: 'I have heard. Now I shall see. I shall see what is true.' Her blind eyes seem to look right into the soul. People say if you lie to her, you'll be dead in a week.

Then there is her name, Eumenides, which she must have found in the pages of *Chaffinch's Ancient and Classical Mythology* – one of her favourite books, crammed full with bookmarks. On the Earth, in Ancient Greece, this was the polite name for the Erinyes or Avenging Furies, terrifying goddesses whose function was to hound the guilty to death; it literally means 'Sweet-Tempered Ladies' and was meant to be flattering to them and reassuring to us, but nobody was ever fooled by that. Her chosen hobby is weaving, which (like the spinning of the Fates) is a traditional metaphor for the way supernatural beings decide human destinies. One tale from the Earth (the medieval Icelandic *Njal's Saga*) tells how twelve valkyries were seen setting up a gruesome loom, just before the great Battle of Clontarf between Vikings and Irishmen in 1014. As they worked, they sang:

We weave, we weave a web of war.
Human guts our warp and weft,
Skulls our loom-weights, spears our shuttles,
Swords to beat the blood-stained cloth.
We decide who lives, who dies.
We weave, we weave a web of war.

Next, her birds. At the time Tiffany was living with Miss Treason, she kept two ravens, which had once worked for Blind Io; one would sit on each side of her head on a wooden perch which fitted like a yoke across her shoulders. The effect was very witchy, and mythic too; no doubt she had been reading about the Norse god Odin and his ravens Huginn and Muninn ('Thought' and 'Memory'), which perched on his shoulders and told him everything they had seen as they flew round Middle Earth.

Before the ravens, she had kept a pet jackdaw. There are no links between jackdaws and Justice, but good precedents for their use as magical familiars. The medieval English chronicler William of Malmesbury wrote in his *Gesta Regum Anglorum* (1125) of a witch who had lived at Berkeley in Gloucestershire some sixty years before his time, in the year 1063. She was skilled in interpreting omens, and had a tame jackdaw as her very great favourite; one day, the bird chattered more loudly than usual, and she turned pale, knowing this was a warning that her own death was at hand. (A Discworld witch wouldn't mind knowing this, but the Witch of Berkeley had made a pact with the Devil, so for her it was not good news.) In much more recent times, in the 1960s, to be precise, a well-known witch in the New Forest in Hampshire, Mrs Sybil Leek, would always appear in public with a tame jackdaw called Hotfoot Jackson perching on her shoulder. Very eye-catching, but (like Miss Treason) she did have to put up with mess down the back of her cloak.

Myth-making is a communal activity, even if most people involved don't see that that's what they're doing. It's built up from fears, rumours, thrills and stories, all driven by powerful doses of narrativium. Miss Treason takes a keen interest in the process, since she has a reputation to keep up. She asks Tiffany:

'Have you heard the stories about me, child?' . . .
    'Er, that you have a demon in the cellar?' Tiffany answered
. . . 'And you eat spiders? And get visited by kings and princes?
And that any flower planted in your garden blooms black?'
    'Oh, do they say so?' said Miss Treason, looking delighted.
'I haven't heard that last one. How nice. And did you hear that
I walk around at night in the dark time of the year and reward
those who have been good citizens with a purse of silver? But,
if they have been bad, I slit open their bellies with my thumbnail like this?'
    Tiffany leaped backwards as a wrinkled hand twisted her
round and Miss Treason's yellow thumbnail scythed past her
stomach. The old woman looked terrifying.
    'No! No, I haven't heard that one,' she gasped, pressing up
against the sink.
    'What? And it was a wonderful story, with real historical
antecedents!' said Miss Treason, her vicious scowl becoming a
smile. 'And the one about me having a cow's tail?'
    'A cow's tail? No!'
    'Really? How very vexing . . . I fear the art of story-telling
has got into a pretty bad way in these parts. I really shall have
to do something.' [*Wintersmith*]

It is to be hoped that she did, for they are indeed splendid stories, and it would be a great pity if they were forgotten. Their historical antecedents have deep roots in the Scandinavian and German-speaking parts of the Earth. The cow's tail is characteristic of elf-women in the mountain forests of Norway and Sweden. From in front, they look beautiful, and many a human huntsman or charcoal-burner has been seduced into making love with one of them. But if he gets a glimpse of her back, he will see either that it is hollow, mossy and rotten like an old tree-stump, or that it ends in a long, dirty cow's tail. If he runs off in horror, she will chase him, and if she catches him she will tear him to bits. They are not to be trifled with, these forest elf-women.

As for the stomach-slitting, here Miss Treason is surely thinking of some Discworld equivalent of a famous supernatural hag known as Frau Holle in Germany and Frau Perchte or Frau Berthe in Bavaria, Austria and Switzerland. Stories about her go back at least a thousand years. Some say she lives on a mountain peak, but others say up in the sky; when it snows in the human world everyone knows that she's shaking out her feather beds until the feathers drift about in the wind. In midwinter, during the Twelve Days of Christmas, she comes to earth and travels round the countryside, checking on whether children have been good and obedient, and whether the village girls have worked hard on the farms, and spun as much flax or wool as they should have done in the course of the year. Then comes Twelfth Night itself, sometimes called Perchtanacht and reckoned to be the last night of the year. At midnight she comes into every house. Those who have been good and done their work properly may find a silver coin in their shoes, or in the milking pail. But as for those who haven't, she will slit their bellies open, remove the contents, and fill them up with chopped straw, pebbles and dirt. Then she sews them up again, using a ploughshare as a needle and an iron chain as thread.

Another notion which Miss Treason picked up from the tales of Earth is that of the External Soul. A good example is the legendary Russian evil wizard Koshchei the Deathless, who placed his Life or Soul in an egg. The egg was inside a duck, and the duck was inside a hare, and the hare was lying in a great hollow log floating in a pond in a forest on an island far, far away from Koshchei's palace. Miss Treason's version is less complicated. She wears a heavy iron clock on her belt, and is always winding it up. There is a story in the villages that this clock is her heart, which she has used ever since her first heart died.

'Miss Treason,' said Tiffany severely, 'did you make up the story about your clock?'

'Of course I did! And it's a wonderful bit of folklore, a real corker. Miss Treason and her clockwork heart! Might even become a myth, if I'm lucky. They'll remember Miss Treason for thousands of years!'

She is brilliant at stage-setting too. Her all-black cottage is thick with cobwebs, though there are no spiders to be seen. The black candles by the loom are set in two skulls, and dribble wax all down them; one skull is carved with the Greek word for 'guilt', the other with the Greek for 'innocence'. This is the kind of thing people expect of her, and it all helps to build her reputation. But the skulls hold a secret. There is a label underneath, and it says:

Ghastly Skull No. 1 Price $2.99
The Boffo Novelty and Joke Shop
No. 4, Tenth Egg Street, Ankh-Morpork
"If it's a Laugh . . . it's a Boffo!"

The cobwebs also came from there, and Boffo does masks and warts and green bubbling cauldrons too.

So, where is the difference between Miss Treason buying skulls from Boffo's catalogue and Mrs Earwig buying silver pendants and crystals at Zakzak's shop? The point is this. Mrs Earwig thinks that power *comes from* elaborate devices, and to think this is to misunderstand the whole essence of the craft. But Miss Treason knows that you don't need a wand or a shamble or even a pointy hat to *be* a witch, but that it helps a witch if she puts on a show. Give people what they expect to see. It's all a form of 'headology', like the hat or Granny Weatherwax's bottle of coloured water. That way, you get respect.

Looking back on her life's work as death approaches, Miss Treason muses:

'Oh, my silly people. Anything they don't understand is magic. They think I can see into their hearts, but no witch can do that. Not without surgery, at least. No magic is needed to read their little minds, though. I've known them since they were babes . . . I see their lies and excuses and fears. They never grow up, not really . . .'

'I'm sure they'll miss you,' said Tiffany.

'Ha! I'm the wicked ol' witch, girl. They feared me, and did what they were told! They feared joke skulls and silly stories. I chose fear. I knew they'd never love me for telling 'em the truth, so I made certain of their fear. No, they'll be relieved to hear the witch is dead.'

As a Roman general said long ago, *Oderint dum metuant* – 'Let them hate me, so long as they fear me.'

If you want to be remembered for generations in folk tradition, whether as a hero, a saint, or a sage, a good death scene is vitally important. Now, one of the minor benefits of being a witch is that you know, months or even years in advance, exactly when you are going to die, so you can stage-manage the event to perfection. (On Earth, legend says that exceptionally holy people have this privilege too.) Having done all the obvious things (cleaned the cottage, made a will, destroyed any embarrassing old letters or spells still lying around), you can throw a really good 'going-away party'. This is like a wake, but with yourself as guest of honour, still taking a keen interest. People, especially other witches, come from miles around to enjoy the food (as Nanny Ogg says, you cannot go wrong with a ham roll) and to let it be discreetly known that they have always rather admired your brass candlesticks, or your big carving-dish with the blue-and-gold border. It saves a great deal of squabbling if you, the soon-to-be-late witch, can organize the distribution of these little mementoes yourself.

And then, when everyone has gone home and there's been a few hours of peace and quiet, you just head for the garden, where some helpful neighbour has dug a neat grave (in Miss Treason's case, it was the Nac Mac Feegles who did the job), climb down into it (watched by an awed but appreciative audience of village folk), lie down carefully, and wait . . . It is a fine thing to be able to organize your own Rite of Passage, and Miss Treason pulls it off perfectly.

And she succeeds in her aim of turning herself into a myth. Within a few weeks of her death, her grave was covered with scraps of paper pegged down with sticks, each bearing a message:

> *'Miss Treason please keep my boy Joe save at see.'*
> *'Miss treason, I'm goin bald please help.'*
> *'Miss Treason, please find our girl Becky what run away I'm sorry.'*

Even though there was a new young witch dispensing justice – and quite impressively too, in her own way – people still put their trust and hopes in what they knew. They brought their small prayers to Miss Treason's grave, just as the shepherds of the Chalk left packets of Jolly Sailor tobacco where Granny Aching's old shepherding hut used to stand:

> They didn't write their petitions down, but they were there, all the same, floating in the air:
> 'Granny Aching, who herds the clouds in the blue sky, please watch my sheep. Granny Aching, cure my son. Granny Aching, find my lambs.'

And so a witch, or a shepherdess, can indeed turn into a myth – a local saint – maybe even a goddess. It's been known before, and it still goes on, and not just on the Discworld. Go visit Biddy Early's cottage.

Chapter 11

THE CHALK

THE LAND

THE REGION KNOWN TO ITS PEOPLE simply as 'the Chalk' lies on the Sto Plains about fifty miles from Lancre. It is a land of gentle, rolling, turf-covered hills with occasional patches of woodland, small villages and scattered farmsteads. Above all, it is good land for sheep.

No other place on Discworld is so patently a thinly disguised part of Earth. The Tiffany Aching/Wee Free Men books are, whatever other splendid things they may be, a hymn to a time and a landscape. And here it's found as it was in the time of our great-grandfathers – open country, unfenced, unploughed, turf-covered, a land fit for sheep.

> Green downlands roll under the hot midsummer sun . . . the flocks of sheep, moving slowly, drift over the short turf like clouds on a green sky. Here and there sheepdogs speed over the turf like comets.
>
> And then, as the eyes pull back, it is a long green mound, lying like a great whale on the world . . . [*The Wee Free Men*]

In both worlds, these lands are full of memories of distant times:

> Men had been everywhere on the Chalk. There were stone circles, half fallen down, and burial mounds like green pimples

where, it was said, chieftains of the olden days had been buried with their treasure. No one fancied digging into them to find out.

There were odd carvings in the chalk, too, which the shepherds sometimes weeded when they were out on the downs with the flocks and there was not a lot to do. The chalk was only a few inches under the turf. Hoofprints could last a season, but the carvings had lasted for thousands of years. They were pictures of horses and giants, but the strange thing was that you couldn't see them properly from anywhere on the ground. They looked as if they'd been made for viewers in the sky.

The oldest and most magical of the carvings on the Chalk is the White Horse, on a steep hillside at the head of a little valley (on Earth, the place is called Uffington, in Berkshire, and it is on the north slopes of the Berkshire Downs). It was cut out of the turf way back in the earliest times, perhaps by the same folk who raised the stone circles and buried their dead in the mounds, and for generation after generation people have kept it clear of grass and weeds. It doesn't look much like a horse, not unless you look at it in the right way. It's just lines – long, flowing lines that don't even join up – but, as Granny Aching told Tiffany's father when he was only a little boy, ''Tain't what a horse *looks* like, it's what a horse *be*.' And if the Chalk has a guardian spirit, this is it.

The landscape is full of stories. A hill near Tiffany's home, for instance:

There was a flat place at the top where nothing ever grew, and Tiffany knew there was a story that a hero had once fought a dragon up there and its blood had burned the ground where it fell. There was another story that said there was a heap of treasure under the hill, *defended* by the dragon, and *another* story that said a king was buried there in armour of solid gold.

There were lots of stories about the hill; it was surprising it hadn't sunk under the weight of them.

In our world, there is just such a Dragon Hill, with just such a flat, bare top where a dragon's blood was spilled – in that case, by St George. It is at Uffington, alongside the White Horse. Elsewhere, on the South Downs, there are many hills and burial mounds in which, according to local tales, there are pots of gold, or dead men lying in their golden armour.

Interesting things can be found in or on the Chalk. There are small sharp flint arrowheads, made by men thousands of years before (on the Discworld, though alas not on *our* Chalk, shepherds still have the skill of chipping flints into very sharp little knives, for their own amusement; it is said that a good flint is sharper than a scalpel). Occasionally, one can pick up a stone with a hole in it; these are called 'dobby stones', just as they are in the Yorkshire Dales, and are said to be lucky. Tiffany keeps one in her pocket, though she is unsure what use it is; if she lived in Yorkshire, she would know you can hang them at your door or window to keep evil spirits out, and over your bed to prevent nightmares. She also keeps a fossilized sea urchin, which she once used as part of a shamble; it is the sort which looks like a bun with grooves on it making a five-pointed star, which on the Sussex Downs is called a 'shepherd's crown'. It's said that if you put them on the kitchen windowsill they will keep thunderstorms away and prevent milk from going sour.

THE SHEPHERDS' LIFE

Iron-wheeled shepherding huts like the one Granny Aching used were once common all along the South Downs, and indeed in other sheep-rearing regions too. Shepherds lived in them at lambing time, when it was essential to stay near the ewes day and night; they were also used at other times of year, but less regularly. They were sturdy wooden structures, warmed by a small stove, with a chair, a table, a simple bunk bed, and plenty of shelves, boxes and hooks to hold the shepherd's gear – a horn lantern, crooks, shears, knives, a hay fork, a feeding bottle for sickly lambs and a saucepan to warm the milk for them, tins and bottles of sheep medicines, one or two spare sheep bells, and so on. The huts would be set up close to the lambing-fold; farm horses could draw them from place to place, if need be. The stove made the hut very cosy indeed, though sheep tended to creep under it on cold nights, their stomachs gurgling and rumbling till the dawn – but the shepherd would probably snooze in his chair at busy times, and be too tired to notice.

To count their flocks, Discworld shepherds have special words and a special way of reckoning, known only to them (and to the Nac Mac Feegle). It begins with 'yan tan tethera' for 'one two three', and goes up as far as 'jiggit' for twenty. There it stops. The same system was used by English shepherds, and sometimes also by fishermen reckoning their catch and women counting the stitches of their knitting. Bits of it are still remembered by children when they are 'counting out' to start a game. The names of the numbers vary a bit, but they are always grouped in fives and make a kind of rhyme; for instance:

Yan, tan, tethera, pethera, pimp;
Sethera, lethera, hovera, dovera, dick;
Yaner-dick, taner-dick, tether-dick, pether-dick, bumfit;
Yaner-bumfit, taner-bumfit, tether-bumfit, pether-bumfit, jiggit.

Maybe one reason children have remembered this ditty is that some of the words do sound a bit rude.

When he reached 'jiggit', the shepherd would cut a notch on a stick, or put a stone in his pocket, and start over again. When all the sheep were counted, he would reckon up his notches or stones; suppose there were 123 sheep, this would mean six notches, plus three extra beasts – 'six score sheep and three'.

It sounds cumbersome, but in fact comes easily to any creature that has two hands, with five fingers on each hand. The idea of reckoning by twenties has left traces on the English language even where the special words are not used, as when a psalm says: 'The days of our age are threescore years and ten, and though men be so strong that they come to fourscore years, yet is their strength but labour and sorrow.' In French too, the word for 'eighty', *quatre-vingts*, means literally 'four twenties'. Come to that, in English currency there used to be twenty shillings to the pound.

At lambing time, shepherds are extremely busy, too busy to come down off the hills. And so they are at sheep-dipping time, sheep-washing time, sheep-shearing time, and in the run-up to sheep fairs. This rather gets in the way of regular religion, and may cause offence to some of the more touchy gods, who dislike being neglected. To make sure there were no unwelcome consequences in the afterlife, precautions were taken at the funerals of Discworld shepherds:

> Granny Aching had been wrapped in a woollen blanket, with a tuft of raw wool pinned to it. That was a special shepherd thing. It was there to tell any gods who might get involved that the person being buried there was a shepherd, and spent a lot of time on the hills, and what with lambing and one thing and another couldn't always take much time out for religion, there being no churches or temples up there, and so it was generally hoped that the gods would understand and look kindly on them. [*The Wee Free Men*]

This was done on Earth, too: in some villages of the South Downs up to the 1930s shepherds were buried with a lock of wool in their hands, so that at the Last Judgement they could prove what their work had been, and why they had so often missed church on Sundays. Occasionally, a crook, shears and a sheep-bell were also put in the coffin. It all added up to the same thing: a hope and also perhaps a belief that one Good Shepherd would recognize another.

Granny Aching's grave was dug on the hill, alongside her hut, and after the funeral there was an additional and very unusual ceremony – the hut was burned. There wasn't any shepherd, anywhere on the Chalk, who would use it after her. This was a mark of respect, almost unparalleled on Earth, where only Gypsies would think of making such a gesture.

THE WATCHING OF THE DEAD

A newly dead corpse must be carefully prepared, watched over, protected – and treated with caution, for it might become dangerous.

> People died. It was sad, but they did. What did you do next? People expected the local witch to know. So you washed the body and did a few secret and squelchy things and dressed them in their best clothes and laid them out with bowls of earth and salt beside them (no one knew why you did this bit, but it had always been done) and you put two pennies on their eyes 'for the ferryman' and you sat with them the night before they were buried, because they shouldn't be left alone.
>
> Exactly why was never properly explained, although everyone had been told the story of the old man who was slightly less dead than everyone thought and rose up off the spare bed in the middle of the night and got back into bed with his wife. [*Wintersmith*]

Things were done in much the same way on Earth, in the days when people died at home (not in a hospital) and were laid out at home (not in an undertaker's parlour). Laying out the corpse was both a practical necessity and a social duty; it was a woman's task, and was often done by the local midwife. It involved washing the body, plugging its orifices, and closing the eyes and mouth – and ensuring that they remained closed, by laying a penny on each eye, and tying up the jaws with a bandage under the chin which was knotted on top of the head. A man would be shaved, a woman would have her hair braided. Then the body would either be dressed in good clothes or wrapped tightly in a winding-sheet, with its legs straightened and tied at the ankles and its arms crossed over the chest. The face would not be covered. That way, everything looked clean and decent when family and neighbours came to 'view the body' before it was coffined.

These actions were not just practical. Washing the body could be seen as a purification which echoes baptism, like the Catholic custom of sprinkling a corpse with holy water; a Suffolk woman who used to lay out the dead told the social historian Ruth Richardson in 1980 that 'the washing is so you're spotless to meet the Lamb of God'.

The pennies had once had a mythical meaning too. In England in the seventeenth century, the antiquarian John Aubrey reported that some old-fashioned people still put a coin in the mouth of the dead 'to give to St Peter' at the gates of Heaven. Way back in Ancient Greek and Roman times people used to put a coin into the dead person's mouth 'to pay the ferryman'; his name was Charon, and he would row the dead across the river Styx, which was the boundary of the Underworld. And so too in the Discworld there is also (sometimes) a Styx to be crossed, and a cowled ferryman to be paid.

> 'I have the money,' Roland repeated. 'Two pennies is the rate to cross the River of the Dead. It's an old tradition. Two pennies to put on the eyes of the dead, to pay the ferryman.'
> [*Wintersmith*]

Nobody had given Tiffany any explanation for the bowls of salt and earth which she had to set down beside the corpse. In many countries on Earth the same thing was done, and various reasons were offered. The most common was that it prevents the body swelling – which might well work, if the dishes were heavy enough and were laid actually on the chest or belly, as they generally were. As one Welsh woman said, 'There's no weight so heavy as salt gets when it is on the dead.' Other people gave a religious explanation. In Highland Scotland in the mid eighteenth century, people said the earth was an emblem of the corruptible body, and the salt of the immortal spirit. In nineteenth-century Sussex, they said that to sprinkle a good handful of salt over the body would prevent the Devil flying away with it. It is common for salt to be used in religion and magic to drive away evil spirits; this may be because it resists decay – salted meat and fish last much longer. (Western people now, who worry that too much salt is bad for one's health, might find it hard to believe how important the getting and keeping of salt was to their ancestors.)

The unspoken reason behind much of the ritual, on the Disc and on Earth too, is the need to prevent any demons who might be around from getting at the corpse before it is safely buried, and to stop the corpse itself from reviving as a malevolent zombie or vampire. So the dead must never be left alone; someone should sit with them, night and day, and there must always be candles or lamps burning. These keep the evil spirits and ghosts away, and light up the deceased's journey to the otherworld. And they keep the watcher safe.

Because sitting up with the dead is – well, just a little strange. Sometimes the body makes little noises in the night, or moves just a bit, and you have to remind yourself firmly that it's simply because it's cooling down. And there are so many stories of worse things. Suppose the candle goes out, and the corpse sits up, saying, 'Isn't it fun in the dark?' They say that happened once in Iceland; luckily the watcher was a strong man, who flung himself on the corpse, forced it on to its back, and held it down till daybreak. Or suppose the Devil gets into the house and tries to carry off the body? Or suppose that, as Petunia tells Tiffany, a thousand vampire demons arrive, each with enormous teeth? (Never chronicled, as far as we know.)

All things considered, it's not surprising that in many parts of the multiverse people prefer to do their corpse-watching in groups and make a proper wake of it, with cards, tobacco, and a nip of whisky to get them through the night. And a prayer or two doesn't come amiss.

An Incursion of Monsters

All regions of the Discworld are at risk of invasion by predatory races from elsewhere in the multiverse, since one universe quite often collides with another. When this happens, the roaming predators may well find some weak or 'thin' place, where people are off their guard, and where they can open a door between the worlds. In the case of the Chalk, as we learn from *The Wee Free Men*, it is the Queen of the Fairies who finds a way through from her own small and icy world, where nothing grows and no sun shines, and everything has to be stolen from elsewhere. And with her come the monsters.

> 'D'you know what'll be turning up?' asked Miss Tick. 'All the things they locked away in those old stories. All those reasons why you shouldn't stray off the path, or open the forbidden door, or say the wrong word, or spill salt. All the stories that give children nightmares. All the monsters from under the biggest bed in the world.'

The first to arrive is Jenny Greenteeth, erupting out of a shallow stream, and trying to snatch Tiffany's little brother. She has long skinny arms, a thin face with long sharp teeth, huge eyes, and dripping green hair like waterweed. She is, as Miss Tick explains, nothing more than a Grade One Prohibitory Monster – that is to say, a creature deliberately invented by adults to scare children away from dangerous places. But though the adults don't believe they're real, the children do, and so they *become* real. (This also happens in Ankh-Morpork, as we shall see later.)

On Earth too, adults have invented many Prohibitory Monsters (also called Nursery Bogeys), including a Jenny or Ginny Greenteeth who lurks in deep pools of stagnant water, hiding under the duckweed. She was well known in Lancashire, Cheshire and Shropshire. Even in the 1980s, elderly people remembered being warned against her as children. In his *Plant Lore* (1995) the botanist and folklorist Roy Vickery records what one Merseyside woman told him:

> 'As I recall, Ginny only lived in ponds which were covered in a green weed of the type that has tiny leaves, and covers the entire surface of the pond. The theory was that Ginny enticed little children into the pools by making them look like grass and safe to walk upon. As soon as the child stepped on to the green, it of course parted, and the child fell through into Ginny's clutches and drowned. The green weed then closed over, hiding all traces of the child ever having been there. This last point was the one which really terrified me and kept me well away from ponds. As far as I know Ginny had no known form, due to the fact that she never appeared above the surface of the pond.'

But another Merseyside woman knew exactly what the Jenny Greenteeth who inhabited two pools in Fazakerley looked like: 'pale green skin, green teeth, very long green locks of hair, long green fingers with long nails, and she was very thin with a pointed chin and very big eyes'. Jenny was not the only creature of this species in England. In Leicester there was a Polly Long Arms hiding in the green murky water of the canal, waiting to drag in any child that came near the edge.

The next menacing creature to arrive in the Chalk country is a dark rider, a horseman who has no face – since he has no head to hang a face on. Now, ghosts that appear as headless horsemen are quite common in the Earthly world, but this creature might be something worse than a mere ghost. Especially as it *breathes* through the windpipe it hasn't got, making a wheezy whistling noise which one really would rather not be hearing. Earthbound headless horsemen tend to be more spectral.

Later, the Queen sends three of her grimhounds – big heavy-built black dogs with orange eyebrows, eyes of red fire, and teeth like razor blades. They are said to haunt churchyards. This would imply a connection with the Church Grim, a sinister animal which, according to Earthly tradition, patrols graveyards and is an omen of death for anyone who sees it. In Britain the Grim is a Black Dog; in Scandinavia, there are also Grims which are lame grey horses, three-legged lambs or black pigs. They are said to be the ghosts of real animals deliberately killed when a churchyard was established and buried on the north side, to be its guardian. If this wasn't done, people thought that the first person buried there would not enter Heaven but would have to remain on duty as a ghostly sentinel till the end of the world.

Most of the Black Dogs of our world are grim creatures, in nature if not in name; some are ghosts (of humans or of dogs), but the majority are demons and devils in animal form. Indeed, the Black Dog or Hell Hound is a universally recognized image of evil in European and American folklore. They are generally large, shaggy creatures with huge fiery eyes (unless they happen to be headless); they may wear collars of flame, or drag heavy clanking chains. However, their eyebrows are never mentioned. Only in the folklore of Estonia is it said that a dog (a real flesh-and-blood one, not a demon) which has patches of different colour on its eyebrows has 'four eyes', and can detect and attack beings that are invisible to humans. This would appear to be a good thing. Nevertheless, the principle 'Never trust a dog with orange eyebrows', discovered on the Discworld, is so self-evidently true and useful that it will surely spread.

FOUND IN A FISH

And then there was that odd business with the fish, as told in *Wintersmith*. You would really think that if someone drops or throws into deep water something small but too heavy to float (a ring, say, or a key), that's the last he or she will ever see of it.

In fact you probably wouldn't, depending on your childhood reading. You might already know that a powerful narrative drive decrees that it will be swallowed by a fish, and one day that fish will be caught, and when it's being gutted something glittery will be found in its belly, and will be brought to the very person who lost it in the first place. Which is precisely how Tiffany's precious silver horse pendant returned to her, although she had thrown it into a river.

Here on Earth, such things have been happening, off and on, for many centuries. Polycrates, who ruled in Samos some two-and-a-half thousand years ago, was so rich and had such constant good luck that they say a friend warned him that the gods would soon be jealous, and advised him to create some deliberate bad luck by losing something he really valued. So Polycrates took a magnificent seal-ring, the finest of his jewels, and threw it into the sea. But a few days later someone sent a beautiful big fish as a gift for the king's table, and in its belly . . . It was not long before Polycrates was treacherously captured and killed.

Or again, in Ireland in St Patrick's time, there was a robber called Macaldus who tried to trick the saint and make a fool of him, but then repented, and promised to do whatever penance was fitting. St Patrick wrapped a chain round him and padlocked it and threw the key in a river, and then set Macaldus adrift in a small boat, telling him to go wherever God sent him, and to wear the chain until the key was returned to him. The boat floated out to sea, and finally came to the Isle of Man, where Macaldus was taken into the Bishop's household and led a holy life. One day the Bishop's cook was puzzled to find a key inside a fish he was cleaning . . . so Macaldus was able to take the chain off. He eventually became Bishop of Man himself, and is reckoned to be a saint. There was also St Egwin, founder of Evesham Abbey and Bishop of Worcester from 692 till his death in 711. Falsely accused of crimes, he put fetters on his legs, threw the key into the Avon, and set off on pilgrimage to Rome to convince the Pope of his innocence. And there, in the market, he happened to buy a fish . . . The Pope duly cleared him of all charges and restored him to his diocese.

It is particularly striking that the fish which swallowed Tiffany's pendant should be a pike, for in the Yorkshire town of Pickering people say it got its name because Pendirus, a legendary king of the Britons who is alleged to have reigned there about 270 BC, lost his *ring* while bathing in the river Costa, but later recovered it from the belly of a *pike*. Everyone knows pikes will swallow just about anything. So will some people. Nevertheless, there is a comfort in these stories, even for the godless. They suggest a kind of cosmic rightness. And they still turn up, every few years.

PS: An odd thing happened to Terry once. He bought a ring in a small shop in Pike Place Market, Seattle. It was slightly over-sized and he soon lost it, and couldn't find it anywhere. A year later he was back in the city, went to the same shop to buy a replacement, and in reaching into his jacket pocket (a jacket which, of course, he'd worn many times during the year) for some loose change, he put a finger through the very same ring. How could it have been otherwise? Rings try to find their way back to their owner. Someone ought to write a book about it.

THE DANCE OF WINTER AND SUMMER

It has long been believed, and may very well be true, that the whole multiverse moves in one perpetual dance, though almost all its motions are either too swift or too slow for the human mind to grasp. Whirling electrons, wheeling galaxies, cycles of time, cycles of energy, the pulsations of the blood, angels in the skies or on the head of a pin – all make patterns in the cosmic dance. This is not a matter of couples moving independently (like a waltz), nor of a group simply dancing hand-in-hand in a ring; it involves complicated figures in which dancers change places and partners, advance and retreat, meet and part and meet again.

Many poets have written about this. Sir John Davies in his *Orchestra* (1596) declared that everything in heaven and earth dances:

> Kind nature first doth cause all things to love,
> Love makes them dance, and in just order move.

And so the sun dances with the earth, flowers with the wind, the tides with the moon:

> And lo the sea, that fleets about the land
> And like a girdle clips her solid waist,
> Music and measure both doth understand;
> For his great crystal eye is ever cast
> Up to the moon and on her fixèd fast.
> And as she danceth in her pallid sphere,
> So danceth he about his centre here.

In John Milton's *Comus* (1637), a magician boasts that by dancing while others sleep, he and his companions are echoing the dance of time and nature:

> We that are of purer fire
> Imitate the starry choir,
> Who, in their nightly watchful spheres
> Lead in swift round the months and years.
> Oceans and seas, with all their finny drove,
> Now to the moon in wavering morrice move . . .

Others too have sensed that the Morris has a particular affinity with the cycles of nature. T. S. Eliot wrote in *East Coker* (1940) of glimpsing ghostly Morris Men round a bonfire on a summer midnight, with their 'music of the weak pipe and the little drum',

> Keeping time,
> Keeping the rhythm in their dancing
> As in their living in the living seasons
> The time of the seasons and the constellations
> The time of milking and the time of harvest
> The time of the coupling of man and woman
> And that of beasts. Feet rising and falling.
> Eating and drinking. Dung and death.

In *Wintersmith* we learn more about the Dark Morris, first brought to our attention in *Reaper Man*, when Tiffany is taken one icy midnight to a clearing in a leafless wood, where six men, their faces blacked and wearing black clothes, dance to the powerful beat of a silent drum, while shadowy forms look on. She already knows the white-clad Morris teams that dance on the village green to bring Summer in, but what is this? Unable to resist the beat, she runs forward and jumps into the dance, weaving to and fro in the space where a team's Fool should go, and becoming aware for a few seconds that someone other than human is dancing with her.

What she has seen is part of the never-ending Dance of the Seasons, in which the Wintersmith and the Summer Lady meet and change places in spring and autumn. Explaining this, Miss Treason shows her a picture in *Chaffinch's Ancient and Classical Mythology* of a tall, blonde, beautiful Summer, carrying a cornucopia and dancing with old grey Winter, who has icicles in his beard.

> 'The year is round! The wheel of the world must spin! That is why up here they dance the Dark Morris, to balance it. They welcome the winter because of the new summer deep inside it!'

The spring and autumn Morris dances are a way of marking the moment when the season of ice and the season of fire meet briefly to exchange their dominion over the world. In our world, other ways have been found of bringing Summer in – a young man dressed in leaves and flowers fights and defeats an older man dressed in furs; girls carry an ugly straw figure called Winter or Death out of the village, tear it to bits or throw it into a river, and come back carrying leafy branches; people bring in the maypole. Frazer's *The Golden Bough* has much to say about all this. At the other end of the year, the secrets are better kept, yet even so one can guess that in the season of bonfires and fireworks, nuts and apples, beer, beef, and new wine, there is an underlying celebration that Winter is taking over the power that is rightfully his – for a while. And at midwinter, there is guising, feasting, mummers' plays, and yes, Morris dancing again. The wheel spins.

But Tiffany has made a serious mistake by entering the dance herself. She has taken the place of the Summer Lady, attracting the attention of the Wintersmith, and now is trapped in her role. She is turning into a goddess, or at least an avatar, or an anthropomorphic personification.

The first symptom is that she develops 'Fertile Feet' – wherever she treads with bare feet, flowers spring up. Even the floorboards in Nanny Ogg's cottage, being wood, start sprouting leaves. Much the same thing happened to Prince Teppic of Djelibeybi as soon as the spirit of his father, a recently deceased pharaoh, entered into him, as is told in *Pyramids*. Even on the cobbled streets of Ankh-Morpork grass appeared where he put his feet, and in the bakers' shops loaves cracked open and grew wheat.

On Earth too, avatars of Spring or Summer are, very understandably, credited with the gift of Fertile Feet. In the medieval Welsh tale of 'Culhwch and Olwen' in the *Mabinogion*, it is said of the lovely young heroine that 'four white trefoils sprang up behind her wherever she went, and for that reason was she called Olwen' – which means 'white track'. The Italian painter Botticelli represents Primavera (Spring) as a beautiful woman walking across a flower-filled glade, throwing down more flowers as she goes, which is the closest a painter can get to the idea that they spring up as she passes. And then there are four famous lines from a poem written by Alexander Pope in 1704, when he was only sixteen:

Where'er you walk, cool gales shall fan the glade;
Trees, where you sit, shall crowd into a shade;
Where'er you tread, the blushing flowers shall rise,
And all things flourish where you turn your eyes.

The poem is one of a set of four seasonal love-poems, and is entitled
'Summer'. These particular lines are so famous because Handel set
them to music in his opera *Semele*, as a song addressed by the god
Jupiter to the human girl he loves. They are so appropriate to
Tiffany's situation that they cross over into the Discworld and into
the mind of the schoolmistressy witch, Miss Tick:

'The myth of the Summer Lady says that flowers grow wher-
ever she walks,' said Granny Weatherwax.
'*Where e'er*,' said Miss Tick primly.
'What?' snapped Granny, who was now pacing up and down
in front of the fire.
'It's where e'er she walks, in fact,' said Miss Tick. 'It's more
. . . poetical.'
'Hah,' Granny said. 'Poetry!' [*Wintersmith*]

The next sign of Tiffany's new status is that a Cornucopia (aka
Horn of Plenty) crash-lands in the garden. It is a curly shell-like
object, of magically variable size, containing every kind of fruit,
vegetable and grain – in fact, it turns out, anything and everything
one can eat or drink. These things it produces on request, in lavish
quantities. It is a definitely mythological object:

'According to Chaffinch,' [Tiffany] said, with the *Mythology*
open on her lap . . . , 'the god Blind Io created the Cornucopia
from a horn of the magical goat Almeg to feed his two children
by the Goddess Bisonomy, who was later turned into a shower

of oysters by Epidity, god of things shaped like potatoes, after insulting Resonata, goddess of weasels, by throwing a mole at her shadow. It is now the badge of office of the Summer Goddess.'

The corresponding myth in Ancient Greece is not *quite* so complicated. As a baby, the god Zeus had to be hidden from his murderous father in a cave in Crete, where he fed on the milk of a nanny-goat called Amalthea (unless this was the name of the nymph who owned her). Later, when he became ruler of the gods, he showed his gratitude by placing the goat among the stars as the constellation Capricorn. But first he broke off one of her horns; it became the Cornucopia, which supplies whatever food or drink one desires. This horn later belonged to Demeter, also called Ceres, goddess of the harvest, and was sometimes carried by Flora, the flower goddess, who scattered corn and wine and fruit and flowers from it. Painters and sculptors are very fond of it, it's such a pretty shape.

Tiffany struggles to cope with these rather embarrassing attributes, and the even more embarrassing compliments lavished on her by the Wintersmith. But where, meanwhile, is the real Summer Lady? It turns out that, like many a goddess before her, she is trapped in the Underworld, powerless to return. Without her presence, the Disc will suffer permanent and catastrophic discal cooling, with incalculable environmental repercussions. It is, in short, time for a Hero and a Descent into the Underworld.

This Descent is one of the most powerful stories in the multiverse. On Earth, for example, it can be found in one form or another in at least a dozen mythologies from ancient Babylonia onwards. Sometimes it is a god or goddess who descends, sometimes a human. Sometimes the purpose is to gain foreknowledge by questioning the dead; sometimes it is to learn the secret of immortality, or to carry off a magical object; but most often, it is to rescue a captive. There have been missions that were entirely successful, as when Odysseus went down to consult the dead seer Tiresias or when Herakles (Hercules) brought Queen Alkmene back from the dead; and others that failed, most famously when Orpheus lost his beloved Eurydice when they had very nearly reached the land of the living, because he looked back at her.

And some myths tell of partial successes – and these, curiously, are linked to the cycle of the seasons, just like the rescue of the Disc's Summer Lady. The oldest comes from ancient Sumeria, about 2000 BC, and tells how the great goddess Ishtar went into the Underworld,

> To the Land of No Return, the realm of Ereshkigal,
> To the house which none leaves who has entered it,
> To the road from which there is no way back,
> To the house wherein the entrants are bereft of life,
> Where dust is their fare and clay their food,
> Where they see no light, residing in darkness,
> Where they are clothed like birds, with wings for garments,
> And where over door and bolt is spread dust.
>
> [*Ishtar's Descent*, transl. John Gray]

She was seeking her human lover Tammuz, who had apparently been kidnapped by Ereshkigal, Queen of the Underworld, and was now among the dead. Ishtar fought Ereshkigal, but was defeated, tortured, and held captive in a corpse-like condition. Without her, there was nothing but famine and sterility on earth, so the High Gods forced Ereshkigal to sprinkle Ishtar with the water of life and let her go free. Tammuz too was revived and freed, but not entirely; every year he died again during the long sterile drought season, and the people wept for him. But then, with the coming of the rains, he returned to life.

Similarly in Classical Greece and Rome, myths told how Demeter (Ceres), the goddess of fertile crops and harvest, was distraught with grief when her daughter Persephone (Proserpina) was kidnapped. Neglecting her divine duties, Demeter went searching everywhere for Persephone, until she found her girdle floating in a pool near a great crevice which was known to be an entrance to the Underworld. This remarkably fortuitous clue proved that it was Hades (Pluto), god of death, who had carried her off. Demeter did not descend into the Underworld herself, but appealed to Zeus for justice. Zeus knew that without Demeter's care all crops would fail, so he decreed that Persephone could return to earth, provided she had eaten nothing while in the realm of Hades. But, alas, she had eaten – a mere trifle, just six pomegranate seeds – but because of this Zeus ruled that she must spend six months of the year in the Underworld, though she could come back to earth for the other six. Which is why there are six months of summer and six of winter.

'They are ancient stories. They have a life of their own. They long to be repeated. Summer rescued from a cave? Very old,' said Granny Weatherwax.

So Tiffany's friend Roland de Chumsfanleigh (pronounced Chuffley) makes the Descent, accompanied by Feegles, and passes through a cave into a gloomy land of shadows and mindless people whose memories have been stolen by bogles. There is a dark river and a dark ferryman who as we have seen has to be paid with two pennies from the eyes of the dead, just as in Earthly myth there is the river Styx and Charon the ferryman who takes coins from the mouths of the dead. And then:

There was a big pile of bones on the path. They were certainly animal bones, and the rotting collars and lengths of rusted chain were another clue.

'Three big dogs?' said Roland.

'One verrae big dog wi' three heids,' said Rob Anybody. 'Verrae popular in underworlds, that breed. Can bite right through a man's throat. Three times!' he added, with relish. 'But put three doggy biscuits in a row on the groound and the puir wee thing sits there strainin' and whinin' all day. It's a wee laff, I'm tellin' ye!'

In the classical myths of Earth, the representative of this three-headed breed is called Cerberus. It is his task to guard the entrance of the Underworld so that no one alive may enter, nor may any of the dead escape – but his attention can be distracted by throwing him soft cakes sweetened with honey (and, preferably, also laced with poppy juice). He was also once lulled by the music of Orpheus, and once he was overwhelmed by the physical strength of Herakles. But mostly he is just sitting there, on guard.

Despite all perils, Roland brings the Summer Lady back to the upper world, and Tiffany finds a way to dismiss the Wintersmith. The Dance of the Seasons resumes, in which Summer and Winter must each die and sleep and wake again, year after year. No one should meddle with it.

'Here is the heart of the summer,' hissed the voice of the Summer Lady. 'Fear me as much as the wintersmith. We are not yours, though you give us shapes and names. Fire and ice we are, in balance. Do not come between us again . . .'

Chapter 12

HEROES!

W E'RE NOT TALKING ABOUT SMALL-H HEROES, here. Given a smidgeon of courage and a suitable crisis, practically anybody could turn out to be a small-h hero. But a capital-h Hero is a star in the firmament of myth and legend, a precious asset to any bard or storyteller who happens to meet him. People hoping for a quiet life are less enthusiastic, since a considerable amount of mayhem erupts wherever a Hero passes, even one who is seeking justice rather than, say, the green eye of the little yellow god.

Heroes come in two main types: the Heir to the Kingdom, and the Barbarian. Both are recognizable by certain signs, well known to anyone who knows anything about folklore and the power of narrativium, and abound in the semi-historical legends of many nations. Less common is the First (or Culture) Hero, found on the Discworld and in certain Earthly mythologies. Yet since he is the most ancient of the three, it is only right to begin with him.

THE FIRST HERO

In the myths and folklore of some lands there are tales of a First Hero who walked the earth at the dawn of time, bringing mankind essential gifts and skills without which society could not survive. Such a hero is more than human, but he is not a god; indeed, he may be acting in defiance of gods who wish to keep men helpless and ignorant. In one way he is the opposite of the Barbarian Hero, since he brings civilization, not mere pillage and carnage; some therefore call him the Culture Hero. His courage is the courage of endurance.

On the Disc, the First Hero's name is Mazda – a remarkable coincidence, since on Earth there is a morally admirable deity called Mazda who is the god of light, truth, and justice in Zoroastrianism, the ancient religion of Persia (Iran). He is the Power of Good, locked in combat with the evil Ahriman, whom he will defeat at the Last Day. The Discworld's Mazda is not so exalted, but he too worked for good, and suffered for it. Of course, much depends on the point of view, since an unsympathetic mind would say that what he did was theft. He stole fire from the gods.

'I thought I'd start off with the legend of how Mazda stole fire for mankind in the first place,' said the minstrel.

'Nice,' said Cohen.

'And then a few verses about what the gods did to him.'

'Did to him? Did to him?' said Cohen. 'They made him immortal!'

'Er . . . yes. In a *way*, I suppose.'

'What do you mean, "in a way"?'

'It's classical mythology, Cohen,' said the minstrel. 'I thought everyone knew. He was chained to a rock for eternity and every day an eagle comes and pecks out his liver.'

'I'm not much of a reader,' said Cohen. 'Chained to a rock? For a first offence? He's still there?'

'Eternity isn't finished yet, Cohen.'

'He must've had a big liver!'

'It grows again every night, according to legend,' said the minstrel.

Cohen stared at the distant clouds that hid the snowy top of the mountain. 'He brought fire to everyone, and the gods did that to him, eh? Well . . . we'll have to see about that.' [*The Last Hero*]

This is indeed, as the minstrel says, a classical myth. In Ancient Greece, it was the story of Prometheus, the benefactor of mankind – maybe even the creator of mankind, for some old writers claimed that he formed the bodies of the first men and women from water and clay, after which the goddess Athene breathed life into them. Whether that is true or not, all agree that he brought them civilization, teaching them the skills he had himself learned from Athene – metal-working, building, mathematics, astronomy, medicine – to the great anger of Zeus, who had intended them to remain ignorant. And then, to cap it all, Prometheus stole fire from the gods. He lit a torch from the chariot of the sun, broke off a smouldering ember, hid it in a hollow stalk of fennel, and so carried it down to the earth as a gift to humanity.

Furious, Zeus had Prometheus stripped naked and chained to a rock in the Caucasian mountains. Every day at dawn a monstrous bird, part griffin and part vulture, would fly down and tear his body open, pecking out and eating his liver; every night, as he lay freezing, his liver would grow again, ready for the dawn. Yet he knew he would be released one day. And so it was. When Prometheus had spent a thousand years fettered to the rock (or, some say, ten thousand), Herakles, a hero of the wild and monster-slaying type, persuaded Zeus to let him shoot the griffin-vulture through the heart and set Prometheus free. The Barbarian Hero came to the rescue of the Culture Hero, on Earth as on the Disc.

THE ROYAL HEIR

The people of Ankh-Morpork know all about heirs who arrive incognito to claim their rightful kingdom and turn out to be ideal rulers, brave, wise and just:

> The throne had been empty for more than two thousand years,
> since the death of the last of the line of the kings of Ankh.

Legend said that one day the city would have a king again, and went on with various comments about magic swords, strawberry birthmarks, and all the other things that legends gabble on about in these circumstances. [*Sourcery*]

What is more, pretty well all of them know the rumour that such an heir is currently living in the city, as a mere watchman. And they can put a name to him: Captain Carrot Ironfoundersson (a conspiracy to groom Nobby Nobbs for the role failed utterly). In fact, the only person who *seems* unaware of the rumour is Carrot himself. He is a foundling; he has a strong sword, well-used, though quite unmagical and lacking any mysterious inscriptions; he has an oddly shaped birthmark, rather like a crown. But *still* he resists the pressures of narrativium, and goes around ignoring his manifest destiny in a most irritating manner.

Perhaps there have been Carrots on Earth, but if so, their strategy has been so successful that nobody has ever heard of them. In that universe, the nearest thing to Carrot's attitude is the naïve simplicity of the teenage Arthur. As is well known, he had no idea he was a dead king's son, and was simply acting as squire to his elder foster-brother Sir Kay. Kay needed a replacement sword to use in a tournament, and sent Arthur to find one. Arthur wandered off into a churchyard, where he noticed something which he thought would come in useful. As Malory writes in his *Morte D'Arthur*:

there was seen in the churchyard . . . a great stone four square, like unto a marble stone, and in the midst thereof was like an anvil of steel a foot on high, and therein stuck a fair sword naked by the point, and letters there were written in gold about the sword that said thus:– Whoso pulleth out this sword of this stone and anvil, is rightwise king born of all England.

Without bothering to read the inscription, Arthur casually pulled the sword out and took it to Kay. When people realized where it had come from, and also that when it was put back nobody but Arthur could get it to move at all, he was acknowledged to be the Long-Lost Heir.

One might easily assume that this was the famed Excalibur which Arthur always bore in battle, but Malory says not – according to his account, the sword drawn from the stone was broken two or three years later in a duel between Arthur and Pellinore, but Merlin promised to find him another:

> So they rode till they came to a lake, the which was a fair water and broad, and in the midst of the lake Arthur was 'ware of an arm clothed in white samite, that held a fair sword in that hand. Lo! said Merlin, yonder is that sword that I spake of. With that they saw a damosel going upon the lake. What damosel is that? said Arthur. That is the Lady of the Lake, said Merlin . . . speak ye fair to her that she will give you that sword . . . And so they went into the ship, and when they came to the sword that the hand held, Sir Arthur took it up by the handles, and took it with him, and the arm and the hand went under the water.

This is the true Excalibur, the one which the dying Arthur ordered Sir Bedivere to throw into a lake:

> Then Sir Bedivere [took up the sword and] went to the water side; and there he bound the girdle about the hilts, and then he threw the sword as far into the water as he might; and there came an arm and an hand above the water and met it, and caught it, and so shook it thrice and brandished, and then vanished away the hand with the sword in the water.

Whether King Arthur ever really died is a mystery. True, there was a tomb for him in the medieval Glastonbury Abbey, but it was a fake, and rumours abounded. As Malory wrote:

Some men say in many parts of England that King Arthur is not dead, but had by the will of Our Lord Jesu into another place, and men say that he shall come again, and he shall win the Holy Cross. I will not say it shall be so, but rather I will say, here in this world he changed his life. But many men say that there is written upon his tomb this verse: *Hic jacet Arthurus, Rex quondam Rexque futurus* ['Here lies Arthur, former King and future King'].

This is no longer the tale of a Lost Heir. This is a Hero of another sort: the Sleeping King under the Mountain, the King who will come back from 'another place' to save his people and achieve heroic feats – a tale we have met already in Lancre and elsewhere. It is a powerful narrative pattern, widely scattered through the multiverse as a consolation and a source of inspiration and hope.

THE BARBARIAN HERO

There was no mistaking that shape. The wide chest, the neck like a tree trunk, the surprisingly small head under its wild thatch of black hair looking like a tomato on a coffin . . . Hrun was one of the Discworld's more durable heroes: a fighter of dragons, a despoiler of temples, a hired sword, the kingpost of every street brawl. He could even speak words of more than two syllables, given time and maybe a hint or two. [*The Colour of Magic*]

Hrun dresses only in a leopard-skin loincloth and numerous gold arm-bands and anklets. It goes without saying that he is totally fearless and unimaginative, while being at the same time as alert to any danger as a cat and as lithe as a panther. His life is one long string of adventures, which don't surprise him in the least:

'Oh,' said Hrun, 'I expect in a minute this dungeon door will be flung back and I'll be dragged off to some sort of temple arena where I'll fight maybe a couple of giant spiders and an eight-foot slave from the jungles of Klatch and then I'll rescue some kind of princess from the altar and then kill off a few guards or whatever and then this girl will show me a secret passage out of the palace and we'll liberate a couple of horses and escape with the treasure.'

Hrun leaned back on his hands and looked up at the ceiling, whistling tunelessly.

'All that?' said Twoflower.

'Usually.'

Earth too knows heroes of this type, notably Conan the Barbarian from Cimmeria, whose many adventures as pirate, mercenary, and eventual war-lord and emperor were chronicled in America in the 1930s by the fantasy writer Robert E. Howard and others. An admirer wrote: 'Conan is a true hero of Valhalla, battling and suffering great wounds by day, carousing and wenching by night, and plunging into fresh adventures tomorrow.' Besides ordinary human enemies, he is forever attacking, or being attacked by, evil lords, sorcerers, witch-queens, magical monsters, dark gods. An indestructible stone toad-thing as bulky as a buffalo, with seven green-glowing eyes, crouching on an altar in a temple of lustreless black stone whose geometry obeys no human laws, is just the kind of thing he *would* meet. He always wins.

A Barbarian Hero, like his Kingly counterpart, often possesses a remarkable sword. Hrun's is called Kring, and he stole it from the impregnable palace of the Archimandrite of B'Ituni. It is forged from black meteoric iron, with highly ornate runes on the blade and rubies on the pommel. Not only does Kring have a name of its own, it has a soul; it talks incessantly in a voice like a claw being scraped across glass, and it has a very irritating personality. In the course of its multidimensional existence it has of course starred in numerous battles, and at one point belonged to a pasha who used it to cut silk handkerchiefs in mid-air; on the other hand, it once spent two hundred years at the bottom of a lake, which was not really fun. Can this possibly mean that Kring has existed on Earth too – that Kring and Excalibur are aspects of a single entity? And is that why Kring remarks, when stuck in a tree branch, that 'it could have been worse, it could have been an anvil'?

Come to think of it, even the tree could be significant. The Volsungs, a family of Norse and Germanic heroes, had as their heir-loom a sword which came to them by way of a test very like Arthur's. Odin, the God of War, had driven it up to the hilt into a tree-trunk, challenging kings and warriors to pull it out: 'Whoso draweth this sword from this tree shall have the same as a gift from me, and shall find in good sooth that never bare he better sword in hand than this.' Sigmund the Volsung was the only one who could draw it out, and it served him well until in his last battle it broke against the spear-shaft of Odin himself. But when Sigmund's son grew up (he is called Sigurd in Iceland, and Siegfried in Germany), he reforged the blade that was broken, naming it Gram, and became an even greater hero than his father had been. Perhaps this too is something Kring knows about.

Many heroes undertake adventures just for the fun of it, while others (young Nijel in *Sorcery*, for instance) see themselves as ruled by a special kind of destiny called a 'geas'. This is a form of the Irish word *geis*, and has nothing at all to do with large, waddling, grey or white birds. It means an obligation, enforced by magical penalties, to do or not to do some particular thing. A hero may be born with a *geis* (or more than one), or someone may lay it on him. Either way, it usually spells trouble, especially if he gets into a situation where two of his *geissa* clash. One great Irish warrior, Cú Chulainn, was trapped in this way. He was under two obligations: one was never to eat dog's flesh, which seems simple enough, but the other was never to refuse an offer of food and hospitality. So when an enemy, knowing this, invited him to a meal of dog-stew he was forced to break either one rule or the other, and was doomed. Nijel, luckily, has no such dilemma.

The greatest by far of the Discworld's Barbarian Heroes is Cohen. Anything others have done, he has done better, faster, more often. He is the bravest, the most famous. He has been an Emperor in the Counterweight Continent, and during this phase of his career was respectfully referred to as Genghis Cohen. There is just one small problem – he is now somewhere around ninety years old. Most of the friends and foes of his younger days are dead. His surviving companions are now known as the Silver Horde. Like him, they suffer a variety of age-related afflictions (piles, deafness, toothlessness, stiff joints), and like him they will never cease to be Heroes.

And yet, in the long run, what does the life of a Hero amount to? Standing on a mountain peak, Cohen surveys the kingdoms of the world as he sets out on his last and greatest enterprise, accompanied by the Silver Horde and a very puzzled minstrel.

'I bin to everywhere I can see,' said Cohen, looking around. 'Been there, done that . . . been there again, done it twice . . . nowhere left where I ain't been.'

The minstrel looked him up and down, and a kind of understanding dawned. I know why you are doing this now, he thought. Thank goodness for a classical education. Now, what was the quote?

' "And Carelinus wept, for there were no more worlds to conquer",' he said.

'Who's that bloke? You mentioned him before,' said Cohen.

'You haven't heard of the Emperor Carelinus?'

'Nope.'

'But he was the greatest conqueror that ever lived! His empire spanned the entire Disc! . . . Well, when he got as far as the coast of Muntab, it was said that he stood on the shore and wept. Some philosopher told him there were more worlds out there somewhere, and that he'd never be able to conquer them. Er . . . that reminded me a bit of you.'

Cohen strolled along in silence for a moment.

'Yeah,' he said at last. 'Yeah, I can see how that could be. Only not as cissy, obviously.' [*The Last Hero*]

And later, trying to explain why he and his companions mean to blow up the mountain of the gods, though they themselves will be killed doing it, Cohen remembers the rage and frustration of Carelinus that the unjust gods have granted such short lives to men:

'I ain't much good with words, but . . . I reckon we're doing this 'cos we *are* goin' to die, d'yer see? And 'cos some bloke got to the edge of the world somewhere and saw all them other worlds out there and burst into tears 'cos there was only one lifetime. So much universe, and so little time. And that's not right.'

Carelinus, the mighty conqueror of distant kingdoms, has a counterpart in the history of Ancient Greece. His name was Alexander the Great, and there are strange similarities in the careers of these two great men. The Knotty Problem, for one. Carelinus once came to the Temple of Offler in Tsort, where there was a huge, complicated knot tying two beams together, and it was said that whoever untied it would reign over the whole continent; Carelinus simply sliced right through it with his sword, and went on to build a huge empire. Was this cheating? Cohen thinks it wasn't:

'It wasn't cheating, because it was a good story. I can just imagine it, too. A load of whey-faced priests and suchlike standin' around and thinkin', "That's *cheatin'*, but he's got a really *big* sword so I won't be the first to point this out, plus this damn great army is just outside." '

Amazingly, exactly the same thing happened to Alexander. As a young general, he led his army into the town of Gordium (near modern Ankara, in Turkey), where there was an ancient ox-cart which their first king had dedicated to Zeus after tying up its axle tree with a weirdly knotted rope. It was prophesied that anyone who could untie it would rule all Asia, but nobody had managed it in over a hundred years. Alexander tried, failed, and then drew his sword and cut it. That night there was a terrible thunderstorm. The priests of Zeus wisely decided this showed the *approval* of the gods.

Another story told of him (if properly understood) shows that he felt just the same way as Carelinus and Cohen did about the limits of his achievements.

It is popularly said that Alexander, at the height of his power, stood on the shores of the Indian Ocean and 'wept to think that there were no worlds left for him to conquer'. Like so much that is popularly said, this is nonsense; it is a medieval legend, not to be found in any ancient source. Alexander was no fool. He knew perfectly well that though he had conquered Afghanistan, reached the borders of Kashmir, and then marched down the Indus Valley to the sea, there remained many more kingdoms in Asia and India which he had not defeated. Come to that, there were large tracts of Europe itself, to the north and west of Greece, where his armies had never set foot. No way could he have thought there was nothing left for him to conquer.

This medieval legend distorts an older and more subtle anecdote, which is to be found in the Ancient Greek author Plutarch – not in his full-scale *Life of Alexander*, but in an essay 'On Contentment of the Mind' in his collection of *Moralia*. Among the members of Alexander's court was a philosopher named Anaxarchus, who by pure reasoning achieved a remarkably modern understanding of the nature of the multiverse. According to Plutarch, 'Alexander wept when he heard Anaxarchus speak about the infinite number of worlds in the universe. One of Alexander's friends asked him what was the matter, and he replied: "There are so many worlds, and I have *not yet conquered even one*." '

Cohen is not alone in sharing the frustration of Carelinus and Alexander. So, in a different way, does the normally cheerful tourist

Twoflower, standing at the rim of the Disc and staring out at the stars.

> 'Sometimes I think a man could wander across the disc all his life and not see all there is to see,' said Twoflower. 'And now it seems there are lots of other worlds as well. When I think I might die without seeing a hundredth of all there is to see it makes me feel,' he paused, then added, 'well, humble, I suppose. And very angry, of course.' [*The Colour of Magic*]

It is also intriguing to note how Fortune (Lady Luck) decided the fate of both Alexander and Cohen by a throw of the dice. Writers in Antiquity and in the Middle Ages argued about the influence of Fortune on the life of Alexander – he had been amazingly successful as a conqueror and ruler, yet he was only 33 when he unexpectedly died, struck down by sickness or, some believed, treacherously poisoned. So was Fortune on Alexander's side or not? Did he owe his achievements to her, or to his own virtues? Did she turn against him in the end? In Chaucer's *Canterbury Tales*, the Monk is certain that she did. He laments over the long list of great men who first enjoyed Fortune's favours, but whom she then betrayed. One of them is Alexander, at one time 'the heir of her honour', till she destroyed him in a game of dice where she magically transformed his winning throw, a six, into the lowest possible one.

> O worthy, noble Alexander, O alas
> That you should ever fall in such a case!
> Poisoned by people of your own you were.
> Your six did Fortune change into an ace,
> And yet she never wept for you one tear.

In the Discworld, Cohen accepts a challenge to roll dice against the harsh god Fate (*not* against Fortune, the Lady). Fate throws a six, and tells Cohen that to win he must throw a seven – though the die is a perfectly normal one with only the regulation six sides.

> 'So . . . seven and I win,' said Cohen. 'It comes down showin'
> seven and I win, right?'
> 'Yes. Of course,' said Fate.
> 'Sounds like a million-to-one chance to me,' said Cohen.
> He tossed the die high in the air, and it slowed as it rose, tumbling glacially with a noise like the *swish* of windmill blades.
> It reached the top of its arc and began to fall.
> Cohen was staring fixedly at it, absolutely still. Then his sword was out of its scabbard and it whirled around in a complex curve. There was a *snick* and a green flash in the middle of the air and . . .
> . . . two halves of an ivory cube bounced across the table.
> One landed showing the six. The other landed showing the one. [*The Last Hero*]

The situation is not without precedent on the Discworld (a five thrown by the Lady turns into a seven in *The Colour of Magic*), or even in our own world, where it is said that King Olaf of Norway played dice against the King of Sweden for a disputed island, and won when his die accidentally split in half, one face showing the six and the other the one. Nevertheless Fate accuses Cohen of cheating, and would have reneged on the bargain if the Lady – whom none of the gods ever opposes – had not intervened on Cohen's behalf. But Cohen does not appreciate the favour.

> 'And who are *you*?' snapped Cohen, still red with rage.
> 'I? I . . . am the million-to-one chance,' she said.
> 'Yeah?' said Cohen, less impressed than the minstrel thought he ought to be. 'And who are all the other chances?'
> 'I am those, also.'
> Cohen sniffed. 'Then you ain't no lady.'
> 'Er, that's not really—' the minstrel began.

'Oh, that wasn't what I was supposed to say, was it?' said Cohen. 'I was supposed to say, "Ooh, ta, missus, much obliged"? Well, I ain't. They say fortune favours the brave, but *I* say I've seen too many brave men walkin' into battles they never walked out of. The hell with all of it.' [*The Last Hero*]

Nothing, not even a marvel that has saved his own life, can persuade Cohen to give up his fury at the injustice of old age and inevitable death.

Those who want a happy ending every time had better steer clear of epic poetry and heroic sagas, for the wages of heroism is death. True, there are a few legendary heroes who vanish into fairyland, but the great majority die by violence, and their deaths are at least as memorable as their lives. Some fall in battle against overwhelming odds, as did Charlemagne's noble warriors Roland and Oliver facing a Saracen army at Roncevalles; some, like the Irish Cú Chulainn and the Danish Hrolf Kraki, die because the enemy host is strengthened by the spells of evil magicians and malevolent deities; some are murdered by the treachery of trusted relatives or comrades, as were Sigurd the Dragon-Slayer and Robin Hood.

On the other hand, death is what offers a Hero the finest chance to display his mettle. An Anglo-Saxon poet put these words into the mouth of an ageing English warrior facing certain defeat and death in battle against Vikings at Maldon in Essex in 991:

Our minds shall mount higher, our hearts beat harder,
Our spirits grow stronger, as strength dwindles.

Always at the last there is the burial mound, the funeral pyre, the death ship – which may be set on fire, or simply pushed out to sea, as was done for Scyld Scefing, a legendary Danish king:

The prince's ship with curving prow,
Glinting with hoar-frost, eager to leave,
Lay in the harbour. They laid their dear lord,
Their ring-giver, in the ship's bosom, beside the mast,
And treasures too, from far-off lands.
High over his head a banner hung,
Gold embroidered. They let the waters bear him away,
Trusted him to the ocean. Sad were their hearts. [*Beowulf*]

Or, as Cohen puts it, remembering one of his old comrades,

'Where would he have been if we weren't there to give him a
proper funeral, eh? A great big bonfire, that's the funeral of
a hero. And everyone else said it was a waste of a good boat!'
[*The Last Hero*]

And where was the boat heading? Well, there was always the possibility of Valhalla or the Elysian Fields or the Happy Isles, but ancient
epics and sagas have little to say on this point. What mattered far
more was that the hero should be *remembered*. It was said of Sigurd
that 'his name will last as long as the world endures', and the same
was – or should be – true of every hero. As the Old Icelandic poem
Hávamál puts it,

Cattle die, kinsmen die,
And each man too shall die.
I know one thing that never dies,
A dead man's reputation.

An eye-catching grave is useful publicity too; not for nothing did
Beowulf's people cover his ashes with a large mound, high on a head-
land where every passing ship would see it. But the centuries roll on,
and memories fade. We can make a fair guess at who lies in the royal
barrow at Sutton Hoo in Suffolk, but there are dozens upon dozens of

mounds along the South Downs and on Salisbury Plain that were raised for men whose names and deeds are now utterly forgotten. Which is wrong. Which is why Cohen is found one day sitting on an ancient burial mound and refusing to come back into camp for dinner, because he 'hadn't finished'.

'Finished what, old friend?'
'Rememb'rin',' said Cohen.
'Remembering who?'
'The hero who was buried here, all right?'
'Who was he?'
'Dunno.'
'What were his people?'
'Search me,' said Cohen.
'Did he do any mighty deeds?'
'Couldn't say.'
'Then *why*—?'
'*Someone's* got to remember the poor bugger!'
'You don't know anything about him!'
'I can still *remember* him!' [*The Last Hero*]

Time also creates a problem for the rare hero who does *not* die young. Is it fitting for him to settle down quietly, while Old Age, the enemy he can never conquer or outwit, advances steadily upon him? Is he to lie in his bed, old and sick, meekly waiting for death – a straw death, as Vikings would mockingly call it? Of course, Fate might send him, even in old age, the chance of a last good fight; Beowulf had been a king for fifty years when he went to face the dragon. But if not . . . well, it is in the nature of heroes to rage against the dying of the light.

In history, one of the great medieval warlords of Asia was the Mongolian Timur-I-Lenk, called Tamerlane by westerners, who was descended on his mother's side from Genghis Khan. His empire was centred in Samarkand, and stretched from Turkey to the Ganges valley and the borders of China; he died a natural death in 1405 at the age of seventy-two, while making plans to invade China itself. According to legend, as told by the Elizabethan playwright Marlowe (who called him Tamburlaine), on his deathbed he declared war on the gods for striking him down:

> What daring god torments my body thus,
> And seeks to conquer mighty Tamburlaine?
> Shall sickness prove me now to be a man,
> That have been termed the terror of the world?
> Techelles and the rest, come, take your swords,
> And threaten him whose hand afflicts my soul.
> Come, let us march against the powers of heaven,
> And set black banners in the firmament,
> To signify the slaughter of the gods.

He may not have been the only one who refused to go quietly. Odysseus may have done the same, though less fiercely. In Homer's *Odyssey* we hear how this resourceful hero, whose cleverness led to the Greek victory in the Trojan War, eventually got home to his island kingdom of Ithaca after ten years of struggling against monsters, enchantments, and shipwrecks. And there Homer leaves him, happily reunited with his wife Penelope, to grow old in peace. But did he?

A thousand years later Dante (who, like all Italians, called him Ulysses) thought his story ended differently. The bonds of family and homeland could not overcome his passion to learn more about the world. So he set sail with a small band of his faithful comrades, all grown old, urging them on towards the lands beyond the sun; men were not made to live like brutes, he said, but to pursue knowledge and excellence. They sailed through the straits of Gibraltar and out into the deep ocean, past the equator, and far southwards, till they saw a towering mountain – which, though they did not know it, was the Mount of Purgatory crowned with the Earthly Paradise. But there came a whirlwind from this unknown land, and spun their ship three times round, and sank it. And thus ended the life of Ulysses.

In Victorian times, Tennyson took up the theme. In his poem 'Ulysses' the aged hero looks back on a life spent 'always roaming with a hungry heart', and resolves never to pause, never to make an end, but still

> To follow knowledge like a sinking star,
> Beyond the utmost bound of human thought.

He gathers his former comrades, urging them to defy the years and the approach of death, and join him on a last voyage into the unknown:

> For my purpose holds
> To sail beyond the sunset, and the baths
> Of all the western stars, until I die.
> It may be that the gulfs will wash us down;
> It may be we shall touch the Happy Isles,
> And see the great Achilles, whom we knew.
> Though much is taken, much abides; and though
> We are not now that strength which in old days
> Moved earth and heaven, that which we are, we are:
> One equal temper of heroic hearts,
> Made weak by time and fate, but strong in will
> To strive, to seek, to find, and not to yield.

Cohen and the Silver Horde would have understood.

Chapter 13

LORE, LEGENDS *and* TRUTH

THE FOUNDATION LEGENDS

ANY SELF-RESPECTING CITY has to have a legend about its own
foundation. Ankh-Morpork, as is right and proper for the
oldest and greatest city on the Disc, has two.

The first is the official one. According to this, there were once
two orphaned brothers, mere babies, who had been left on the shores
of the Ankh to die. There they were found by a she-hippopotamus,
who suckled them. When they grew up, they decided to build themselves a home, and so founded what must at the time have been a
very small city indeed. In memory of this, the shield on the coat of
arms of Ankh-Morpork has as its supporters deux Hippopotâmes
Royales Bâillant, un enchainé, un couronné au cou. Which, stripped
of its aristocratic herald-speak, means two royal hippos yawning,
one wearing a chain and the other with a crown round its neck. The
conventions of heraldry do not permit the sex of the beasts to be
clearly indicated, but in view of the tale we can safely state that at
least one of them is female. The legend is also commemorated by
eight hippo statues on the city's Brass Bridge, facing out to sea. It is
said that if danger ever threatens the city they will run away.

Some people have expressed doubts over this ancient and uplift-
ing tradition. Why and how, they ask, would a she-hippo suckle
human babies? And how could they thrive on this eccentric diet? Did
they but know it, these doubters could find a tale on Earth proving

that such things are perfectly possible. It tells of twins, Romulus and Remus, who were the sons of Mars the God of War and a human princess. Their evil great-uncle, having just usurped his brother's throne, seized the boys and threw them into the Tiber, for fear they might grow up to challenge him.[11] But the river washed them safely to the bank, where a she-wolf fed them with her milk until a kindly shepherd found them. Later, they built the city of Rome. Considering what wolves normally eat, this tale is even more wondrous than that of the hippo, but the Romans had no difficulty in believing it. And, naturally, making a statue about it.

The second legend is not told *quite* so often by the citizens of Ankh-Morpork, but is surprisingly widespread in other towns. It is said that way back in the fogs of time there was once a great flood sent by the gods, and that a group of wise men survived by building a huge boat into which they crammed two of every type of animal then existing on the Disc. After a few weeks the combined manure was beginning to weigh the boat low in the water, so – the story runs – they tipped it over the side and called the heap Ankh-Morpork. Anybody who doubts the truth of this should go and stand on one of the bridges over the Ankh, preferably on a warm day, and breathe deep.

SUNKEN CITIES AND VANISHING ISLANDS

There is also the legend of the Lost City, the City-before-the-City. It is not an uncommon tale – indeed, there are variants in all the cities of the Sto Plains – but hardly anyone takes it seriously.

There had been a city once, in the mists of pre-history – bigger than Ankh-Morpork, if that were possible. And the inhabitants had done *something*, some sort of unspeakable crime not just

---

[11] Tyrants insist on doing this, despite the fact that it never works.

against Mankind or the gods but against the very nature of the universe itself, which had been so dreadful that it had sunk beneath the sea one stormy night. Only a few people had survived to carry to the barbarian peoples in the less advanced parts of the Disc all the arts and crafts of civilization. [*Moving Pictures*]

According to the dreaded grimoire *Necrotelecomnicon*, there had been a hill at the edge of the city:

... and in that hill, it is said, a Door out of the World was found, and people of the City watched what was Seen therein, knowing not that Dread waited between the universes ... for *Others* found the gate of the Holy Wood and fell upon the world, and in one nighte All Manner of Madnesse befell, and Chaos prevailed, and the Citie sank beneath the Sea, and all became one with the fishes and the lobsters, save for a few who fled.

The hill is still there, on a lonely stretch of coast about thirty miles from Ankh-Morpork. It is not very high, yet high enough to be visible for miles, standing out from the wind-blown sand dunes all around. It is covered with wretched scrubby trees. People call it Holy Wood. And they say that if you stand on the beach at Holy Wood on a stormy night, you can still hear the bells of old temples ringing under the sea. The events chronicled in *Moving Pictures* would suggest that there is after all rather more than a grain of truth in these old tales.

There are many, many legends about sunken cities on Earth, where islands bob up and down like the chorus in *HMS Pinafore*. The oldest on record was told by the Greek philosopher Plato about 2,400 years ago, and according to him it was true, and had happened some 9,000 years before *that*. And it was not just one city that had sunk, but the whole large island of Atlantis – rich, civilized, with

many mighty cities, harbours and palaces. There, men had at first
been wise and virtuous, but in time they became obsessed with
wealth and power, so the gods destroyed their land in a single day
and night.

> There occurred portentous earthquakes and floods, and one
> grievous day and night befell them when the whole body of
> warriors was swallowed up by the earth, and the island
> of Atlantis in like manner was swallowed up by the sea and
> vanished; wherefore also the ocean at that spot has now
> become impassable and unsearchable, being blocked up by the
> shoal of mud which the island created as it settled down. [Plato,
> *Timaeus*, transl. R. G. Bury]

Plato does not mention any door or gate, for the large-scale
destruction he describes must have involved some great natural
disaster – an earthquake, a volcanic eruption, a tsunami – and was
the direct work of the gods. There are other, more recent traditions
along the sea-coasts of western Europe telling of lands and towns
submerged by the foolish or treacherous act of someone who opened
a sluice gate. In Wales, for instance, they talk of the lost land of
Cantre'r Gwaelod under the waters of Cardigan Bay – forty miles
long by twenty wide it was, with sixteen fine towns on it. There was
a great dyke protecting it from the sea, but Seithenhin, the keeper of
the dyke, was a drunkard, and one night forgot to close the sluice
gates. The way others tell it, Seithenhin was lord of the land, and it
was his daughter who let in the sea, curses upon her! Or it was God's
doing, because Seithenhin was a proud and presumptuous ruler.
Whatever, you can still see the pebble ridge which was once the
protecting wall; you can still hear bells ringing underwater.

Then there is the Breton tale of the drowning of Kêr-Is. This, they
say, was a magnificent city built on land reclaimed from the sea in
what is now the Bay of Douarnenez in Brittany, and ruled by a King
Grallon or Gradlon. He himself was a virtuous man, but his courtiers

and subjects were drunken and debauched, though a holy man warned them that there would be a reckoning:

> After happiness, grief!
> Anyone who eats the meat of the fish,
> By the fish he will be eaten.
> And anyone who swallows will be swallowed.
> And anyone who drinks wine and mead
> Will drink water like a fish;
> And anyone who doesn't know will learn.
> [*Livaden Geris*, transl. James Doan]

Yet the king let the revellers go on feasting, while he took himself quietly to bed. Now, the king had a daughter named Dahut, and she had a lover (some say he was the Devil himself, but they always say that sort of thing) who coaxed her into stealing the golden key which her father wore on a chain round his neck as he slept. This was the key to the gate in the dykes protecting the city from the sea. They were opened, and the ocean swept in and submerged everything; only Grallon himself escaped, thanks to the saint's warning and to his fine horse. Dahut tried to mount behind him, but the saint miraculously appeared and struck her with his crozier, so that she fell into the raging waters and drowned. As for the sunken city, its buildings can sometimes be glimpsed when the sea is calm and clear, and its bells are heard ringing. Legend loves the sound of sunken bells.

In Cornwall, tradition tells of the lost land of Lyonesse, which once stretched all the way from Land's End to the Scilly Isles, though no one now remembers just why it sank. The strange rocky outcrop of St Michael's Mount overlooks Mount's Bay, where the lost land once began and where one can still, at very low tides, find fossilized bits of wood from the trees which once grew there. In the Cornish language, four hundred years ago, the Mount was called Carrack Looz en Cooz, 'The Grey Rock in the Wood'. The drowned forest was important, once. Maybe it was a Holy Wood.

Such legends have always been particularly popular among fishermen. They are the ones who, peering down through unusually clear water, sometimes glimpse curious structures that look more like streets and ruined buildings than simple rocks; they are the ones whose nets sometimes snag on underwater obstacles where, according to their charts, no obstacles should be. Oddly, the fishermen of Ankh-Morpork do *not* have such legends. So it came as a total surprise to Solid Jackson and his son, out fishing by night in the middle of the Circle Sea, when a sound came from below the surface, the sound of a bell or gong slowly swinging ... followed by a weathercock ... a tower ... a surge of huge, weed-encrusted buildings ... a whole malevolent-looking city on an oozy, weedy island rising up out of the sea. They had discovered the Lost Island and City of Leshp.

They did not like it. In fact, it gave them the willies. Partly, this was because of the smell of sulphur and rotting seaweed. Partly, because of nasty little ripples and soft splashing noises in the dark pools that lingered in the deeper cellars. But mainly it was because of the city itself. There were *some* buildings which looked more or less as human buildings should, with pillars and arches and steps and suchlike, and nice tiled floors with patterns of shells and squid and octopuses. But besides these, there were the remains of massive structures which had nothing to do with human architecture. It came as a relief when the island, after a few weeks, settled back down on to the seabed.

Some faint awareness of these events, chronicled in *Jingo*, may have reached parts of the Earth. There is talk there of a 'Green Land of Enchantment' which occasionally rises to the surface in the Bristol Channel, and then vanishes again. A certain Captain Jones had a curious experience in the 1890s which was reported in the *Pembroke County Guardian*:

Once when trending up the Bristol Channel and passing Grassholm Island, in what he had always known as deep water, he was surprised to see to windward of him a large tract of land covered with a beautiful green meadow. It was not, however, *above water*, but just a few feet *below*, say two or three, so that the grass waved and swam about as the ripple flowed over it, in a way quite delightful to the eye, so that as one watched it made one feel quite drowsy. 'You know,' he continued, 'I have heard old people say there is a floating island off there, that sometimes rises to the surface, or nearly, and then sinks down again fathoms deep, so that no one sees it for years, and when nobody expects it comes up again for a while. How it may be, I do not know, but that is what they say.'

There are similar tales of intermittent islands off the coasts of Norway and Ireland. If you want to make them stay permanently above water (since they offer good grazing), the thing to do is to throw a knife, or a burning torch, or a lit tobacco-pipe on to them before they can sink again, but this is very hard to achieve. The largest and loveliest Norwegian one is called Utrøst, inhabited by kindly beings; it only becomes visible to humans if their lives are in deadly danger, when its harbour offers them safety. Those who shelter there will have good luck all their lives.

These are *nice* islands, of course, even if they are imaginary. One that was undoubtedly real and very Leshpian in its effects appeared in July 1831. It was a pumice island, and it rose to the surface off the coast of Sicily, due to volcanic action. A British fleet landed on it and claimed it for Britain, naming it Graham Island, but the Italians also claimed it, naming it Ferdinandea. The French and Spaniards showed interest too. The ensuing diplomatic dispute was still not settled when the island sank back into the sea in December of the same year, which was rather a shame, but averted a possible war.

Finally, it should be noted that an island which pops up and then sinks again is, as Leonard of Quirm remarked, rather like a certain type of folklore current among sailors on the Discworld:

'It puts me in mind,' said Leonard, 'of those nautical stories of giant turtles that sleep on the surface, thus causing sailors to think they are an island. Of course, you don't get giant turtles that small.' [*Jingo*]

In our world, in the absence of any turtles larger than, say, a decent-sized dining-table, traditional nautical lore warns instead of the risks involved in landing on a really, really big fish or whale which happens to be dozing on the surface. In particular, it is very unwise to light a small fire and start cooking breakfast. St Brendan the Navigator, who was Abbot of Clonfert in Ireland in the sixth century, is said to have done just that while sailing far out in the Atlantic. Suddenly what he'd thought was an island began to twitch, and then to sink. Brendan and his crew were lucky to get back to their ship in time.

Exactly the same thing happened to Sindbad the Sailor on his first voyage in the Indian Ocean, as is told in *The Thousand and One Nights*. The ship came to a little island which seemed as fair as the Garden of Eden, where the passengers disembarked; some wandered off to explore, while others busied themselves cooking, eating and drinking.

> While we were thus engaged we suddenly heard the captain cry out to us from the ship: 'All aboard, quickly! Abandon everything and run for your lives! The mercy of Allah be upon you, for this is no island but a gigantic whale floating on the bosom of the sea, on whose back the sands have settled and trees have grown since the world was young! When you lit the fire it felt the heat and stirred. Make haste, I say; for soon the whale will plunge into the sea and you will all be lost!' [transl. N. J. Dawood]

According to the poet Milton, the enormous creature is none other than Leviathan, mentioned in the Bible –

> . . . that sea-beast
> Leviathan, which God of all his works
> Created hugest that swim the Ocean stream.
> Him, haply slumbering on the Norway foam,
> The pilot of some small night-foundered skiff,
> Deeming some island, oft, as seamen tell,
> With fixèd anchor in his scaly rind
> Moors by his side under the lee, while night
> Invests the sea, and wishèd morn delays.

Atlantic, Indian Ocean, seas off Norway . . . the monster (or the story) certainly does get around.

In Cambridge University Library and in the British Library there are manuscripts of a Latin Bestiary (that is, a Book of Beasts) dating from the early twelfth century. It includes a section about the sea-monster which gets mistaken for an island, beginning thus:

> There is an ocean monster which is called an *aspido delone* in Greek. On the other hand, it is called an *aspido testudo* in Latin. It is also called a Whale . . . This animal lifts its back out of the open sea above the watery waves . . . [transl. T. H. White]

Testudo is Latin for 'tortoise'. *Delone* makes no sense, and must be a mistake for *chelone*, which is indeed a Greek word, meaning 'turtle'. Why on earth should English monks a thousand years ago get the traditional whale mixed up with tortoises and turtles? Some echo from the Discworld, maybe? As for *aspido*, this must refer to a snake of some sort, so it would seem that the Sea Serpent has somehow got into the mix. It makes a good yarn even better.

KINGS AND HEROES

A certain legendary glow surrounds the (rather vague) memory of the Kings of Ankh, a dynasty which came to an end some 2,000 years ago. They are said to have been thoroughly wise, just, charismatic, and so on, plus being of course extremely powerful. As for the later Kings of Ankh-Morpork, they are remembered in many a merry anecdote, for recurrent lunacy, sadistic cruelty, and general bloody-mindedness. (These anecdotes, being factually accurate, do not count as folklore.) If a ruler made himself too disagreeable to the rest of the aristocracy, the Guild of Assassins would eventually be contacted, and he would be discreetly inhumed. Curiously, this tactful and civilized procedure is seen by some as the survival of something extremely archaic:

> There was a tradition once, far back in the past, called the King of the Bean. A special dish was served to all the men of the clan on a certain day of the year. It contained one small hard-baked bean, and whoever got the bean was, possibly after some dental attention, hailed as King. It was quite an inexpensive system and it worked well, possibly because the clever little bald men who actually ran things and paid some attention to possible candidates were experts at palming a bean into the right bowl.
>
> And while the crops ripened and the tribe thrived and the land was fertile, the King thrived too. But when, in the fullness of time, crops failed and the ice came back and animals were inexplicably barren, the clever little bald men sharpened their long knives, which were *mostly* used for cutting mistletoe.
>
> And on the due night, one of them went into his cave and carefully baked one small bean.
>
> Of course, that was before people were civilized. These days, no one has to eat beans. [*Night Watch*]

That, at any rate, is a theory of kingship put forward by speculative folklorists in Ankh-Morpork, and enthusiastically adopted by people who feel tradition must always be bloodthirsty, or about sex, or (preferably) both. Naturally, when dealing with such a remote period one can't expect to find documentary evidence to back up one's hypothesis (cave-dwelling clans don't keep diaries or committee minutes). But Quoth the Raven, who is a member of an occult species with links to the gods and therefore knows what he's talking about, does mention a midwinter custom, thousands of years ago, which sounds rather similar. It involved some poor bugger finding a special bean in his food at the Hogswatch feast. It made him king, but also meant he'd be killed off a few days later. A merry reign, but a short one. (We have more to say about this in the section on the Hogfather.)

To return to the early kings of Ankh. Theirs was a Golden Age, from which little remains – some well-built ancient sewers, a few ruined walls, a worm-eaten throne, and, if legend can be believed, a very special Sword. Nobody has set eyes on it for centuries, and many think it must be lost.

And yet, there are always rumours. Although they are so proud of being modern and living in an Age of Reason, the citizens of Ankh-Morpork have surprisingly romantic imaginations. Their minds are littered with mangled myths and fragmented fairy tales. Deep down, they feel sure that one day a long-lost heir will turn up, brandishing the Sword and displaying a birthmark, to claim the throne. He will right all wrongs, and the Golden Age will return.

Since the rules of fairytale narrative are known to every child in the multiverse (even in worlds where the books of Grimm and Andersen are not to be found), the people of Ankh-Morpork naturally assume that the heir will have begun life as a humble swineherd, and/or revived a princess who has been asleep for a hundred years, and/or proved how royal he is by sleeping on a huge pile of mattresses and a few very small peas. His hands will have sensational, but highly specialized, healing powers, though there appears to be some uncertainty about what exactly it is that he cures.

Some citizens think a true king can cure baldness by his touch, while the aristocratic Lord Rust mentions dandruff, and scrofula, a disease of the throat glands. On Earth, it was definitely scrofula, which was therefore known as 'king's evil'. Several kings of England, from the time of Edward the Confessor to the end of the Stuart dynasty, made a point of ceremonially touching sufferers; so did the kings of France.

Best of all, if the heir to a kingdom encounters a dragon he will most certainly slay it. As Cut-Me-Own-Throat Dibbler says to the sceptical Vimes:

> 'You've got no romance in your soul, Captain. When a stranger comes into the city under the thrall of the dragon and challenges it with a glittery sword, weeell, there's only one outcome, ain't there? It's probably destiny.' [*Guards! Guards!*]

In the same way, people know just how things will go if a dragon appears. It will fly around, flaming and ravening; it will want a pile of gold to sleep on; it will expect people to give it virgins to eat, chained to rocks; it will speak, quite likely in riddles; *but*, it will have one vulnerable spot, which a good archer can hit as it flies overhead. That's what always happened in the old stories, and so that's what will happen again.

These expectations are moulded by all the dragon-lore which has been drifting from one universe to another from the dawn of time. There is no mythology in any world which doesn't have dragons in it, together with gods or heroes to kill them. The tales known in Ankh-Morpork are just as famous on Earth. There, it was the Ancient Greek hero Perseus who was the first to rescue a virgin who had been left chained to a rock for a dragon to eat; her name was Andromeda. Later, St George did the same, though he, being a Saint, didn't marry the girl. Several great warriors of Anglo-Saxon and Scandinavian legend – Beowulf, for instance, and the two Volsung heroes, Sigmund and Sigurd (whom Germans call Siegfried) – slew dragons which lay on hoards of treasure. One of these, the one named Fafnir which Sigurd killed, did indeed speak, and could ask and answer riddles.

As for the one vulnerable spot, this is sometimes on the belly, as it was with Fafnir, and with Smaug in the tale of Bilbo the hobbit. More often, it is when a dragon opens his mouth that he becomes vulnerable to a well-aimed spear or arrow going down his gullet and into his vitals; this technique was pioneered by the Babylonian god Marduk, who destroyed the primeval dragoness Tiamat by hurling deadly winds down her throat. And then there is the sad case of the Yorkshire Dragon of Wantley, whom More of More Hall kicked in the arsehole with a spiked boot:

> 'Murder, murder!' the dragon cried,
>   'Alack, alack for grief!
> Had you but missed that place, you could
>   Have done me no mischief!'
> Then his head he shaked, trembled and quaked,
>   And down he laid and cried;
> First on one knee then on back tumbled he,
>   So groaned, kicked, shat, and died.[12]

SOME MORE LEGENDS

Many town-dwellers have, lurking in the corners of their minds, various half-remembered tales and no-longer-properly-believed beliefs which pop up again in the right circumstances. The tale of the shifting shop, for instance:

> Glod looked up at a blank wall.
>   'I knew it!' he said. 'Didn't I say? Magic! How many times have we heard this story? There's a mysterious shop no one's

---

[12] It's the little details that charm.

ever seen before, and someone goes in and buys some rusty old curio, and it turns out to—'

'Glod—'

'—some kind of talisman or a bottle full of genie, and then when there's trouble they go back and the shop—'

'Glod—?'

'—has *mysteriously disappeared* and gone back to whatever dimension it came from— yes, what is it?'

'You're on the wrong side of the road. It's over here.' [*Soul Music*]

But in fact Glod was right. This shop *was* magic, and contained, among other things, a flute which you mustn't blow unless you want to be knee-deep in rats, a trumpet which can make the world end and the sky fall down, and a gong which can make seven hundred and seventy-seven skeletal warriors spring up out of the earth. Two out of the three would work on Earth too. Not the gong, since according to Greek myth, the correct way to make warriors spring up out of the earth is to sow the ground with dragon's teeth, as the heroes Cadmus and Jason did. But the Bible does mention a Last Trump with which, according to prophecy, an angel will announce that Doomsday has come; and the flute is clearly a pair to the fife with which the Pied Piper of Hamlin summoned rats.

The Hamlin story is a fine example of the weird power of narrativium. It seems reasonably certain that something did happen in the German town of Hamlin in 1284, something involving a stranger and the children of the town, and that everyone found it very upsetting. There are sober, reliable chronicles, written less than a hundred years after the event, which declare that someone marched into the town on 26 June in 1284 and marched away with 130 of its children. But they do *not* say anything about rats, or a pipe, or curiously coloured clothes. In fact, there's no magic involved at all. He marches in, he marches away, taking the children . . . that's all there is to it, at first.

· But that won't do. Surely, people thought, something so terrible as the loss of all those children must have more to it than that. It must be due to sorcery, or a punishment for some sin – or both. Now, it was widely believed throughout Europe that some men had an uncanny power over snakes, or rats, or mice; they would summon the vermin by playing on a flute or pipe, and then lead them into deep water or order them to leap into a bonfire, and so destroy them all. Perhaps a man who could lure rats could also lure children? Could one of these legendary ratcatchers have come to Hamlin in great-great-grandfather's time? Could something have angered him? Maybe the townsfolk tried to cheat him of his pay, and he took his revenge?

And so the story of the Pied Piper was born. Back in 1284, people said, the town had been overrun with rats, until a stranger arrived, proclaiming himself a ratcatcher. He was dressed in a multi-coloured coat and carried a small fife, so they called him the Pied Piper, and promised him a great deal of money if he would help them. As soon as he started playing rats came running out of every house, and followed him as he marched out of town. He led them down to the river Weser and waded in; they followed, and drowned. But then the citizens regretted having promised so much money, so they made excuses not to pay, and he went off in a furious rage. On 26 June he returned, this time dressed as a hunter. Again he played his fife, but this time it was children who came running to him, and he led them out of the town, where they disappeared with him into a cave in a mountain, and were never seen again – though some said they came out alive, hundreds of miles away, in Transylvania.

By the middle of the sixteenth century this had become the official explanation. The Mayor had the entire story illustrated in stained-glass windows in the main church; a new city gate erected in 1556 carried an inscription stating that it was put up '272 years after the sorcerer abducted 130 children'; another inscription on the City Hall commemorated '130 children lost by a piper inside a mountain'.

Of course, there are always some people who prefer a rational explanation to a magical one. With the Hamlin story, it's not difficult to think of something that could fit, and many modern commentators have offered suggestions. There were wars going on in thirteenth-century Germany, so maybe a recruiting sergeant passed through the town and led away 130 young men, and maybe they were all killed in battle. Or maybe the date is wrong, and the story really recalls how friars came preaching wild sermons to get youngsters to join the so-called Children's Crusade to Jerusalem in 1212; they never got there, and those who did not die on the road ended up as slaves. Or maybe it refers to the forced emigration of local families to colonize new territories far away. For example, Bishop Bruno of Olmütz recruited families from Lower Saxony to build up a German population in his diocese in Bohemia; a comparison of city records in Hamlin and Olmütz reveals a startling agreement in the family names in each place, which bears out the rumour that the lost children of Hamlin reappeared safe and sound in Transylvania.

Be that as it may, it's the rats, the pipe, and the pied coat that we remember now. And only a beastly spoilsport would point out that rats can swim.

As for drums . . .

There was even an Ankh-Morpork legend, wasn't there, about some old drum in the Palace or somewhere that was supposed to bang itself if an enemy fleet was seen sailing up the Ankh? The legend had died out in recent centuries, partly because this was the Age of Reason and also because no enemy fleet could sail up the Ankh without a gang of men with shovels going in front. [*Soul Music*]

There is a curiously close parallel here with the patriotic English legend of Drake's Drum. After the great Elizabethan seaman Sir Francis Drake died off Panama in 1595 a drum painted with his coat of arms was brought back to his home at Buckland Abbey in Devon, and is still kept there. It is traditionally believed to have come from the ship on which he had once sailed round the world. In 1895, for the three-hundredth anniversary of the hero's death, Sir Henry Newbolt wrote a vigorous poem telling how Drake on his deathbed promised that if the drum was struck when England was in danger, he would return to save the country once again, as he had done when the Spanish Armada came.

> Drake he was a Devon man an' ruled the Devon seas,
>   (Capten, art tha sleepin' there below?)
> Rovin' tho' his death fell, he went wi' heart at ease,
>   An' dreamin' arl the time o' Plymouth Hoe.
> 'Take my drum to England, hang et by the shore,
>   Strike et when your powder's runnin' low;
> If the Dons sight Devon, I'll quit the port o' Heaven,
> An' drum them up the Channel, as we drummed them long ago.'

In 1916, when England was at war, a poet named Alfred Noyes gave this story an even stronger patriotic twist. Writing an article in *The Times* about submarine warfare, he declared that Devon fishermen believed that the drum had sounded of its own accord in times of crisis, and that Drake would always hear and answer its call. It had been heard when Nelson's fleet went to meet the French at Trafalgar, and again in that very year of 1916 before the naval battle of Jutland in the North Sea. And this, the fishermen said, showed that Drake had returned to inspire Nelson and Admiral Jellicoe and guide them to victory. Whether Noyes really had heard Devon fishermen saying this, or whether he made it up himself, hardly matters. It's folklore now. And now people say Drake's drum was heard in 1940 at the evacuation of Dunkirk.

The citizens of Ankh-Morpork show in their legends an appreciation of virtue which is rarely evident in their lives. They can in fact be downright sentimental. Take the story of the famous dog Gaspode –

not to be confused with the mangy, flea-ridden speaking cur of the same name, who was simply called after him. The reason the *famous* Gaspode is famous is his devotion to his master.

> 'It was years and years ago. There was this ole bloke in Ankh who snuffed it, and he belonged to one of them religions where they bury you after you're dead, an' they did, and he had this ole dog—'
>
> 'Called Gaspode?'
>
> 'Yeah, an' this ole dog had been his only companion, and after they buried the man he lay down on his grave, and howled and howled for a couple of weeks. Growled at everybody who came near. An' then died.' [*Moving Pictures*]

Strangely, there are two cities on Earth – Edinburgh and Tokyo – where almost the same story is told, the main difference being that the dog survives for many years, fed by passers-by, though still faithfully grieving. In Edinburgh, this model of doggy devotion is a terrier called Greyfriars Bobby, after the graveyard where his master, a night-watchman called John Gray, was buried in 1858, and where there is now a statue of him (the dog, that is, not John Gray). He lived on for fourteen years; some say he spent all day at his master's grave, but others say he was regularly fed in a nearby restaurant. When he died, a place was found for him near the entrance of Greyfriars Kirkyard, though not actually in consecrated ground. The stone is inscribed: 'Let his loyalty and devotion be a lesson to us all.'

In Tokyo, the faithful dog, named Hachi-koh, used to go daily to Shibuya Station to meet his master, a professor, when he got off the train on his return from work. The professor died in 1925, but the dog lived on for ten years more, loyally meeting the train every day at the usual time, and resisting all attempts to re-home him. A statue of him was set up in the station even in his lifetime, and a special section of the concourse was set aside as his home; his stuffed body is now in the Natural Science Museum in Tokyo, and his statue is always garlanded with flowers on the anniversary of his death.

What Gaspode – the modern, mangy, flea-bitten Gaspode – would make of these stories is not hard to guess, considering his cynical ideas about his famous namesake:

> 'That's very sad,' said Victor.
>
> 'Yeah. Everyone says it demonstrates a dog's innocent and undyin' love for 'is master,' said Gaspode, spitting the words out as if they were ashes.
>
> 'You don't believe that, then?'
>
> 'Not really. I b'lieve any bloody dog will stay still an' howl when you've just lowered the gravestone on his tail,' said Gaspode.

The modern Gaspode takes good care to keep his skills hidden, which is relatively easy since most people refuse to believe that any dog can talk. Even so, rumours get around. William de Worde, editor of the *Ankh-Morpork Times*, who is professionally inclined to scepticism, struggles (in vain) against that strange phenomenon, the urban myth:

> A couple of months ago someone had tried to hand William the old story of there being a dog in the city that could talk. It was the third time this year. William had explained that it was an urban myth. It was always the friend of a friend who had heard the talk, and it was never anyone who had seen the dog . . . There seemed to be no stopping that kind of story. People swore there was some long-lost heir to the throne of Ankh living incognito in the town. William certainly recognized wishful thinking when he heard it. [*The Truth*]

Alas for William, who has chosen the wrong city in which to be an enlightened thinker . . .

Meanwhile, other people, even more cynical, know how to take a legend and turn it into a nice little earner. One is the con-man known as the Amazing Maurice (who may in fact, according to rumour, be a remarkably cunning cat). He travels from town to town with his gang of Educated Rodents, who infiltrate the buildings. A musical confederate then undertakes, for a good fee, to summon them with his magic pipe and lead them all far, far away. It has always worked. Here, we know this as a rather inverted version of the Pied Piper story.

TREACLE MINES

Embedded in place-names, lurking like hidden diamonds, are precious traces of past history and traditions. There is, for example, a street in Ankh-Morpork called Treacle Mine Road, running from Misbegot Bridge to Easy Street. It takes its name from the treacle mines which used to be worked in this area, which are ancient, very ancient indeed. The deepest levels contain the remnants of pig-treacle measures that are estimated to be 500,000 years old, intermingled with basalt slabs carved with archaic trollish pictograms. The mines were abandoned many years ago, and most people believe that this was because they were exhausted. However, when some deep-down dwarfs (grags) bought property on that street and began mining below it, for reasons of their own (as told in *Thud!*), they reopened old tunnels and galleries, and their bores struck some residue of deep treacle.

Up in the mountains, on the borders of Uberwald, there are still very productive treacle mines, enabling the dwarfs of that region to make a handsome profit exporting both raw pig-treacle and luscious treacle-based confectionery to the cities of the plain. Far away in the hot and swampy realm of Genua, there are lakes of liquid treacle fermenting happily only a little way underground, and occasionally bursting out under pressure to create springs of rum. Near Quirm, there are toffee beds. The origin of all this succulence goes back to the Dawn of Time, when the Fifth Elephant collided with the Disc with so great an impact that thousands of acres of prehistoric wild sugar cane was buried under massive landslides, and compacted into a dense crystalline mass.

Those who study the effects of cosmic resonance in the space-time continuum of the multiverse often cite the Treacle Mine Phenomenon with amazement and awe, for it has been shown without doubt that these mines, which are a plain fact of geography on the Disc, have insinuated themselves into the folklore of a world where they do not actually exist, and never have done. In England, there are at least thirty villages reputed to have a secret treacle mine tucked away somewhere on their territory. Even more astonishing, there is one place, the village of Patcham in East Sussex, where people have a fairly accurate idea of how the treacle was formed (allowing for the fact that this world sadly lacks any cosmic elephants). A Mrs Austen told the *West Sussex Gazette* in 1973 the tale she knew, and had passed on to her children:

> Millions of years ago, when England was a tropical country, before the Ice Age, sugar cane grew here. Year after year it grew, ripened and rotted unharvested, the molasses draining away down into the folds of the hills, where it accumulated above an impermeable layer of clay. The centuries passed, the colder weather came, and sugar cane no longer grew on the Downs, but the underground layer of treacle lay patiently waiting until in 1871 Peter Jones, a scientist who had long suspected its existence, sank the first shaft. The ensuing treacle gusher spouted for three days, covering the countryside for several miles around with a fine rain of treacle, until it was at last brought under control.

Elsewhere, other explanations are offered. At Chobham in Surrey, military incompetence is alleged to be the cause. It is said that soldiers who encamped on Chobham Common before setting out to the Crimean War (others say, American troops stationed nearby during the First World War) buried vast stockpiles of supplies, including drums of treacle and molasses, and forgot to remove them when they left. The drums corroded, and a subterranean reservoir of treacle was formed.

Other places do not attempt to account for the origin of the precious substance, but tell ingenious tales about its discovery and use. The mine at Jarvis Brook near Crowborough (Sussex) was supposedly begun by the Romans, who carved the solid treacle rock into jewellery, but never found out how sweet it was; this was discovered accidentally when a medieval baby prince was visibly soothed by sucking his mother's necklace. At Sabden (Lancashire) it is claimed that boggarts (a species of goblin) are employed in the mine to lick up any spilt treacle; cards and souvenirs about the mine are sold to tourists.

Yet, sad to say, the people who tell these tales do not take them seriously. It is all a poker-faced joke, a hoax, a leg-pull, used by the locals to hoax gullible outsiders, by parents to entertain their children, by older children to make fools of young ones. While all the time, did they but know it, the remains of a *real* treacle mine lie below the streets of Ankh-Morpork.

WIZARDRY AND CEREMONIAL MAGIC

Any comment upon wizardry in a book with 'Folklore' in the title will have to be made *very quietly*, since there is nothing that infuriates a scholar more than to be mistaken for a member of the folk, after he has spent all his waking hours for the past fifty years with his nose in a book (mealtimes partially excepted). Naturally, he may have come across the odd scrap of folklore in the course of his reading, but he will make it very plain that he does not *believe* it. Arch-chancellor Ridcully, for example, has heard of the kind of monster called a Sciopod by Ancient Greeks and a Uniped in Latin:

a humanoid with only a single leg and foot, this being so huge that if it lies on its back and sticks its leg in the air, the foot makes an excellent sunshade. But he thinks it's just something travel writers invented.

> 'They always make up that sort of thing. Otherwise it's too boring. It's no good coming home and just saying you were shipwrecked for two years and ate winkles, is it? You have to put in a lot of daft stuff about men who go around on one big foot and the Land of Giant Plum Puddings and nursery rubbish like that.' [*The Last Continent*]

Magic as actually practised by wizards generally consists of transformation spells, the skilled hurling of fireballs, the creation of illusions, and the occasional summoning of demons or, in extreme cases, of Death himself. These things are done as rarely as possible. But the theory underpinning these few simple acts is immense, and subdivided into innumerable branches – divination, theurgy, runes ancient and modern, cabbalistic rites, gramarye, knowledge of amulets and talismans, magianism, thaumatology, astrology, morbid spellbinding, sortilege, invisible writing – and so on and so forth. Not necromancy, however; this is frowned upon, and has been replaced by a far more acceptable Department of Post-Mortem Communications. The very heart and soul of Unseen University is its Library. With over 90,000 volumes of grimoires and magical texts, it is by far the largest concentration of magical scholarship anywhere in the multiverse, and so dangerous that most of the books have to be chained up.

Folklore? Oral tradition? Old wives' tales? Tchah! It is an insult to the grand intellectual achievements of wizardry to think their work has anything in common with the foolish ways of the peasantry.

No doubt the famous and learned occultists of medieval and Renaissance Europe – such men as Albertus Magnus in the thirteenth century, or Paracelsus, Cornelius Agrippa, and Dr John Dee in the sixteenth – would have been just as dismissive. They wrote books which straddled the ill-defined boundaries between magic, science and philosophy – massive, expensive tomes in Latin, the international language of the wise. Albertus, for instance, wrote a treatise on the practical procedures of alchemy, and was also reputed to be the author of a much simpler *Book of Secrets* which described the magical properties of stones, herbs, and beasts. For example:

> *If thou wilt know whether thy wife be chaste or no.* Take the stone which is called Magnet, in Englishe the Loadstone. It is of a sadde blew colour, and it is found in the sea of Inde, and sometime in part of Almaine. Lay this stone under the head of a wife. And if she be chaste, she will embrace her husband. If she be not chaste, she will fall forth of her bed . . .
>
> *If thou wilt Overcome thine Enemies.* Take the stone which is called Draconites, from the dragon's head. And if the stone bee drawne out from him alive it is good against all poisons, and he that beareth it on his left arme shall overcome all his enemies . . .
>
> *The Marygold.* The vertue of this herbe is marvellous for if it be gathered, the Sunne being in the Signe Leo in August, and wrapped in the leafe of a Lawrell, or May tree, and a wolf's tooth added thereto, no man shall be able to speake one word against the bearer thereof, but only words of peace. If anything bee stolen, and the bearer of the things before named shall lay them under his head in the night, he shall see the theefe in a vision.

And so on. It must remain one of the mysteries of trans-dimensional correspondence whether this Albertus Magnus of medieval Europe has any connection with Alberto Malich, the exceptionally powerful wizard who founded Unseen University some two thousand years ago, and disappeared while performing the Rite of AshkEnte backwards. He had intended to achieve immortality, and so he did, in a way. He now exists (one can't *quite* say 'lives') as cook, valet and gardener in the House of Death, which suits him nicely.

On Earth, grimoires were often attributed to prestigious figures from legendary times, such as King Solomon the Wise and Hermes Trismegistus. As time went on, the practice of magic slid down the social scale; by the eighteenth and nineteenth centuries cheap, simple books of spells and conjurations were selling in thousands to village cunning men and wise women, and to ordinary households. In Germany, there was *The Sixth and Seventh Books of Moses*; in France, *Le grand Albert* and *Le petit Albert*, *Le dragon rouge*, *La poule noire*, and the splendidly named *Abracadabra monumentissima diabolica*. Intellectual wizardry was being drawn into the vast melting-pot of folk tradition.

This has not happened in Ankh-Morpork, nor is it likely to, so long as the Librarian has an ook to say in the matter. Nevertheless, far outside the hallowed walls of Unseen University, lurking in shadowy and insalubrious back-alleys and keeping out of sight of qualified wizards, are magical practitioners of a lower sort. Their ambitions are great; their skills are not. They know far less than they suppose. They band together in secret societies with imposing titles, and attach vast importance to ritual, ceremony, and magical tools. They are led by pompous, bullying men, calling themselves Supreme Grand Masters. Such are, for instance, the Elucidated Brethren of the Ebon Night, guardians of the sacred knowledge since a time no man may wot of.

Such groups would be just as indignant as the academic wizards at the notion that what they were doing had anything in common with folk magic. No, their Grand Master had been taught profound secrets from the Heart of Being while undergoing tuition from Hidden Venerable Sages on a distant mountain. Furthermore, the Sages had given him a book of ancient wisdom . . . actually, he had arranged for it to be stolen from the Unseen University Library, but no matter, it was a Book. And it was ancient.

But it would be a mistake to think that everyone in Ankh-Morpork has such a highbrow approach to magic. There are people who need no books, no apparatus, no complex rituals – people with a natural inborn talent for the occult, like the redoubtable medium Mrs Evadne Cake, noted for her precognition and her numerous spirit contacts. In some ways she is very like a witch, and every community needs its witch.

Even in Unseen University itself the housekeeper, Mrs Whitlow, dabbles in the occult. She loves trying to peer into the future, and owns a crystal ball which she keeps under a sort of pink frilly tea cosy, several sets of divinatory cards, a pink velvet bag of rune stones, an ouija board, and special dried monkey turds which can be thrown in such a way as to reveal all the secrets of the universe. Granny Weatherwax, for purposes of her own, offered Mrs Whitlow her services as a reader of tealeaves. No doubt she had her own opinion of such amateurish goings-on, but she kept it to herself.

SATOR SQUARE

Most of those who walk through the streets of Ankh-Morpork never pause to wonder why the square in front of Unseen University is named Sator Square. There is indeed a reason, though you have to search the annals of a different universe to discover it: on Earth, Sator Square is the most famous of all magic squares. But it's no use looking for it on the street map of any city, for it is not *that sort* of square. It is a palindromic word square.

These are talismans, difficult to invent, but very powerful. You have to choose a group of words which can be laid out as a square of letters and which (this is the hard bit) will remain the same whether you read it downwards, upwards, from the left or from the right. Most of them are mere gibberish, but the Sator formula does make sense, of a sort. It goes:

```
S   A   T   O   R
A   R   E   P   O
T   E   N   E   T
O   P   E   R   A
R   O   T   A   S
```

Four out of the five are normal Latin words, meaning 'the sower holds the works [and] the wheels', but *arepo* is either pure nonsense or the mysterious, mystical name of the mysterious, mystical Sower who controls the Wheels (of Fate? Of the heavenly spheres?). The earliest known example of the square is in one of the houses of Pompeii, buried by the eruption of Vesuvius in AD 79; another early one was found scratched on wall plaster in a Roman villa at Cirencester in Gloucestershire. At these dates, both homes could have belonged to Christian families, and the square could have served as a coded signal of their faith. It can hardly be a coincidence that its letters can be unpacked to reveal the first words of the Our Father (*Pater noster*) twice over, plus A and O twice. The latter could mean Alpha and Omega, the Beginning and the End, which is a title of Christ in the Apocalypse, the Bible's Book of Revelation. What's more, the whole thing can be laid out as a cross, thus:

```
                    P
                    A
        A           T           O
                    E
                    R
        P A T E R N O S T E R
                    O
                    S
        A           T           O
                    E
                    R
```

The Sator-Arepo Square was known all over medieval Europe, and in some countries (Russia, America and Germany, for example) was still being used in folk magic right up to modern times, almost two thousand years after it was invented. People said it would put out a fire, if you wrote it on a piece of wood and threw the wood into the flames; if you cut it into dough, baked it, and swallowed it, it would cure the bite of a mad dog; in the United States in the nineteenth century, a cheap book of spells recommended it as a fire precaution, a detector of witches, a protection against disease, and good for the cows.

Some echo of all this must surely have filtered through to the wizards of Unseen University, but whether they actually use word squares themselves remains unknown.

THE BLACK SCHOOL

For centuries, Earth has known rumours of a Black School where magic was taught, though none quite matches the venerable antiquity of the Disc's Unseen University, now some two thousand years old. The only possible contenders would be certain secret academies where (if we can believe the rather unreliable Roman author Pomponius Mela in the first century AD) druids trained pupils for twenty years on end 'in sequestered and remote places, whether in a cave or in secluded groves'.

Once real universities became established in the Middle Ages, there soon grew up the legend of their secret counterpart, a college called the Black School where one could learn all the occult arts. It was deep underground, windowless, and pitch dark. Nobody ever saw the Teacher, for that was the Devil himself. Students never went outside. Every evening, they would say aloud what they wanted to learn, and by next morning the right books would have appeared magically on their desks, written in fiery letters that glowed in the dark; or the information would be written in fire upon the walls. And when the course of studies ended, the students would rush to escape through the single door, for it was known that the Devil would take the hindmost – unless he was cunning enough to trick him into seizing his cloak, or his shadow, instead.

And where was this wondrous Black School? Usually it was said to be in one of the great medieval universities, but not of course in one's own country. The learned French scholar and scientist Gerbert d'Aurillac (946–1003), who became Pope Sylvester II, was rumoured to have studied magic at the Islamic university in Cordoba, Spain. The Icelander Sæmundur the Learned (1056–1133) was said to have attended a Black School somewhere in France. In Romania, folk tradition tells of an underground academy called Scholomance, near Sibiu in the mountains of Transylvania (Bram Stoker had heard of this). Others have talked of a Black School in Paris, Padua, Salamanca, Prague, or Wittenburg (Faust studied there). Probably students at Wittenburg and Prague whispered about the fearful occult activities at Oxford and Cambridge.

An aside: It has been suggested by the learned science fiction writer Isaac Asimov that the general western antipathy towards witches is at least partly to do with teeth and beards. The hypothesis runs like this: until the advent of modern dentistry, people who lived to a great age tended to lose their teeth – to get gummy, in fact. For the old widow, perhaps with no family to care for her, that added another problem. She *looked* like a crone, with the lower part of the face dished in and the nose appearing to hook. Of course, the same thing happened to the old men, but *they* could grow long white beards to hide the wrinkles behind, and looked as wise as an Old Testament prophet. Wise wizard, wicked witch . . . what a difference a razor makes.

Chapter 14

MORE CUSTOMS, NAUTICAL LORE *and* MILITARY MATTERS

THERE IS A WIDESPREAD FEELING among folklorists that city-dwellers do not have customs. Maybe there had been some in the very old days, when the city was little more than a collection of villages, but they are long forgotten now. Of course there are various civic and academic occasions which require serious-minded men to process through the streets in outdated ceremonial robes and plumed helmets, but these aren't proper *folk* customs. They are all too obviously well organized and official. They are not archaic and bloodthirsty, nor, on the other hand, do they involve jolly yokels and winsome maidens prancing around with many a merry fol-de-rol. Folklore collectors therefore feel free to ignore them.

However, there comes a time in the history of most cities when somebody says, 'We really ought to have a few customs. They could do wonders for the tourist trade.' Books are consulted. Ideas from elsewhere are forcibly uprooted and shamelessly reworked to fit their new environment. And lo! Suddenly, there are Morris dancers everywhere, and age-old traditions spring up overnight like mushrooms.

This is beginning to happen in Ankh-Morpork. There is a team of folk dancers who have revived the Morris – probably more than one, since Morris dancing is essentially a competitive pastime, sometimes quite dangerously so. Nobby Nobbs is known to be a participant. There are also enthusiastic and delightfully melodious wassailers, who put in weeks of practice before setting out to spread seasonal cheer through the streets of Ankh-Morpork at Hogswatch.

The custom was referred to by Anaglypta Huggs, organizer of the best and most select group of the city's singers, as an occasion for fellowship and good cheer . . .

The singers were halfway down Park Lane now, and halfway through 'The Red Rosy Hen greets the Dawn of the Day' in marvellous harmony. Their collecting tins were already full of donations for the poor of the city, or at least those sections of the poor who in Mrs Huggs' opinion were suitably picturesque and not too smelly and could be relied upon to say thank you . . .

In fact the hen is not the bird traditionally associated with heralding a new sunrise, but Mrs Huggs, while collecting many old folk songs for posterity, had taken care to rewrite them where necessary to avoid, as she put it, 'offending those of a refined disposition with unwarranted coarseness'. Much to her surprise, people often couldn't spot the unwarranted coarseness until it had been pointed out to them.

Sometimes a chicken is nothing but a bird. [*Hogfather*]

Thanks to the humorous workings of narrative necessity, these well-bred singers, so beautifully free from anything that could distress either the musical ear or the moral susceptibilities of their audience, find themselves face to face with what may well be the last vestige of pure, raw wassailing in the city, the makers of the Rough Music of Time – Foul Ole Ron and the Canting Crew of deranged beggars, singing and swearing at the tops of their voices, and banging saucepans together. The beggars are not well versed in folkloric theory, but they do know this is the sort of thing one does at midwinter, and have good reason to believe that if you make enough din people will give you money to stop.

Those who have looked into the history of folklore of western Europe over the last couple of hundred years will notice some quite astonishing similarities to this situation. There too, some genteel Victorian collectors, while professing their deep love of tradition, took for granted that it must be stripped of all coarseness and daintily repackaged. There too, some customs slipped down the social scale till they were little more than a way for the poorest of the working class (or even beggars) to extract a little beer-money from their betters at festive seasons. And there too, these same customs might be rediscovered, imitated, revived and updated by later and more sophisticated generations.

As soon as people begin to *notice* a custom (as opposed to just doing it), they start wondering where, when and why it began. They weave wonderful theories. But this is futile, since folklore is almost always unaccountable:

> Very few people do know how Tradition is supposed to go. There's a certain mysterious ridiculousness about it by its very nature – *once* there was a reason why you had to carry a posy of primroses on Soul Cake Tuesday, but *now* you did it because that's what was Done. [*Jingo*]

> The ceremony still carries on, of course. If you left off traditions because you didn't know why they started you'd be no better than a foreigner. [*Hogfather*]

In both worlds, old customs discarded by adults are often kept going for a few generations by children. According to the Bursar, when he was a boy there was a custom on Soul Cake Tuesday that children would roll boiled eggs down the Tump, a large steep hill on the outskirts of the city. Naturally, nobody can say what the point of it is, apart from the fairly obvious fact that it is fun, and that the eggs are nice to eat, even if they are a bit cracked and muddy. As Nanny Ogg would say, with surprising Biblical insight, 'We all have to eat a peck of dirt before we die.'

Since children in Lancre and other rural areas also get given eggs on this date, as we mentioned earlier, there is every reason to think the custom is genuinely folksy – possibly even mythic, if the Soul

Cake Duck is involved. If so, it would have begun as something serious, to be done by adults. There are some people, including the compiler of *The Discworld Almanak*, who claim that the duck plays a major role in primeval mythology:

> Curiously written out of early legends of the creation of the Universe is the *Great Duck*, from whose single egg the whole of Creation was hatched. However, truth will out, and it is now known that, from the outside, infinity is duck-egg blue.

It turns out that this was written in haste by a member of the *Almanak* staff to justify an error elsewhere in the book, but there once were similar myths scattered throughout our own world (in ancient Egypt, Finland, India, Greece and Persia, for example), telling how the universe was hatched from an egg laid by some Great Bird, often a duck or goose. And *that*, in a roundabout sort of way, might explain those chocolate eggs people buy at Easter, without quite knowing why.

Folk custom also explains why one occasionally sees visitors to Ankh-Morpork leaning over the Brass Bridge in a meaningful manner. They are acting upon an old superstition that if you throw a coin into the Ankh you'll be sure to return to the city – or is it if you just *throw up* into the Ankh? Probably it is a coin after all, since a remarkable number of supposedly rational species in various worlds feel compelled to toss coins into rivers, fountains, wishing-wells, and even oddly shaped cascades in airport terminals, in a vague expectation of good luck and wishes fulfilled. Why? Well, in the case of airports it is a convenient way of getting rid of small change you won't need in Sydney while at the same time getting a small smug feeling of having done some good, but in the other cases? What mechanism is operating here, in the twenty-first century? On the Discworld, though, they know why. The Lady is a real presence.

*

Unseen University has a whole clutch of traditional ceremonies and festivals of its own, carried out with unfailing regularity. These of course have nothing whatever to do with anything or anybody beyond the University's walls. They are 'gown', not 'town', and emphatically not 'folk'. Those which involve processing through the public streets do so as a way of inspiring due respect in the uncultured masses. A prime example is the Convivium, when the Archchancellor, Council, and entire senior staff proceed ceremonially from the University to the Opera House, where new graduates are awarded their degrees in the presence of the Patrician. The procession then returns, rather more quickly, for a large banquet.

But one ceremony which has a certain impact on the townsfolk is the Beating of the Bounds every 22 Grune. This involves a choir, all able-bodied members of staff, and a gaggle of students retracing the exact route of the boundaries of the University, as originally laid down centuries ago. They walk through or if necessary climb over any buildings that have since been built across the route, while ceremonially striking members of the public with live ferrets (in memory, for reasons unknown, of a long-ago Archchancellor Buckleby).

> Any red-headed men encountered are seized by several strong young men and given a 'plunking'; this tradition has, most unusually – and subsequent to an incident which left three wizards hanging precariously from a gutter – been amended to read 'any red-headed men except of course Captain Carrot Ironfoundersson of the Watch'. After the progress, the entire membership of the University heads back to the Great Hall for a huge breakfast at which duck must be served. [*The Discworld Companion*]

Why red-heads? In Ankh-Morpork the reason, if there ever was one, is forgotten. On Earth, folklore asserts that red hair was the mark of Judas, and is found in descendants of Jews and of Viking raiders. They were distrusted, though there is no record of people plunking them.

In Britain and Europe, processions to Beat the Bounds (also known as Rogation Processions) were mainly found in country districts, where priests led the people round the parish boundaries, blessing the fields and praying for a good harvest. The custom was legally useful too; when local administration was organized by parishes, it was important that everyone knew just where one parish ended and another began. That way, taxes and tithes could be fairly assessed, and if a penniless beggar dropped dead on the road one knew whose job it was to bury him. Boundary markers on walls, stones or trees were inspected, renewed if necessary, and ritually 'beaten' with rods. Sometimes boys were upended and beaten too, to make sure the next generation remembered everything quite clearly.

The custom does not often survive in towns, but in Oxford on Ascension Day two parishes still provide a spectacle remarkably similar to what can be seen in Ankh-Morpork (but without the ferrets, alas). In the words of folklorist Steve Roud:

> The boundary markers in Oxford can be set into walls, high or low, or even into the floor, and can be down narrow alleyways, in basements, and behind or inside buildings. The routes take in the college buildings within the parish as well as shops and pubs, much to the surprise of people they meet on the way. They stop for refreshments at various locations, and at one point students throw coins and sweets for the choristers to scramble for. [*The English Year* (2006)]

In Ankh-Morpork there are also traditional student activities, notably the dreaded Rag Week, which has all the normal perils of student humour with the additional seasoning of magic. Prudent citizens take evasive action, but the event is welcomed by the landlords of the Mended Drum, the Bunch of Grapes, and other hostelries, since much alcohol is traditionally consumed.

The even more dreaded mass football match is now discontinued. This used to involve teams of fifty students apiece from the University itself and from each of the Guild Colleges attempting to kick or carry a football from the outskirts of the Shades to the Tower of Art. Goals were scored by kicking the ball through the door (or more often the window) of landmarks along the way, most of them having names like the Mended Drum, the Bunch of Grapes, etc. The scoring team had then to be bought drinks by the other teams. Much alcohol was traditionally consumed. There were occasions when the match went on for a month.

Something very similar used to happen on Earth, and in some cases still does. For, just as there is a whole area of folklore that concerns singing very loudly until being given money to stop, or at least to go away and infest some other street, so there is an area chock-full of folk games that consist of two sides trying to get a ball (or similar token) into an opposing goal by means of, apparently, a bout of all-in wrestling.

In many towns of Britain, some five or six hundred years ago, the streets would periodically be jammed tight with a heaving mass of young men shoving, kicking and head-butting one another. If you watched long enough, you would probably work out that it was not a fight after all, but some kind of game played between two teams. Somewhere down out of sight there would be a ball being kicked or carried, for this was the true, the original, form of British football. No rules worth mentioning, no limit on the number of men crazy enough to play for one team or the other. No goal posts either; the 'goals' would be at opposite ends of the town, at least a mile apart, and might just as likely be ponds or streams as buildings. It was a wild, violent type of game, and might very well last all day. In Derby in 1829 a writer explained how it was done:

> The game commences in the market-place, where the partisans of each parish are drawn up on each side, and about noon, a large ball is tossed up in the midst of them. This is seized on by some of the strongest and most active men. The rest of the players immediately close in upon them, and a solid mass is

formed. It then becomes the object of each party to impel the crowd towards their own particular goal. The struggle to obtain the ball, which is carried in the arms of those who have possessed themselves of it, is violent . . . It would be difficult to give an adequate idea of this ruthless sport. A Frenchman passing through Derby remarked that if Englishmen called this playing, it would be impossible to say what they called fighting.

If you asked the players what the point was, they'd probably tell you it celebrated the defeat of some Scotsmen (or Englishmen, or Vikings, according to taste), whose heads were then kicked round the battlefield.

The tough young fellows who played it absolutely loved it. Others were less enthusiastic. People got injured, as the respectable citizens of Chester complained in the 1530s, 'some having their bodies bruised or crushed, some their arms, heads or legs broken, and some otherwise maimed or in peril of their lives'. Worse still, windows got broken, which was expensive. The town authorities stopped the Chester game in 1539, but in some other places people were more stubborn; in Derby it took soldiers, special constables, and the reading of the Riot Act to finally subdue the footballers in 1849. Some towns kept their mass football till late in the nineteenth century. Indeed, there are a few places where it is still vigorously played. It can be seen at Alnwick in Northumberland and Ashbourne in Derbyshire every Shrove Tuesday, and at Kirkwall in Orkney at the New Year.

The 'Haxey Hood Game' at Haxey in Lincolnshire every January is similar, though it is surrounded by more ceremonial, and though the object tussled over is not a ball but a roll of leather, like a truncheon. Allegedly, this represents the hood of a long-ago medieval lady which blew off, causing twelve or thirteen labourers to go chasing after it. Who knows, but for that unthinking piece of gallantry we might now be watching Association Archery on Saturday afternoons.

GHOST SHIPS

In *Small Gods* there's a description of a shipwreck. When the captain cries, 'We'll have to abandon ship!' Death replies, NO. WE WILL TAKE IT WITH US. IT IS A NICE SHIP. And so, though the ship has been completely smashed up and everyone aboard is drowned, it seems to become whole again (in a way) and sails away, grey and slightly transparent, through darkness and silence, bearing the ghosts of men and of rats.

Sailors on Earth also find it perfectly natural that a ship can become a ghost, since before it sank it had been a living creature, with a soul of its own – a 'she', in fact, not an 'it'. She's got a name, hasn't she? And wasn't she christened, just like a human being, with somebody blessing her and smashing a bottle of champagne over her? In French fishing villages, there would be a full-scale religious ceremony for a new boat, with a godfather and godmother, and a priest to sprinkle holy water; everyone was given blessed bread, including the boat herself – scraps of the bread would be put into holes in the mast.

Many also thought that a ship had a guardian spirit. Some said it lived in the figurehead. Others, from Ancient Egypt to modern China and the Mediterranean, have painted huge eyes on the prow; these are the eyes of its guardian, to bring luck, to see the way ahead, and to outstare any evil spirits. The Swedes have a different notion; they say that when boat-builders cut a tree down to make the keel, the tree's guardian gnome follows it, and becomes the boat's luck-bringer.

Ships and death go well together. Vikings thought a dead man should sail in his own boat to the land of the dead. So some of them buried or burned the man and the boat together; others lit a pyre for the corpse on board a ship, which was then set drifting out to sea; others marked the site of the man's grave by an oval of standing stones, forming the outline of a boat. An English poet, D. H. Lawrence, wrote in the 1920s of 'The Ship of Death':

We are dying, we are dying, so all we can do
is now to be willing to die, and to build the ship
of death to carry the soul on its longest journey.

A little ship, with oars and food
and little dishes, and all accoutrements
fitting and ready for the departing soul.

There are also the phantom ships doomed to sail the seas of
Earth for ever, because of some crime or sin committed on board, or
because of the tragic circumstances in which they sank. To see one is
an omen of disaster, or at least of very bad weather. You can recognize them because they are sailing at full speed against the wind, or
when there is no wind at all. Often they have no crew; if there is one,
they are skeletons. They never reach a port; they never answer when
hailed. There is at least one, at Porthcurno in Cornwall, which has
been seen to sail straight for the shore at dusk, rise up into the air,
and go on sailing *across dry land*.

The most famous of the phantom ships is the *Flying Dutchman*.
She haunts the seas around the Cape of Good Hope, because her
captain blasphemously swore he would round the Cape, despite a gale,
even if it took him till Doomsday. In Britain, several ghost ships haunt
the Solway Firth, as a result of crimes. Two were pirate vessels; one was
deliberately wrecked by a jealous murderer as it carried a bridal party;
one was a slave trader, homeward bound, whose rich but godless
captain refused to go ashore to attend church on Christmas Day. There
is also the *Lady Lovibund*, which is supposed to appear on 13 February
once every fifty years, heading for the Goodwin Sands (in the Channel,
off Deal), because the first mate deliberately ran it aground there, being
driven crazy with jealousy because he was in love with the captain's
newly wedded bride. This is said to have happened in 1748, and some
people claim the spectral ship was sighted at fifty-year intervals up to
and including 1948. Oddly, when boatloads of journalists went looking
for it in 1998, it failed to appear.

The derelict ghost ships in *Going Postal* are real, or rather, the way they hang suspended in the depths of the sea was once thought to be a real scientific possibility. But the wonderful image of skeletons crewing rotting hulks faded in the light of deep oceanic research in the nineteenth century. Until then, it was quite respectable to assume that water, like air, got denser with depth, and that a stricken ship would sink only until it encountered water at a density slightly higher than its own, where it might then drift on the interface until it rotted. In fact water does not compress like air, which is why fish at the bottom of the sea don't have to drill holes in it. When you sink, you sink.

FEMALE SOLDIERS

Folk songs, most notably 'Sweet Polly Oliver', keep alive the theme of the cross-dressing girl who goes off to war in men's attire:

> As sweet Polly Oliver lay musing in bed,
> A sudden strange fancy came into her head:
> 'Nor father nor mother shall make me false prove,
> I'll 'list for a soldier and follow my love.'

> So early next morning she softly arose,
> And dressed herself up in her dead brother's clothes.
> She cut her hair close, and she stained her face brown,
> And went for a soldier to fair London Town.

The songs were based on fact, and *Monstrous Regiment* was only an exaggeration for comic effect – very little which is said in that book about the girls' cross-dressing experiences was made up.

There are plenty of references to such women in the eighteenth and nineteenth centuries[13] (up to 1,400 of them in the American Civil

---

[13] Indeed, more or less throughout recorded history, but this is when it happened in a major way.

War, it has been suggested, but 500 or fewer seems more acceptable). They made the decision out of love, for adventure, or from a desire to escape from a burdensome life. They came to light as a result of falling in love, betraying themselves by lack of acting skill, or being wounded somewhere that obliged the surgeon to remove the patient's trousers; or, quite often, by proudly admitting it much later on. When some of them were grandmothers. Obviously, we will never know about ones who didn't own up.

The subject is a fascinating one, and well documented. We give a couple of titles in the bibliography, but there are many more. What is interesting is how easily women could get away with it (after the not-really-serious were weeded out very early on). The Pollys often did well, acting as spies, where their wonderful skill at dressing up as women was a great help, and even getting promoted. There is a whole slew of explanations as to how they kept their secret while living with hundreds of men, and some of these turn up in *Monstrous Regiment*. For instance, in an age long before unisex fashions, trousers meant 'man' and skirts meant 'woman'. Trousers plus high-pitched voice meant 'young man'. People didn't expect anything else, and saw what they expected to see. Many Pollys joined up as boys, and if the lad was a little shy, no one thought that odd. People did not often see one another naked, and the surgeon amputating a foot might only roll the trouser leg above the knee. But the big reason is that, if they are determined and careful, women can easily fool men.

However, there was one thing, according to accounts, that many of them just could not manage. It was swearing. Many could not bring themselves to cuss, and found the ripe language of their comrades hard to bear, let alone imitate. So . . . a bit of a change there, at least!

Chapter 15

KIDS' STUFF . . . YOU KNOW, ABOUT 'ORRID MURDER *and* BLOOD

THERE ARE MANY LINKS between folklore and the mental world of children, but they do not always follow the paths one might expect. Theoreticians in the Ankh-Morpork Folklore Society (and indeed in similar institutions here) love to think that some age-old memory, preferably of something quite horrible, lurks in the background of the simplest rhyme or game. They claim, for example, that when children shape big fat figures out of piled-up snow and push in lumps of coal as eyes, these are 'obvious survivals' of primitive idols representing the dreaded Ice Giants with their tiny, deep-set black eyes who, according to mythology, will one day overwhelm the world. Of course, the children say they just do it for fun – they would, wouldn't they? But a theoretical folklorist rarely if ever takes note of what the folk themselves have to say. It stands to reason that he or she is far better equipped than they are to roll back the mists of time. And in two shakes of a duck's tail, the theory is accepted as a proven fact. If the moving pictures enterprise once begun at Holy Wood had succeeded, by now every audience in Ankh-Morpork would know that when a film-maker shows a brief shot of a snowman he means everyone to shudder at this sinister symbol of ecological doom and the imminent End of the World. Meanwhile, the kids go on throwing snowballs and lumps of coal around, regardless.

In our Earthly culture, many parents and teachers worry whether fairy tales and nursery rhymes and children's games and customs are respectable, morally and educationally sound, and fully in accord with health and safety regulations. Judging from existing records, few adults on the Disc are bothered by these issues. There, at least in the poorer parts of Ankh-Morpork, children freely play brutal and unhygienic street games, hallowed by long tradition. These include Dead Rat Conkers and Tiddley-Rat, though a recent observer has noted that Turd Races in the gutter appear to have died out, despite an attempt to take them upmarket with the name Poosticks. Hopscotch too is popular, especially a variation which Captain Vimes played in childhood, in which you kicked the least popular kid from one square to another, singing 'William Scuggins is a bastard' – actions and words which do not figure in handbooks designed for games teachers.

Throughout the multiverse, parents have repeatedly discovered the useful fact that the best way to control a child is by working on its imagination to create a gruesome anthropomorphic personification: 'Don't you dare play in the cornfield! If you do, the Corn Mother will come with her long iron teeth and her long iron claws, and tear you to bits' – 'Behave yourselves while I'm out. Remember that Rawhead-and-Bloody-Bones is watching you!' Used in moderation, these Frighteners and Prohibitory Monsters have a great deal to recommend them. If Nanny Ogg's grandchildren believe there's a demon inside the copper in her wash-house,[14] and if country children everywhere are scared of deep pools because there's something down there with green eyes and big teeth just *longing* to pull them in, a lot of nasty accidents will be avoided.

But there are snags, particularly on Discworld. Even though the adults don't believe the Frighteners are real, the children do, and the high magic quotient built into the very fabric of the Disc ensures that whatever is powerfully believed in will, very shortly, exist. ('If

---

[14] In this particular case, the demonic warning might well be justified.

only people would *think* before they invent monsters,' sighed Miss Tick, the teacher-witch of the Chalk country.) The problem seems to be at its worst in cities. True, there are fewer natural dangers there, but semi-sadistic adults still enjoy inducing irrational fears, as Susan Sto-Helit found when she became a governess in Ankh-Morpork. Since she was one of the rare adults capable of seeing the resulting monsters, she knew how to deal with them:

> One of the many terrors conjured up by the previous governess's happy way with children had been the bears that waited around in the street to eat you if you stood on the cracks [in the pavement].
>
> Susan had taken to carrying the poker under her respectable coat. One wallop generally did the trick. The bears were amazed that anyone else saw them . . .
>
> The previous governess had used various monsters and bogeymen as a form of discipline. There was always something waiting to eat or carry off bad boys and girls for crimes like stuttering or defiantly and aggravatingly persisting in writing with their left hand. There was always a Scissor Man waiting for a little girl who sucked her thumb, always a bogeyman in the cellar. Of such bricks is the innocence of childhood constructed. [*Hogfather*]

It is impossible to describe what bogeymen look like, since they are skilled shape-shifters and mould their appearance to match whatever horrors they find lurking in their child-victim's subconscious. But one *can* say how to get rid of them – at any rate, on the Discworld. They are terrified of blankets, especially those with blue fluffy bunnies on. Even a small square of blanket fabric drives them off. Which stands to reason, for if you can protect yourself from a bogeyman by hiding your head under the blanket, how much more effective it will be to drop a blanket on *his* head!

Most of the Frighteners exist on Earth too. A poem by A. A. Milne tells how Pavement Bears lurked in the streets of London in the 1930s; sensible children watched their feet as they walked, taking care to tread only on the square paving stones, never on the cracks between them.

The Earthly Scissor Man, a monstrous tailor, was first described in nineteenth-century Germany by Heinrich Hoffman in *Struwwelpeter*, a book of verses known in English as *Shock-Headed Peter*. There, he is a tailor, a 'great, long, red-legged Scissor Man'.

> One day Mama said, 'Conrad dear,
> I must go out and leave you here.
> But mind now, Conrad, what I say,
> Don't suck your thumb while I'm away.
> The great tall tailor always comes
> To little boys that suck their thumbs;
> And ere they dream what he's about,
> He takes his great sharp scissors out,
> And cuts their thumbs clean off, and then,
> You know, they never grow again.'

On the Discworld, he looks different:

> When Susan turned to go up the stairs the Scissor Man was there.
>
> It wasn't man-shaped. It was something like an ostrich, and something like a lizard on its hind legs, but almost entirely like something made out of blades. Every time it moved a thousand blades went snip, snip.
>
> Its long silver neck curved and a head made of shears stared down at her.
>
> 'You're not looking for me,' she said. 'You're not *my* nightmare.' [*Hogfather*]

Then there's the Sandman. He sweeps right across the world at the speed of dark, just as dusk falls, and gets inside every house where there are children. It's up to him to make sure that they go up the wooden hill to *Bed*fordshire the *very minute* they're told, and get straight into bed and go straight off to sleep, no fooling about. If the mother is kind-hearted and modern in her views, she will say he does this by sprinkling magic sand which makes them so sleepy that they can't keep their eyes open. Those who are less soppy know that the bag of sand he carries is small, but heavy, and he doesn't bother to take any out before he swings it against the child's skull.

These days, on our world, he has been 'dwindled'; mums all have the same idea of a *nice* Sandman. But go back a couple of hundred years, to a time when people really knew how to keep children in a constant wholesome state of terror, and listen to what a nanny says in a story by another German author, E. T. A. Hoffman:

> 'Oh, the Sandman is a wicked man, who comes to little children when they won't go to bed, and throws handfuls of sand in their eyes, so they jump out of their heads all bloody; and he puts them in a bag and takes them to the half-moon as food for his little ones; and they sit there in the nest and have hooked beaks like owls, to pick at the eyes of naughty little boys and girls.'

The magic of childhood is not what it was.

Thankfully, not all Anthropomorphic and Theriomorphic Personifications are so sinister. Jack Frost, an elderly man who draws ferns and paisley patterns on window panes at night, has no dealings with children at all. The Soul Cake Duck lays chocolate eggs for them, in gardens, on the Tuesday of the Soul Cake Days in the month of Sektober; she hides them well (but not too well), so that the kiddies can have fun hunting for them. In spite of her name, she does *not* lay cakes. Her equivalent on Earth is the German and Swiss Easter Hare, who has been laying eggs for children to find since the sixteenth century. Nowadays he is known in Britain and America under the name of the Easter Bunny – a terrible come-down. At first the Hare only laid real eggs, often brightly painted; more recently he has been producing chocolate ones. German and Swiss children enjoy building little nests of moss and flowers and hay, ready for the Hare to use. Just how a hare – and a male hare at that – can *lay* chocolate eggs will be no mystery to anyone who has noticed certain little brown oval objects in the corner of the rabbit hutch.

Then there are the ever-welcome tooth fairies. Everybody knows what *they* do – when a child loses a tooth, he or she must slip it under the pillow, and a tooth fairy will come in the night to take it away, leaving at least half an Ankh-Morpork dollar as payment. Despite the name, they do not belong to the same species as elves, or even gnomes. They are human-sized, rather plain and dumpy, and none too bright.

> Fairies aren't necessarily little twinkly creatures. It's purely a job description, and the commonest ones aren't even visible. A fairy is simply any creature currently employed under super-natural laws to take things away or, as in the case of the Verruca Gnome, to bring things. [*Hogfather*]

Tooth fairies are to be found chiefly in towns (there are at least half a dozen in Ankh-Morpork alone), and then only in moderately well-off homes. This is probably due to socio-economic factors, since it is generally supposed that the coins the fairy brings have been re-cycled (by bogeymen) after being lost in the very same house. You won't find many coins under the furniture of a cottage in Lancre, where the basic unit of currency is the chicken. Nor, come to that, in the poor quarters of Ankh-Morpork, in a place like Cockbill Street. Pennies were precious in Cockbill Street; if you had any spare ones you put them by to get you a decent funeral; you didn't lose them under the settee, because you didn't have one. The Tooth Fairy rarely visits Cockbill Street.

Actually, it is wrong to speak of *The* Tooth Fairy, as if there was only one of her. The mistake originated in America somewhere around 1960, and has mysteriously leapt across the dimensions in an attempt to gain a footing in the Discworld. Fortunately, in Ankh-Morpork Violet Bottler and her fellow workers are united in loyalty to one another and to their weekly wage, insisting that they are all, each and every one of them, tooth fair*ies*.

In Britain, it is certain that fairies (in the plural) have been collecting children's shed milk teeth from under pillows for about a hundred years, leaving money in exchange. What happened earlier is a mystery. Victorian folklore books do not mention tooth fairies, but this is probably because the collectors spent their time hunting for excitingly unusual customs and beliefs; it did not occur to them that the everyday stuff in their own homes was interesting too.

Nowadays, owing to pervasive American influence, British children believe in one single Tooth Fairy. She is immensely popular. Even dentists talk about her, and keep a stock of dinky little envelopes with her picture on, so that when children have a tooth professionally extracted, they can take it home and pop it under the pillow just the same.

So, how long have tooth fairies been around? There is one small scrap of evidence that in seventeenth-century England elves and fairies were already busy collecting pretty little items in the human world and carting them off to fairyland to decorate their dwellings – which answers the question, 'What exactly do the fairies *do* with the teeth?' This evidence comes in the poem 'Oberon's Palace' by Robert Herrick, number 444 in his book *Hesperides* (1648). The poem describes a charming little cave or grotto where Oberon the Fairy King goes to make love to Queen Mab. They are very small fairies, possibly the same species as are often mistaken for wasps on the Disc. The cave walls are decorated with bits of peacock feathers, fish scales, blue snake skins, dewdrops etc. The floor is a mosaic of plum-tree gum, dice, brown toadstones, human fingernails, warts, and the teeth of squirrels and children 'lately shed'. These bits and pieces, says Herrick, are 'brought hither by the Elves'. They are not following *quite* the same procedure as a modern tooth fairy, since they don't leave money, but they're well on the way.

There is another way of dealing with shed teeth, and this too goes back to the seventeenth century. Children would just rub the tooth with salt and throw it in the fire. This was still done in some homes in the 1950s, especially in the north of England, sometimes with a verse:

Fire, fire, burn a bone,
God send me a tooth again,
A straight one, a strong one,
A white shiny bright one.

In many parts of Europe, especially Germany and Russia, it wasn't fairies that took the teeth, but mice or rats. And what they gave in exchange was not a coin, but lovely new teeth to grow in place of the old – teeth as strong, sharp and well shaped as their own. So children would shove the tooth as far as they could down a mousehole, with some suitable rhyme:

Mousey, mousey, mousey,
Here's my tooth of bone,
Mousey, bring a new tooth,
A tooth as hard as stone.

Tooth Mice didn't care whether a home was rich or poor, and they were one hundred per cent reliable. No child who put a tooth in a mousehole ever failed to find a new one growing through its gums.

Unfortunately, the same magic law of like-to-like meant that if people were careless about shed teeth, the unlucky child could end up with something very ugly indeed. According to the folklorist Charlotte Latham, writing in 1878 about superstitions she had noted in Sussex ten years earlier:

> A servant girl said children's cast teeth must never be thrown away, because if an animal found and gnawed them, the new tooth would grow just like that animal's. 'Look at old Master Simmons,' she said, 'with that gurt big pig's tooth in his upper jaw. He allus says 'twas his mam's fault, she having dropped one of his baby teeth in the hog's trough, accidental like.'

Poor Master Simmons! If he had lived on the Disc, people would have told him how lucky he was to look just like the Hogfather, whose teeth are remarkably tusk-like.

But there is an older, darker reason why shed teeth must either be entirely destroyed by fire, or be hidden somewhere where nobody can ever lay hands on them. It has to do with power, and control, and magic – a magic so old and so simple it's hardly magic at all. In our world, this is explained by Sir James Frazer in his famous work *The Golden Bough*:

> The most familiar example of Contagious Magic is the magical sympathy which is supposed to exist between a man and any severed portion of his person, such as his hair or nails; so that whoever gets possession of human hair or nails may work his will, at any distance, upon the person from whom they were cut. This superstition is worldwide.

Exactly the same principle works on the Discworld, as the assassin Teatime knows only too well, especially as regards teeth. So does Archchancellor Mustrum Ridcully, who remarks, with reference to his own toenails,

'You can't be too careful. Get hold of something like someone's nail clippings and you've got 'em under your control. That's real old magic. Dawn of time stuff.' [*Hogfather*]

HOGSWATCH

In the bleak midwinter, frosty winds make moan. People, on the other hand, make as much loud and cheerful noise as they can:

> People have always had the urge to sing and clang things at the dark stub of the year, when all sorts of psychic nastiness has taken advantage of the long grey days and the deep shadows to lurk and breed. Lately people in Ankh-Morpork's better districts had taken to singing harmoniously, which rather lost the effect. Those who really understood just clanged something and shouted. [*Hogfather*]

They also gather to eat and drink and dance, to light bonfires, and to give one another presents. This happens in many parts of the multiverse, provided the climate is suitable. Obviously, you've got to have a midwinter before you can have a midwinter festival, so there's no point looking for one in hot regions like Djelibeybi or the Rimward hinterland of Klatch, but wherever there's a cold dark season you can find something pretty much like Hogswatchnight. It's a way of telling the Sun what you expect of him – 'Rise and shine, Sun, start to grow strong again, drive back the Ice Giants, bring us the warmth of Spring.' The Sun needs a little encouragement, whatever astronomers may say.

The Disc is a lucky world in that the sensible arrangement of its sun, its disc, and its supporting elephants has ensured that the dates of its solstices can be easily observed without any need for complicated maths – unlike Earth, where the hours of sunrise and sunset stay apparently the same for three or four days around midsummer and midwinter, giving rise to muddled arguments over whether Midsummer Day is 21 June or 24 June, and why the Romans chose 25 December rather than the 21st as the Feast of the Unconquered Sun. It is also lucky for the inhabitants of Lancre, Ankh-Morpork and the Sto Plains that some sensible ruler in ancient times decided that the night of the winter solstice, Hogswatchnight, would also count as New Year's Eve. Would that all calendars were as simple and rational! As a result, it is *both* the time of the darkest shadows, *and* the time when all the old year's occult rubbish has piled up and must be cleared away, *and* the time for the largest, loudest feast of the year.

The name 'Hogswatch' makes perfectly good sense for the Discworld, where the festive fare at midwinter is centred on pig-meat in one form or another – roast boar, pork joints, pork pies, sausages, hams, pigs' heads, black puddings – and where the Hogfather, the seasonal gift-bringer, gallops across the skies in a sledge drawn by wild boars. This is a world where pigs (at least, certain special pigs on a certain special night) can and do fly. Oddly, in Scotland and northern England there is a rather similar-sounding name for New Year's Eve, Hogmanay – a word which has been known since the sixteenth century, but which nobody has managed to explain. Moreover, British Methodists call Christmas Eve and New Year's Eve the *Watch* Nights, and hold midnight services. There are parts of Europe (notably Romania, Serbia, Sweden and Norway) where roast pig or a pig's head is *the* thing to eat at Christmas. All this surely proves that echoes of the great Discworld festival drifted across the dimensions and became fruitfully confused in receptive Earthly minds.

Be that as it may, there is a good practical reason why midwinter feasting is so lavish – it's the season for a mass slaughter of livestock. Why use up large amounts of fodder keeping *all* your animals alive through the winter? Come the spring, a single young healthy bull, ram and boar will be enough to service all your cows, ewes and sows. So, kill off the surplus males, and for once everyone can eat as much fresh meat as they like, and then salt or smoke the rest, and with luck they'll have enough to last all winter. Farmers have been doing this for thousands of years. The people who built Stonehenge, about 2500 BC, left enormous piles of half-eaten bones littering a village some two miles away – bones of cattle, and many, many pigs. The pigs' teeth show they were young beasts, killed at about nine months old, just right for the winter solstice. And there were so many bones that people must have been gathering from miles around for this annual feast. Whatever its name may have been, it was the Hogswatch of its time.

Very likely, it went on for more than just one night and day. There's not much work needed on farms at midwinter, so why not spread the fun out for as long as possible? Many peoples have had this idea. The Ancient Romans managed to turn most of December into one long festive season. First came the Saturnalia, a period of five or six days of revelry beginning on 17 December and honouring Saturn, god of new-sown crops. Shops were closed, work was forbidden (except cooking and baking), people gave one another presents, and everyone was expected to be full of jests and japes and jollity. There were parties, at which men drew lots to see who would preside as 'king' of the feast; his word was law, and he could order the guests to do all kinds of ridiculous things – dance naked, for instance, or pick up the flute-girl and carry her three times round the room. Often, social distinctions were turned topsy-turvy: slaves sat at table and gorged, while their masters waited on them. We suspect that the slaves were magnanimous in office, though; tomorrow the masters would be the masters again.

Then came the Feast of the Unconquered Sun on the 25th, a relatively sober affair. And then the wild three-day celebration of the Kalends, beginning on New Year's Day, 1 January. All Romans, rich or poor, ate and drank the best they could afford. Adults gave one another presents yet again (children are not mentioned). Houses were decked inside and out with evergreens – holly, ivy, laurel, branches of conifers, whatever was still alive and green in the dead season. There were torches and lamps everywhere. People hardly went to bed, but roamed the streets disguised in masks and weird costumes of animal skins. A great deal of wine was consumed.

So powerful were these traditions that when the Roman Empire became Christian most of its midwinter customs were adapted so as to fit in with the new religion. Christ's birth was being celebrated on 25 December in Rome as early as the year 354, while in 567 a Church Council at Tours laid down that the whole period of twelve days from 25 December to 6 January (feast of the Epiphany) would be one long festal cycle, during which all but the most essential work must cease. And so the Twelve Days of Christmas were born.

There are echoes of all this on the Disc. There are songs about what gifts one's true love sends on the Twelve Days of Hogswatch, involving partridges and pear trees, and others about the rising of the sun and the running of the deer. Homes are decorated with special Hogswatch trees, not to mention holly, ivy, mistletoe. The mistletoe is felt, obscurely, to be especially significant, even in Unseen University, where there can be no question of anyone kissing anyone:

'Well, er . . . it's . . . well, it's symbolic, Archchancellor.'

'Ah?'

The Senior Wrangler felt that something more was expected. He groped around in the dusty attics of his education.

'Of . . . the leaves, d'y'see . . . they're symbolic of . . . of green, d'y'see, whereas the berries, in fact, yes, the berries symbolize . . . symbolize white. Yes. White and green. Very . . . symbolic.'

He waited. He was not, unfortunately, disappointed.

'What of?'

'I'm not sure that there *has* to *be* an *of*,' he said.

'Ah? So,' said the Archchancellor, thoughtfully, 'it could be said that the white and green symbolize a small parasitic plant?'

'Yes indeed,' said the Senior Wrangler.

'So mistletoe, in fact, symbolizes mistletoe?'

'Exactly, Archchancellor,' said the Senior Wrangler, who was now just hanging on.

'Funny thing, that,' said Ridcully, in the same thoughtful tone of voice. 'That statement is either so deep that it would take a lifetime to fully comprehend every particle of its meaning, or it is a load of absolute tosh. Which is it, I wonder?'
[Hogfather]

Not tosh, probably. Plants which insist on staying green, and even bearing white berries or red berries, when others are bare and dry are, in their own way, as unconquered as the midwinter sun. They are life, and they refuse to die.

Unseen University observes another age-old custom at Hogswatch, the appointment of a Boy Archchancellor. A first-year student is selected to be the Archchancellor for a whole day, from dawn till dusk. During this period he can exert the full powers of that office, and there are many tales of japes played on senior members of the College Council. Yet inevitably, inexorably, dusk will come. For this reason the student selected for the honour is usually the most unpopular boy in the University, and his life expectancy the following day is brief.

On Earth too there are traces of this urge to turn normal authority upside down during midwinter and New Year celebrations. At the Roman Saturnalia, as we have said, slaves feasted while masters acted as servants. In medieval France, low-ranking clergy sometimes took charge of the services in cathedrals on New Year's Day or Twelfth Day and turned them into a Feast of Fools or Asses' Feast. Their leader would call himself 'bishop' or 'pope' for the day. Theologians in Paris in 1445 complained that these clerical revellers came into church dressed up in ridiculous costumes and masks, pretending to be women and minstrels; they ran up and down the aisles, leaping and dancing; worse still, they sat round the altar eating black puddings, gambling, and singing wanton songs, and then went out into the streets to entertain the crowds with their foolery.

There was another medieval 'reversal ritual' known in towns all over western Europe, but this one was absolutely respectable, well controlled, and full of charm – the custom of the Boy Bishop. Either on 6 December, the feast of St Nicholas (the patron saint of children), or on 28 December, the feast of the Holy Innocents (the babies Herod killed), the choirboys had a day off, and chose one of their number to be the Boy Bishop. He held office until Twelfth Night. Dressed in full episcopal robes, he could sit in the bishop's throne and preside at certain services, while the rest of the boys also wore fine robes and sat in the chapter stalls; the real bishop (if present) and the other higher clergy had to go and sit in the choir-stalls. The custom was especially popular in England, where it spread to abbeys, some Oxford and Cambridge colleges, and many wealthy parish churches. Henry VIII forbade it, but it survived (or was revived) in some places. It is still done in Hereford Cathedral, where the Boy Bishop preaches a sermon on St Nicholas's Day.

Meanwhile, out in the countryside, people have their own little ways, as Albert explains when Death talks about the 'real meaning' of Hogswatch:

'What, you mean that the pigs and cattle have all been slaughtered and with any luck everyone's got enough food for the winter?'

WELL, WHEN I SAY THE *REAL* MEANING—

'Some wretched devil's had his head chopped off in a wood somewhere 'cos he found a bean in his dinner and now the summer's going to come back?'

NOT EXACTLY THAT, BUT—

'Oh, you mean that they've chased down some poor beast and shot arrows up into their apple trees and now the shadows are going to go away?'

THAT IS DEFINITELY *A* MEANING, BUT I—

'Ah, then you're talking about the one where they light a bloody big bonfire to give the sun a hint and tell it to stop

lurking under the horizon and do a proper day's work?'
YOU'RE NOT HELPING, ALBERT.
'Well, they're all the real meanings that *I* know.'

It is amazing how much of all this used to happen in our world too, in the days when farming *was* farming, and no one had invented Health and Safety Regulations and Prevention of Cruelty to Animals. Bonfires blazed; burning barrels and cartwheels were rolled down steep hills into watching crowds; men ran through the streets carrying barrels of flaming tar on their heads. In regions where cider apples were grown, villagers would come at midwinter to 'wassail' the trees. This meant they would beat the trunks with sticks, fire guns up into the branches, pour ale over the roots, yell, howl, and blow horns. And they told the trees what was expected of them:

> Here stands a jolly good old apple tree.
> Stand fast, root; bear well, top.
> Every little bough, bear an apple now;
> Every little twig,
> Bear an apple big!
> Hats full, caps full,
> Three-bushel-sacks full!
> Whoop, whoop, holloa!
> Blow, blow the horns!

The trees had better take notice, or else . . .

> Apple-tree, apple-tree,
> Bear good fruit,
> Or down with your top
> And up with your root!

As for 'chasing down some poor beast', there was plenty of that too. In the nineteenth century, bricklayers from Sussex towns would get a day off at the end of November, and go in gangs to the nearest woods armed with short, heavy sticks which they would hurl at squirrels and any other small animals they saw. If they *did* manage to hit a squirrel, they took it home to eat. Foxes, on the other hand, are quite inedible. Which has never discouraged generations of English from going fox-hunting on 26 December, a date called Boxing Day or St Stephen's Day.

Then there was the very curious custom of hunting the wren, which was once widespread in England, France, the Isle of Man, Wales, and especially in Ireland; it happened on St Stephen's Day, or Christmas Day, or Twelfth Day. One would hardly think this tiny bird worth hunting, even though it is nicknamed 'king of the birds'. What makes it odder still is that on any other date it would be *extremely* wicked to kill one, a crime which only the lowest coward would stoop to, and which would bring terrible bad luck.

But on the *right* day, a dead wren was the luckiest thing in the world. The young men who had hunted and killed it would make a big display of it. Some fastened it to a long pole, with its wings extended; others hung it by the legs between two crossed hoops garlanded with greenery; others carried it on a little bier decorated with ribbons. Then they formed a procession and solemnly carried it from house to house, chanting:

> We hunted the wren for Robin the Bobbin,
> We hunted the wren for Jack the Can,
> We hunted the wren for Robin the Bobbin,
> We hunted the wren for everyone.

and:

> The wren, the wren, the king of the birds,
> On Stephen's Day was caught in the furze.
> Although he is little, his family's great,
> I pray you, good lady, give us a treat.

Those who did give the 'wren-boys' money or a drink would get one of the wren's feathers to keep for luck, and as a charm against shipwreck.

What can all this mean? Was it just a way of getting beer and money? Or a joke (for the humans, if not for the bird), making fun of upper-class huntsmen who are so proud of trophies? Or was it a survival of some incredibly ancient magic ritual involving the sacrifice of a sacred animal at midwinter? On the Discworld, there's no doubt at all, as Quoth the Raven explains:

> 'Blood on the snow, making the sun come up. Starts off with animal sacrifice, y'know, hunt some big hairy animal to death, that kind of stuff. You know there's some people up on the Ramtops who kill a wren at Hogswatch and walk around from house to house singing about it? With a whack-fol-oh-diddle-dildo. Very folkloric, very myffic.'
>
> 'A *wren*? Why?'
>
> 'I dunno. Maybe someone said, hey, how'd you like to hunt this evil bustard of an eagle with his big sharp beak and great ripping talons, sort of thing, or how about instead you hunt this wren, which is basically about the size of a pea and goes "twit"? Go on, *you* choose.'

But killing a bird or beast, however sacred, is not half as impressive as killing a human, especially an important one, especially a king. The Raven says that once, long ago, that's what used to happen, up to a point – the king was not a *real* king, presumably because real kings don't take kindly to being killed off after just one year on the throne, and have bodyguards to see no one tries it.

> 'Then they start this business where some poor bugger finds a special bean in his tucker, oho, everyone says, you're *king*, mate, and he thinks "This is a bit of all right" only next thing he's legging it over the snow with a dozen other buggers chasing

him with holy sickles so's the earth'll come to life again and all this snow'll go away.'

This is a very remarkable piece of information, which probably explains what happened when Sir James Frazer, that most famous of Victorian speculative folklorists, turned his attention to a cheerful, innocent little Christmas custom, and came up with a splendidly melodramatic theory. In England and France, from Tudor times onwards, people used to round off the Twelve Days of Christmas with a lavish party on Twelfth Night. There was a big, rich cake. In that cake was a bean. Whoever got the slice with the bean in it would be 'King of the Bean' for the rest of the day, and would preside at the celebrations. It was simply a bit of fun – no violence, no sinister implications. But Frazer decided that it was *really* the survival of a bloodthirsty primitive ritual, long, long ago, in which the King of the Bean had been put to death when the revels were over. He had no shred of evidence, just a powerful hunch that mock kings must some-how also be sacred sacrificial victims. In the light of what we now know to be the case on the Discworld, it seems certain that Frazer's mind had been invaded by some drifting inspiration from that distant universe.[15]

Way back in the early centuries of the Disc's existence, the Hogfather had been a sacred victim, hunted and slaughtered in animal or human form so that the sun would rise and the snows melt. He had been the boar, the wren, the Bean King. But times change, and old gods must find new jobs. Nowadays, the Hogfather is the Midwinter Visitor, the Gift-Bringer, and Hogswatch is meant to be, on the whole, just for kids. Toys, stockings on the end of the bed, crackers and puddings, holly and cards, jolly little figures of elves and fairies. But he still lives in a Castle of Bone, far away in the icy

---

[15] Both the authors discovered Frazer in their teens and were bowled over, as probably most readers are, but became more sceptical later on. Folklorists have learned to be careful; if it looks like a jolly good story, it may very well *be* one.

regions near the Hub. People still make offerings to him, of a sort –
the glass of sherry and the pork pie left on the mantelpiece, the
carrots for the boars that pull his sledge. His colours are red and
white, even if nobody now thinks about blood on the snow. And he
is, still, just a little scary, even when he is handing out toys in a
sparkly grotto in Crumley's Emporium:

> HAPPY HOGSWATCH AND BE GOOD. I WILL KNOW IF YOU'RE GOOD
> OR BAD, YOU KNOW. HO. HO. HO.
> 'Well, you brought some magic into *that* little life,' said
> Albert.
> IT'S THE EXPRESSION ON THEIR LITTLE FACES I LIKE, said the
> Hogfather.
> 'You mean sort of fear and awe and not knowing whether to
> laugh or cry or wet their pants?'
> YES. NOW *THAT* IS WHAT I CALL BELIEF.

The Hogfather's duties include moral judgement. Has the child
been good or bad, naughty or nice? A good little boy gets, say, a
model Klatchian war chariot with real spinning sword blades. A bad
little boy traditionally gets nothing but a bag of smelly old bones,
though modern and enlightened parents are beginning to back off
from this practice, on the grounds that (a) it causes a nasty complex,
and (b) you really do *not* want to be woken up by all this weeping
and wailing at six in the morning.

On Earth, supernatural midwinter visitors have been around in
Europe for centuries. They are a very mixed lot – saints and angels
and even the Child Jesus on the one hand, hags and goblins and
mock-terrible monsters on the other – and they turn up on various
dates from November through to Twelfth Night. One of the first to
arrive is St Martin (11 November), who comes to Antwerp, Ypres,
and other Flemish towns. He wears a red cloak, and rides a white
horse. Children hang up stockings stuffed with hay in their bed-
rooms; by morning the hay has disappeared, replaced by apples,

nuts, and little cakes shaped like horseshoes. That's assuming the children have been *good*, naturally; if they haven't, all they find is a cane to beat them.

Then there is St Nicholas, patron saint of children, who brings them gifts either on the eve of his own feast day (6 December) or on Christmas Eve. He is famous in Holland and Belgium, and in the Catholic parts of Germany, Switzerland and Austria. He comes in the night riding a white horse (or donkey); he is dressed as a bishop in red robes embroidered with gold, and has a fine white beard. Children put out hay and carrots for his steed, and a glass of schnapps for his servant who carries the bag of presents, whose name is Scruffy Johnny, or Black Peter. Often there is someone else with them – the hideous Krampus or Klaubauf, a shaggy monster with horns, black face, fiery eyes, and chains that clank as he moves. Children who know their catechism will be rewarded with sweets; those who don't had better look out, for Krampus and Black Peter both carry a stick to beat them.

The Protestant parts of Germany disapproved of saints, so St Nicholas is not mentioned there. Instead, it is the Christ Child, imagined as a radiantly lovely little boy, who comes at midnight on Christmas Eve to bless the good children and leave presents for them. However, it wouldn't do for things to be all sweetness and light. So in north Germany there is also Knecht Ruprecht, a weird figure dressed in skins or straw; if children have been good and can sing a hymn nicely, he rewards them with apples and gingerbread from his wallet, but if they can't he beats them with a bag of soot and ashes. In some parts people call him Rough Klas or Ashy Klas; since 'Klas' is short for 'Nicholas', they must think he is an avatar of the saint.

Nowadays, the mood has changed. It is not now thought to be good for little children to be scared out of their wits, even if it does make them behave themselves. So in the course of the twentieth century some of the worst bogey-figures have reinvented themselves as comic and kindly. Take the Icelandic Gryla, for example, who has been around for some seven hundred years. She is a huge ugly she-troll with fifteen tails, carrying a sheepskin sack and accompanied by her thirteen sons, the Christmas Lads, who are smaller but equally ugly. Until fairly recently, the whole point about Gryla was that she was hunting for naughty children, to carry them off in that sack, and eat them; a fine old tradition with the smack of authenticity. Now she brings sweets and goodies in the sack, and the thirteen Lads slip into a child's room, one by one, during the thirteen nights before Christmas, to pop something nice under the pillow . . . They still *look* like goblins, though.

The best-known of all the gift-bringers on Earth, and most like the Hogfather, is the one whom some call Father Christmas and others Santa Claus and others Le Père Noël. He has been around for over 600 years, and is now stronger than ever. The myth just grows and grows and grows, since it is powered by money.

When first glimpsed, in England at the end of the Middle Ages, he had nothing to do with children, and little to do with gifts. He wasn't even necessarily called *Father* Christmas, but could be 'Captain Christmas', 'Prince Christmas', or 'Sir Christmas'. His job was to personify all the joys of eating, drinking and general jollity. In the 1460s the rector of Plymtree in Devonshire wrote a lively carol about Sir Christmas singing 'Nowell, Nowell!' outside the door, and urging everybody to drink as much as possible:

Buvez bien par toute la compagnie,
Make good cheer and be right merry!

He was still at it in the early seventeenth century (in spite of Puritan disapproval), when he was featured in Ben Jonson's play *Christmas his Masque* (1616), coming on stage followed by his equally jolly sons, whose names were Misrule, Carol, Mince Pie, Pots-and-Pan, New Year Gift, Mumming, Wassail, and Baby Cake. He wore doublet and hose and a high-crowned hat with a brooch, and had a long thin beard.

It was Charles Dickens who gave the finest account of a

personified Christmas Spirit who embodies the joys of food and drink, in his *A Christmas Carol* (1843). He told how Scrooge came face to face with a 'jolly Giant, glorious to see', in a room thickly hung with holly, ivy and mistletoe, and piled high with food:

> Heaped up on the floor, to form a kind of throne, were turkey, geese, game, poultry, brawn, great joints of meat, sucking-pigs, long wreaths of sausages, mince pies, plum puddings, barrels of oysters, red-hot chestnuts, cherry-cheeked apples, juicy oranges, luscious pears, immense twelfth-cakes, and seething bowls of punch, that made the chamber dim with their delicious steam.

This Spirit looks like a younger version of Father Christmas, or indeed of the Hogfather. Like them, he wears a long simple robe, trimmed with white fur, but in his case it is *green*, not red, and has no hood; he has long curly brown hair, and is wearing a wreath of holly set with icicles. And though he takes Scrooge on a visionary journey through the night, wandering invisibly from house to house to watch the celebrations, he does *not* bring presents for the kiddies.

Even so, the idea of Father Christmas as a gift-bringer started infiltrating Victorian Britain, probably from Germany. He became quite a familiar figure – an old man, bearded, trudging through the snow with his sack of presents, dressed in a long hooded gown which was often, but by no means always, red. He did not have a companion to beat or threaten naughty children, as his Continental kinsmen had.

Meanwhile, on the other side of the Atlantic, something quite extraordinary had been happening. The Dutch settlers in New Amsterdam (later renamed New York) had kept up the tradition that St Nicholas would come in the night of 5/6 December to pop presents in the shoes or stockings of sleeping children, just as he did in their old homeland. In 1809 the very popular writer Washington Irving drew attention to this, but transferred the idea to Christmas Eve.

And then in 1822, suddenly, inexplicably, inspiration gripped a clergyman and professor of Hebrew and Oriental Languages called Clement Clark Moore, and he wrote a little poem for his children. He called it 'A Visit from St Nicholas', but most people now think of the first line, not the title:

'Twas the night before Christmas, and all through the house . . .

Moore probably disapproved of saints, and even bishops, since his Nicholas is not a bishop in full regalia on a white horse, but a fat little gnome, hurtling through the sky in a miniature sleigh drawn by eight tiny reindeer. (Why reindeer? Nobody knows. There are no reindeer in Holland.) He comes and goes by way of the chimney. He carries a sack of presents. As for his appearance:

He was dressed all in fur, from his head to his foot,
And his clothes were all tarnished with ashes and soot . . .
His droll little mouth was drawn up like a bow,
And the beard of his chin was as white as the snow;
The stump of his pipe he held hard in his teeth,
And the smoke it encircled his head like a wreath;
He had a broad face and a little round belly,
That shook when he laughed, like a bowlful of jelly.

Before too long, the folk imagination got to work. Bishops were forgotten, and the gift-bringer's name was shortened to Santa Claus. In the 1860s the artist Thomas Nash began drawing him. Nash dropped the furs, preferring the typical Dutch costume of a belted jacket, blue breeches, and a flat sailor's cap. But by the end of the nineteenth century red became the standard colour (with or without white trimmings), and the cap became a red one, long and floppy. In the twentieth, Santa Claus acquired a team of elves as little helpers, and a home near the North Pole.

This American Santa Claus arrived in England in 1854, by way of a fictional story by Susan and Ann Warner, 'The Christmas Stocking'. Little by little he became popular, and he and the native Father Christmas blended together, sometimes using one name, sometimes the other; sometimes in a long robe, sometimes in a jacket. And now the combined figure is spreading all over the world.

This extraordinary history shows beyond doubt that a truly powerful idea bounces to and fro across space and time, from mind to mind and from one universe to another. In a way, both Santa and the Hogfather are communal 'Shakespearean' creations. As we point out elsewhere, Will would happily drag some fragments of myth and folklore together and weld them into something new in such a way that the end result suits our sense of narrative grammar.

Did people in northern Europe make sacrifices at the winter solstice? Yes. Human? Could be, long, long ago, to the extent that as a species we have occasionally indulged in human sacrifice, but later the most likely sacrifice would have been a horse or a farm animal. And the King of the Bean? A good story, which satisfies our desire for a thrilling narrative, but almost certainly untrue. The evolution of the proto Hogfather? Indeed, the person seen by Susan going through his different personifications does add up to the 'festive spirit'. And the suggestion that, via some deep visceral means, the colours of the said spirit have become the colours of blood on snow? That's a happy coincidence, and a good story, but it's not folklore!

One final thing. The Coca-Cola company is often credited with the 'modern' look of Father Christmas, but it is much truer to say that it popularized, over much of the world, one 'look' among many that already existed. Exposure wins. (For example, as Terry mentions in his introduction, the 'magpie rhyme' that introduced the ITV children's series in the late 1960s and the 1970s almost certainly did a lot to wipe out the existing regional variations of the rhyme.) But across the Channel, at least, older avatars often appear alongside, or even instead of, the red and white demigod of Christmas expenditure. Ho. Ho. Ho!

Chapter 16

DEATH

DEATH MAY WELL BE THE ONLY SUPERNATURAL entity (strictly speaking, an anthropomorphic personification) which is known and acknowledged throughout the entire multiverse. His arrival is quite, quite certain – and yet, most people secretly hope that for them and their friends it will be indefinitely delayed, and his actual manifestation generally comes as a surprise. On the Discworld only wizards and witches can foresee his arrival; on Earth, only exceptionally holy men and women.

Some people try to bargain with him, staking lives on the outcome of a game of chess or cards. This rarely succeeds, though Granny Weatherwax did once win against him at Cripple Mr Onion (of course, he knew she would). Others try to run away. This is quite hopeless, since Death keeps an appointments diary, and knows precisely where and when he is scheduled to find them.

A story is told about this on our world. It is part of the age-old traditions of Muslim lands, and reached English-speaking countries in the 1930s through a play by Somerset Maugham and a novel by John O'Hara. It tells of a servant who was buying food for his master's household in the street market in Baghdad one morning when someone jostled him, and he turned to find himself face to face with Death, who made an abrupt gesture. Terrified, the servant ran home, begged his master for the loan of a horse, and galloped off to Samarra, which is about 75 miles away. The master then went to the market-place himself, and there he too saw Death. 'Why did you raise your hand to threaten my servant?' said he. 'That was no threat,' answered Death, 'only a start of surprise. I was astonished to see him here in Baghdad, for I have an appointment with him tonight in Samarra.'

Something similar happened once on the Disc, as we learn from *The Colour of Magic*, when Rincewind jostled a tall dark figure in the bazaar of Ankh-Morpork, and was told I WAS EXPECTING TO MEET THEE IN PSEPHOPOLOLIS. Actually, it turned out to be a misunderstanding.

On both the Disc and the Earth Death manifests himself to humans and humanoid races (e.g. dwarfs) as a very tall human skeleton, every bone pleasantly polished, with remote but piercing points of blue light in his eye sockets. His deep resonant voice has been compared to many things of a funereal nature, such as the clang of the leaden doors of a crypt when slammed deep underground, yet no comparison really does it justice. He wears a hooded robe woven of absolute darkness. Normally he carries a scythe, but also owns a sword for use on kings; both weapons have shimmering semi-transparent ice-blue blades, for separating souls from bodies. There is usually an hourglass hidden in the folds of his robe; this is a lifetimer, which measures the life-span of the person he is about to visit.

On Earth there are some countries in whose languages 'death' is a feminine word (*la mort, morte, muerta*). This has no effect at all on the manifested appearance of Death in those lands. In any case, it takes a calm, well-trained eye to tell a male from a female skeleton, and black hooded robes are unisex attire.

There was a time when Death thought it polite to appear in whatever form the client expected – at least, for human clients; what shape he assumes when manifesting himself to, say, a sea anemone, a mayfly, or a nettle is beyond conjecture. However, he discovered that most people have no clear expectations at all, probably because in their hearts they never *really* believe they will die. And those who do think they know what they will see have some pretty strange ideas. For example, King Teppicymon XXVII, Pharaoh of Djelibeybi, found that the hooded robe lacked a certain something:

'I understood that Death came as a three-headed giant scarab beetle,' said the king.

Death shrugged. WELL, NOW YOU KNOW.

'What's that thing in your hand?'

THIS? IT'S A SCYTHE.

'Strange-looking object, isn't it?' said the pharaoh. 'I thought Death carried the Flail of Mercy and the Reaping Hook of Justice.'

Death appeared to think about this. WHAT IN? he said.

'Pardon?'

ARE WE STILL TALKING ABOUT A GIANT BEETLE?

'Ah. In his mandibles, I suppose. But I think he's got arms in one of the frescoes in the palace. Seems a bit silly, really, now I come to tell someone. I mean, a giant beetle with arms. And the head of an ibis, I seem to recall.' [*Pyramids*]

There have been times and places on Earth where Death would have found it just as tricky to fit in with his local image. For the Ancient Egyptians, he would have had to appear as Anubis, a man with the head of a jackal or wild dog; for certain South American peoples, as a cross between a jaguar and an eagle; for some Hindus, as the ferocious many-armed goddess Kali, adorned with garlands of skulls. So he decided to stick to what he liked best, using the costume and attributes he had been gradually collecting over the past 2,000 years or so.

His starting-point was the Bible, specifically the sixth chapter of the Apocalypse (or Book of Revelation), which speaks of a 'rider on a pale horse' whose name was Death, wearing a crown, and flourishing a sword. The same passage mentions three other riders as his companions, War, Famine, and Pestilence. On the Discworld too, in suitable circumstances, he teams up with them and they appear together as the Four Horsemen of the Apocralypse, as a sure sign that the world is just about to end – probably. Some of their doings on the Disc are recorded in *The Light Fantastic*, *Sourcery*, *Interesting Times*, and *Thief of Time*; and on Earth in *Good Omens*.

Death liked the idea of a horse, and got himself a handsome white steed named Binky, who is real flesh-and-blood, though capable of galloping in the air and across the dimensions as well as on land. He did briefly experiment with skeletal horses, but found bits kept dropping off; and fiery horses, which tended to burn down the stable. Binky is far more practical, and more reliable. He is well fed and well groomed (Death strongly disapproves of artists who represent the Pale Horse as a mangy, starving creature). From time to time he requires new horseshoes, and on these occasions Death takes him to the best farrier on the Disc, Jason Ogg of Lancre. Jason's gift as a craftsman is that he can shoe anything, *anything*, that anyone brings him – a horse, a goose, a unicorn, an ant. But the price to be paid for the gift is that he *must* shoe anything anyone brings. So on certain nights, when he hears a certain knock and a certain voice, he does as his father and grandfather did before him: he puts on a blindfold, and shoes what must from the feel of it be the finest horse in the world – and certainly the most docile.

As far as is known, Death has not made similar arrangements on Earth. But apparently the Devil did, once. It's said that there was once a blacksmith at Keenthorne in Shropshire who was so proud of his skill that he boasted that 'if the Devil himself came to his forge he would shoe his horse for him, aye, and shoe him to rights too!' And then, one dark midnight, a traveller on a great black horse arrived, demanding that it be shod – and the smith noted with horror that the rider himself had a hoof. The smith ran off in a panic and roused the parson, begging him for help. The parson answered that he must fulfil his boast, but should accept no payment, for that would be selling himself to the Devil. So the smith did shoe the Devil's horse, most efficiently, but though the Devil repeatedly offered him good payment, he would take nothing. The Devil and his horse vanished in a flash of fire.

To return to Death. In the course of the Middle Ages he became dissatisfied with the idea of himself as the crowned and sword-wielding Rider of the Pale Horse. He disliked the idea of kingship, even though it appealed to many artists and poets – to Milton, for example, who in *Paradise Lost* describes Death as a dark, faceless but menacing shadow:

> What seemed his head
> The likeness of a kingly crown had on.

On one occasion on the Discworld, Death (who at the time had become more or less human and was calling himself Bill Door) encountered an entity which had taken on his role, and had adopted much the same wraith-like manifestation as Milton described. This filled him with fury:

> The new Death raised his cowl.
>   There was no face there. There was not even a skull. Smoke curled formlessly between the robe and a golden crown.
>   Bill Door raised himself on his elbows.
>   A CROWN? His voice shook with rage. I NEVER WORE A CROWN!
>   *You never wanted to rule.* [*Reaper Man*]

And so Death went looking for another image from our world. He decided he liked the look of Old Father Time, an old man carrying a scythe and an hourglass. This figure had evolved out of a god called Cronus in Ancient Greece and Saturn in Rome, who carried a sickle or a scythe because he was a god of agriculture, and an hourglass because he had also become the god of Time (this happened because 'Cronus' sounds almost exactly like *chronos*, meaning 'time' in Greek). Now, harvesting and death are two faces of the same thing, depending on the point of view. If you are the farmer reaping corn or grass, you're looking ahead to the bread, the beer, the hay for the cattle, and you go home for a cheery Harvest Supper with plenty of drink and a hey-nonny-no, and maybe a barn dance. But if you are the plant being reaped, what you're going through is death. Seeing the sense in this, Death copied the scythe and hourglass of Cronus, and adopted the title of the Grim Reaper. It was, after all, his job to separate the wheat-germ of the soul from the chaff of the mortal body.

Both the Rider and the Reaper were thought of, at first, as having the normal body of a living man. However, the European Middle Ages had a rather morbid interest in physical decay, so for a while Death adopted the appearance of a rotting corpse, with split belly, peeling skin, and crawling worms, wearing (if anything) a shroud. Many medieval painters and sculptors showed him in this form. Then, little by little, he changed over to something more hygienic – just clean, gleaming bones. His new idea of himself as a Skeleton Reaper seeped into the minds of Italian artists during the fourteenth century. He can be seen in this guise, for example, on early packs of Tarot cards (he is Number 13 among the Greater Trumps, which accounts for a lot). Then, soon after 1400, painters in the Netherlands who had to do the illustrations for manuscripts of the Apocalypse got the message, and started drawing the Rider on the Pale Horse as a skeleton too. At first they kept the sword (after all, that's what the Book *said*), but by the end of the century woodcuts in German Bibles were giving him the scythe instead. And that, give or take a black cloak and hood, is how Death still usually chooses to be seen: a skeleton on a white horse, with a scythe and an hourglass. He allows himself one touch of luxury – the robe is fastened with a silver brooch engraved with an omega, which is the last letter of the Greek alphabet and so very definitely signals The End. Also, it's a pretty shape.

It was also towards the end of the European Middle Ages that Death learned how to dance. He is famed for it. Any dance, every dance – square dances, round dances, reels, the polka, the mazurka, the waltz, the tango, the Quirmish bull-dance (oh-lay!):

A high-speed fusillade of hollow snapping noises suddenly kept time with the music.

'Who's playing the maracas?'

Death grinned.

'MARACAS? I DON'T NEED . . . MARACAS.' [*Reaper Man*]

That was on the Disc. He can be just as energetic on Earth too, judging by old prints of skeletons wildly leaping about, and by a story told in Sussex in the 1860s, as recorded by Charlotte Latham:

> There stood upon the Downs close to Broadwater an old oak tree, and people said that always on Midsummer Eve, just at midnight, a number of skeletons started up from its roots and, joining hands, danced round it till cock-crow, then as suddenly sank down again. They said several persons had actually seen this dance of death; one young man in particular, having been detained by business at Findon till very late, and forgetting that it was Midsummer Eve, had been frightened out of his very senses by seeing the dead men caper to the rattling of their own bones.

On other occasions, his dancing is sedate and courtly. In Europe in the fifteenth and sixteenth centuries, the Dance of Death was often painted on the walls of cemeteries and churches; it showed a line of men and skeletons, hand in hand, pacing along in a slow and stately chain-dance. In England there was a famous mural in the cloister of London's Old St Paul's Cathedral (the one that burned down in the Great Fire of 1666), and there is still a set of carvings on the ceiling of Roslyn Chapel near Edinburgh. The Dance was also painted in the margins of prayer books, and acted out in religious pageants. Nowadays, it is best remembered as the closing shot of Ingmar Bergman's film *The Seventh Seal*.

On the Discworld, Death has often tried to act in human ways as a relief from his unremitting memory of both past and future, but he rarely gets much satisfaction from it. Fishing, gambling, getting drunk and joining the Klatchian Foreign Legion in order to forget have not really worked for him. His greatest success was his spell as a farm labourer (harvesting a speciality), as described in *Reaper Man*; he also on one occasion enjoyed riding a rather special motorbike:

> There were two small cart-wheels, one behind the other, with a saddle in between them. In front of the saddle was a pipe with a complicated double curve in it, so that someone sitting in the saddle would be able to get a grip.
>
> The rest was junk. Bones and tree branches and a jackdaw's bouquet of gewgaws. A horse's skull was strapped over the front wheel, and feathers and beads hung from every point. [*Soul Music*]

Death is clearly the patron saint of album covers. And in some cultures a saint is just what he is – or rather *she* is: Santa Muerte, a (female) folk saint. Devotees say she is an offshoot of the Catholic Church; the Church dismisses them as a cult. The case continues, but one follower delivered a quote with a near Discworld pragmatism: 'It's better to make her your friend.'[16]

Sainted or otherwise, Death is attracted to Mexico, where he takes part in all kinds of human activities, expertly and with great enjoyment. This is especially obvious around the time of the Day of the Dead (1 and 2 November). At this season, streets and shops are full of cheerful images of male and female Deaths not just dancing but playing all kinds of musical instruments, flirting, fighting, drinking, showing off their fine clothes, working at any and every trade. Nothing, in short, could be more alive than Death, in Mexico.

And what of the dead themselves, on the Discworld? What happens when Death comes to them? Well, that usually seems to be

---

[16] Perhaps she recalled the words of St Francis: 'By your holy death, help us to live each day as our last and to welcome sister Death.'

up to them. The only group who had no say in the matter were the luckless pharaohs of Djelibeybi, mummified and immured in pyramids which were supposed to ensure a blissful afterlife but which simply imprisoned them inside a time-distortion. After centuries of excruciating boredom, they broke free and passed over into Death's world (with great relief, and forming an orderly queue). It is not known whether the Ancient Egyptian pyramids had the same unwelcome side-effect on *their* pharaohs.

On Earth, according to the myths of Ancient Greece, the gods would occasionally, as a mark of great favour, take someone newly dead and turn him or her into stars. The hero Perseus is a constellation now, as is Andromeda, the girl he rescued from a sea-monster, and indeed Cetus the monster too. So is Orion the hunter, lover of at least two goddesses; so is Amalthea the Goat, who became the constellation Capricorn. Some people on the Disc are aware of this possibility, though as far as is known the Disc gods have never actually done it – Cohen and his Horde rode for the stars because *they* wanted to, and gods had nothing to do with it. In any case, becoming a constellation is not a permanent solution:

Mrs McGarry looked up at the stars.
   'In the olden days,' she said, 'when a hero had been really heroic, the gods would put them up in the stars.'
   · THE HEAVENS CHANGE, said Death. WHAT TODAY LOOKS LIKE A MIGHTY HUNTER MAY LOOK LIKE A TEACUP IN A HUNDRED YEARS' TIME. [*The Last Hero*]

There are a few who, when Death comes to them, refuse to move on, preferring to become ghosts – certain kings of Lancre who haunt their ancestral castle, for example, and dwarfs who may choose to walk the earth in torment if they have not been buried with their finest weapons. According to the myths and folklore of our world, such situations are pretty common here; people linger as ghosts because they have not been properly buried, or have been particularly wicked, or have died by violence, or are looking for money they buried, or simply can't bear to leave home. But nobody, in any universe, can match the obstinacy of the political activist Reg Shoe, who insists on remaining a zombie in order to campaign for the rights of the dead and the undead.

The normal course of events is that Death escorts those who die to the edge of a vast desert of black sand under a brilliant starry sky, where he informs them that what they do next, or what happens to them next, is not his responsibility – for in the universe of the Discworld Death is never the supreme reality. It appears that no two people have the same experience, since it will accurately reflect the beliefs and personality of each one.

In *Small Gods*, for instance, five deaths are described. One, a sea-captain who believes that the souls of sailors become friendly porpoises (in British lore, it would be seagulls), sails away in search of paradise in a ghostly ship (for ships too have a soul), with a ghostly crew, and ghostly rats, and an escort of ghostly porpoises. The second and third are soldiers – Fri'it, an Omnian general who secretly disbelieves the hell-fire doctrines of that church, and Ichlos, a private who has never given much thought to religion. Both remember a childhood song:

> You have to walk a lonesome desert,
> You have to walk it all alone . . .

Fri'it asks Death: 'What is at the end of the desert?' and is told, JUDGEMENT.

> The memory stole over him: a desert is what you think it is. And now, you can think clearly . . .
>
> There were no lies here. All fancies fled away. That's what happened in all deserts. It was just you, and what you believed.
>
> What have I always believed?
>
> That on the whole, and by and large, if a man lived properly,

not according to what any priests said, but according to what seemed decent and honest *inside*, then it would, at the end, more or less, turn out all right.

You couldn't get that on a banner. But the desert looked better already.

Fri'it set out.

It is the same for Ichlos, though he puts it more simply:

'My mum told me about this,' he said. 'When you're dead, you have to walk a desert. And you see everything properly, she said. And remember everything right.'

Death studiously did nothing to indicate his feelings either way.

'Might meet a few friends on the way, eh?' said the soldier.

POSSIBLY.

Ichlos set out. On the whole, he thought, it could have been worse.

The next who dies is Vorbis, the single-minded, pitiless, utterly unshakable Omnian Exquisitor. When he sees the desert, his certainties drain away. Though he has taken for granted that there would indeed be a Judgement according to the rules of his religion (and that he would do very well in it), all he can feel is the echo of his own thoughts, and when he looks inside himself all he can see is the horror of what he has done, and the terror of emptiness and solitude.

The last to die is the compassionate monk Brutha. He too follows Death to the black sand under the starry sky.

'Ah. There really *is* a desert. Does everyone get this?' said Brutha.

WHO KNOWS?

'And what is at the end of the desert?'

JUDGEMENT.

Brutha considered this.

'*Which* end?'

Death grinned and stepped aside.

It's only natural to want to know what lies at the far end of the
desert. But this, as Tiffany told the hiver in *A Hatful of Sky*, is something no words can describe, which is why you have to cross the
desert to find out. But before you can even begin, there is something
important to be done. You must face and accept Judgement, the
Judgement you pass on yourself in the light of clear self-knowledge
and accurate memory. And *that*, as Brutha guessed, begins as soon as
you die, at *this* end of the desert.

And then Brutha sees Vorbis, hunched on the sand, too paralysed
with fear to have even started the journey.

'But Vorbis died a hundred years ago!'

YES. HE HAD TO WALK IT ALL ALONE. ALL ALONE WITH HIMSELF.
IF HE DARED.

'He's been here for a hundred years?'

POSSIBLY NOT. TIME IS DIFFERENT HERE. IT IS ... MORE
PERSONAL.

'Ah. You mean a hundred years can pass like a few seconds?'

A HUNDRED YEARS CAN PASS LIKE INFINITY.

Whereupon Brutha, true to his own nature, offers companionship to
Vorbis, and they set out to cross the desert together.

It may come as a surprise to those whose notion of Christian
teaching about the afterlife is based on, say, the famous hell-fire
sermon in James Joyce's *Portrait of the Artist as a Young Man*, that
what is described in Discworld terms in *Small Gods* is pretty well
what many modern theologians say – at any rate, as regards Brutha,
Vorbis, and Fri'it, though maybe not the ship's captain. Such teachers
say that a lifetime's daily choices determine what we are at the
moment of death, and that God's 'Judgement' consists in letting us

see, accurately and fully, what we have chosen to become. He does not hurl punishments; those who suffer, like Vorbis, do so because they have imprisoned themselves in their own evil. It is to be hoped that every Vorbis finds a compassionate Brutha.

The same point emerges from the post-mortem experience of the brutal, murderous, but mentally subnormal thug Mr Tulip (in *The Truth*). Death makes him see the value of the many lives he had destroyed, and once he understands the truth about himself he is filled with huge remorse and passes his own judgement on himself, saying he wishes he could go back in time to kill himself before he could do such harm, but as that's impossible he wants to spend the rest of his afterlife feeling 'really sorry'. As Death notes, Tulip has 'something in him that could be better', given enough time. His purgatory is not harsh. Since he has been taught to expect reincarnation, reincarnation is what he gets, in a form agreeable to the best part of him, his love of good craftsmanship and beautiful antiques. He becomes a woodworm in a fine old desk.

However, there is nothing good in the other thug, Mr Pin, who puts his trust in a lucky potato and whose remorse is simply pretence. He too reincarnates, but the outcome will not be pleasant. He becomes a potato, and is fried, since 'Reincarnation enjoys a joke as much as the next philosophical hypothesis.'

But to Death, a nature like Mr Pin's is no joke.

Death sighed deeply. WHO KNOWS WHAT EVIL LURKS IN THE HEART OF MEN?

The Death of Rats looked up.

SQUEAK, he said.

Death waved a hand dismissively. WELL, YES, OBVIOUSLY *ME*, he said. I JUST WONDERED IF THERE WAS ANYONE ELSE. [*The Truth*]

One who *may* have answers to the questions that trouble Death's lonely mind – questions about goodness and evil, and justice – is

Azrael, his Lord. On Earth, 'Azrael' is the name given in the traditions of Islam to the Angel of Death, whose name is nowhere mentioned in the Bible itself. Muslims say he is one of the great Archangels, equal to Michael, Raphael or Gabriel in rank, and greater than them in wisdom. His name is Arabic, and means 'Help of God'.

But the nature of Azrael is best seen on the Discworld. He is known there as the Great Attractor, the Death of the Whole Multiverse, the Beginning and End of Time. He is so vast that he can only be measured in terms of the speed of light, and whole galaxies are lost in his eyes. *Our* Death, the Death who harvests all lives on Earth and on the Discworld, is only a *little* Death, and Azrael is his Lord.

And at the end of all stories, Azrael, who knows the secret, thinks: I REMEMBER WHEN ALL THIS WILL BE AGAIN. [*Reaper Man*]

Bibliography and suggestions
for further reading

Barber, Paul. *Vampires, Burial and Death: Folklore and Reality* (Yale University Press, 1988. ISBN 0-300-04126-8 hardback, 0-300-04859-9 paperback)

Briggs, Katharine M. *A Dictionary of Fairies, Hobgoblins, Brownies, Bogies and Other Supernatural Creatures* (Penguin Books, 1977. ISBN 0-14-00-4753-0 paperback)

Briggs, Katharine M. *The Vanishing People: A Study of Traditional Fairy Beliefs* (Batsford, 1978. ISBN 0-7134-1240-2 hardback)

Davies, Owen. *A People Bewitched: Witchcraft and Magic in Nineteenth-Century Somerset* (Bruton, 1999. ISBN 0-9536390-0-2)

Frazer, Sir James G. *The Golden Bough: Abridged Edition* (Macmillan & Co., 1922, frequently reprinted)

Lenihan, Edmund. *In Search of Biddy Early* (Mercier Press, 1987; paperback 1995)

MacManus, Dermot. *The Middle Kingdom; the Faerie World of Ireland* (London: Max Parrish & Co., 1959. Paperback edition: Gerrards Cross: Colin Smythe & Co., 1973. ISBN 0-900675-82-9)

Maxwell-Stuart, P. G. *Witchcraft: A History* (Tempus Publishing, 2000. ISBN 0-7524-2305-3 paperback)

Miles, Clement A. *Christmas Customs and Traditions: Their History and Significance* (1912; reprinted by Dover Books, New York,

1976. ISBN 0-486-23354-5)

Roud, Steve. *The Penguin Guide to the Superstitions of Britain and Ireland* (Penguin Books, 2003. ISBN 0-141-00673-0)

Roud, Steve. *The English Year: A Month-by-Month Guide to the Nation's Customs and Festivals* (Penguin Books, 2006. ISBN 0-140-51554-2)

Russell, Jeffrey B. *A History of Witchcraft* (Thames and Hudson, 1980. ISBN 0-500-27242-5 paperback)

Ryan, M. *Biddy Early: The Wise Woman of Clare* (Mercier Press, 2000)

Silver, Carole G. *Strange and Secret Peoples: Fairies and Victorian Consciousness* (Oxford University Press, 1999. ISBN 0-19-512199-6)

Simpson, Jacqueline. *British Dragons* (Batsford, 1980. ISBN 0-7134-2559-0 hardback. Wordsworth paperback, 2001. ISBN 1-84022-507-6)

Simpson, Jacqueline, and Steve Roud. *A Dictionary of English Folklore* (Oxford University Press, 2000. ISBN 0-19-2100019-x hardback, 0-19-860766-0 paperback)

Westwood, Jennifer, and Jacqueline Simpson. *The Lore of the Land: A Guide to England's Legends* (Penguin Books, 2005. ISBN 0-141-00711-7 hardback, 0-141-02103-9 paperback)

Wills, Barclay. *Shepherds of Sussex*, 1938.

Yeats, W. B. *Fairy and Folk Tales of Ireland* (Gerrards Cross: Colin Smythe Ltd, 1973; paperback Pan Books, 1979. ISBN 0-330-25769-2) Originally published as two books, 1888 and 1892.

Not folklore but never mind

Blanton, De Anne, and Lauren M. Cook. *They Fought Like Demons: Women Soldiers in the American Civil War* (Louisiana State University Press, 2002. ISBN 0-8071-2806-6)

Dekker, Rudolf M., and Lotte C. Van De Pol. *The Tradition of Female Transvestism in Early Modern Europe* (Palgrave MacMillan, 1997. ISBN13 978-0312173340)

And for those who want to go further

Burn, Lucilla. *Greek Myths* (British Museum Publications, 1990. ISBN 0714-120-618)

Evans, George Ewart. *The Horse in the Furrow* (Faber and Faber, 1960; paperback Faber and Faber, 1971. ISBN 0-571-08164-9)

Hart, George. *Egyptian Myths* (British Museum Publications, 1990. ISBN 0714-120-642)

Hughes, Thomas. *The Scouring of the White Horse* (1859; reprint Alan Sutton, 1989. ISBN 0-86299-563-9)

Judge, Roy. *The Jack in the Green* (D. S. Brewer, 1979; revised edn FLS Books, The Folklore Society, 2000. ISBN 0-903515-20-2)

Opie, Iona and Peter. *The Lore and Language of Schoolchildren* (Oxford University Press, 1959. ISBN13 978-0940322691)

Opie, Iona and Peter. *Children's Games in Street and Playground* (Oxford University Press, 1969. ISBN13 978-0192814890)

Page, R. I. *Norse Myths* (British Museum Publications, 1990. ISBN 0714-120-626)

Pegg, Bob. *Rites and Riots: Folk Customs of Britain and Europe* (Blandford Press, 1981. ISBN 0-7137-0997-9)

Philip, Neil. *The Penguin Book of English Folktales* (Penguin Books, 1992. ISBN 0-14-013976-1)

Philip, Neil. *The Penguin Book of Scottish Folktales* (Penguin Books, 1994. ISBN13 978-0140139778)

Quiller-Couch, Arthur. *The Oxford Book of Ballads* (Clarendon Press, 1910, many reprints)

Thomas, Keith. *Religion and the Decline of Magic* (Weidenfeld and Nicolson, 1971. ISBN 0-297-00220-1)

Wilson, Stephen. *The Magical Universe: Everyday Ritual and Magic in Pre-Modern Europe* (Hambledon and London, 2000. ISBN 1-85285-251-8)

We have put in a couple of the pioneering regional studies, as they give a taste of the whole *range* of folklore in a community (tales, beliefs, customs, sayings etc.). The hyphen isn't a mistyping, that was the way the word was spelled then:

Burne, Charlotte. *Shropshire Folk-Lore A Sheaf of Gleanings* (London, 1883)
Leather, Ella Mary. *The Folk-Lore of Hereford* (London, 1912)

Index